Margaret Dickinson

Welcome Home

PAN BOOKS

First published 2015 by Macmillan

First published in paperback 2015 by Pan Books,
an imprint of Pan Macmillan
20 New Wharf Road, London N1 9RR
Associated companies throughout the world
www.panmacmillan.com

ISBN 978-1-5098-9561-8

1 3 5 7 9 8 6 4 2

A CIP catalogue record for this book is available from the British Library.

Typeset by Palimpsest Book Production Limited, Falkirk, Stirlingshire
Printed and bound by CPI Group (UK) Ltd, Croydon, CR0 4YY

Visit www.panmacmillan.com to read more about all our books
and to buy them. You will also find features, author interviews and
news of any author events, and you can sign up for e-newsletters
so that you're always first to hear about our new releases.

For Mandi

With My Love Always

ACKNOWLEDGEMENTS

Many sources have been used for information for this novel but I would like to pay tribute to the wonderful book, *The Secret Ministry of Ag. & Fish* by Noreen Riols (Macmillan) and also to acknowledge use of the newspapers of the day, particularly the *Grimsby Telegraph* and its *Bygones* publications.

My special thanks to the staff of the North East Lincolnshire Local History Library in Grimsby Central Library – Jennie Mooney, Debbie Grundy, Tracey Townsend and Simon Balderson – who so kindly helped me with my research. Also my grateful thanks to Vanessa Dumbleton and to Carol and Garry Sidney for their interest and help. And, as always, my sincere thanks to the staff at Skegness Library for their continuing support.

My love and thanks to my family and friends for their constant encouragement, especially those who read the script in the early stages; David Dickinson, Fred Hill, Pauline Griggs and Scott Heath. And never forgetting my wonderful agent, Darley Anderson, and his team, and my editor, Trisha Jackson, and all the team at Pan Macmillan.

Prologue

'Edie! Edie – are you there?'

Lily Horton pushed open the back door of her neighbour's home and stepped into the scullery.

Edie Kelsey, in her late forties, was tall and well built with a round face and short, glossy dark brown hair. When she washed it, she pinched it into neat waves with her fingers and secured them with metal wave clips. The only time she ever visited a hairdresser was to have a trim. Until the beginning of the war, there had not been even a hint of grey, but the last six years had brought unending worry and now there were little wings of silver hair at her temples. She was standing at the deep white sink, scrubbing her husband's shirt collar. She paused, thankful for the respite, resting her arms on the edge of the sink.

'Put kettle on, Lil, there's a duck. I'm parched. How my Archie gets his shirts in such a state, I don't know.'

'It's not easy being at sea, Edie.'

'I reckon he doesn't take his shirt off from one day to the next, Lil. I bet he even sleeps in it.'

Lil, smaller, thinner and three years younger than her friend, had fair, naturally curly hair. Once, she had been described as a 'pretty girl', with smooth skin, blue eyes

1

and a smile to melt ice, but the years of hardship had etched lines into her face and deep in her eyes was a sadness that would never quite go away. She moved through Edie's scullery and into the room that was a cross between a kitchen and a living room. To one side was a black polished range with a fire, oven and hob for the kettle, but this room was also where the family ate at the table in the centre or sat in one of the two fireside chairs.

Lil set the kettle to boil and then, from the sideboard, laid out cups and saucers. Edie's tea drinking was legendary in the street, but today there was a very good reason for a celebratory cup.

Lil went to stand in the doorway between the scullery and the living room. 'He's really dead, then.'

Edie had resumed her vigorous scrubbing.

'Who is?' she said absently, still concentrating on removing the last unsightly dirty mark from Archie's shirt collar.

'Hitler, of course. They're saying now that he committed suicide. Haven't you heard? But the Russians are doubting that he's dead at all. They think it's a trick to allow him to escape capture by the Allies.'

This was probably the only thing that could have made Edie stop and turn round slowly to stare, wide-eyed, at Lil. 'No – no. I hadn't heard. I don't listen to the wireless – well, not the news – or read the papers when Archie's at sea. You know I don't. I'll know soon enough if . . .'

Lil nodded in sympathy. Her husband, Tom, had been lost in 1919 when, it was believed, the trawler on which he was serving had hit a mine left floating in the sea from the Great War. No hands had survived the disaster. Since then she had struggled to bring up their

2

only child, Irene, who had been born five months after
the tragedy. Sadly, Tom had never seen his daughter –
and now that daughter was married with a little boy
of her own, Tommy. But through all that dreadful time,
Lil had had the help and support of her next-door
neighbours, Edie and Archie Kelsey. Lil had always
worked; she'd had to. Fisherfolk looked after their own
and Lil had never been short of nets to make or mend,
fastened to the wall in her backyard in fine weather or
in her living room in winter. She was employed by The
Great Grimsby Coal, Salt & Tanning Company Ltd,
who manufactured all sorts of equipment for the fishing
industry and was allowed to be a home worker because
of her young daughter. But still, times were hard and
the recent war had not improved matters, though she'd
always had a roof over her head, her daughter Irene
and good friends next door. Indeed, all the inhabitants
of their street were friendly; a close-knit community,
many of whom were involved in the town's fishing
industry. The men went to sea together and the women
supported each other when their menfolk were away.
The street, where Edie and Lil lived side by side, was
a long road of red-brick terraced houses not far from
the fish docks. The front doors were painted brown,
the doorsteps and windowsills worn by constant
scouring with donkey stone by the house-proud women.
Every so often, a passageway ran between the houses,
one of which was on one side of Edie's house. On the
other, Edie shared the wall between her house and Lil's.
Often, they could each overhear what was going on
next door. The back door opened from the scullery
on to a small, concreted area where a tin bath hung
on a hook near the outside privy and then there was a
long strip of ground where most householders grew

vegetables. At the end of the 'garden' was a shed and a fence with a door in it leading out to an alleyway shared not only with the other houses in their own road but also with the occupants of the terraces in the adjacent street.

Lil wasn't the only widow on the street whose husband had been drowned in the course of his dangerous work. Now there were so many more who'd been lost; husbands, fathers, brothers and sons, killed in the war. Lil never complained, however; she accepted her lot in life and 'got on with it'. But what she would have done without her good friend, Edie Kelsey, Lil didn't know.

Lily Bailey had been born in the back streets of the town with an indolent father and a care-worn mother. The eldest of six children, she had frequently been kept at home from school to help with the younger ones and the never-ending housework. When Tom Horton – a handsome, hardworking deckie – had proposed to her, she had accepted gratefully, but, sadly, she wasn't to escape the hard life as she had hoped to do, for only two years later Tom was gone and Lil was a widow at only twenty. When they'd married, Tom had found them a terraced house as far away from her former home as he could, but Lil had still felt obliged to visit her family to help her mother when Tom was away at sea.

'You would go and get yourself married and leave me to do all this,' Norma, the next sister in line, who had had to take on the household duties from Lil, had grumbled. Norma was a cheerless, plain girl, resentful that she had none of Lil's prettiness. 'And I'm not likely to snare a husband with all them young fellers not coming back from the war, am I? You've been lucky.'

That had been the Great War; the war that had been

supposed to end all wars, and yet here they were just emerging from a second conflict that had robbed them of another generation of young men. In the First World War, Grimsby had been devastated by the losses sustained by their local pals' battalion – the Grimsby Chums – when men from the same families, the same workplaces, even the same streets, had been lost. This time, when the authorities realized what heartbreak had been caused to communities, there had been no pals' battalions. But it didn't mean that towns and cities didn't lose their loved ones and Grimsby was no exception. And the civilian population had been hit hard too. Situated on the north-east coast of Lincolnshire and just across the Humber from Kingston Upon Hull, the town had taken its share of the bombing.

The Bailey family were all scattered now. Their parents were both dead and only Norma – apart from Lil – still lived in Grimsby on her own in the old family home. Yet the sisters hardly saw each other. Norma worked as a cleaner in two or three of the grander houses on Bargate and was well thought of by her employers as a conscientious worker, albeit rather dowdy in the black coat and felt hat she always wore, her sensible low-heeled shoes and her perpetually grim expression that did nothing to alleviate her plainness.

'If you'd only smile a bit more,' Lil had said daringly on one occasion, but her kindly efforts were met with a baleful glare and a dismissive sniff.

'What have I got to smile about? Scrubbing – that's all I'm good for. I never had the chances you had, Lil.' It was Norma's constant grumble on the rare occasions that the two sisters met. And so perhaps it was only natural that Lil felt closer to her neighbour, Edie Kelsey, whom she saw every day, than she did to her sister.

'Sit down, Edie, while I tell you. Tea's mashed.'

Edie dropped the shirt into the soapy suds, dried her hands and sat down with a sigh. She smiled across the table. 'What would I do without you, Lil, to pop in and make me a cuppa just when I need it?'

The two women sat in companionable silence for a moment, savouring the hot tea and the broken biscuits Lil had laid out on a plate.

'Come on then, Lil, spit it out.'

'Evidently he killed himself along with his mistress – well, his wife by then, it seems.'

'Eva Braun? He married her?'

Lil nodded. 'At the last minute. Then they both killed themselves the very next day. In his bunker in Berlin. She'd taken poison and he'd shot himself – through the mouth, the papers say.'

Edie was silent. She'd never considered herself a spiteful woman and yet at this moment she was tempted to say, Good job, an' all.

'So, is it all over, then, or is there some other bugger ready to step into his shoes? Mussolini, I suppose.'

'Oh no. He's dead too. He was shot several days ago by Italian partisans. He was hung upside down by his heels with his mistress beside him in the Piazza Loretta in Milan. Gruesome end for a man who used to be called *Il Duce*, wasn't it?'

'Ee, hark at you with your Italian,' Edie teased, but then she sighed. The war might be nearly over but already revenge killings had started.

'There're all sorts of rumours flying round about the German leadership,' Lil went on. 'They reckon Doenitz has taken over.'

Edie blinked. 'The Commander-in-Chief of the German Navy? I'd've thought it would have been Goebbels,

Himmler or even Goering.' Despite her declaration that she rarely listened to the news, Edie was remarkably well informed. When he was at home from the sea – often only for about thirty-six hours and then he was off again on the next tide – Archie followed the news avidly, listening to every bulletin and devouring the newspapers. Edie couldn't help but overhear, or be obliged to listen to, Archie ranting when he read or heard something with which he disagreed. A mild, good-tempered cuddly bear of a man most of the time with thinning fair hair and blue eyes, Archie could become surprisingly incensed by controversial news items.

Lil shrugged in answer to Edie's comment. 'You'd've thought so, wouldn't you, but it seems that Hitler fell out with Himmler because he'd tried to negotiate with the Allies and with Goering because he wanted to take over the leadership.'

'What about Goebbels?'

'He died in the bunker with Hitler, apparently. Anyway, everyone seems to think the war's over – at least in Europe. We're all just waiting for Mr Churchill to make an official announcement. And the German forces in Italy have surrendered.'

'What about the war with Japan?'

Lil shook her head. 'That's still going on.'

There was a long silence before Edie murmured, 'They'll not be coming home yet, then.'

Edie's eldest son, Laurence, had been killed at Dunkirk and, though she would never get over the loss, she had, along with many more mothers, learned to live with her grief. Like her friend Lil, she just 'got on with it'. But now, when there had been a glimmer of hope that her second son, Frank, still serving in the army – God alone knew where – would soon be back, she was sensible enough to know that although one theatre of war might be over, whilst there was still another enemy to defeat, demobilization was unlikely. 'Frank won't be home until it's all finished with, will he?'

Lil shrugged. 'Your guess is as good as mine.'

'But it'll be over for us here, won't it? I mean, we're not likely to get kamikaze pilots over Britain, are we?'

Lil gave a wry laugh. 'I don't expect so, duck, no.'

'So your Irene and little Tommy will be coming home. Ee, I can't wait to see him. He must have grown. All that good country air and farm food – he'll have shot up since we last saw him. And my Reggie too. Oh Lil, I can't wait to have all my family back together.' Her face fell. 'There'll be one missing, of course, but to have everyone else back safe and sound . . .' Her voice faded away. Dare she begin to count the days just yet?

Lil touched her hand. 'Just be patient a bit longer, Edie. All we can do is hope and pray. Just like we've been doing for the past six years. And then they'll all be home, the boys and your Shirley and Beth too.'

'It'll be five years at the end of this month since Laurence . . .' Edie said and then fell silent again as she remembered that dreadful morning the telegram had been delivered.

'I know, duck, I know. I hadn't forgotten.'

Archie had been at sea when the news had arrived and Lil had been the one to whom Edie had turned. Never had Edie needed her good friend more than she had at that moment.

One

Edith Riley had been born and brought up on the same street in which she still lived. The elder daughter of Jim Riley, a trawler skipper, and his wife Patricia, she'd always longed to be part of a large family. Patricia, however, had had high expectations for her two daughters, Edith and Jessie. She dreamed of them both taking shorthand and typing lessons and working in a nice office, so she was not too pleased when Edie fell in love with the tall and handsome deckie learner, Archie Kelsey. When Edie fell pregnant, Patricia's hopes for her were finally dashed and a wedding was hastily arranged. Edie married at nineteen, and her son Laurence had arrived six months to the day after their marriage and Archie had found a house to rent just up the road from Edie's parents. Before many years had passed, the little house was bursting at the seams, the children sleeping top to toe: the boys in one bed, the girls in another.

After Laurence had come Elizabeth – Beth, as she'd soon become known. She was a pretty, merry child with dark curls and soft brown eyes. Archie had been her willing slave from the moment of her birth, for which he had been home from the sea to witness. He had been the first to hold the wriggling infant and the bond formed in that moment had never been broken.

In September 1919, Lily and Tom Horton had moved into the house next door. The two young women had

9

soon become firm friends and helped each other when their menfolk were at sea. Only two months later, though, Tom was tragically lost and the young mother-to-be leaned on Edie's broad shoulder, both literally and metaphorically. The birth of Lil's daughter, Irene, brought joy and sorrow in equal measure and Lil wept in Edie's arms. 'She'll never know her dad. He'll never play with her like Archie plays with your two.' She'd given a tremulous smile as she'd added, 'Three soon.' For Edie was heavily pregnant with her third child.

Frank Kelsey had been born two months later and with two children almost the same age, the young mothers grew even closer. Beth, though a year older than Irene, became the younger girl's friend and pro-tector. It was Beth's hands that Irene clung to as she learned to walk and the older girl's hand she held on to tightly on her first day at school alongside Frank. Beth watched out for both of them in the rough and tumble of the playground and stuck up for them if there was the slightest sign of bullying from anyone, no matter how much bigger than her they might be.

'She's a fiery piece, that Beth Kelsey,' was the general consensus in the playground. 'Don't lay finger on her little brother – or Irene Horton either – else she'll 'ave yer.'

Beth was a motherly little girl who not only cham-pioned her brother and the little girl from next door at school or out playing in the street, but also now had a baby sister – Shirley – to help feed and bath and dress.

'That's the last,' Edie declared to Lil as they sat watching Beth and Irene amusing the new baby.

'I'll believe that when I see it,' Lil said, smiling.

'No, no, I mean it, Lil. Four kids in six years – I mean it. I've got the family I always wanted. And she'

– she nodded towards the most recent arrival – 'isn't an easy baby like the other three. She's still waking up two or three times in the night. She's a grizzly baby, an' all. I hardly knew I'd got the others, but this one . . .' she cast her eyes to the ceiling – 'and she's keeping Beth awake. The boys seem to sleep through anything, but Beth's losing sleep and she's only five. She's too tired to go to school some mornings.'

'Oh, don't let her miss school, Edie,' Lil said swiftly, mindful of the gaps in her own education because of being kept at home to help with younger siblings. 'Tell you what, let her come and sleep at our house on school nights, if that'd help until little Shirley gets more settled. Irene'd love it and we've plenty of room.' The last few words were spoken without any hint of self-pity, yet Edie was aware of their poignancy.

'Well, if you're sure. She'd have all her meals at home, of course, but if she could come round some nights just to sleep, that'd be a huge help, Lil. Ta, duck.'

Edie was sensitive to the fact that Lil didn't have any spare money to be feeding her neighbour's child, though the children ran freely between the two houses, always sure of a welcome, always sure they were loved by their adopted 'aunties'. And happily, the children liked each other too. Though Laurence found playmates of his own age in their street and beyond, he was nevertheless a kindly boy and was not above entertaining his younger brother and sister and Irene too, who followed him about with the devotion of a little puppy. He was tall for his age, with fair hair like his father and blue eyes that, for the most part, twinkled merrily. But Laurence was no good with the baby, Shirley. With a bemused and wary expression, he would look at her in the battered pram that had served all the Kelsey babies, at her little red face screwed up, at her tiny fists waving and her feet kicking in anger. He just didn't know how to cope with a screaming infant, but he would take Frank into the street and teach him to kick a football, he would play Ludo or Draughts with Frank, Beth and Irene, patiently explaining the rules.

'But no cheating,' he would say firmly, trying hard not to laugh, 'else I won't play.'

Watching them fondly, Edie would say, 'He's a good lad, Lil. He'll make someone a lovely husband one day.'

God willing, Lil would think, but she was not going to voice such thoughts aloud. No doubt Laurence would be destined to follow his father into the fishing industry and they all knew what dangers that job held.

Despite Edie's adamant pronouncement that her family was complete, it had been no surprise to Lil when, over five years after Shirley's birth, Edie had come through the door in the fence between their two back-yards one morning looking bemused and strangely sheepish.

'Put kettle on, Lil, I've had a bit of a shock.'

'Oh Edie, what is it?' Lil was at once anxious. 'It's – it's not Archie, is it?'

Edie gave a wry laugh that told Lil that the news, which Edie was about to impart, was nothing very terrible. 'He's got summat to do with it, yes, but not the way you mean.'

'What is it, then? One of the kids? Or your Jessie? Don't tell me – she's fallen pregnant at last. Oh, how lovely—' But Edie was shaking her head.

Jessie was Edie's younger sister. She still lived in the same street, too, at the far end in the house where both the sisters had been born. She'd married a lumper. Harry Charlton worked nights unloading the fish from the trawlers, sorting it and preparing it for sale at the early morning auctions on the pontoon. He was a big, strong man, who said very little but who adored his vivacious, gregarious wife and shared her sorrow that they had not had children.

'No, no, it's not Jessie who's been caught. It's – me.' Lil's mouth dropped open. 'But you said . . .'

'I know what I *said*, Lil – me an' my big mouth – but there it is. I'm in the family way – again.'

Lil sat down at the table and reached across it to touch her friend's hand. 'But you're pleased, aren't you, Edie? I mean . . .'

'Oh, I expect I will be – once I've got used to the idea. But what Archie'll say when he gets home, I don't know. I've given all me baby stuff away. I'll have to get new.'

'Archie'll be as pleased as punch,' Lil tried to reassure her, though she couldn't quite keep the note of wistfulness out of her tone. She'd have loved more children, but there was no way it was ever going to happen now. 'He loves his kids and this one'll be no different.'

Seven months later, Beth, at eleven and Irene, ten, had another little baby to play with, though six-year-old Shirley was not so pleased to see the arrival of a tiny infant who usurped her coveted position as the youngest of the family. Reginald, who swiftly became known as Reggie, was a placid little chap, quite the opposite of what the fretful Shirley had been. Shirley now scowled every time she heard his gurgles and saw his round, beaming face.

'He never cries,' she overheard Edie telling Lil with amazement and took it as a personal insult when her mother added, 'Not a bit like Shirley was. As long as he's warm, dry and fed, I don't hear a peep out of him.'

So the two households grew, sharing their joys and troubles together as if they were all indeed part of the same family. They lived amongst fishing families and they all knew the hazards of that life; a hard life, but one the men wouldn't change for the world. Out at sea in atrocious weather, Archie would yearn to be home sitting in his armchair by the fire, cossetted by Edie and with the chance to spoil his children of whom he saw little. But after two days ashore, he – and many fishermen like him – would long to be back at sea.

Edie never went to the docks when Archie left on yet another trip, though the children, Laurence, Beth and Frank and later Shirley and Reggie too – and usually with Irene in tow as well – would wave him off.

'Don't forget to look at the listings in the *Grimsby Evening Telegraph* to see when we're due back,' he would remind them as he boarded his ship. And they'd always be there to welcome him home, even if it was late at night, for Edie knew what it meant for all of them. They didn't have long with him, his shore leaves were short, but for a day or two they had his full attention. They'd be waiting on the dock, ready to rifle through his sea bag for sweets and chocolate whilst he collected his settlings from the dock offices. If his catch had been plentiful, with his pay in his pocket, he would buy them gifts from the shops in Freeman Street, never forgetting to bring home something for Edie and even a little gift for Lil.

Freeman Street teemed with life; it was Beth's favourite place in the whole of Grimsby. The street thronged with people; fishermen, dressed in their best suits, home for sometimes as little as thirty-six hours before they were out with the tide once more. Women trying to shop for that extra tasty meal for their menfolk, children on bicycles weaving in and out of the path of the trolley buses. Cars towing trailers and window cleaners with handcarts; a busy, happy street and Beth loved it.

'Come on, Irene, let's go down Freeman Street. You too, our Shirl.'

'I've no money,' Irene would say quietly.

'Neither have I,' Beth would say cheerfully. 'But it doesn't cost owt to look, does it? And we can all see what we want to buy the next time Dad has a good catch.'

'I can't keep taking presents off your dad,' Irene said. 'It's not right.'

Beth would link her arm with her friend's and say, ''Course you can. You're like a member of our family, Irene Horton, and don't you forget it. Next time he comes home, he said he'll look out for two second-hand bikes – one for each of us. So there you are, you see. Dad always thinks of you too.'

'What about me?' Shirley had piped up. 'Am I getting a bike too?'

'I expect so, darling, but maybe not until you're a bit older, eh?'

'But I will get one?'

'Of course you will. Dad wouldn't miss you out, now would he? And when he's old enough, he'll get one for Reggie an' all.'

'What about Frank?' Irene asked in a soft voice. 'He ought to have one before me.'

Beth laughed, a merry sound that had the folks passing by them smiling at the sound. 'Frank's already got one. Dad got it after his last trip. He knows a chap in the next street who does up second-hand bikes.'

'I haven't seen it.'

'It's in the shed at the bottom of the yard, but he'll

not let you see him with it until he's learned how to ride it properly. And he hasn't yet. Laurence takes him up and down the street on it after dark. You watch out of your mam's bedroom window and you'll see them. But don't let on I told you.'

And so Archie continued to spoil his children; they were the centre of his world for the few days he was at home, and he theirs.

'I'm a millionaire for a day,' Archie would tell them with a deep chuckle, but he was a careful man and whilst he spent freely on the day of his return from sea, there was always enough saved for his wife who would have to manage the housekeeping until he returned from his next trip. And on the occasions when his catch was poor, he explained carefully to the children why, this time, there would be no presents. He'd say, 'And I can't afford to take you to the ice rink this time, but we can go to the park or to the beach at Cleethorpes. What would you like to do?'

Whilst Edie washed and ironed his clothes ready for his return to sea, Archie would spend time playing with his children. But she was careful never to wash on the day he left. Even fishermen's wives were superstitious. But their mother, anxious that Edie and Jessie would know nothing of the life, had kept them cocooned from such tales, dismissing them as nonsense.

'You'll wash him to a watery grave,' a new neighbour had told Edie when she was first married. 'And you'll see he'll never sail on a Friday, it's bad luck.' The woman had jabbed her finger towards her. 'You'd best get rid of that green jumper, an' all. We don't have owt green in Grimsby. Even the Mariners' goalie never wears a jumper that colour. Green is for grief. And, when you're cooking, don't forget to smash your eggshells into smithereens.'

Edie had blinked. 'Whatever for?'

The woman had cackled with laughter. ''Cos, duck, half an eggshell is big enough for a witch to sail out to sea and bring disaster to trawlers.'

Edie had laughed, but she knew better than to defy any belief no matter how ridiculous it sounded. She learned them all. She wouldn't toy with Archie's life; he was too precious to her.

And his time ashore was treasured too. But besides having fun with his children, Archie would make time for lessons too, teaching them Morse code and semaphore with his big torch and with flags. 'It'll come in useful if you go to sea, lads,' he said to his sons, but Beth was not to be left out.

'I want to learn it too, Daddy.'

Archie had smiled indulgently. 'You'll not be a fisherman, duck. Girls don't go to sea.' But when Beth had pretended to pout, he had relented and included her in the lessons. As it turned out, she had been the quickest learner of them all and soon she was sending perfect messages by both the flickering torch and the flags. She stood in front of her brothers and Irene, arms outstretched whilst Archie watched her. Pity she's not a lad, he thought, but then he reminded himself sharply that she would not be his pretty little Beth if she were. But her quickness, her brightness and her eagerness to learn made his heart swell with pride.

'Are you taking Laurence on your next trip, Archie?' Edie had asked when their eldest son was nearing school-leaving age, but her husband had shaken his head adamantly. 'No, love. You know I won't ever take any member of my family to sea with me. The lads can go when they're ready. I'll find them a good skipper, but it won't be me.'

Laurence had gone to sea twice before he left school and had found the experience harrowing. He suffered appalling seasickness.

'It'll disappear when you go to sea for real,' Edie had tried to reassure him. 'You'll be far too busy to think about being ill.'

Frank, however, first went to sea with one of Archie's trusted pals at the age of twelve. He came home, excited and elated. 'I weren't sick at all,' he told them all proudly. 'I want to be a skipper like me dad.'

Archie had laughed and ruffled his hair. 'Well, you have to start as a galley boy and work your way up, but if it's what you really want to do, lad, then I'll not stand in your way.'

'What's Laurence going to do now he's about to leave school?' Lil asked Edie in the summer of 1932.

'What else can he do? It's no use him staying on to take examinations. He's a practical sort of chap.' Edie smiled fondly, if a little sadly. 'He's not one for book learning. I expect he'll go to sea like most of 'em do.'

Lil eyed her friend. 'But you don't want him to,' she said quietly, sensing that there was something troubling Edie.

Edie wriggled her shoulders. 'I wouldn't mind if only he could go with his dad, but Archie won't hear of it.'

Lil blinked. 'Why ever not?'

'He doesn't agree with folks from the same family going to sea together.' Edie bit her lip, knowing she was touching on a painful subject for Lil, but it had to be said. 'You know what it's like, duck, don't you?'

Lil nodded. On that dreadful night not only had Tom been lost, but two of his cousins had perished on the same ship. The whole Horton family had been devastated three times over. 'I can see his point,' she said quietly.

'So can I, I suppose.' Edie sighed. 'But I just wanted to feel that someone was keeping an eye on the lad, you know. Anyway,' she added, brightening a little, 'he's not going to sea straightaway. Harry's found him work on the dock so that should keep him out of trouble for a bit.'

Three years later, in the summer of 1935 – the same year that Beth left school – Laurence went to sea as a member of a crew for the first time. Beth, reckoned by them all to be the clever one in the family, had stayed on at school to take her School Certificate. That summer she found work locally as a nursemaid to a Mr and Mrs Forster's two young children, aged four and two.

Beth had grown into a lovely girl, with long brown hair curling to her shoulders and her dark eyes were soft and gentle. When she was anxious she would twist a strand of her hair round and round her forefinger. Yet, she did not look her age; she was slim and not very tall and many mistook her for a schoolgirl still. Perhaps this is what endeared her to young children; they felt she was one of them, not a grown-up at all.

'The kiddies are so sweet, Mam,' she told Edie and Lil when she arrived home after being interviewed for the position. 'And Mrs Forster's French – so pretty and dainty, but she can't deal with two lively kids. You'd never believe it, Mam, how those two little imps run rings around their mother. They fluster her, but they seemed to take to me. I spent the afternoon with them and Mr Forster was ever so pleased with how I got them to do as I told them, and Mrs Forster' – Beth laughed – 'she just couldn't believe it. "Why do they not do that for me?" she said.' Beth imitated the French woman's accent perfectly. 'And,' Beth added, her eyes sparkling with excitement, 'best of all, I might get the chance to go to France to look after the children when they go to visit Madame's parents.'

'Oh dear,' Edie moaned. 'I'm losing my chicks. Laurence is going to sea and you're going across the water too.'

'You've still got Frank and Shirley and little Reggie. They'll not be leaving home for ages yet. And there's Irene too. She's here more often than not.'

Lil and Beth laughed together, but Edie could only raise a weak smile.

'And just think, Aunty Lil, Irene will have her bedroom all to herself.' Beth had often continued to sleep next door even after Shirley's restless nights had ceased. With Reggie's arrival, Edie's little house was overflowing.

Lil grimaced. 'I don't think that'll please her. She'll miss you, Beth, sharing her room with you, whispering and giggling way into the night. We'll all miss you.'

'I'll come back often – every day I get off. But this is the perfect job for me. You know how I love looking after little ones.'

Whilst the Forsters still lived in Grimsby, Beth kept her promise, but the day came which Edie had feared. Mr Forster's job – 'something in imports and exports,' Beth told her family – took him back to France and, with great thankfulness, his wife insisted that the family should move back to her home country permanently.

And she was also adamant that Beth should go with them.

'I cannot possibly manage without you,' Simone Forster declared, her expressive hands fluttering in the air.

In the same week that Beth left for France, Laurence, who had done his best to overcome debilitating seasickness as a fisherman, vowed he would go to sea no more.

'I might be able to get a job down dock. Mebbe as a barrow lad.'

'That's hard work.'

'It's all hard work, Mam, but it pays a pound a week, don't forget. That's good money for someone of my age.'

'Talk to your Uncle Harry. He'll likely be able to put in a good word for you. Mebbe he could get you work alongside him as a lumper.'

Harry was willing to help, but warned his nephew, 'It's tough being a lumper, Laurence. It's wet and cold and dangerous working on ice-covered boards through the night whatever the weather. Mind you,' he added swiftly, 'it's better than going to sea, specially if you've got the seasickness bad.'

'Did you never want to go to sea, Uncle Harry?'

The older man shook his head. 'No, I didn't. I lost me dad and a brother to the sea. I don't like it. It's a cruel mistress.'

'Me dad loves it.'

'Aye, well, there's plenty of fishermen do and I suppose I can understand it. It's in their blood, somehow. And your dad's a good skipper. He's well-liked and trusted. Blokes who get into his crew hang on to their place as long as they can.'

'I guessed that. Several of them have been with him for years.'

'Aye, his mate's been with him ten years or more, I reckon. One little tip, lad, when you start as a lumper: wear gloves, else your hands'll be red raw in a day.' Harry grinned. 'But you'll soon get hardened to it.'

But Laurence did not take to the life on the docks any more than he had going to sea and not many weeks after Beth had gone, he left Grimsby to join the British Army.

Now, two of Edie's fledglings had left the nest.

Two

Whilst it had been Laurence whom the infant Irene had followed devotedly, had idolized as the big brother she would never have, as they all grew older, it was Frank with whom she fell in love. They'd always been a threesome, Beth, Irene and Frank, though sometimes with Shirley in tow. But once Beth had gone to France with the Forster family, the two younger ones were thrown together even more.

'I miss Beth so much, Frank,' Irene told him as they walked home from school together just as they always had done. But their school days were coming to an end too. In the summer, they would sit their School Certificate and then, they too, would have to look for work. They had both stayed on at school to take the examinations even though Irene had protested that she should leave and start bringing home a wage.

'You'll do no such thing, love,' Lil had said firmly. 'I want you to have the chances I never had.'

So, at sixteen, Frank and Irene, though they had dutifully worked hard at their schoolwork, were both itching to leave school, to find work and at last feel that they were 'grown-ups'.

'Yeah, me too,' Frank said, kicking a stone so that it bounced and rattled along the pavement as they walked. 'We made a good trio, didn't we? It's not quite the same with our Shirley, is it? She's such a mardy cow.'

Irene had giggled. 'Poor Shirley. I feel sorry for her. She's always been the odd one out, but she's only twelve. She's still a kid. I've tried hard with her, but she's – well, she's not Beth. She was like a big sister to me – just as Laurence and you are like my brothers.'

Frank was silent, looking down at the ground and giving the stone another kick.

'I don't want to be your brother, Irene,' he muttered. 'I – I want to be your boyfriend.'

'Eh?' Startled, Irene had stopped and turned to face him. 'What did you say?'

Frank was blushing, not daring to look up to meet her gaze. 'I said, I want to be your boyfriend, not a sort of brother.'

'Oh!' Irene said and then, after a long pause, she smiled and continued to walk on as she said softly, 'I think I'd like that, but—'

'Aye, I thought there'd be a "but",' Frank said, disappointment in his tone. His brown eyes were sad and his dark hair flopped endearingly over his forehead.

Irene giggled. 'I just think we should keep it secret. I reckon our mams would say we were too young.'

Frank's head shot up as he grinned at her. 'Oh, right. I get you. But they won't think anything of it if we're always together, will they?'

Irene laughed and now it was she who blushed. 'We always are, but we just won't have to let them see us – um – well, holding hands or – or—'

'Kissing.' Frank stopped again and took hold of her arm, turning her gently to face him. He planted a clumsy kiss on her mouth, but their noses bumped and they ended up laughing.

'Reckon we need a bit of practice at that,' Frank said.

24

It didn't take very long for Frank to become a lot more expert at 'this kissing lark' nor did it take many weeks for their families to find out.

It was Shirley who was the talebearer.

On leaving school, Frank had gone straight to sea. There had been no problem of seasickness for him, though his choice of career had caused an argument between his parents.

'I don't really want him going to sea at all,' Edie had said, 'but if he's set on it, then he can be with you, can't he, Archie? You can keep an eye on him.'

To her disappointment Archie had shaken his head and added, 'I don't believe in families sailing together. You know I don't. I know it's done, but I don't like it.' Archie Kelsey was a respected skipper and able to choose his own crew. He would never take men who were related – even distantly – to one another.

Some trawlermen ridiculed him. 'I can't get a crew together without 'em being related, Archie. How d'you do it?'

Archie had smiled enigmatically. He'd been a fisherman for a long time and a skipper for several years. He was known as a safe pair of hands and fair with the men under him. He never needed to look far for a crew; they returned time after time to serve under Archie Kelsey. He was saddened when, only a few years later, a trawler was lost at sea skippered by that very same trawlerman who had questioned his rules with the loss of all the crew, which had included three members from the same family. It was one of those occasions when Archie had been sorry to be proved right.

So Frank never sailed with his father, but he took to the life and soon earned the reputation of being a good and reliable worker.

Irene had grown into a pretty young woman with long blond curling hair, sparkling blue eyes and dimples in her cheeks when she smiled. And she smiled often. Irene had had no trouble in finding work in a department store in Freeman Street.

'She's got such a nice job at Oldroyd's on the hosiery counter,' Lil had enthused to Edie. 'They're all very kind to her there and I know she'll work hard and do well. No mending nets for her if I have anything to do with it.'

Edie had nodded and smiled. 'She deserves it, Lil. She's a good girl. I think of her like one of me own – you know I do. I'm pleased for both of you. Mebbe you'll be able to take it a bit easier now.'

But Lil had shaken her head determinedly. 'Oh no. I wouldn't want her thinking she's got to support me. She's going to give me a bit towards the housekeeping, but I've told her she ought to start saving for her bottom drawer.'

Edie had laughed. 'But that's a long way off yet, Lil. She's got to meet a nice young man first.'

'True, but she's a pretty girl – though I suppose I shouldn't say it about me own daughter.'

'Well, if she wants to meet a prospective husband, Lil, she'll have to stop going around so much with our Frank.'

Whenever he was at home from sea, Frank, feeling rich and important with money in his pocket, would splash out on his girl. They'd go to the cinema for a bob's worth of dark, as he put it, sitting in the back row of the stalls, holding hands and even sneaking a kiss whenever they thought no one would see them. But someone did see them and couldn't wait to get home to tell her mother. Shirley, on a special treat with her school friends one Friday evening, spotted her brother and Irene cuddling in the back row of the cinema.

'Our Frank's got himself a girlfriend, then,' she announced, almost before she was through the scullery and into the living room. Edie was sitting near the range with a pile of socks for mending on her knee. She was on her own, Archie was at sea and, although the wireless had been tuned to one of her favourite programmes, Edie had turned it off before the late news came on. She glanced up at Shirley, but the girl went back into the scullery to make cocoa for them both, deliberately keeping her mother in suspense. But Edie was used to Shirley's dramatics and she calmly carried on with her mending and waited patiently until the young girl could contain her news no longer.

'Did you enjoy the pictures?' Edie asked mildly as Shirley carried two mugs back into the living room and placed one beside her mother. 'What did you see?'

'We went to the Savoy. It was Charlie Chaplin in *Modern Times* and then there was a Mickey Mouse cartoon. But it was what was going on in the back row that was even more interesting than the films.'

Edie said nothing, keeping her gaze firmly fixed on her sewing.

'Didn't you hear what I said? Frank's got a girlfriend.'

'I heard.'

'I thought you'd say he was too young,' Shirley said, miffed because her mother wasn't displaying the interest – or the sense of shock – the girl had hoped for.

Edie dipped her head so that Shirley wouldn't see her wistful smile. She'd been sixteen when she'd started walking out with Archie Kelsey, even though it had been in secret to start with; her mother had not approved.

'He's a working man now. I just hope she's a nice girl, that's all.'

Shirley smirked. 'Oh, she's nice all right.'

Now Edie didn't try to contain her interest. 'You know her, do you?'

'Yes – and so do you.'

'Me?' Edie raised her eyebrows. 'I don't know any girls Frank's age except . . .' She stared at Shirley. 'Oh no! You don't mean it's – it's . . . ?'

Shirley nodded. Now she was getting the reaction she'd wanted.

'Oh well, now, I don't know about that.' For a brief moment, Edie was still and then, throwing her mending aside, she stood up. 'I'll have to have this out with Lil.'

'It's late, Mam. Aunty Lil might have gone to bed.'

'I doubt it,' Edie said grimly. 'She always sits up to wait for Irene coming home and if you say she's out with Frank and he's not home yet, then neither will she be.'

'What about your—' Shirley began, but Edie was gone, out of the back door and through the door in the fence. 'Cocoa?' Shirley said to the empty room. Already she could hear the sound of Edie banging on Lil's back door, the sound echoing through the night air.

Shirley finished her drink, set her mug down and followed her mother, catching up with her just as Lil opened her back door.

'Whatever's the matter?' she asked at once, her eyes dark with fright. Fisherfolk didn't like late-night knocks on their door.

'It's all right, Aunty Lil, it's nothing very terrible, but Mam's got summat to tell you.'

Edie grasped Shirley's arm firmly. 'Well, now you're

here, miss, you can do the telling, seeing as you're the one who's seen it for yourself.'

'Seen what?' Lil asked.

'Let's get inside, Lil, and we'll tell you.'

'Oh sorry, Edie. Come in, duck. I'm not thinking straight. You've got me worried. I thought it was bad news.'

''Pends how you look at it. It's about Irene.'

Lil drew in a startled gasp, but as Shirley added, 'And Frank,' the woman's anxiety turned to puzzlement.

'I – don't understand.'

'Shirley's just been to the pictures with some of her friends from school – a gang of them went – and she saw your Irene and our Frank—'

'Sitting in the back row—'

'Kissing.'

Lil's mouth dropped open as she glanced from one to the other. But then she began to smile. 'Well, that's nice,' she began, but sensing Edie's disapproval, she faltered. 'Isn't it?'

Edie shook her head. 'They're too close.'

'More like brother and sister,' Shirley put in slyly.

'They've grown up together.'

Lil was frowning. 'I don't see that that matters. I – I think it's lovely. Childhood sweethearts. What could be more romantic?'

Edie wriggled her shoulders. She hadn't reckoned on Lil disagreeing with her. 'Tell you what, we'll not say owt to them – not yet. We'll wait till Archie gets back. See what he says.'

'All right, but . . .' Lil agreed reluctantly. She was more than happy with the news. She'd spent sleepless nights worrying that her pretty daughter might get in with the wrong crowd or start going out with someone totally unsuitable. She was very relieved to hear that Irene might be falling in love with the boy next door, the boy whom Lil already loved as a son. What could be better? But Edie didn't seem to think so and though Lil, at the moment, couldn't understand why, she hoped this wouldn't come between her and her dearest friend.

'And I'll write and tell our Beth,' Shirley said. 'She'll talk some sense into them. They'll listen to her. And Laurence. I'll write to him an' all.'

As Lil closed her back door behind her departing neighbours, she was thoughtful. She couldn't understand Edie's objection to the blossoming love story, if it was indeed serious. She thought it was wonderful news. And now, knowing that Irene was with Frank and would be seen home safely, there was no longer any need for her to sit up into the early hours waiting for her daughter. She began to get ready for bed, a small smile playing on her mouth. Just as she was about to fall to sleep, she heard the back door close softly and Irene creep up the stairs.

Oh how wonderful it was, she thought, to be young and in love. Her only sadness this night was that Tom was not here to delight in how his daughter had grown into a wonderful young woman, loved by a fine man.

If only, she thought, Edie comes round.

But her friend remained adamant. 'They're more like brother and sister,' Edie persisted, picking up on what Shirley had said. 'There can't possibly be that same excitement of meeting someone and falling in love. They know too much about each other already. Where's the thrill?'

'It's different, I grant you,' Lil said, 'but surely there's something to be said for the fact that they *do* know each other.'

The two women discussed the matter endlessly over the next few days but said nothing to Irene or Frank and swore Shirley to silence.

'I'm telling Beth, though,' the young girl said. 'She'll agree with us, Mam. And Laurence.'

But Beth did not agree, as she made clear in her letter.

What marvellous news, she wrote. *We'll still be one big, happy family. And they'll be able to live with Aunty Lil and when the little ones come along . . .* On and on her letter went, rambling over four pages; she was obviously ecstatic to think that her best friend would become her sister-in-law.

'Well, your dad won't agree,' Edie said, tossing Beth's letter to one side in disgust.

But to Edie's surprise and disappointment, Archie did agree with his elder daughter.

'Oh, I might have known you'd side with Beth,' Edie snapped. 'Whatever she says'll be right with you, won't it?'

'Now, now, Edie, love,' Archie said placidly, glad to be back home from sea. This last trip had been difficult and he'd been grateful to think he'd have a few days respite, but he hadn't expected to walk into a storm at home.

'So,' Edie said, folding her arms over her ample bosom – a sure sign that she was spoiling for an argument, 'you're in favour of it, are you?'

'I'm not *against* it, love. I can't see any harm. Let's see how it goes, shall we? I mean, it's not as if they're talking about getting married yet, is it? They are too young for that, I'd agree with you there. And it might all fizzle out anyway, given time. And just remember, Edie, the more you try to separate a young couple, the more determined they'll be to stay together.' He caught her eye and winked at her, silently reminding her of the opposition their own courtship had faced and, eventually, overcome.

With that, Edie was unable to argue.

Three

It was Laurence who finally won Edie over, though it took him several months. When he came home on leave the following May, he slapped Frank on the back and kissed Irene on both cheeks. 'When are you getting married, because I want to be your Best Man?'

'What about me? I want to be a Best Man too,' Reggie piped up. He idolized both his older brothers and didn't want to be left out.

'You're too young, Shrimp,' Laurence teased, tweaking his nose. 'But you can be an usher.'

'What's one of them?'

'They show the guests to their places in the church. It's a *very* important job. We don't want anyone sitting on the wrong side of the church, now do we?'

Edie hid her smile; she could always rely on Laurence to make everyone feel valued, but aloud she said, 'Now steady on there, who's talking of marriage? They're far too young for one thing and for another—' Edie repeated yet again her misgivings about their closeness.

'I reckon that's a good thing – oh, not the brother and sister bit,' Laurence added hastily, 'but isn't it better that they know all about each other? There're no skeletons going to pop out of the cupboard and Irene's a lovely girl. And she could do a lot worse than our Frank.'

Edie bristled. 'She couldn't do any better, let me tell you.'

33

'And besides,' Laurence said, his expression sobering, 'I know it's been euphoric just lately with the coronation—'

'The papers have been full of it,' Edie said, her expression softening, 'such lovely pictures of the little princesses. And tomorrow me and Lil are going to see a film about it at the Queen's cinema. I can't wait. They seem such a happy family. It's lovely to see, after all the trauma of the abdication.'

'And yet you'd deny our Frank the chance of such happiness, Mam?'

'Of course I wouldn't.' Now his mother was indignant, 'it's just – oh, I don't know. I seem to be the odd one out around here. You're all so pleased about it, all except me and Shirley.'

Laurence put his arm around Edie's shoulder. 'Mam, dearest Mam, Shirley's just jealous, that's all. And there's another thing,' he added softly and, for the young man who normally laughed his way through life, he was strangely serious. 'You know things are very unsettled in Europe, don't you? With all the civil fighting that's going on in Spain.'

'But that's got nothing to do with us, has it?'

Laurence shrugged but didn't answer her directly. 'And then there's this little corporal in Germany, who's talking about his country needing more "living space". I don't deny he's done wonders for the morale of the German people since their defeat in 1918, but now it seems he's not happy to leave it at that. He and his pal Mussolini are posturing that they want peace and yet want to extend their territories. And how d'you think they're going to do that? Mussolini invaded Abyssinia over a year ago and Nazi Germany, led by Adolf Hitler, has been secretly rearming – only it's not so secret now.

34

He's rebuilt the German navy and unlawfully created a military air force that he's been bragging is equal to Britain's and, probably spurred on by Mussolini's success in Abyssinia, he has reoccupied the Rhineland.'

'But I thought – I mean – there were Treaties and – and whatever – after the war, weren't there?'

Soberly, Laurence nodded. It seemed he took an interest in world affairs just like Archie did. 'Yes, Mam, there were. The Treaty of Versailles, but that doesn't seem to matter any more to Herr Hitler. I think he's hell bent on marching into whatever country takes his fancy. And we can't let that happen, now can we?'

Edie blinked as she gaped up at him. 'You don't mean there might be another war? Oh no, Laurence, not again. Surely they won't let it happen again?'

'Of course, we all hope not, but—'

'Then you must leave the army right now.'

Laurence gave a wry laugh. 'I can't, Mam, I signed on for nine years and even if I could leave – which I don't want to and I won't – I'd soon be called up again. In fact, if it does come to war, all able-bodied men would be called up eventually. Even Frank.'

'And me?' Reggie said. 'I'd like to be a soldier.'

Laurence laughed and ruffled his brother's floppy brown hair. 'Well, Shrimp, I hope it won't last until *you're* old enough to go.'

Edie was quiet for a moment before saying softly, 'So you reckon I ought to give in gracefully and give Frank and Irene my blessing, do you?'

'I do, Mam. We'll all be there for them. We'll help them and – if I know Aunty Lil – they'll only be living next door. Frank won't really be leaving home at all,' Laurence added with a coup d'état worthy of the most seasoned negotiator, 'not like if he married some girl, who took him right away from here. And besides, Aunty Lil's all for it. You don't want to upset her and lose her friendship, now do you?'

'No, I don't,' Edie said swiftly, a sliver of fear coursing through her at just the thought of such a preposterous idea.

'Oh, I know you've got Aunty Jessie down the street,' Laurence went on, 'but let's face it, Mam, you're closer to Aunty Lil than you are to your own sister.'

Edie gave a huge sigh as she knew herself beaten. Perhaps they were all right; it would be nice to have Irene as her daughter-in-law. So Edie capitulated and made no more objections to the blossoming romance between Frank and Irene, but, for a little while longer, she held out against their marriage. 'They're only seventeen. They're far too young.'

But by 1939, war seemed inevitable and Frank and Irene pestered both families to be allowed to marry before Frank might be conscripted, Edie once more found herself the only one holding out against the idea. This time, even Shirley had accepted the idea especially since the day Irene had asked her to be a bridesmaid.'It wouldn't be a bad thing for Frank to be married, you know,' Archie argued.

'You've heard about the Military Training Act that's just been passed, haven't you, that requires all men aged twenty and twenty-one to take six months' military training?' Edie nodded. She'd read about it in the newspapers Archie had shown her. 'Well, now they're saying in the papers that if war does come, it's likely that all men aged eighteen to forty-one will be liable for conscription, though single men would probably be called up before married men.'

'But it *hasn't* come yet,' Edie retorted, but already

she knew she was losing the battle. 'Frank's only eighteen, so he's safe for another two years at least even without getting married.'

'He'll be nineteen next month,' Archie reminded her quietly.

'But won't fishing be a reserved occupation?' was Edie's last salvo. Archie's reply had been only a shrug. 'Yes, it will be – to a point, but they can be called up into the Navy and, besides, fishing's going to get less and less the longer a war lasts.'

'But we'll always need fish,' Edie tried to argue. 'Even more so if there's a war on, though I expect the prices will rocket.'

Archie had remained silent. He didn't want to tell her that the North Sea would be a dangerous place and that already there was talk of trawlers being commandeered by the Navy to be turned into minesweepers to help the war effort if it became a reality. And fishermen would be volunteering to undertake such work. But fishing would continue, Archie knew, even if the number of vessels putting out to sea to fish were seriously depleted. And that would seriously affect employment in the town; many of the jobs on shore depended on the industry. But it would have to go on; the nation would need to be fed. Archie hoped – as a skipper of some years standing now – that he would be able to hang on to his job but he seriously doubted if young men like Frank would be able to find regular employment. And if they couldn't, no doubt they would be called up.

In July, the authorities began issuing Public Information Leaflets on what to do if war broke out. The threat was coming closer and closer.

And then, Beth arrived home unexpectedly.

Edie was ironing one Saturday afternoon, swapping her two flat irons in turn as they heated on the range. Archie was dozing in his chair by the fire whilst Shirley sat at the table polishing her mother's copper kettle, when they all heard the sound of light footsteps tripping down the passageway.

'If I didn't know better,' Edie murmured, 'I'd think that was our Beth . . .'

She glanced up at the window that looked out over the backyard and saw a slim figure heading to the back door.

'It is her,' Shirley said, flinging down her polishing cloth and rushing into the scullery.

'Eh? What?' Half asleep, Archie struggled up from his chair whilst Edie stood with one iron suspended in mid-air, staring at the door leading from the living room into the scullery and listening to the excited voices of her two daughters. Archie was already holding his arms out wide. 'Beth, my lovely, you've come home to us.'

'Looks like I won't get my ironing finished now,' Edie murmured, but she was smiling as she put the iron back on the hob and went forward to meet her daughter.

When the first flurry of welcome had settled down and Archie had carried her suitcase up the stairs, Edie bustled about setting out the tea. 'You must be hungry. You sit down in my chair, Beth, and tell us all about it. Have you left the Forsters? Are you home for good?'

Before she could answer, the back door burst open and Reggie came in, panting heavily and grinning widely. 'I thought it was you. I was playing footie up the end of the street and I saw you. Have you come home for Frank's wedding?'

Beth's eyes widened. 'Are they getting married soon, then? How lovely.'

38

'Only if they elope, 'cos there's been a lot of argy-bargy in this house about it,' Reggie went on before anyone else could speak. 'Mam dun't want 'em to get wed, but the rest of us do. Laurence is going to be Best Man and I'm going to be an usher.' The nine-year-old was a gangly boy with scuffed knees and short trousers. He had brown hair, like Frank, and the same dark eyes.

'And I'm going to be Irene's bridesmaid,' Shirley said importantly, but then her smile faded a little. 'Though I expect she'll want you instead, now you're home.'

Beth put her arm round her sister. 'Not instead, *chérie*, but maybe as well. That'd be all right, wouldn't it?'

Shirley nodded and smiled again. She gazed at Beth, drinking in the sight of her – she was taller than her elder sister already. She was still the same Beth, and yet there was a difference about her and not only in the stylish cut of her hair – swept back from her face but falling in shining waves and curls to her shoulder. She was wearing a fitted pink jacket with a pink and grey flared skirt. A pale blue scarf, tied in a bow at her neck and a jaunty pink hat completed what was a very smart and fashionable outfit.

'Is that what they're wearing in France just now?' Edie said, eying the fancy clothes with a mixture of envy and anxiety. 'It must have cost you a small fortune.'

'*C'est très chic, Maman,*' Beth laughed and added, 'Madame treated me to this outfit as a thank-you for all my work with the children.'

'Well, don't let your Aunty Jessie see it. She'll have it off your back as soon as look at you.'

'It wouldn't fit her. She's rather more' – Beth struggled to find the English word – 'voluptuous than I am.'

Edie sniffed. 'Maybe so, but if she knows that it's a Paris fashion, she'll squeeze herself into it.'

But Jessie, when she saw Beth's finery a little later in the afternoon, merely clapped her hands. 'Oh darling, you look wonderful. So like me, isn't she, Edie?'

Edie smiled thinly. There was no denying that Beth resembled her aunt in so many ways. She had the same prettiness and the same vivacious personality. She just hoped that Beth would be lucky enough to find a husband as good as Harry but that she, unlike poor Jessie, would be blessed with children.

As they all sat down around the tea table, they pressed Beth to tell them why she had come home. 'Not that we're not delighted to see you and hope you're back for good,' Archie added, trying hard not to let his favouritism for his elder daughter show in front of the rest of his family.

'When Frank gets married,' Reggie said, 'you could have our attic bedroom all to yourself. I wouldn't mind sleeping down here in Mam's front room.'

'Now, you just hold your horses, young man,' Edie said firmly. 'It's not definite that they're getting married – at least not yet anyway?'

Beth gazed across the table at her mother, her soft brown eyes suddenly very serious. Her smile had faded from her face. 'Mam,' she said softly, 'there is a war coming, you know. That's why I've come home. Czecho-slovakia has been overrun and now Hitler's got his sights on Poland. If that happens, we'll go to war and the French are very afraid that yet another war is going to be waged in their homeland.'

There was silence around the table as Beth finished

speaking. Slowly, Edie raised her eyes to meet her daughter's gaze. 'Then you think – you all think – I should allow them to get married?'

Slowly, Beth nodded. 'The sooner the better, I'd say, Mam.'

'All right. You win. You all win.'

'Don't look at it like that, Mam,' Beth pleaded, but it was Archie who chuckled and said, 'If I know your mam, Beth, once she gets started planning this wedding with your Aunty Lil, she'll forget she was ever against the idea.'

They all laughed and then Archie prompted Beth, 'So, with all that's happening in France, you thought it best to come home. Very sensible, love.'

Beth laughed. 'I can't take the credit for that, Dad. It was Mr Forster – Alan – who decided we should all come back here. But you should have seen Madame's reaction. She was almost hysterical at the thought of leaving her parents to the mercy of the Nazis. So Alan said we'd all come – her parents and her brother, Emile, too.'

'And have they?'

Beth shook her head. 'Her parents wouldn't leave their farm and Emile' – she paused and Edie was sure she detected a softer tone and a note of anxiety when she spoke the young man's name – 'he's determined to stay and fight for his country if it comes to that – and I think it will.'

'So, who's come back, then? Just Mr Forster, his wife and the children?'

Beth nodded. 'But they're settling down south, near London, this time. As a fluent French speaker, Alan thinks he can be helpful to the War Office.'

'Won't he be called up?'

'It's very doubtful he'd pass the medical. Evidently he had rheumatic fever as a child, which has left him with a mild heart condition. It was nothing serious in terms of being life threatening, but it was enough to keep him from ever being called up to active service. But with his background knowledge of France, he thinks he could be very useful here in the event of Britain becoming involved in the war.'

'What about you, love?' Archie asked softly, already fearing the answer he guessed he was about to hear. 'What are you going to do? Are you still needed down south to look after the Forster children?'

'No, Simone is enrolling them in boarding school, so I intend to offer my services to the authorities wherever I can be of use.'

At this, there was silence around the table.

Four

'Get kettle on, Lil,' Edie called as she stepped into her neighbour's living room the following morning, where Lil was rolling out pastry and Irene was hanging her underclothes on the airer suspended by ropes and pulleys from the ceiling. 'Our Beth's home – though how long for, I don't know – and it looks like we've got a wedding to plan.'

Irene turned round and her mouth dropped open, but Lil looked puzzled. 'What d'you mean? Is Beth getting married?'

Edie chuckled, nodding towards Irene. 'No, I mean these two rascals. Everyone else seems to think it's a good idea, so, I'm beaten.'

'Oh Aunty Edie, please don't say that,' Irene said, moving towards their friend and neighbour. 'We both want you to be pleased for us.'

Edie sighed. 'I am, love, it was just that I had doubts at first and you're both so young, but if Frank is old enough to have to go to fight for his country, then I suppose he's old enough to get married. And we'll all be on hand to help you both. By the way, where are you going to live? Here with your mam?'

'It makes sense,' Lil said. 'Frank's away at sea a lot and, if he does get called up, it would be silly for Irene to be paying rent to live on her own, now wouldn't it?'

'That's what we all thought.'

'Oh Aunty Edie, thank you – *thank* you.' Irene hugged her and then stood back, her eyes shining. 'And you say Beth's home. Do you think she'd be another bridesmaid alongside Shirley?'

'I'm sure she'd love it,' Edie said, beaming.

Arrangements for the wedding moved swiftly and a date was set for Saturday, 9 September.

'Now,' Beth said, 'you're not going to mind me being a bridesmaid too, are you, Shirley?'

Shirley was the misfit in the Kelsey family. She was an unattractive child with straight mousey hair, not helped by a permanently sulky expression. Although Archie tried valiantly to hide his favouritism of Beth – he never spoiled her any more than he did the others – Edie did not hide the fact that she idolized her three boys. Challenged, she would have hotly denied showing any preference, but Shirley felt it. Beth – pretty, lively and able to make friends easily – felt sorry for her younger sister and always tried to compensate. She and Irene had always included the younger girl in their outings and tried to involve her in their girlie chats and their experiments with make-up and clothes. But when Beth had left home and Irene had started seeing more of Frank, the younger girl had felt lonely. She didn't make friends easily and had few school chums.

Now, though, Beth was back and both she and Irene were including Shirley in the wedding preparations.

'Are you staying on at school until next year, *chérie*?' Beth asked, as she wielded a pair of curling tongs. Sitting in front of Irene's dressing table, Shirley meekly submitted to Beth's valiant efforts to instil some curl into her sister's short hair.

Shirley grimaced into the mirror. 'Mam says I ought to. She says if I leave, I'll only get drafted into some sort of job to do with the war effort.'

'Maybe you could get a job at Oldroyd's with me,' Irene said. 'Do you want me to ask? I mean, you are old enough to leave school now, aren't you? Or do you want to take the exams?'

'It'd be a good idea to stay on,' Beth advised. 'If you get any sort of qualification, no one can ever take it away from you, you know. Alan Forster was very keen to know what subjects I'd passed when he interviewed me – and that was only to look after his kids.'

'Mm. Trouble is, I don't like school much. I wouldn't mind leaving now.'

'I'll ask Miss Townsend at work if they've any vacancies, if you like,' Irene said.

'Right,' Beth said giving Shirley's hair a triumphant flick. 'Don't you think that looks nice, Irene?'

All three girls scrutinized Shirley's new look in the mirror.

'It does. Curly hair really suits you,' Irene said. 'You'll have to learn how to do it up in rags at night.'

'To sleep in, you mean?'

Irene nodded.

'Won't it be uncomfortable?'

'Well, yes, a bit but—'

'Oh, how we have to suffer for our beauty, *chérie*,' Beth said, dramatically putting the back of her hand against her forehead.

Shirley giggled. 'What's this "sherree" you keep calling me?'

'It's French for "darling".'

'Can you speak a lot of French now?'

'Oh yes.' Beth pulled a face. 'In fact, I'm having a job to think of English words sometimes.'

Irene kept her promise to ask about vacancies in the department store where she worked, but, the next evening, she came round to see Shirley. 'I'm sorry,' she said in a low voice out of range of Edie's sharp hearing. 'But they're not taking on any new staff at the moment because of all the uncertainty over the war.'

'It's OK,' Shirley said. 'I'll stay on until next summer. Things might be better by then.'

Irene smiled wanly and nodded. She was very much afraid that, by then, things might be a whole lot worse.

The date for the wedding – 9 September – had been decided and the church booked, but a venue for the reception had still not been decided on.

'We'll have it in my front room,' Edie said.

'Or mine,' Lil put in. 'I'm the bride's mother. I'm supposed to be whatever-they-call it. The hostess, I suppose.'

'Now, Lil, we've had all this out before; you're to let me and Archie help you and not be embarrassed about it. We're one big happy family. Remember?'

'Mebbe we could hire a hall somewhere,' Lil said, but Edie could hear the doubt in her tone. Hiring a hall would be expensive. The young couple couldn't afford it and neither could she.

'No need, duck,' Edie was adamant. 'We'll squeeze everybody in. There won't be that many more than we have round the table at Christmas. And we'll do the catering between us. In fact, if you're not doing owt now, how about a trip round the shops to see what we can get to put by for the big day?'

Now that she had given in to the idea, Edie embraced it with the fervour of the converted.

The two women set off together and joined a queue outside the butcher's. 'I wonder if . . .' Edie began but she was interrupted by a merry voice from the front of the line.

'Edie – and Lil – how fortuitous,' Jessie greeted them, her hands spread wide in welcome. 'I was thinking of coming round to see you two.'

'She always did use big words where a simple one would do,' Edie muttered in Lil's ear. 'Though I expect she'd say "would suffice".'

Lil had difficulty in stifling her laughter as Jessie gave up her position and came to stand by them. She was wearing a kind of uniform; a green tweed coat and skirt and a matching felt hat with a red band. 'I've joined the Women's Voluntary Service and we need more volunteers, you know,' Jessie was saying, 'and I thought you two would be just perfect.' She nodded towards Lil and added, 'Your sister, Norma, has already joined us.'

Lil pulled a face. 'Getting everyone organized, is she?'

Jessie chuckled. 'She's trying.'

'Oh, very trying, I'd say,' Lil muttered.

'But I bet she's no match for you, Jessie, is she?' Edie put in.

'Absolutely not, Edie. We'll be very busy if they evacuate all the kiddies like they're saying might happen. Will you send Reggie, Edie?'

Edie shook her head firmly. 'No, he'll stay at home with me.'

Jessie pulled face. 'You ought to think about it seriously. Grimsby'll be right in the line of fire, if you ask

47

me. Anyway, there's no reason why the two of you can't help out now and again. Do come along some time.'

'We'll see,' was all Edie and Lil would promise. 'We've got a wedding to organize, Jessie.'

'I heard,' Jessie smiled, 'but I'm still waiting to be asked.'

Edie chuckled. 'Don't hold your breath for an official invite, Jessie. Printed ones cost money. Just take it that you and Harry are invited.'

Impishly, Jessie said, 'And would you like me to extend the invitation to your Norma when I see her, Lil?'

Lil sighed. 'Aye, you might as well. I suppose she'll have to come.'

The three women glanced at one another and began to laugh.

Five

On Sunday, 3 September, a sunny, sultry day, Britain officially declared war on Germany and Laurence sent word that he would not be able to attend the wedding; he was likely to be amongst the first British soldiers to be sent to France with the British Expeditionary Force. A cloud settled over the family, not only because the whole country's fears had been realized, but also because Laurence would not be with them for their special day.

'It's starting,' Edie moaned to Archie. 'My wonderful family'll be split up before we know it. They want to evacuate the youngsters. Jessie came round last night and she was telling us that a lot have gone already, but where are they sending them, that's what I'd like to know? I'm not letting Reggie go to live with strangers.'

'They're not going far,' Archie tried to console her, but he had his own worries, concerns he had not yet shared with his wife. Just what was going to happen to his livelihood now? The North Sea and beyond would be an even more dangerous place. 'It's true some are going to Derbyshire,' he went on, trying, for the moment, to concentrate on Edie's anxieties. 'But a lot are only going as far as Skegness, Alford or Spilsby or even just into the Wolds. Reggie could stay relatively near home, just so long as he's out of the town.'

'It'll be far enough. Transport to get to see him will be difficult.' Edie paused and then asked in a small voice, 'You think I should send him?'

'To be honest, love, I don't know. Let's just see how things work out, eh? He can always go later.'

'I don't know whether he can. They're already saying that if they miss the first evacuations, they might not have the chance again.'

Archie put his arm around his wife's shoulders. 'Let's not worry about it now. In fact, let's not worry about anything except enjoying this wedding.'

'I can't now. Not when Laurence won't be with us.'

'Just try, Edie love. For Frank and Irene's sakes, just try.'

When the news had reached them from Laurence, Frank had sought out Reggie. 'You'll have to be my Best Man now. Think you can do it?'

'Of course I can – if you tell me what I've got to do.'

Frank laughed. 'Stick close to me and make sure I don't run away at the last minute.'

Reggie blinked and asked solemnly, 'You're not going to, are you?'

'Of course I'm not. I want to marry Irene more than anything in the world and, if I'm likely to get called up, then the sooner, the better. By the way, has Mam said whether she's going to send you into the country with the rest of the kids?'

Reggie shrugged. 'She's not said owt, though I reckon Dad thinks she ought to.'

Frank squeezed his brother's shoulders. 'You wouldn't be far away. Anyway, let's forget all about that. We've got a wedding to enjoy first. Oh, and you have to keep the ring safe. I'll give it to you when we get to the church. You have to hand it to me in the service.'

Reggie nodded, feeling important.

'Oh, you look beautiful, Irene,' Shirley said, as the three girls readied themselves in Irene's bedroom on the morning of the wedding. 'That dress fits you a treat. You've got such a lovely figure.'

'And you don't look so bad yourself,' Irene said. 'Your hair looks really pretty, curled up like that. And you're getting a very nice shapely figure too.'

Shirley blushed, whilst Beth grimaced comically. 'More than can be said for me. I can't seem to get any voluptuous curves, however much of Mam's cooking I put away.'

'Thanks for doing my hair, Beth,' Shirley said. For once, she was feeling involved with the excitement of the day. 'I can't seem to get it right myself. I get this side all nice and then this side seems to flop.'

'When you leave school, *chérie*, I'll treat you to a perm,' Beth promised. 'Now, Irene, it'll soon be time we were leaving. Let's have a last look at you. Dad'll be round in a minute.'

Archie was to give Irene away.

'You were Tom's best friend, Archie,' Lil had said. 'It's what Irene and I both want – and it's what he would have wanted too.'

Irene was wearing a full-length, long-sleeved gown of ivory satin with a heart-shaped neckline and a small train. She had a full-length veil, held in place by a pearl tiara, and was carrying a bouquet of pale pink roses and fern.

'You look amazing,' Beth said now, a catch in her voice. Even Shirley had tears in her eyes. She envied both Irene and Beth their good looks, but they were both doing their best to show her how to make the most of herself.

'Come on, Shirley. Time we were going.'

They all enjoyed the day; even Norma unbent enough to accept a glass of sherry and then seemed to be laughing rather loudly.

'Is your Aunty Norma drunk, d'you reckon?' Frank asked his new wife.

Irene giggled, a little tipsy herself. 'I wouldn't know, though I've never seen her laughing like that before. And just look at Mum's face. It's bright red. I think she's had one too many.'

'Come on, let's leave them to it.' Frank squeezed her hand. 'Time we were going.'

Frank had splashed out on a couple of nights in a nice hotel in Cleethorpes and he had no intention of wasting a minute of the money it had cost him. It wasn't far away but distant enough to make them feel they were really on honeymoon. The couple made their farewells and left in a taxi to the sound of everyone's good wishes ringing in their ears.

As the vehicle drew away, only Edie said sorrowfully, 'Another one of my family gone.'

'Come on, Mam,' Beth said, linking her arm through Edie's, 'don't get maudlin. They'll soon be back and living next door. He's not exactly gone very far, now has he?'

'No, but for how long? How long will it be before Frank is called up? And I expect you'll be the next to be off to London or somewhere to join up.'

Beth did not answer.

*

52

Immediately after the wedding, Jessie came round to see both Edie and Lil.

'Now, you two, you'll have to do some sort of war work sooner or later, so how about sooner?'

Jessie explained everything that the members of the WVS were likely to be involved in. 'There are plans for us to run a mobile canteen,' Jessie told them. 'The meals are going to be prepared in Doncaster and brought over here and then we distribute them. And thanks to Harry, I can drive.'

Edie frowned. 'But who are we taking meals to?'

Jessie ticked them off on her fingers. 'Gun crews, barrage balloon personnel – anyone stationed in and around the town, really. And then, if we do get bombed – Heaven forbid, but it's very likely it'll happen sooner or later – there'll be the rescue parties to be fed and watered. And I understand that the Town Hall will be a centre for families who get bombed out and we'll be in charge of looking after them.'

Edie said, 'I have to say, it sounds worthwhile work and the sort of thing we could do. What d'you think, Lil?'

'I'm doing my bit, Edie,' Lil protested. 'I've still got my nets to do.'

'I know, I know, but surely there won't be so much demand for fishing nets, will there? Archie was saying he expects a lot of the trawlers will be commandeered by the Royal Navy.'

Lil smiled. 'Well, I was just coming to tell you summat when Jessie arrived. I saw Mr Blake from Coal Salt yesterday and he said the authorities are looking for folk to make camouflage nets and they want them just like we make our fishing nets. They're taking on women to work in the old bus sheds in Cleethorpes, but I've got permission to work from home.'

'Eh, Lil, that's grand for you, duck. Me an' Archie have been worried that your work might fall off a bit. I hope they pay you well.' Then her face fell. 'So, I s'pose you won't have time for voluntary work, then? We'd make such a good team, you an' me.'

Lil chuckled at the thought of them walking side by side to the centre. They looked a comical pair when they were out together. Edie walked with a straight back and a stately gait, her head held high and her dark hair dressed in tight waves beneath her felt hat. Lil, whose head only came up to Edie's shoulder trotted along at the side of her, her short, fair curls blowing in the wind.

'Oh, I'll come along, Edie. It'll give me a break now and then from housework and the nets.'

Edie nodded. In the early days of her marriage she, too, had made and mended nets in her backyard. However, when Archie was promoted and the children came along – the first four in fairly quick succession – she was able to give up the work and concentrate on looking after her family, which fell heavily upon her when Archie was at sea for weeks at a time. When he became a skipper, the Kelsey family could have moved to the outskirts of the town, to a bigger and better house with a proper garden at the back, but Edie loved the neighbourhood where she lived. She knew nearly everyone down the long street of back-to-back terraced houses and they knew her. Besides, she hadn't wanted to leave Lil. And it was nice to have her sister, Jessie, living at the opposite end of the road too. There were only the two of them left now, their parents having succumbed to the dreadful Spanish flu pandemic of 1918 and 1919. The sisters were very different. Edie was a fine figure of a woman but it was Jessie who was the prettier of the two. Her sweet face was framed with dark brown curls and she was vivacious and bubbly. She'd married Harry Charlton, a soldier who had survived the carnage of the Great War, and they'd rented the very same terraced house where Edie and Jessie had grown up. Much to the sadness of both Jessie and Harry, they had no children, but Jessie had compensated for that by being involved with Edie's growing brood. She'd always been on hand for baby-sitting duties, though always second to Lil, and had taken care of the whole family whenever Edie had been unwell or had been having another baby! And Harry had been a doting uncle-by-marriage.

'So,' Jessie prompted the two friends. 'Can I count on you both?'

As they glanced at each other and then nodded, Jessie beamed. 'That'd be great and I can assign you work together, if that's what you'd like.'

'We would,' the two friends chorused.

The three women laughed and, with the matter settled, their thoughts turned to other topics as they sat around Edie's table drinking tea and eating biscuits. Jessie loaded a teaspoon with sugar from Edie's sugar bowl and then paused. 'I suppose we'll have to cut down on all this sort of thing.' She was still hesitating, the spoonful hovering over her cup.

Edie smiled and nodded. 'Go on, Jessie. It's not happening yet.'

'But it will,' her sister said, serious for a moment. 'I remember the last time. I was sixteen when it started.'

'And I was eighteen and courting Archie in secret. It was easy really, with him being away at sea such a lot. Mam didn't find out for months.'

'You went to work at the Victoria Flour Mills, didn't you – in the war?'

Edie chuckled. 'Much to Mam's disgust. And you weren't much better – in her eyes anyway.'

'No, she didn't like me working at the local War Hospital Supply Depot but I so wanted to be a nurse and I thought that would be a way in, but she was against that too.' Jessie pulled a face. 'There wasn't much I could do about it and by the time I was old enough not to need her permission to apply for training, the war was over. Besides,' she shrugged, 'I'd met Harry by then, so I ended up working in Ticklers' jam factory. She wasn't best pleased about that either, but it's a lovely place to work.' There was a pause before Jessie asked, 'What about you, Lil?'

Lil's shoulders sagged as she remembered the drudgery of her young life. 'I was at home helping my mam. She wasn't strong and having six children hadn't helped. I didn't get involved with anything in the war, I'm afraid, but,' she added with a new determination in her tone, 'I will this time.'

'That's the spirit,' Jessie said. 'We'll soon have old Adolf licked.'

'What do you think we should put by?' Edie said, her mind returning to providing for her family. 'Food, I mean.'

'I remember our mam sending me out to buy extra sugar and tea,' Jessie said. 'And soap. She was terrified we'd run out of soap.'

Lil laughed wryly. 'That didn't bother anyone in our house. We must have been a mucky lot, looking back. No wonder I never had any friends.'

Edie reached across the table to touch her hand. 'You've got plenty of friends now, duck.'

Lil smiled gratefully at her. 'I think the only thing we bought extra of was Dad's baccy. Selfish to the last, he was.'

'I know what I'm going to do,' Edie said suddenly. 'I'm going to clear the top shelf in my pantry and put some extra things there that will keep – tins of corned beef, salmon, mebbe cocoa and tinned fruit that I can bring out on special occasions.'

'Just be careful it's not too much of any one thing, Edie,' Jessie warned, 'or you might get accused of hoarding.'

Edie waved her hand dismissively. 'That's when you stockpile stuff – far more than you could ever need. I won't be doing that, Jessie.'

On the day that Edie and Lil had presented themselves at the WVS centre, they found that Jessie was already there, organizing with a cheerful firmness that had everyone following her orders without question. All except one person, who stood on her own at the back of the room, her mouth pursed in disapproval.

'Oh heck! *She*'s here?' Lil had muttered to Edie.

Edie glanced around. There were several women from their street and from the surrounding area too. And then she saw Norma.

'Let's ask Jessie what she wants us to do,' Lil said, firmly, leading the way across the busy room towards her.

'Aren't you going to speak to your sister?'

Lil paused and glanced once more across the room before saying tersely, 'Eventually.'

That first day was taken up with everyone getting to know each other. And gradually, Norma was included in the work, though it was obvious to Lil, if to no one else, that her sister resented anyone else taking charge.

It was true what they said about leopards and their spots, Lil thought, hiding her smile. Norma had always been the bossy one even though she was two years younger than Lil.

So, too young to be conscripted, and now also married, Frank continued to go to sea whenever he could, though as the weeks and months passed more and more trawlers stopped fishing. Many were turned into minesweepers to assist the war effort.

The time came when Frank could no longer find regular work.

'You could take him with you, Archie. You've still got a ship,' Edie pleaded once more.

'You know my feelings about family members on the same ship. I won't do it, love.'

And then, Edie broke her golden rule never to quarrel with Archie just before he put to sea. 'You'd sooner see your own son be shot by Hitler's Nazis than take his chances with you at sea, would you?'

Archie had sighed heavily, patiently holding on to his resolve. 'Edie, love, you know fishermen are a super-stitious lot. I'm not, in general, but in this one thing I am. I always have been and I won't break my rule now.' He took a deep breath. 'Not even for Frank.'

Six

'Archie Kelsey, if you think I'm going to let you dig up the only strip of garden I've got – or am ever likely to get – for a shelter then you've got another think coming.'

'We could have moved to a better part of the town years ago,' Archie said mildly with a twinkle in his eyes, for he knew very well what was coming next. 'You could have had as big a garden as you wanted.'

'There's no better part of town than our street, let me tell you. I've lived here all me life and I aren't going to live anywhere else. Besides, I wouldn't leave me neighbours. Salt of the earth, they are, each and every one of them. And you know I couldn't bear to be living anywhere else but next door to Lil. Really, Archie, fancy bringing that up again.'

Archie chuckled. 'I was really asking you about me digging a hole for an Anderson shelter in the yard. I want to keep you, Shirley and Reggie safe, especially when I'm not here.'

'Then you can ask Lil if you can put one in her backyard and we'll share it.'

'You'll not get everyone in there. Not while Frank's still here.'

'How many folk do they hold?' Edie was determined not to be outdone.

Archie wrinkled his brow as he studied the leaflet.

'Well, if you pack 'em in like sardines, you can get four adults and four young children in. But in our case, there'd be too many grown-ups.'

Edie chewed her lip. 'But we're complying with the instruction that we should grow all the vegetables we can. I'm already losing all me flowers. Me sweet peas – everything – just so you can grow potatoes and carrots and the rest.'

'I've let you keep your rose bush.'

'I should think you have, an' all. You planted that for me when Laurence was born. You were that thrilled to have a son.' They smiled at each other as they remembered.

'But to get back to the Anderson shelter—'

'I don't want one, Archie, and that's final.'

'But what about Reggie and Shirley?'

'Reggie won't be here, if you have your way about him being evacuated and Frank'll no doubt be gone soon' – there was a catch in her voice as she was forced to face the facts – 'so there'd be plenty of room for the rest of us in Lil's shelter, if she agrees to you putting one up in her backyard.'

'Except when I'm home.'

Edie sniffed. 'Which isn't often, let's face it.'

He sighed. 'I'll talk to Lil, then.'

'You do that.'

And, as far as Edie was concerned, the matter was closed.

Lil was quite happy for Archie and Frank to dig up the strip of ground – it hardly warranted the title of 'garden' – in her backyard. She'd never been a gardener, though she intended to do her bit for the war effort by growing a few vegetables now. But when she stood watching the two men beginning to dig the huge hole, she understood Edie's refusal to have one in her own backyard.

'I'll finish it, Dad, if you have to go back before we're done.'

'If you get down to water – and you're likely to, lad – get in touch with the council. Harry's digging one in their yard and he told me that they help towards concreting it. And don't forget to cover the top with earth deep enough to grow vegetables. Your mam and Lil are going to keep that going when I'm not here.'

And so the Anderson shelter took shape in Lil's backyard and was made as comfortable as possible. Edie sewed some old blankets together to make sleeping bags and together the two women collected 'emergency' rations and first-aid items.

'I really don't know what Archie wanted to do all this for. We haven't even had any bombs.'

'He's just being cautious,' Lil said. She was grateful for the help she'd received; she couldn't have constructed such a shelter on her own.

'We'd better make the most of Christmas this year, Edie,' Lil warned. 'They're starting rationing in the New Year. Butter and bacon'll be first, they say.'

'I know,' Edie nodded grimly, 'but it's sort of started already. There's a lot of things you can't get even now.'

'I've made me Christmas cake,' Lil said. 'I had the ingredients put aside before the war started.'

'And I've made the puddings.'

The two households always spent festive seasons – Christmas and Easter particularly – together and the two women pooled their resources; something that was going to be even more useful as the war progressed and shortages really began to bite.

It was a strange time, this first Christmas of the war. They couldn't help but look back and remember what they'd been doing this time last year, and Edie and Lil looked back even further, recalling the Christmases of the Great War, and now here they were almost four months into another.

'Well, we're all still here apart from Laurence,' Edie said, trying to make light of the fact that one of her brood – her eldest boy – would be missing from the celebrations. 'Even Archie reckons he'll be at home this year, but he's due away on Boxing Day.' Laurence was already somewhere in France with the BEF – the British Expeditionary Force. 'But we'll make the best of it. We couldn't have bonfire night because of the blackout, they're saying we won't get Easter eggs, and it's very doubtful we'll be able to have summer holidays next year, so I'll be blowed if they're going to take Christmas away from us an' all.'

'Mind you,' Lil said, 'it'll be very different. We can't put a lit-up Christmas tree in the window like we usually do.' The decorating and lighting up of their own tree in the front room had always been one of Lil's favourite times; a time she spent just with her daughter, an intimate, private moment when she remembered Tom so poignantly and wished he could see what a lovely daughter they had. And now that little girl was a married woman and her husband was living with them. Not that Lil wasn't enjoying having the young couple with her – they were great company. Frank had them both in stitches with his teasing and his jokes. And she had Irene to herself again when he was at sea.

'You can still do your tree, Lil,' Edie soothed, 'but just mind your blackout's tight, that's all.'

That's all! Lil thought mournfully. Christmas in complete blackness; it wasn't her idea of the festive season. 'And I expect the next thing'll be they'll be plastering anti-blast tape over the windows in all the shops and we won't be able to see all the Christmassy things.' That had always been another of Lil's simple pleasures when she and Edie walked the full length of Freeman Street in early December 'oohing' and 'aahing' over all the wonderful displays.

So on Christmas Day they gathered around Edie's table. Edie and Archie, who had docked on Christmas Eve, four of their five children, Jessie and Harry and, of course, Lil and Irene. It was a squeeze in Edie's front room but that only seemed to add to the closeness of the Kelseys and their neighbours, who now really were part of the family. Edie realized she was luckier than many this first Christmas of the war. Scores of children had already been evacuated from the town and would not be at home for Christmas. The mere thought made Edie shudder.

Archie stood at the head of the table carving the roast pork. Edie and Lil had bought the biggest joint they could find between them. Lil had brought the stuffing, apple sauce and the vegetables and Edie had supplied the plum pudding and brandy sauce.

'My, this smells good,' Frank said. 'I won't want no tea.'

Edie smiled. If she knew her family, they'd be tucking into nuts, fruit and crystallized figs all afternoon – even the youngest Reggie – yet they'd still be asking for sandwiches at teatime. And Edie had even found a greengrocer with some oranges for sale, and she doubted there'd be many available in the future.

There was no hiding the fact that there'd be all sorts of changes soon. Frank – despite his age and being married now – would no doubt be called up eventually. Every day, Edie urged him to try to find a reserved occupation that would keep him safely at home. And Beth – they all wondered what Beth would do. She'd said very little, and there was a restlessness about her and she seemed to be putting off finding work locally. But at least she was still here. She hadn't volunteered for one of the services or disappeared back to London, Edie comforted herself. At least, not yet.

Shirley seemed to be the only one whose plans for her future were settled. At the beginning of December, Irene had arranged for her to see Miss Townsend at Oldroyd's and Shirley, with Beth's guiding hand, had been quite presentable on the day of her interview.

'You need to look your best, Shirl,' Irene had said. 'Miss Townsend is the one who hires and fires the women staff and she's a stickler for a neat appearance.'

As several of the older girls were now leaving the store to join the forces or to take up war work of some kind, Miss Townsend was desperate to fill the vacant posts with reliable young girls.

'You haven't left school yet, though, have you?' The woman, dressed in a smart, yet serviceable costume, regarded the young girl over her spectacles.

'No, Miss Townsend,' Shirley said. 'My mam would like me to stay on at least until the end of next summer.'

'That sounds very sensible. Any employer will look favourably on someone who has stayed on at school a little longer. Education is never a waste of time.'

'So – you would advise me to do that?'

Miss Townsend nodded. 'I would.' She was thoughtful for a moment and then she leaned forward, resting her arms on the desk. 'But you are, of course, already the statutory school-leaving age, so there is something we could do. Would you be interested in working during the school holidays and perhaps on Saturdays in term time? That is usually our busiest day of the week. It would also ease you into the work very nicely if you still want to come to us full time next year. And,' the woman smiled, acknowledging her own advantage in the idea, 'we could see how you shape up too.'

'I'd like that, Miss Townsend. I'd like that very much. Thank you.'

'That's settled, then,' the personnel manager said, straightening up and shuffling a few papers on her desk. 'You can start at the beginning of January. You'll get thrown in at the deep end because that's our traditional sale time, but I'll mind I put you with one of our senior members of the sales staff, who'll look after you.'

And so, Shirley was the happiest member of the family to sit down to Christmas dinner that day. 'Let's play charades this afternoon,' she suggested.

'I want to play with my new board game,' Reggie said. 'Snakes and Ladders.'

Reggie's woolly stocking had been bulging when he woke up that morning, quite pulled out of shape with all the different presents: colouring books and paints, a whip and top, a small boat with white cotton sails, chocolate and, pushed into the toe, were three bright new pennies. He'd been a lucky boy – the family had spoiled him – but there was one gift he'd turned his nose up at – a gas mask container.

'But I like charades,' Shirley said. 'We played it last year.'

Beth laughed. 'We play it *every* year, Shirl. But don't worry, we'll have time to play everything.'

'It's a tradition that we play charades, isn't it?' Shirley persisted. 'We don't need to stop doing things just because there are no Christmas lights up this year and the blackout'll have to go up before tea.'

Edie sighed as she glanced around her best parlour. That was another tradition; they always had Christmas dinner in the front room. Christmas Day and Easter Sunday were the only times they ate in this room, though it was used on other occasions, as it had been for the recent wedding. Now, coloured paper chains were looped across the room between the picture rails and a spindly artificial tree sat in one corner. They'd made the effort and yet there was not the same spirit in the room.

Something – and someone – was missing.

Word came from Laurence spasmodically. They knew he was somewhere in France by now and the news was bleak. And at home – just as Lil had warned – rationing began in January 1940.

'How are we supposed to feed our families on this?' Edie moaned to her friend as they spread out their ration books on the table and totted up just how much they could get each week.

'It says here,' Edie went on, reading from a piece of paper, 'that meat is likely to be rationed next month but for the time being we don't need coupons for brawn and sausages.'

'Mebbe so, but what sort of rubbish will they put into sausages and the like?' Lil muttered morosely.

'They'll feel the sharp end of my tongue, if they do,' Edie said and then carried on with her reading aloud. 'We can also get poultry, game – and fish. Oh well, that's all right, then.' She smiled. 'We'll be all right in Grimsby, won't we?'

'I read somewhere that even if you don't need coupons, it's going to be rationed on the basis of value.'

'There's got to be some sort of control, else people will start to hoard.'

'It's going to be an offence to do that, so I've heard.'

'Quite right too,' Edie said with asperity. 'We've all got to pull together to get through this.' Her face fell as she added, 'I just hope my Laurence comes back safe and sound. I can't help being selfish about that.'

'Of course you can't. By the way, what's Shirley going to do when she leaves school this summer? I hear you've persuaded her to stay on until then.'

Edie laughed wryly. 'Yes, we have – at least, Beth did – but it was a struggle. She's a little madam, that one. I understand that it was Irene who tipped the balance, though.'

'Was it?' Lil raised her eyebrows. 'That's the first I've heard.'

'Shirley wanted to leave school as soon as she could and Irene asked at Oldroyd's if there were any jobs going. She had an interview with someone in December and they advised Shirley to stay on. But they offered for her to work Saturdays to see how she gets on. She starts this week.' Edie gave a thoughtful sigh. 'Funny, really, how life pans out, isn't it? My mam would have given her eye teeth for me to have stayed on and taken exams. She wanted both me and Jessie to work in an office. She thought it would be a "nice" job.'

'You've done a much better job, duck, raising a wonderful family,' Lil reassured her.

'Aye, but they're all going to be leaving me now, one way or another, aren't they?' Edie said sadly.

Seven

Beth was still at home, but she was restless. The Forsters hadn't asked her to go back to London yet, much to Edie's relief but to Beth's increasing agitation.

'I must do *something*,' she said, her warm, brown eyes troubled. 'They'll start conscripting single young women soon – I'm sure of it – and if I'm not careful, I'll get drafted into something I don't want to do.'

'What *do* you want to do?' Edie asked, though she feared the answer. She bent her head over her knitting as she sat beside the fire. Archie, on the opposite side of the hearth, was pretending to read the newspaper but his attention was divided. He was listening to Edie and Beth.

'I don't really know,' Beth sighed. 'That's the trouble. I only know I must get involved. I can't bear sitting about doing nothing.'

'You could come down the WVS with me an' Lil. They're always glad of another pair of hands.'

Beth laughed. 'No offence, Mam, but it's hardly my scene, is it? A lot of old ladies knitting and gossiping.'

Behind his paper, Archie chuckled softly, but he said nothing whilst Beth stared into the fire thinking hard. At last, her mind made up, she said, 'I'll write to Alan and find out if there's any work for me in London. The War Office, maybe. That's where he is now. If not, I'll look at one of the services and join up. I won't wait for conscription – I'll volunteer.'

Archie and Edie glanced at each other across the hearth, their hearts sinking.

'I tell you what you could do, love,' Archie said with seeming casualness, but the motive behind his suggestion was to try to keep his beloved Beth here at home for as long as possible. 'You could ask your Uncle Harry to teach you to drive.'

Harry Charlton was the only one in the family to own a car. He'd always been generous and had often taken Edie's children out in it for a Sunday afternoon drive to the seafront at Cleethorpes where they'd spend a happy afternoon building sandcastles on the beach or running in and out of the waves, shrieking with laughter at the cold water.

'Do you think he'll be able to spare the petrol for something like that?' Beth asked doubtfully. Petrol rationing had started the previous September.

'You can only ask, love,' Archie said mildly and returned to reading his newspaper, but the print blurred before his eyes. Had he done the right thing in suggesting she should learn to drive? Perhaps not, if it meant she might end up driving ambulances through the bombed streets of the capital.

But Harry was only too happy to teach his niece to drive.

'I don't use my car much and I'm thinking of taking it off the road while the war's on, but before I do, we'll get you driving.'

The two of them spent several happy hours bowling along the country lanes on the outskirts of Grimsby.

'You're a natural,' he told her. 'I've never seen anyone pick it up so quickly. Are you planning to volunteer? Is that it?'

'I must do something, Uncle Harry. I'm bored to

tears at home. Sorry, that sounds awful, but I am, and I thought driving might be useful. Actually, it was Dad who suggested it, but I think he's right.'

Harry said nothing. Archie had had a quiet word with his brother-in-law and Harry knew the reasoning behind her father's idea. But he wasn't sure it was going to help; Beth wanted involvement and excitement and nothing and no one was going to stand in her way. Harry sighed inwardly. He loved all his nephews and nieces, but like Archie, he recognized that Beth was someone special – very special. He just hoped and prayed she would stay safe.

At the beginning of April, when the disturbing news came that Hitler had invaded Denmark and Norway, Irene, however, had a piece of good news.

'Mam,' she said shyly one morning. 'I went to the doctor yesterday.'

'Oh ducky, what's wrong?'

'Nothing's wrong, Mam. I'm going to have a baby, that's all.'

Lil stared at her for a moment before hugging her and saying, '"All", she says. "That's all", as if it isn't the most marvellous news ever. Oh, wait till Edie hears this!'

'D'you want to tell her, Mam? I don't mind if you do.'

Lil was bursting with pride, but she steeled herself to say, 'No, no, that should be Frank, though I don't know if I'll be able to contain myself until he gets home tonight. I'd best stay out of her way. She'll read it in my face.'

'But aren't you meant to be going to the WVS centre with her today?'

'Oh dear, yes, it's Thursday, isn't it?'

Now Lil was faced with a dilemma. She knew she wouldn't be able to keep Irene's secret if she was to be with Edie for more than a few minutes, let alone most of the day.

'Oh, go on, Mam. It won't matter if you do let the cat out of the bag. Frank won't make a fuss. He was that thrilled when I told him last night after we went to bed, I reckon he wanted to wake the whole street up there and then.'

Frank had gone out early to look for work but neither of them knew what time he might return.

'I just didn't want to spoil his surprise. I'm sure he'd like to tell his family himself.'

'If you can keep it to yourself, do, but don't worry if she winkles it out of you. I know what Aunty Edie's like – and so does Frank.' She laughed. 'He used to tell me when we were kids at school that he could never keep anything he'd done from her. "I shall find out," she used to say to him, "so you might as well tell me yarsen."'

'I remember,' Lil murmured and then sighed. 'Oh well, I'll do my best.'

As it happened, Edie had some news of her own and she was so wrapped up in telling Lil all about it that she didn't seem to notice Lil's happy smile or the extra twinkle in her eyes.

'Beth's going away again.'

'Oh Edie, no! Where? Back to the Forsters?'

'I'm really not sure where she's going, Lil, but it seems it's Alan Forster's fault – oh, dear, I shouldn't say that, because she'll have to do some sort of war work eventually. She might even get called up. They're already trying to persuade women to volunteer for the services.'

'But there are other things she could do, aren't there? What about the WVS or even the Land Army?'

Edie pursed her lips and shook her head. 'No, she's determined to go to London. It seems this Alan Forster is now involved in some sort of work in the War Office. She wrote to him asking if there was anything she could do and he's written back to say that she could be an enormous help there because she can speak French fluently.'

'I don't think I like the sound of that, Edie.'

'No, and neither do I.'

'What does Archie say?'

'He doesn't know yet, but he'll be home tonight. I'm hoping she'll listen to him.'

But the evening in the Kelsey household was taken over by Frank and Irene's arrival with their exciting news. All day, Edie had been preoccupied with her own worries and Lil had escaped any awkward questions.

Frank and Irene had arrived together after tea. 'You're going to be a grandma, Mam. How does that sound?'

Edie had given a shriek and enveloped first Frank and then Irene in her embrace. 'That's wonderful news! I'd better start knitting. And Archie, you can get the old cot down out of the loft and make sure it's in good repair. And me and your mam can watch out for a decent second-hand pram, Irene.'

The family laughed at her joy, but they all shared it and in the midst of it, Beth's news went unsaid and it wasn't until they were getting ready for bed together that Edie remembered to tell Archie.

'You'll have a word with her, won't you? Try to stop her going. I don't want her down in London.'

Much to her surprise – and not a little disappointment – Archie said, 'I won't be able to stop her, love, and besides, even if I could, I'm not sure I'd want to. As a single young woman, she's going to have to do something. It might be better if she does something now which is her own choice.'

'But living in London, Archie . . .'

'I'm sure Mr Forster will make sure she's all right.' He chuckled. 'Besides, she might be working in a nice office. What would your mam have said to that, eh?'

Edie had the grace to smile.

Archie insisted that they all went to the railway station to see Beth off.

'I'd rather you didn't, Dad. I don't like goodbyes.'

He forced a laugh, though her words sounded prophetic. 'It's not "goodbye" only – what is it you'd say now?'

She smiled weakly. '*Au revoir.*'

'Doesn't that mean "till we meet again"?'

'Sort of.'

'There you are, then. See, even I know a bit of French.'

It was quite a gathering on the platform. They were jostled by soldiers going back to camp from leave and all their families who'd come to wish them well. There was laughter, but plenty of tears too with wives and sweethearts clinging to their menfolk until the very last second. Young children – those who had not already been evacuated – sensed the pathos of the moment and cried loudly.

'I'll write,' Beth promised, giving each member of her family a swift hug, and Lil and Irene too, but it was Archie who held her just a little longer than the rest and who whispered in her ear. 'Take care of your-self, lass, and come back to us.'

Beth hadn't replied but she'd squeezed him tightly and then turned away quickly and boarded the train. As it left the station and began to gather speed, people began to drift away, but Archie refused to move until the train was out of sight.

'Things are getting serious in France, you know, Edie,' Archie said early in May, prodding his finger at the newspaper he was reading. 'Holland and Belgium have been invaded. I don't think it will be long before they fall and then I reckon poor old France will be next.'

'What?' Edie had stared at him, wide-eyed. 'But – but Laurence is over there.'

'I know.'

'Are they bringing our lads back home, then?'

Archie had been about to say, 'Of course not; they'll stay and fight to the bitter end', but the words remained unspoken. He couldn't say that to Edie. Instead he said mildly, 'Let's hope so, love.' Then he added, 'But there's one bit of brighter news. Mr Churchill's become Prime Minister. We'll be all right with him at the helm.'

Again he didn't say that in the report he was reading of the new Prime Minister's speech to the House, all Winston Churchill could promise was 'blood, toil, tears and sweat'.

Defeat, it seemed, was not a word that was in Mr Churchill's vocabulary.

When Archie returned to sea, Edie no longer read the newspapers or listened to the news bulletins on the wireless, so she didn't hear when Holland and Belgium surrendered to the Nazis or how the German army pushed on into France and surrounded the remnants of the British army at a place called Dunkirk, trapping them against the sea. Though Lil heard and trembled to think of Laurence, she said nothing to Edie. But even Edie could not remain oblivious to Operation Dynamo at the end of the month, the unbelievable evacuation of over three hundred thousand troops from the Dunkirk beaches.

'It's nothing short of a miracle,' Jessie enthused when Edie and Lil arrived at the WVS centre and even Norma said, 'I wish we were there. I'd love to be meeting the soldiers coming ashore, giving them tea and blankets. Poor things.' For a brief moment they saw a softer side to Norma.

'Our colleagues in the area will be doing everything they can and we're doing our bit, Norma,' Jessie said, for once in agreement with Lil's surly sister, 'by sending supplies, even if we can't be there in person.'

Edie stood still, trying to close her ears to the talk buzzing around her; it was all about Dunkirk and when Jessie asked her, 'Have you heard from Laurence?' she shook her head, turned and walked away.

'Leave it, Jessie,' Lil whispered. 'She never wants to know news of any sort when Archie's away. And he's been away longer than normal this time. She'll hear soon enough if . . .'

Lil left the dreadful words hanging in the air.

Eight

The arrival of a telegram boy on his bicycle in the street struck fear into the hearts of all those who saw him. Jessie saw him as she walked towards the town centre to join the queues and haggle with the shopkeepers over the rations. Norma saw him as, dressed in her WVS uniform, she walked along the street where her sister lived with the intention of calling on Lil to see if she was helping out today. But when she saw the boy pedalling towards her, Norma carried on walking. Lil saw him as he slowed his bicycle, stopped and actually leaned it against the wall of her house. Watching him from her front-room window, she saw him search in the bag he carried over his shoulder and pull out the telegram. Then, slowly, as if he already knew the contents, he knocked on Edie's front door.

'Oh no,' Lil whispered, her fingers covering her mouth. She turned and hurried through to the back room where Irene was ironing and Frank – still unable to find work – was cleaning shoes. As she opened the door, they both looked towards her, seeing at once that something was wrong.

'Frank – there's a telegram boy just – just gone next door. To your mam's.'

Frank stared at her for a moment and then, galvanized into action, flung down the shoe and the brush he was holding and ran out of the house, through both yards and in at the back door of his former home. He only stopped when he saw the pitiful sight of his mother standing in the centre of the living room holding the telegram in her hand, too afraid to open it. Gently, Frank eased the paper from her stiff fingers and tore it open. He stared down at it for a long time before he raised his eyes and said huskily, 'Oh Mam, it's Laurence. He was killed on the beach at Dunkirk. It – it says a letter will follow.'

The colour drained from Edie's face as Frank helped her to sit down in the easy chair by the fire. Despite its warmth, Edie began to shake. 'Fetch – fetch Lil,' she gasped.

'I'm here, duck,' Lil spoke from the doorway. She had followed Frank and had been hovering in the scullery. Now she stepped into the living room and went to kneel at Edie's side to take her hand. Edie clung to it like a drowning person.

There was nothing Lil could say or do to lessen the pain for her friend, but she was there for her.

The promised letter arrived the following morning and gave a little more detail. 'He was killed as he waited to get on board one of the little ships. The enemy were dive-bombing the beaches,' Frank explained to Lil, but Edie just sat beside the range staring at nothing. She didn't weep or wail; in fact, she was eerily silent. She hardly seemed able to speak and Lil stayed at her side all day and through the night until Archie was due home.

But Archie did not arrive on the day they'd expected him and when Lil read in the paper about all the 'little ships' that had gone across the Chanel, she began to worry even more.

Frank went each night to the docks in the hope of

meeting his father but when there was still no sign of Archie's trawler, Frank went to the dock offices.

'Mr Reeves,' he asked politely of the man in charge, 'have you heard any news of my father's ship? He was due back three nights ago.'

Jack Reeves avoided meeting Frank's steady gaze. 'You'd best go to his employers' offices. They'll tell you.'

Frank stared at the man, a shaft of fear coursing through him. 'You know something, don't you?'

Jack shook his head. 'I know where he is – or rather where he went – but I don't know where he is right this minute, Frank. Like I say, go and ask at the owners' offices.'

Frank knew most of the office employees of the owners of Archie's trawler and he was pleased to see one of his former schoolmates behind the enquiry desk.

'Luke, me dad's trawler is late back. Have you any news?'

The young man glanced around him to make sure no one could overhear before he came round the desk and said quietly, 'I'm not supposed to say too much, Frank, but you're one of us, so I can tell you. A lot of our ships have gone down to Sheerness and then across the Channel.' He paused and then whispered, 'You understand what I'm saying, don't you?'

The room around him seemed suddenly unsteady and Luke's face swam before Frank's eyes. He thought for one dreadful moment that he might pass out; a very unmanly thing to do in Frank Kelsey's book. But the news was shocking and disturbing. They'd just had news that Laurence had been killed on the beaches, were they now to hear that another member of their family had perished trying to rescue the soldiers?

In a cracked, none-too-steady voice, Frank said, 'I do, mate.'

'The Admiralty issued appeals for skippers, engineers and crew of small craft and anyone with knowledge of coastal navigation.'

Hoarsely, Frank said, 'And I suppose trawlers were an obvious choice. Weren't they?'

Soberly, Luke nodded.

'I didn't hear anything, Luke. Me mam won't listen to the news bulletins when me dad's at sea.' He paused, then frowned, 'But he's on a regular trip – he won't have . . .' He stared at Luke. 'Will he?'

'He came back earlier than expected.' Frank blinked and focussed on what Luke was saying. 'You should have seen it on the docks that night, Frank, after the appeal. We were inundated with volunteers. They were queuing out of the docks and down the street. The skippers were choosing their crews and men were jostling each other to be picked. Old men who shouldn't really have gone, but they skived the medical and joined the ships. It was a sight to see, Frank, I don't mind telling you. Your dad got his usual crew, so he was lucky because they'll all work so well together and ships were leaving on every tide – dozens of them. For the first time in me life, Frank, I wished I'd been a fisherman and then I could have gone.'

'But he never came home.' Frank was amazed. But then he realized; Archie wouldn't have wanted his family to know what he was going to do.

'Thanks for telling me,' he said quietly. 'Will you – will you come to the house yourself if – if there's any news?'

'I will, Frank,' Luke promised solemnly. 'But I'd keep it to yourself for the time being, if you can. The ships are on their way home as we speak. We'll know soon enough.'

'Haven't you heard by radio who's coming back?'

Frank shook his head. 'Use of ship-to-shore radio is restricted now. You know that.'

Frank nodded. 'Of course. I'm – just not thinking straight.'

He turned to go, his heart heavy. The thought uppermost in his troubled mind was: *Whatever am I going to tell Mam?*

As it happened, Frank was spared saying anything to his mother. Edie was so sunk in grief that she was unaware of the passage of time, even oblivious to the fact that Archie was late back. She just sat, staring into space with Lil sitting beside her or trying to tempt her to eat. But Edie could eat nothing, though she did drink the endless cups of tea that Lil made.

Frank confided his fears for his father's safety to his young wife. 'But don't say owt to your mam. She might feel she's got to tell her. They don't have any secrets from each other.'

Irene sat down suddenly in a chair and put her hand protectively over her swelling belly. Now, her baby would never know its Uncle Laurence. Would it also not have either granddad? The thought was unbearable.

Frank knelt at the side of her chair. 'Are you all right, love? You've gone awfully white. Mebbe I shouldn't have told you either. Let me get you a glass of water.'

'I'm all right – honest. It – it was just the shock.'

'If you're sure, then I'd best get back to Mam. Just you rest now. Promise?'

Irene nodded, but when Frank left the house and she was alone, she let the tears flow, not only for Laurence, whom she'd loved as a brother, but also in her dread for Uncle Archie's safety.

When Frank stepped back into Edie's living room, he saw Jessie sitting opposite her. He went to stand behind his mother's chair. Jessie bit her lip, glanced up at Frank and then her gaze came back to her sister's face. 'Does she know about – about Archie?'

Lil looked up sharply. 'What about Archie?'

Behind his mother, Frank made urgent signals that Jessie should say no more, but whilst Lil was anxious to know what Jessie meant, Edie didn't even seem to have understood.

'Oh, nothing, nothing.' But Lil was acutely aware that there was something and that Jessie, and possibly Frank, too, knew what it was. It was to do with Archie and the reason for his late return, she was sure, but Lil, in her overriding concern for her dear friend, never considered that Archie could have been involved in what she thought of as the greatest rescue mission ever under-taken.

Frank squinted through the darkness at a young woman standing in the shadows, her gaze fixed on the lock gates, watching the ships coming through. He had come again to the docks, but there was still no news from the dock master. Frank hadn't seen the girl before and he thought he knew all the pretty girls around here. Not that he could see much of her face through the gloom, nor the colour of her hair, which was covered with a headscarf, but he could tell she was slim, her hands pushed deeply into the pocket of her mackintosh. He sidled over to her.

'You waiting for someone too?'

She jumped, startled by his voice. 'Y-yes,' she stammered. 'I am waiting for – for my boyfriend. He is on a trawler, but it is late.'

Frank frowned uneasily. The girl had a strong foreign accent.

'Oh aye,' he said, deliberately sounding casual. 'What ship's he on?'

The girl laughed nervously. 'I don't know. He goes on a different one sometimes. I don't know which one this time.'

The girl spoke very good English, but there was no hiding the accent.

'You're not from around here?'

She shook her head, avoiding his gaze. 'I am Swiss,' she told him hurriedly. Perhaps she was a little too eager to impart the information to convince him that she was no threat. 'But I live here now. I am a freelance reporter for the local paper. That's why I am here. There are several ships late back. Do you know where they have been?'

Frank opened his mouth, but somehow the words stuck in his throat. Whether it was because he didn't want to tell anyone else before his mam knew or whether it was some instinct that made him cautious, he couldn't have said. All he knew was that he didn't want to tell this girl. Her accent troubled him even though he told himself that she was a Swiss national; she wasn't the enemy. Instead, he forced himself to say, 'I haven't a clue. They're all very secretive about where they fish now.'

He couldn't see her expression but he heard her mutter, 'I know', and there was a resentful edge to her voice as she added, 'it makes my job very difficult. I rely on news for my livelihood.'

'It must do,' Frank murmured, but still he wasn't going to tell her anything.

The evening high tide was just before ten and so it was very late when the first trawler limped into number one fish dock and moored at its berth. But tonight there would be no fish to unload and Frank could see the lumpers standing in readiness even though they were already realizing they probably wouldn't be wanted tonight. Frank stepped closer to the ship that had moored; it wasn't his father's ship, *The Havelock*. He turned away but instead of going back to stand near the girl, he approached the group of lumpers and sought out his uncle who, of course, knew exactly where the trawlers had been.

'Any news?' he said softly.

Harry shook his head. 'Does your mam know?'

'No, I thought it best not to say owt till we know.'

'You do right, lad. Jessie told me you'd managed to stop her saying anything to Edie.'

Frank and Harry stood side by side, waiting for what seemed an eternity.

'He'll have to be here soon,' Harry muttered, 'else he'll miss the tide.'

Ten minutes later, another trawler came through the lock and seemed to be heading towards *The Havelock*'s berth.

'God willing,' Harry murmured, 'this is Archie.'

Nine

It was indeed Archie's ship and Frank and Harry slapped each other on the back with relief, but then their euphoria sobered as Harry said, 'But what dreadful news he's coming back to after being a hero himself. I think I'd best leave you to it, Frank. You know where me an' Jessie are if you want anything. Anything at all.'

'Thanks, Uncle Harry,' Frank murmured, but his gaze was now on the men coming down the gangway. The last one off, as always, was Archie. He staggered off the ship, his face grey with fatigue, his eyes large with the horrors he had witnessed. Frank went at once to his side and put his arm around his father's waist. The older man leaned on him with gratitude.

'Frank,' he said hoarsely, 'I've just been to Hell and back. And God knows, I'm lucky to be here.'

'I know, Dad, I know.' Frank hesitated. How was he to tell the poor man the terrible news?

'Does your mam know where I've been?'

Frank shook his head and then haltingly added, 'Dad, there's bad news . . .'

Archie stopped and turned to face him. 'What is it? Tell me.'

'It's Laurence. There was a telegram and then a letter. He was killed on the beaches at Dunkirk.'

Archie closed his eyes and let out a low growl of pain. 'I was there, Frank, and to think I couldn't save me own son. There were thousands and thousands of men on the beaches, lines of them wading into the sea to be picked up by the little ships. And there were Stukas dive-bombing them every three quarters of an hour or so. Maybe I could have . . .'

'Dad, don't think like that. Of course you couldn't possibly know where Laurence was, but you've saved a lot of other mothers' sons.'

'Aye, aye, we have, but not me own, eh?'

As they walked slowly home, Frank supporting his father, Archie said, 'Don't tell your mam where I've been. We've never had secrets all our married life, but this is something I can't tell her, lad, 'specially now. At least, for the time being. Promise me?'

'Of course, Dad, and I'll see that Irene says nothing either, not even to her own mam.' He smiled wryly, ''Cos you know those two. Lil wouldn't be able to keep it from her, so it's best she doesn't know either.'

Even though it was late when they walked through the door, they found that Lil, just as she had done for the past three nights, had a meal waiting and the kettle on the hob, but Archie went at once to kneel beside his wife's chair and put his strong arms around her. Slowly, Edie turned to face him and then she let out an anguished cry of pain, like the yowl of a wounded animal and sobbed against his shoulder, the tears flowing fast.

Lil nodded and turned away, tears in her own eyes. 'I'll leave 'em to it, Frank love. She'll be all right now Archie's home and she's letting go. It's what she needed to do.'

'I'll come with you, Aunty Lil. It's high time I made sure that Irene's all right.'

The whole family were grieving; Shirley and Reggie tried to carry on as normally as they could, but they were devastated to think that they would never again see their adored older brother. Shirley sat in her bedroom and composed a letter to Beth, but the letter was blotchy, stained with her tears. She sent it to the only address they had for Beth, the Forsters' home in South London, but she had no idea when or even if it would reach her sister. Though they'd received letters from her since she'd left home, they had no idea exactly where she was or what she was actually doing.

'She'll be living with the Forsters, I reckon, if she's working with him,' Edie had tried to comfort herself when Beth had first left home. But no one actually knew. They all feared she could already be doing something very different.

As for Reggie, he felt lost and lonely. He played football in the streets with the other boys, but his heart was no longer in it; he'd always liked playing with Laurence best, but now he'd never be able to do that again.

'Have you sent word to Jessie?' Archie asked his wife gently when the first storm of weeping had subsided into a dull ache in her chest.

Edie nodded. 'Frank went to see her that night. I think she came round, but I was in such a daze, Archie, I can't really remember who was here and who wasn't. Only Lil. She stayed with me all the time.'

Of course, the Kelsey family were not the only ones to lose a loved one; all over the country similar telegrams were being delivered and there were other losses in Grimsby too. And whilst they sympathized and felt an affinity with all those who were suffering the same devastation, it didn't really make it any easier for them. Laurence was *their* boy, *their* son.

'My beautiful boy. He was such a bonny baby, Lil,'

Edie said as she sat with a box of old photographs on her knee. 'You didn't know him when he was really little, but here, look at this photo we had done at the photographer's in town. Look at his fair hair and chubby little legs. Oh Lil, I was just reckoning of the day when he would come home again, but now he never will.'

Very slowly, life returned to some sort of normality. Once she was over the initial, searing shock, Edie's natural strength and resilience rose to the surface once more. She'd grown up alongside families who had lost their menfolk at sea; fisherfolk, sadly, were used to tragedy, but it didn't make it any easier. This was something different. War took countless numbers of men, a whole generation. Grief from the losses in the last war still overshadowed so many lives – especially in Grimsby where the pals' battalion, the Grimsby Chums, had lost so many local boys. And now it was all happening again.

When Archie had to go back to sea, Edie, with Lil beside her, returned to the WVS centre and threw herself into the work.

'I'm doing it for my boy – I'm doing it for Laurence,' she said bravely. 'It's what he would have wanted – and would expect – me to do.'

Now she had other worries at the back of her mind. Frank was finding it harder and harder to find regular work and soon, she knew, he would be called up. Beth had obviously received Shirley's letter for when she replied, Edie could tell she felt the loss keenly. She had been the closest to Laurence in age and they had always been good 'mates'. Edie tried to comfort herself with the fact that Beth must still be living with the Forsters.

But life, as Edie was always being told, had to go on. And it did. Whilst she would forever mourn

Laurence's death, the living must be cared for. And there was Irene's baby coming, due in September. It was like her mother's old saying, she thought. When someone goes out of a family, another comes into it. Edie wondered if they would call it after Laurence, if it was a boy. She hoped so.

It was in late June 1940 when the first bombs fell on Grimsby. The very same day that the French signed the armistice with their invaders, and, with engineered irony, in the same railway carriage used in 1918 for the German surrender. Adolf Hitler was gleeful, his revenge for what he saw as the humiliation of his own country was complete. Britain stood alone and the war was coming even closer to home; casualties were to be expected amongst the civilian population. It was not just soldiers who would lose their lives now.

Talk began again of evacuations into the relative safety of the Lincolnshire countryside for youngsters and mothers and babies.

'You ought to go,' Frank urged Irene. 'I'll be going any day now and—'

'I'm going nowhere until this baby is born. I want him – or her – to be born in Grimsby, preferably here at home.' Irene was determined and nothing – and no one – would change her mind. She could be remarkably stubborn when she wanted to be, Lil thought. More bombs fell on the town in July when the enemy targeted the docks, but as the missiles all fell into the river, no damage was done. The Battle of Britain had begun and the RAF was valiantly trying to prevent the Luftwaffe attacking coastal ports, radar stations and airfields in the south of England.

Early in September, Frank got his call-up papers and the next morning, Irene went into labour.

'Must have shocked her into it,' he joked, but his eyes were worried as he listened to Irene's cries from the room upstairs. 'I just wish the midwife would hurry up.'

'No need for any midwife,' Edie said, coming through the door. 'If me and her mam can't see this babby into the world, it's a pity. Now, Lil, have you got everything ready?'

Lil nodded, but Frank still wasn't sure. 'Oh but, Mam, I don't think—'

But Edie was already on her way up the stairs carrying towels and a bowl of hot water.

The baby boy slipped easily into the world with a minimum of fuss in the afternoon of 5 September and two days later, three hundred German bombers flew over London; the blitz on London had begun in earnest.

'They'll be back here,' Frank warned. 'Once they've had a go at the capital they'll start systematically on all the major cities and the ports'll be a major target. We've already had a taste and so has Hull.' The city across the river had been bombed for the first time three days before Grimsby had been targeted in June. 'Irene, you've got to go and take our son with you. This time I won't take no for an answer.'

'But what about Mam? I can't leave her here all on her own.'

'She wants you to go as much as I do. You've got to think of the baby now, love.'

'All right, you win,' Irene said, with a wan smile.

*

90

'I'm sending our Reggie with your Irene,' Edie announced the day before another batch of evacuees were due to leave the town. Reginald Kelsey was now ten and Edie didn't like him running wild through the streets, especially now that there was the real fear of bombing. A new pastime had developed for boys of his age; scrambling over bomb sites, searching for bits of shrapnel as souvenirs. And if their house took a direct hit, not even hiding in the cupboard under the stairs was going to save them. 'Shirley won't go now she's working full time.'

'Do you think the authorities'll make her do some sort of war work?' Lil asked.

Edie shrugged. 'I don't know. She's a bit young yet, but our lives do seem regimented by the war effort, I grant you. Mind you,' she added, laughing wryly. 'It'd do that little madam good if they did call her up. She'd have to do as she's told for once in her life.'

When Beth had been at home for the wedding and for a little while afterwards, she had taken Shirley to the cinema or shopping, encouraged her to curl her hair and experiment with make-up. But when she'd left home again, Shirley slipped back into her old ways, and now took little interest in her appearance – apart from keeping herself neat for work – or in making friends. And her tongue had become sharp and, it had to be said, spiteful. Edie sighed over her younger daughter. It seemed she was only happy when Beth was at home. And now, with Irene going too, Shirley would be even lonelier than she had been already.

'She'll be missing her sister,' Lil said and, as she was perhaps the only person who could raise such a painful reminder, added, 'and she's lost Laurence too. She idolized both of them. And now, because of his loss, she'll be frightened the same thing might happen to Beth, especially now the bombing in London is so appalling.'

'She's not the only one who's worried,' Edie replied tartly and then her tone softened. 'Sorry, Lil, it's just that it's always there, you know. I think about Laurence all the time and now there's Beth to worry about too, to say nothing of the fact that we're getting bombed here, an' all. That's why I've decided to send Reggie to the country. Archie said I ought to and I think he's right. It's not so bad now I know he'll be going with Irene and little Tommy.'

Edie had been gratified to hear that her grandson was to be called Laurence Thomas but that he would be known as Tommy. A christening had been hastily arranged for the previous Sunday and, with Frank reporting for duty the day after, there was nothing keeping Irene, Tommy and now Reggie, too, from joining one of the evacuation parties.

'They're not going far away,' Lil reported to Edie. 'Only to a farm in a little village near Louth. Won't that be grand, Edie? They'll have good food and fresh air.'

'They might as well be on the moon for all that we'll be able to visit.' Edie was not to be comforted.

'We might be able to go now and again,' Lil said, trying to be positive. 'Maybe your Harry could take us.'

'His car's laid up now for the rest of the war. He can't get the petrol.'

'Then we'll find out about bus or train times. The train might be easier. Irene said the last halt before Louth is Fotherby and that's near where the farm is,' Lil said, determined not to be beaten. 'At least we can go and see them somehow and no doubt Frank will be in this country for a while, training. He'll get leave.'

Edie sighed. 'But they'll not be *here*. They'll not be at home where they should be, will they?'

The following morning, Edie watched her youngest child walk down the street away from her, the box containing his gas mask slung around his thin shoulders. He carried his little suitcase in one hand, but the other was clinging to the handle of the pram, which Irene was pushing.

'Now, you stick with Irene,' Edie had warned him, trying to give Reggie's face yet another wash and to smooth his hair, but he'd wriggled away from her.

'Aw, Mam, don't.'

'Hold tight to the pram. I don't want you getting lost. I think I ought to come to the station . . .'

'He'll be all right, Auntie Edie,' Irene had said, 'I promise. The billeting officer has said we're going to the same place. A farm right out in the countryside. He'll soon be running around in the fresh air and – hopefully – there'll be plenty of food.'

'I wouldn't bank on it, duck. Farmers have to abide by the rationing just like the rest of us.'

Irene had laughed, her long blond hair blowing in the wind, her cheeks dimpling prettily. 'Oh aye, and you reckon they'll send men from the ministry to scour the hedgerows counting just how many eggs the hens have laid.'

Edie had laughed with her, but as her young son, daughter-in-law and brand-new grandson walked away from her, she felt her heart constrict.

'They're all going, Lil,' she'd said with a catch in her voice, though she was determined not to cry. 'First Laurence and then Frank and Beth and now those three. I've only got Shirley left.' The words were left unspoken, but Lil was in no doubt that of her five children, Shirley was the last one Edie would have wanted left at home. Lil knew Edie well enough to be able to say gently, 'Mebbe you and Shirley will grow closer now.'

Edie's 'Mm' was non-committal.

'Come on in to my place and I'll make you a nice cup of tea,' but Edie resisted the invitation until her family rounded the corner at the end of the street and disappeared from her sight.

'There they go,' Edie said shakily. 'How am I to bear it?'

Tactfully, Lil did not remind her friend that it was the same for every mother in the land as Edie added mournfully, 'And when we'll see Beth again, I don't know.'

Ten

Despite the terrible news about Laurence, which she must learn to live with, Beth was enjoying herself, though she felt a little guilty at admitting it when the country was plunged into war, when the blackout increased motoring accidents and even pedestrians in the darkened city didn't feel safe. Rationing was now beginning to bite and the black market was a temptation many could not resist as even goods that were not on ration soared in price. She wrote home to her family reassuring them that she was fine and that she was still with the Forsters, which, at the moment, was the truth, even though she was no longer acting as a nanny to the children. Each day, she travelled into the city with Alan Forster and acted as his secretary, though she could tell her family none of this. Alan Forster, because of his knowledge of France, was getting more involved in secretive work.

'I want you with me, Beth,' Alan told her as they journeyed to work together one morning in late October. 'I can't tell you much at the moment, but it's all very exciting and I think you're the right sort of person we need, if only,' he added, his voice dropping almost to a whisper, 'we can persuade the authorities that women are capable of taking an active part.'

Beth laughed, 'I don't understand what on earth you're talking about.'

Alan chuckled. 'All will be revealed in due course, but first, I want you to join the FANYs. I need to get you into uniform. That's the first step.'

'What on earth are they?' Beth asked.

'First Aid Nursing Yeomanry.'

'But I don't know the first thing about nursing and I don't think I'd be a very good one anyway.'

'You've been an excellent nursemaid to the children.'

'That's a bit different. That was looking after them, playing with them and getting them to bed on time. But at the first sign of a sniffle, I was calling the doctor.'

'Quite right too, but the FANYs would only be a cover. You wouldn't actually be doing any nursing.'

'A cover for what exactly?' Beth was suddenly suspicious.

'Ah, now I can't tell you that yet. All in good time,' he added as he drew the car to a stop in the place where he parked. 'Not a word to a soul though. Oh, and by the way, can you drive?'

'Yes, yes, I can,' Beth said, as mystified as ever, but Alan would reveal no more.

Three days after his conversation with Beth, Alan Forster, along with other personnel, moved into premises in Baker Street. And Beth went with him.

It was all very hush-hush. There were several offices in the building and plenty of people walking about with files under their arms and looking very serious, but no one said very much. No one, not even Alan, told her exactly what was happening. She was interviewed and accepted as a recruit into the FANYs and began to wear a khaki uniform comprising a tunic, a skirt and a cap. At once, it seemed to give her some kind of status.

People talked to her more, included her in their conversations, and yet still she didn't really understand what it was all about.

'I want you to talk to some young men who are being trained for special duties,' Alan said one day. 'I need you to test their French.'

Beth opened her mouth to say, 'But you speak better French than me,' but something stopped her and then she was glad that she'd remained silent for at Alan's next words she began to glean a little of what lay behind all this cloak-and-dagger stuff. He leaned towards her over his desk and spoke in a low voice, even though they were quite alone in his office. 'They are being trained to be agents. If they pass muster, they'll eventually be dropped into France behind enemy lines to create circuits and to help local resistance groups and to sabotage the enemy. They'll be receiving all sorts of physical training and learning other skills, but they need to be fluent in the language – as you can guess – and not make mistakes in any situation. I need you to mix with them socially and possibly carry out a few of the spot tests. Do you think you can do that?'

Beth's eyes shone. 'Of course.'

She knew that France was now divided into two parts. The southern part was still under the rule of Vichy France led by Marshal Pétain, but the north-eastern part was occupied by the Germans.

'Our organization,' Alan went on, 'has been personally authorized by the Prime Minister and though it meets with disapproval in some quarters, there's not much they can do about it in the circumstances. We're known as the Special Operations Executive.'

Beth chuckled, catching on at once. Who would dare to question Mr Churchill's decision?

They talked for another half an hour whilst Alan gave her detailed instructions as to what he wanted her to do. As she left his office, she paused with her hand on the door knob. Before opening it, she turned briefly and smiled at him. 'If you ever decide to use women in the field, let me know, won't you?'

Without waiting for his reply, she left the office, closing the door quietly behind her. She did not see his satisfied smile; her words were exactly what he had wanted to hear.

'Oh yes, Beth,' he murmured to the empty room. 'You'll be the first to know, believe me.'

'Is she still looking after the children, then?'

'I don't know, Lil.' Edie was holding Beth's most recent letter. 'She doesn't really say what she's doing. Except that she's joined the FANYs, so I don't suppose she can still be with the family. Anyway,' Edie said more briskly, tucking the letter behind the bracket clock on the mantelpiece for Archie to see when he came home, 'no good wishing for the moon. It'll be Christmas soon and I'm late getting me puddings done this year.'

'It'll be worse than last year,' Lil mourned, 'with all the shortages.'

'We'll make a go of it somehow,' Edie said, attempting cheerfulness, but inside her heart was breaking. It would be the second Christmas since the war had started, but their first since Laurence had been killed and now she wouldn't have Reggie or Irene and the baby here either. And she doubted that Frank or Beth would get home.

It was going to be a very quiet Christmas.

'It's certainly going to be very different this year, Lil,' Edie went on, trying to concentrate her mind on eking out their meagre rations. 'We didn't really feel the pinch last year, but it's going to hit hard this time.'

Edie said nothing about the people who would be missing around the table this year. Her thoughts were with them all, especially Laurence, who was gone for ever.

As if sensing her friend's feelings, Lil said gently, 'Will Beth get home, d'you think? And what about Reggie?'

'I don't know. Have you heard what Irene intends to do?'

Lil bit her lip. 'She's not coming, but she said the Schofields have asked us all to go out there, if we want to.'

'It'd be nice, but it's hardly fair on the poor woman for the four of us to descend on her.'

Lil shrugged. 'I don't think she'd mind. Irene says she's used to catering for a lot of folk. They've got land army girls staying, but they might be going home for Christmas so it wouldn't be many more than usual.'

'Mm, I'll ask Archie. How would we get there?'

'I haven't a clue,' Lil replied comically, and then added more seriously, 'probably by train. That's how they went, isn't it?'

When Edie talked it over with Archie when he was next at home, he shook his head. 'If Harry had got his car running I'd've asked to borrow it, but he's got it laid up now. Besides, I don't think we should unsettle young Reggie – he might start begging to come back with us. Irene'll see that he has a good Christmas and the Schofields sound nice people.'

Edie could understand his reasoning, but she wasn't happy and Christmas this year looked like being a miserable affair.

Through the year Edie and Lil had saved foodstuffs

for the festivities – if indeed they could call them that, Edie thought morosely.

'This isn't classed as hoarding, is it, Edie?' Lil asked worriedly. She was terrified of disobeying regulations and scanned each leaflet that appeared through her front door with a frown on her face.

'No, Lil, it isn't. We're just saving up a bit to use on a special occasion. Hoarding's when you buy and put away loads of stuff you're probably never going to use. We'll have to make mincemeat last minute this year, because of putting more apple in it. It's likely to ferment if we do it too early.'

'What about puddings?'

'Ah, now, let me tell you.' Edie opened a hand-written notebook she'd started compiling at the beginning of the war. It contained all sorts of snippets of useful information, amongst which were wartime recipe ideas. 'It seems,' she went on, 'that we'd be lost without good old Doctor Carrot. There's a recipe for carrot pudding, but I shall have to make it early on Christmas morning.'

'Not beforehand, like you always do?'

'It says it's best done on the day because it's what they call a "one-boil" pudding.'

'Eh?'

'If you make it on the day, it saves fuel by not having to heat it up again.'

'Oh,' Lil said uncertainly. 'I've made a cake already and it's got carrot in it.'

'It'll be fine. We'll soon all be able to see in the dark if we go on eating carrots at this rate.'

The two women laughed together, not taken in by the propaganda that carrots helped the RAF's night-flying. The myth had come about because of a temporary glut of carrots earlier in the year, which the authorities wanted used up, but not wasted. Not only did they want the public to eat the carrots but they wanted the enemy to believe that British pilots' flying capabilities had been improved by eating them and not because of the use of secret new inventions, such as radar.

Two days before Christmas, there was a knock at Edie's front door. Only strangers or the telegram boy bearing bad news ever knocked at her front door and she was trembling as she hurried to answer it. She wished Lil was with her. She opened it to see a burly man standing there, dressed in plus-fours and a checked cap and carrying two dead cockerels in his hand.

'I'm Joe Schofield,' he said, stretching out a calloused hand. 'Me and the missis'd be glad if you'd accept these.'

Edie stared at him, dumbstruck for a moment before coming to her senses and realizing who he was. She invited him in. 'Please come in, come in. The kettle's on the hob.' She led the way into the living room and then turned to face him again. 'You – you didn't bring Reggie to see us?'

The man shook his head, realizing at once that the woman was disappointed. 'We didn't know what to do for the best, missis, to tell you the truth. We didn't want to unsettle him, like.'

'But he's all right?' Edie's tone was anxious now.

'Oh, he's champion. Taken to the country life like one of my ducks to the pond.'

Edie didn't know whether to be pleased or sorry. Pleased because her little boy was happy, yet she couldn't help feeling a twinge of disappointment that he wasn't the tiniest bit homesick.

'Of course, he's missing his family,' Joe added hastily, 'but it helps him having Irene and the babby there too.'

'Are they all right?'

'Champion.' It seemed to be one of Joe Schofield's favourite words. 'Babby's growing into a fine little chap. You must come out and see them. You and Irene's mother, when the better weather comes.'

'We'll try. Now, sit down and have a cuppa. And thank you so much for the cockerels. We'll have them for Christmas dinner.'

'I'm a bit late bringing them but I couldn't get into Grimsby afore today. Mebbe you've already got your dinner organized.'

Edie pulled a face. 'Only if you can call a cheap cut of meat, which has been pot roasted to try to make it tender, a Christmas dinner. No, Mr Schofield, these will be splendid. We'll have a real feast. Thank you.'

As soon as he'd supped his tea, Joe got up. 'I must be going.'

'Oh, can't you stay and see Lil – Irene's mam? She's gone into town to do a bit of queuing.' She laughed wryly. 'But she should be back soon.'

'If you don't mind, missis, I'll be on me way. I don't like strange towns in the dark and I don't know Grimsby all that well. Give 'er my regards and tell her that Irene and the little one are fine.'

'I will and thank you again for the birds. Lil will be sharing them with us on Christmas Day.'

'That's what Irene said.' He picked up his cap from the table and nodded his farewell as Edie saw him out of the front door again, making sure that he left by the same way that he had entered her home and thus didn't take the good luck out with him.

'My goodness,' Lil exclaimed when she saw the two

birds lying on Edie's draining board. 'What a lovely gift.'

'You know, Lil, I'm thinking we should share our good fortune,' Edie said slowly. 'Jessie and Harry will come as usual, but what about your Norma? She'll be all on her own, won't she?'

Lil pulled a face. 'She always is. I've asked her countless times in the past but she always says she prefers her own company. She can't abide all the daft games folks play at Christmas.'

'She could just come for her dinner and then go home again, if that's what she wants. We wouldn't be offended. Besides, I doubt we'll be playing many games with only Shirley here.'

Lil laughed. 'Shirley won't let Christmas pass without a game of charades and your Jessie's always up for a bit of fun. But, yes, I'll ask Norma. Thanks, Edie. Now, let's get plucking.'

The day after the arrival of the cockerels, Edie at last received a letter from Beth.

I'm so sorry, she wrote, *but I won't be able to get home for Christmas. The children are home from school and are so excited that Madame really can't cope with them.*

There was truth in this statement, but it was not the whole truth. Work in Baker Street did not stop just because it was Christmas, but Beth kindly insisted that Alan took two days to spend with his wife and children, of whom he saw little enough these days. Simone never complained. She knew his work was important and that the fight was to save her beloved France. At least he was with her occasionally, unlike the poor soldiers who were abroad and away from their families for months – even years – at a time.

And, in truth, Beth was a little nervous of going home. It was relatively easy to keep silent about the secret work she was involved in whilst she was living amongst it, but she was so afraid that once home again in the bosom of her family, she would be asked awkward questions and her very evasiveness would arouse their suspicions. And the worst to resist would be her father's gentle probing.

But at least Edie had seven people round her table for Christmas dinner.

'We've brought our week's rations for you, Edie,' Jessie greeted her as soon as they stepped into the house. 'They've doubled the tea ration for Christmas week and upped the sugar too. Did you know?'

Edie nodded. 'Me 'n' Lil have got ours, but thank you, Jessie. It's most generous of you.'

Jessie flapped away her thanks with a smile. 'It's the very least we can do. My word,' she added, as she sniffed the air. 'What a delicious aroma is emanating from your oven, Edie, and Harry's managed to bring two bottles of wine – though you can't obtain anything French now for love nor money. A white and a red. I hope that's acceptable.'

'It's lovely, Jessie – thank you, Harry.'

Rather sheepishly, Harry drew out a small bottle of whisky from his inside pocket. 'And a little nip of the hard stuff for me and Archie. To keep out the cold, you know,' he added with a broad wink.

Edie laughed. 'Of course, Harry. Would I think anything else? Come in, come in and make yourselves at home. Oh, and here's Norma.'

Lil's sister had brought gifts of food too, though Edie

noticed that there were no rationed goods amongst her offering. But what she had brought would have cost her far more than pre-war prices and Edie was grateful for the gesture.

Whilst Edie and Lil, red-faced and anxious, scurried between the scullery, the living room and the front room carrying steaming dishes of vegetables, Archie played the magnanimous host.

'Now, Norma, how about a little pre-dinner sherry for you?'

'Oh, I shouldn't really, Archie, but it is a special occasion.' She held out her glass, which Archie generously filled to the brim, remembering the wedding reception. Norma, it seemed, was quite partial to a sherry or two.

When he had poured a sherry for Jessie and a beer for himself and Harry, Archie sat down by the fire.

'No use you sitting down, m'lad,' Edie said. 'You'll have to come and carry these two birds to the table.'

'No rest for the wicked, eh, Harry?' Archie said good-naturedly as he heaved himself out of his chair again.

Minutes later they were all seated around the table, admiring the two cockerels.

'They're plump birds,' Norma said. 'The ones in the butcher's were skinny. Hardly any meat on them.'

'It was a generous gift, no doubt,' Harry said. 'Did Mr Schofield say how the family are? I expect they'll be having a real farmhouse feast. Here's to 'em, I say.' And he raised his glass.

The conversation continued around the table until, one by one, they fell silent as they began to eat. Then there was Edie's pudding to follow and Lil's mince pies, freshly baked that morning.

'I couldn't eat another thing,' Jessie declared.

'Nor me,' Norma agreed, standing up a little unsteadily. 'And now we must help with the washing-up.'

'Oh, there's no need—' Edie began, but Norma and Jessie insisted.

'And you, young lady,' Jessie added, tapping Shirley on the shoulder, 'can give us a hand. That's if you want us all to play charades with you later.' Everyone laughed but, although she pulled a face, Shirley got up and began to help clear the table.

After everything had been cleared away, it was present-giving time. Most of the gifts this year were of a practical nature. Because Harry didn't go to sea and was able to run an allotment as well as the strip of garden at the back of his house, he was given gardening tools and seeds. But it was Lil's gift to Shirley that caused the girl to squeal with delight. 'Oh, Aunty Lil, soap! Wherever did you find it? I hope you didn't pay a fortune for it.'

'Not – exactly.' Lil bit her lip and then confessed. 'It's some I'd been saving from before the war.'

'That's kind of you, Aunty Lil. Are you sure?'

''Course I am, duck.'

'And what are you glancing at the clock for, Archie Kelsey?' Edie smiled. 'As if I didn't know.'

Archie shifted uneasily in his chair and exchanged a glance with Harry. 'Well, we – er – were just wondering—'

'If you could go to the match,' Edie finished his sentence for him with a chuckle as she turned to her sister. 'What d'you reckon, Jessie? Shall we let 'em go?'

Jessie waved her hand airily. 'I don't see why not, Edie. We can have a good old gossip if they're out of the way. Who are they playing?'

'Hull,' both men chorused promptly.

'They're playing at Scunthorpe,' Harry put in, 'but Bert Platt down the street has still got his car on the road. He said he'll give us a lift.'

Both men glanced at the clock. There was still time to reach the ground before the kick-off.

'Then you'd better get off.'

'You're a good 'un, Edie Kelsey.' Archie kissed his wife soundly on the cheek. 'Come on, then, Harry.'

The two men hastily donned their jackets and black and white scarves knitted by their wives in Grimsby Town's colours and scuttled out of the back door before Edie or Jessie could change their minds.

'Now,' Shirley said firmly, as the door closed behind the two men. 'How about a nice game of charades?' But it wasn't quite the same without Beth's hilarious antics and Frank and Reggie playing up to her.

It had been a good day in a lot of ways, Edie thought, as she got ready for bed that night, but not the same. It would never be the same unless all her family were around her. And now that could never happen again.

Quietly, she shed a few tears into her pillow whilst Archie snored gently beside her.

Eleven

Shirley was lonely now that both Beth and Irene had gone away. She even missed Reggie. Although she enjoyed her work, she didn't mix with the other women and girls from Oldroyd's and it wasn't much fun going to the cinema or dancing on her own. But several times, as she walked home from work, she saw a young woman with blond curly hair – so fair that it was almost white – going into one of the houses at the opposite end of the street to where Shirley lived. They began to nod to each other, then to say a tentative 'hello' and finally, one evening, Shirley smiled and stopped. 'I keep seeing you – do you live here?'

'I lodge here.' The girl nodded towards one of the nearby terraced houses. 'With Mrs Porter.'

Shirley grimaced. 'I don't envy you. She's a miserable old cow.'

'She is unhappy woman, I think.'

Shirley was startled by the strange accent and, as if seeing a question in Shirley's eyes, the girl said swiftly, 'I am Swiss. I am freelance reporter for the local paper.'

'Ah, I see,' Shirley said. 'Well, if you fancy a night out sometime, to the pictures or something . . .'

The girl smiled. 'I would like that.'

And that was how it had started. Shirley was a chatterbox and soon Ursula knew quite a lot about the Kelseys and the Hortons. 'What about your family?'

Shirley asked one evening as they walked home from the cinema. 'You never say much about them.'

Ursula shrugged. 'I haven't seen them recently.'

'Are they still in England?'

Ursula shook her head. 'No – no. They went back to Switzerland just before the war started.'

'Why didn't you go back with them?'

Again, Ursula gave a nonchalant shrug. 'I like it here and besides, back then I had a boyfriend I didn't want to leave.'

'Had?' Shirley asked carefully.

'He – he was killed at Dunkirk.'

Shirley put her arm through her friend's. 'Like our Laurence,' she said softly. 'I am sorry.'

Ursula turned her head away as if to hide tears.

They paused outside the gate of the house where Ursula had lodgings. 'Haven't you found it difficult here in England? Because you do have a bit of an accent.'

Ursula laughed ironically. 'Sometimes, but as soon as I show my Swiss papers people accept that I am who I say I am.'

'I'm surprised you haven't been snapped up by the war office to help them with translating and such. Still,' Shirley added as she squeezed the girl's arm. 'I'm glad you haven't or you wouldn't be here.'

Ursula was thoughtful for a moment. 'Perhaps that is what your sister is doing. You said she speaks good French.'

'Maybe. Whatever it is, she's not very bothered about the rest of her family,' Shirley said bitterly. 'She hardly ever writes now, though when she first went away, her letters were several pages long. She doesn't even tell us where she is. Anyway, I'd better go. Mam'll whinge if I'm later than I said. 'Night, Ursula. See you.'

As Shirley disappeared into the darkness of the blackout, Ursula waited a moment before turning and walking back to the end of the road, but this time, instead of turning towards the town again, she took the way that led to the docks.

Archie's was one of the few trawlers still going to sea to fish. Many had been requisitioned by the Navy and had been turned into minesweepers.

'I'm pleased you're not going on one of those,' Edie had said. 'At least you're doing what you've always done. We're all used to that. Minesweeping must be ever so dangerous.'

Archie said nothing. The North Sea was now an even more perilous place. He did not tell his wife that his ship had been fitted with guns in case of attack, nor about the trawlers that were already being lost – and not only those which had been turned into minesweepers for the duration of the war. The Nazi planes had no compunction in attacking innocent fishing vessels wherever they found them. Although he felt guilty keeping yet another secret from Edie, he didn't want to worry her; she had enough anxieties already. His trips were mainly confined to a strip down the east coast of the country, much of the North Sea being closed to fishing now. But there were times when he went to the west coast of Scotland and the Hebrides and even into the Irish Sea, though in the early months of the war, several trawlers had been sunk off the north and northwest coast of Ireland by U-boats. Mines, too, were a constant threat. All this Archie kept to himself and he certainly never told her if he was venturing into Icelandic waters. Luckily for him, it was a tradition that fishermen's wives never asked where their husbands were going; another superstition that Edie respected.

'Edie, love,' Archie said, when he was at home for longer than usual in March, 1941, 'You know you refused to have an Anderson in the yard . . .'

'I most certainly did, Archie. I hope you're not going to bring that argument up again.'

'No, love, I'm not, but I really would like you to have something here.'

'But it's only a step away into Lil's yard,' Edie argued.

'I know, love, I know, but I've heard there's a new type of shelter available – one you can have in the house. It's called a Morrison shelter after the Home Secretary, Herbert Morrison. They say he designed it. If you really won't let me build you an Anderson in our yard—'

'I won't.'

'Then at least let's consider this. It sounds like a good idea. '

'What is it?' Edie was suspicious. 'What's it like and where will it go?'

'It's a big metal cage about the size of our dining table – mebbe a bit bigger. In fact, that's where it would be best. We don't use that room a lot —'

'We do at Christmas and Easter,' Edie argued, determined not to let Hitler spoil all their fun.

'I know, love,' Archie said patiently. She was a grand wife, his Edie, and she was coping remarkably well with all the hardships. When he had to be away he was glad that she had Lil close by, but even Lil couldn't take away the constant worry Edie had when he was at sea. Archie knew Beth and Frank were never far from her mind either, just as they weren't from his, and she was still struggling with the loss of their firstborn. He just

111

hoped that Reggie, Irene and the baby were as safe in the countryside as they believed them to be.

'But if I take the dining table down and store it in the shed,' he went on, 'the Morrison will serve as a table too.'

'I'll tell you when I see it,' was all Edie would promise. She didn't want to argue with her husband; he was only thinking of their safety and she had to admit it had been very scary hiding under the table or squeezing into the cupboard under the stairs when the town was targeted by the Luftwaffe.

The monstrosity, as Edie came to call it, arrived the following week and she watched Archie erect it with a sour expression on her face. It was a large metal cage the same height as their dining table but a little longer and wider and had a sturdy iron frame and a steel top. The steel mesh, put up from the inside when an air raid happened, gave extra protection.

'You'll never get that in there,' she said, making one last ditch attempt to thwart Archie.

'You just watch me,' he said with a grin.

'Now,' Archie said, standing back at last to admire his handiwork, 'Just fetch one of your pretty tablecloths, Edie, and let's see how it looks.'

Moments later, Edie's biggest cloth almost covered the shelter. 'There you are,' Archie said. 'Not so bad, is it? And it will keep you and Shirley safe. There's plenty of room for you both, though it'll be a bit of a squash when I'm at home. We'll put a mattress in and pillows and blankets to make it comfy. You can sleep in there.'

'Oh aye, when there's bombs dropping all around us. I don't see us getting a lot of sleep. But it's not as bad as I thought, Archie,' Edie said, giving in gracefully.

'Though it'll be even more of a squeeze to get us all round it at Christmas. Still, like you say, it's handy to get to – no rushing through the dark streets to find a public shelter – and it looks strong enough. Does Lil want one?'

'No, she's happy with the Anderson.'

And so the 'monstrosity' found its place in the Kelsey household and doubled as a dining table for the first time on Easter Sunday.

This time there were only the four of them sitting in Edie's front room, trying to make the best of a bad job. Edie had shed a few tears as she cooked their dinner, but by the time Lil arrived, carefully carrying the trifle she had made, Edie had dried her eyes and pasted a welcoming smile on her face.

'There,' Lil said, setting it carefully on the table. 'Home-made sponge cake, bottled fruit, jelly made with powdered gelatine and a custard made with dried eggs. No cream, I'm afraid, but what do you think, Edie?'

'It's a triumph, duck. You're so inventive.'

Lil pulled a comical face. 'You've got to be these days, haven't you?'

But the day dragged for all of them and there was no word from any other member of the family. After they'd finished eating, Shirley announced. 'I'm off out to the park. I've made a new friend. She's called Ursula and she's lodging at the end of our street. Ta-ra.'

'Bring her back for tea, if you like, love,' Edie said, but Shirley had left, banging the back door behind her.

Edie glanced at the other two. Archie was settling in his easy chair in front of the range for his Sunday afternoon nap, his eyelids already drooping.

Edie and Lil exchanged an amused look. 'Fancy a game of Rummy, Edie?' Lil said softly.

*

In the autumn of 1941, Alan Forster finally asked Beth if she'd like to train to be an agent in occupied France. 'It'll be very dangerous work. Have no illusions about that, but you're perfect for the job. You speak the language fluently and you've actually visited the area where we want to send you to when you were with us in France.' He hesitated and then added, 'We want you to go back to the farm – to Simone's parents. We've come up with what we think is a good cover story. You look very young for your age, Beth, and we think we could pass you off as a girl who's only just left school.'

Beth gasped and stared at him. 'But won't it be awfully dangerous for Monsieur and Madame Détange?'

Alan shrugged. 'It's what they want to do. They're appalled at the invasion of their country. They've hardly recovered from the last war and now they're overrun yet again and by the same enemy too. And Emile – their son whom you've met . . .'

Beth smiled inwardly at the memory of the handsome young Frenchman. Instantly, she could picture him in her mind's eye as vividly as if he were standing in front of her. His black hair swept smoothly back from his forehead, his dark blue eyes flirting with her. He was slim in build and yet had a wiry strength from working on the farm from an early age. The young Beth – she felt so much older now, even though in reality it was only three years since she'd last seen him – had been more than a little bit in love with him.

'. . . has joined the local resistance group,' Alan went on, interrupting her thoughts. 'In fact, I think it was he who set that particular circuit up. But these groups will need help and support from us. They're hiding in the woods and forests. We've already sent an organizer, but he needs a lot more support. In the meantime, we've sent him a wireless operator, but it's only for a certain length of time. There are other areas where both those people would be more useful eventually. So we need to train replacements for both of them and we'd like you to train as a wireless operator and, in due course, be dropped by parachute into France.' He paused and met her steady gaze. 'It'll be a while before you actually go – the training is intensive, but will you do it?'

Without hesitation, Beth said, 'Of course I will.'

'You'll need to talk to Sybil Carpenter. She's the second in command in charge of women recruits under Vera Atkins.' He smiled as he added, 'Maurice Buckmaster is the Head of F Section – the French Section – and Vera is his Assistant. Both Vera and I answer directly to him.'

Beth's eyes shone.

On the morning she was to meet Miss Carpenter, Beth dressed carefully, but, remembering what Alan had said, not as one might have supposed for an interview for a job. She applied Ponds cold cream to her face but no other cosmetics. Then she tied her hair into two bunches. She would have liked to have plaited it, but it was scarcely long enough yet. Then she put on a gingham dress that reached to just above her knees.

'Good job I'm not massive in the bosom department,' she murmured, as she looked at herself in the full-length mirror. She had a slim figure that was perfectly proportioned, but she would never be described as buxom. And now she was glad of it. White ankle socks and brown, lace-up shoes completed her outfit. She smiled as she checked her appearance. It was like looking back down the years to her fifteen-year-old schoolgirl self.

'I look younger than our Shirley,' she giggled and

then, sobering, put on her coat and left her lodgings to make her way to Baker Street.

As she stepped inside, a voice accosted her. 'You can't come in here, girl. What d'you think you're doing?'

Beth turned to see the man who regularly greeted her every morning. 'Jim, it's me.'

The middle-aged man's mouth dropped open. 'Good Heavens, so it is, Miss Kelsey. Whatever have you—?' Then he paused, as if suddenly catching on. 'Ah, you'll be wanting to see Miss Carpenter, I take it?'

Beth smiled and nodded. This man saw all the comings and goings in and out of the buildings in Baker Street that had once been the offices of Marks and Spencer. But now they had a very different purpose and Jim Lovatt was at the heart of it. He probably knew more about what was going on here than any other individual in the building.

'I don't need to take you to her office, do I? You know the way.' Beth was about to turn away when he said quietly, 'Just be careful what you sign up for, love, won't you?'

'I will,' Beth promised huskily, touched by the older man's concern.

Moments later she was knocking at Sybil Carpenter's door, her heart beating a little faster than its normal rate.

'Come in,' a voice called and Beth opened the door to what was to become a very different way of life for her.

Twelve

'Mam – this is Ursula Werner. She works for the local newspaper as a freelance, covering events and news items when their regular reporters are busy. I've brought her home for tea like you said I could.'

Normally, Edie would have been welcoming but she had queued half the morning outside the butcher's and then again at the grocer's. Her feet hurt and she was not in the best of tempers. Shopping was boring and it was so tiring trudging from shop to shop.

As if sensing a problem, the girl said cheerfully. 'I have brought you some tea, Mrs Kelsey, and some butter.'

Edie blinked at the girl. Although she spoke perfect English, she had a strange accent. Sensing her mother's disquiet, Shirley laughed. 'Ursula is Swiss – from Zurich. That's right, isn't it, Ursula? She's been in England a long time, but some of the accent still comes out now and again. Do you remember when Beth first came back from France, she couldn't remember some English words?'

Edie nodded, still staring at the stranger. She was unnerved by Ursula's accent – and her name, if it came to that. She wished Archie was at home. Still, if the girl was being employed by the local paper she must be genuine. The editor would have vetted her, Edie was sure.

'That's kind of you,' Edie said, trying to instil some

warmth into her tone. It was a nice gesture on the girl's part, she had to admit. 'Sit down, duck. Make yourself at home while I get the tea on.'

The two girls sat down at the table whilst Edie moved between the scullery and the living room, setting the table and bringing in the food.

'So,' she heard Shirley say, 'what have you got lined up for the paper next – anything interesting?'

Ursula laughed. 'My pieces are always interesting.' She paused and then asked casually, 'Will Beth be home soon? I'd like to meet her.'

Edie, coming in at that moment, almost dropped the plates she was carrying. That strange accent again, she thought. Maybe she had some kind of speech impediment. She couldn't sound certain letters of the alphabet like some folk couldn't sound their 'r's.

'No – no,' Shirley said uncertainly, not meeting the girl's questioning gaze. 'She's – away.'

'In the forces?' Ursula was evidently not going to let the subject drop.

'We don't know,' Edie said, banging the plates down onto the table in a gesture of frustration at the newcomer opening up a topic of conversation that was rarely raised. Each member of the family had their own thoughts – and worries – about Beth, but for some strange reason not one of them wanted to voice them aloud. But now, she and Shirley were being forced to confront uncomfortable thoughts.

'When she first went to London,' Shirley said, 'we had long, newsy letters, but now it's just a short note – and not very often at that.'

'Perhaps she is on a secret mission.'

Edie and Shirley stared at her. Seeing their startled looks, Ursula said swiftly, 'I was only joking.'

'Aye, well, mebbe so,' Edie muttered and turned back to the scullery, wondering if the girl's teasing had actually been somewhere near the truth. Where *was* Beth? Was she safe and would she ever come home? Or was she, too, lost like Laurence?

At first, Sybil Carpenter frowned as she looked Beth up and down. 'I see you've taken it upon yourself to design your own style of dress to fit the cover story.'

'It's just a suggestion, Miss Carpenter. I'll abide by whatever decision is made – if I'm accepted and pass the training, of course.'

'That goes without saying.'

Sybil Carpenter was tall and thin with short brown hair and smooth skin. She was neatly dressed in a dark blue costume and a white cotton blouse. She had a brisk manner that sometimes bordered on being brusque, but she had an important job to do and it was not melodramatic to say that people's lives depended on her decisions and on those of her colleagues. She continued to regard Beth thoughtfully, biting her lower lip until Beth began to feel slightly uncomfortable. Had she overstepped the mark? Been too forward?

'Take your coat off, please.' Beth removed her coat and then Sybil said, 'Turn round – slowly.'

When Beth stood facing her once more, the woman's face suddenly broke into a smile, making her look years younger and far less severe. 'Actually, Beth, I think it's a very good idea, particularly in view of what Alan is suggesting. Sit down and let's talk things through.'

The next hour passed quickly whilst Sybil explained all that would be expected of Beth. When she had finished, she asked the same question that Alan had asked. 'Will you do it?'

Once again, Beth said firmly, 'Yes, I will.'

'We want you to start training straight away. You're already in the FANYs so it makes it a lot easier,' Sybil added.

'What happens about letters to our families while we're away?' Beth knew, of course, that she could say nothing to her family.

'If you wish, we can send postcards, which you will have written before you go. Postcards are easier because you won't be required to say too much, not like you would if you were writing a letter.' Sybil smiled. 'Families expect long, newsy letters, but with a short postcard, they accept you can't say much.'

'Mm.' Beth was sceptical. Her letters had been epistles of the highest order, as her aunt, Jessie, would have said, and the difference between them and a few brief postcards would be markedly noticeable. But just lately she had not written so effusively. It had been difficult when she could no longer talk about what she was doing, let alone what she would be doing in the future. But she still doubted that her eagle-eyed mother, or her perceptive dad, would accept brief postcards as 'normal'. More than likely they had already begun to ponder the brevity of her recent letters. Anyway, she comforted herself, it had to be done. Training as an agent was what she wanted to do.

Four days later, Beth was on a train to Wanborough Manor in Surrey, dressed once more in her FANY uniform. She was greeted in French by the woman in charge of the establishment and quickly told that she must speak the language at all times. It seemed to Beth that the atmosphere was very relaxed for a training school for agents, but she had worked with Alan long enough to know that this first part of a four-stage training was to weed out any who were unsuitable. Beth knew that the candidates were being observed every minute of the day, yet no mention was actually made about why they were really here. For the following three weeks, Beth took part in the physical training and laughed with the others during the lessons in sabotage, the teacher making the bangs a matter for levity. Yet underneath they all knew there was a very serious reason. They enjoyed throwing each other about in the unarmed combat lessons, but when it came to learning silent killing they all realized the grim reality of what they were undertaking. They were taught map reading and how to communicate in Morse code, in which, much to everyone else's surprise, Beth excelled.

'Of course this isn't enough for those of you who are going on to train as wireless operators,' their instructor said, 'but all of you should have a basic knowledge.'

When they went out in the evenings, there was always a member of the staff with them, observing their behaviour, as Beth well knew, for she had done it herself several times at Alan's request. But now *she* was being observed. At the end of the three weeks, Beth was one of those chosen to proceed to one of the paramilitary schools based in north-west Scotland.

Now it was getting serious.

'You can all go home for Christmas,' their instructor told the chosen few, 'but not a word about what you have been doing or what you are training for. Not one word. Being in the services' – he nodded towards the small number of women, who were now all in the FANYs, to include them – 'you have the protection of what that stands for.'

Beth felt torn. She longed to go home to see her family, but she was nervous too. Her family – and her father in particular – were very astute and she doubted her own capability of keeping such secrets. Still, she reminded herself wryly, it'll be good practice. If I can dupe my nearest and dearest, I can fool anyone.

Thirteen

'1941's been a funny year, hasn't it, Lil?' Edie mused as they sat together to finalize their plans for Christmas.

'Irene and the little one – and Reggie, of course – have been away such a long time and we haven't even been able to get out to see them.'

'I know, duck, but Archie's adamant that we shouldn't upset Reggie and, of course, we're not encouraged to make unnecessary journeys, are we?'

'I don't think seeing our family is "unnecessary",' Lil replied with surprising asperity.

'Tell you what, you write and ask Irene to come home for Christmas and I'll write to Reggie. Surely he's been there long enough not to get "unsettled", as Archie calls it.'

That decided, the two women turned their thoughts to how the war was going.

'Most of the year seems to have been taken up with Rommel's siege of Tobruk. Thank goodness the Allies won in the end.'

'Yes, but to me the worst thing that's happened this year has been the Japanese attack on America's fleet in Pearl Harbour last week. Who'd have thought anybody could be daft enough to attack a huge country like that?'

Lil laughed wryly. 'Only Hitler, when he attacked Russia. If he beats them, Edie, I'll eat my hat.'

'He won't – but at least we've got both the big powers on our side now.'

'That's true – we're no longer alone, are we?'

Edie sniffed. 'Only here at home without our families.'

At the end of his final trip to sea before Christmas – the third Christmas of the war – Archie stepped into the back door of his house to be greeted by Edie waving a letter under his nose.

'She's coming home for Christmas. Beth's coming home.'

'Ah, now that's the best news I could have had, love. We'll make it the best Christmas we've had since all this started, eh?'

'Aye, we will – as much as rationing will let us. It's going to be even harder this year. I don't reckon it can get much worse. I just hope Beth brings her ration book home with her.'

'She will,' Archie said confidently.

'But there'll be no sherry for Norma this time – even if she was joining us this year, which she isn't – and hardly any chocolates or fruit. And I've had such a job to get you even a bit of baccy, Archie.'

He patted his wife's shoulder. He could see that the shortages were bothering Edie. She couldn't look after her family any longer in the way that she always had.

'I'm sure you and Lil will work miracles. You always do. And chin up, love. Things are looking better than they did this time last year. Adolf was an idiot to invade Russia – at least from his point of view. I don't know what he was thinking of but at least it diverted his Luftwaffe away from us. And he's had to abandon his attack on Moscow now. I expect the Russian winter defeated him just like it did Napoleon. And it'll have depleted his resources and lowered the morale of his troops. And we're not alone now, Edie. We've got the Yanks with us. You mark my words, love, it'll take us a while yet but we'll win. One day – we'll win. And best of all, Beth's coming home!'

For the rest of the day, the smiles never left either of their faces and Lil, when she heard, clasped her hands together and breathed an ecstatic 'Oh!'

Shirley, too, grinned from ear to ear. 'I'll be able to introduce her to my friend.' Shirley had had few real friends in her life other than Irene and, of course, her sister, but she seemed to have found one in Ursula.

'Oh aye.' Archie smiled as he sat down in his armchair with a satisfied sigh and shook open his newspaper. 'And who's this, then? A boyfriend?'

'Don't be daft, Dad,' Shirley laughed wryly. 'Who'd look at me?'

'Aw, don't do yourself down, love.' Archie glanced up at her over his paper but couldn't for the life of him think what to say to encourage his plain-looking daughter without sounding patronizing. 'Beth'll help you with the make-up and curl your hair and all that when she comes home. Your hair looks pretty when it's curled up.' Now he could be truthful, for it did.

Shirley felt a lump in her throat. It wasn't often her dad took much notice of her and he hardly ever commented on her appearance. But she was honest enough with herself to know that it was a difficult task to pay her compliments when she was compared to her lovely sister!

They were all at the station to meet Beth on Christmas Eve, but this time it was a happy occasion. And Lil was there too. After she'd hugged them all and Archie had picked up her suitcase, Beth glanced around her. 'Where's Reggie? And Irene and Tommy? Have they come for Christmas? Are they waiting at home?'

Edie bit her lip and shook her head but it was Shirley who said, 'They've not come, Beth. Irene said that little Tommy's got a cold and she doesn't want him riding on draughty buses or trains. And Reggie, well . . .' she paused and glanced at her mother, then took a deep breath and said bluntly – 'he doesn't seem to *want* to come home.'

'Of course he does,' Edie said, valiantly trying to persuade herself as well as everyone else. 'Mr Schofield brought a letter from him when he brought us two birds – geese this time – and a lovely piece of ham this year. Oh, we'll have a feast, Beth, and no mistake.'

'And what did Reggie say in his letter?'

Edie shrugged, trying to make light of it, but she'd been hurt. 'He said that the land army girls are going home for Christmas and Mr Schofield won't have anyone else to help him on the farm, so – he felt obliged to stay. I'm sure he really *wanted* to come home, though.'

'Of course he did, Mam,' Beth said gently.

Comforted, Edie linked her arm through Beth's and Shirley took her sister's other arm and they walked along the road arm in arm, leaving a smiling Archie and Lil to bring up the rear.

'You'll meet my friend Ursula,' Shirley chattered. 'She's got no family in this country and the woman she lodges with at the top of our road is a right old misery. There'll be no merrymaking in *that* house.'

'Ursula? Who's Ursula?'

'I told you – my friend.'

'I know, but who is she?'

'She's Swiss and came to live in England years ago.'

'She's got a funny accent,' Edie murmured, 'but she seems nice enough.'

'And what about you?' Shirley asked. 'What have you been doing? I must say, I like the uniform. You look awfully smart, though I'm surprised they've let you grow your hair even longer. I thought you had to have it all chopped off when you went into the services.'

Beth laughed, her low, deep chuckle that had everyone smiling. How they'd all missed Beth and that laugh of hers. 'All sorts of things,' she said, answering the first part of Shirley's questions and deliberately keeping her replies vague. Neatly, she avoided any comment on her hair. She was growing it longer for a reason, but she didn't want her family to know what that was. 'I've been taking a first-aid course.' This at least was true and Beth felt she was on safe ground. It fitted in with the nursing theme that the FANYs stood for. 'And it's been very useful knowing how to drive. I must remember to thank Uncle Harry tomorrow. They are coming to us for Christmas Day, I take it?'

'Yes, but Norma's got other plans this year,' Edie replied.

'Well, she won't be missed,' Shirley said, without stopping to think that Lil was walking close behind them. Edie shot her younger daughter a warning glance, but Lil called out merrily, 'It's all right, Edie. Actually, I quite agree with Shirley.'

And all five of them burst out laughing, attracting some curious glances as they walked home.

'Poor Norma,' Beth said kindly. 'Just so long as she's not going to be on her own for Christmas Day. I wouldn't like to think of anyone being on their own at Christmas.'

'That's why I want to invite Ursula,' Shirley said promptly.

'What about the lady she lives with, though? Does that mean she's going to be alone?'

Shirley shook her head. 'She's going to her sister's, but they didn't ask Ursula.'

'Then she must come to us,' Edie said firmly. 'You can pop up the road and ask her before the blackout needs to go up.'

Later that night when Lil had gone home and Edie, weary with all the preparations for the following day, had gone to bed – Shirley too – Beth and her father sat together in front of the dying embers.

'Now, love,' he said gently, 'are you really all right? You can tell your old dad, y'know.'

'Dad, I'm fine – honestly.' And Archie had to admit she looked it. Her skin was clear, her long brown hair was glossy and her eyes were shining as if she were thoroughly enjoying her life in the FANYs.

'Er – what is it you do exactly?'

'All sorts, Dad.'

'But it's nursing, isn't it? Is that what you're doing?'

'Not exactly.' Beth shook her head. She'd rehearsed her answers to any probing questions so they slipped glibly off her tongue with no awkward hesitation whilst she concocted an answer. 'I'm a general dogsbody, I suppose, but thanks to good old Uncle Harry, I can drive an ambulance if needed.'

Archie leaned forward and tapped his pipe out on the hearth and then set it on the mantelpiece. He avoided looking directly at Beth now as he stared into the fire and said softly, 'Well, whatever it is you're doing, lass, just take good care of yourself and – and come back safely to us, won't you?' He was on the point of asking her to write more often, to keep them posted about where she was and what she was doing, but Archie Kelsey had his own instincts – just like his daughter – and he remained silent.

Beth felt a lump in her throat and she was on the point of confiding in her father, but she stopped herself just in time and instead whispered huskily, 'I promise.' She stood up and kissed the top of his head. 'I'm off up now. I need my sleep to cope with a heavy afternoon of charades tomorrow. Night, night, Dad.'

As the door closed softly behind her, Archie sighed. Her replies to his gentle probing hadn't fooled him for one moment.

Despite the absence of several members of the family, they all enjoyed Christmas Day. At first, Ursula seemed shy and somewhat disconcerted by having to meet several more members of the family at once for the first time. She seemed especially nervous when she found that Beth had joined one of the forces.

'Shirley says you've been living in this country for some time.' Beth smiled at her, trying to make the girl feel welcome and yet, she was puzzled by her. She wanted to find out more. 'But where are you from originally?'

'I told you, Beth, she's from Zurich.'

Beth grinned. 'So you did, Shirley. Sorry, Ursula, I'm just naturally nosey.'

Archie, carefully carving one of the geese from the

129

Schofields' farm, pretended to be concentrating on the job in hand, but his sharp ears were missing nothing of the conversation around the table. He was wondering what Beth was playing at. He'd always thought her the least 'nosey' person he knew and yet here she was asking the stranger in their midst quite probing questions. Maybe she was just trying to make the girl feel welcome and at home – or was it something else? Had Beth's training – whatever that had been – taught her to ask questions of anyone and everyone?

'So how long have you been here? You speak wonderful English.'

'I came when I was twelve,' Ursula said. Suddenly, her foreign accent sounded more acute. Perhaps, thought Archie, Beth's questions were unnerving her and she was feeling under pressure.

'Here? To Grimsby?' To the casual observer, Beth's questions sounded innocent enough, as if she was merely making conversation, involving the girl in their midst, but Archie wondered . . .

'No, I was in London for many years, but when the bombing started I came north.'

'Not the safest place you could have chosen, duck,' Edie said, piling potatoes and carrots on to Ursula's plate. 'They've sent folk *out* of Grimsby – not to it.' And she added under her breath, 'As if we didn't know.'

'So, what made you come here?' Beth laughed and, trying to lighten her probing questions, added, 'It can't be that you like the smell of fish.'

'Well, I'm glad she has come here,' Shirley put in. 'She's become my best friend now that you and Irene have gone away.'

Beth smiled at her sister, sensing the poignancy in

the girl's tone. She guessed that Shirley must have felt very lonely, but she hoped she hadn't latched on to just anyone who'd shown her the slightest sign of friendliness.

'I – I got a job on the local paper. At least, I work freelance for them,' Ursula added swiftly. 'If I hear a story, I write it and take it to the newspaper offices.'

'Well, there're plenty of stories just now,' Edie said, with a bitter edge to her tone. 'Ones we'd rather not be having.'

'So, you haven't been interned, then?'

Ursula frowned. 'Interned? What is that?'

'It's when someone living here – even if they've been living here for some time – is sent to an internment camp because they're thought to be an enemy alien.'

Ursula's frown deepened and her cheeks were suddenly tinged with pink. 'I am Swiss,' she declared firmly, 'not German. I speak German because that is what is spoken in Zurich – where I come from. That is all.' Her accent was even more pronounced.

'That's enough, Beth,' Edie said suddenly, aware that their guest was becoming agitated. She felt sorry for the girl, many miles away from her folks and at Christmas too. She must be feeling very homesick. She wanted her to feel part of their family even if only for a day. She hoped that the Schofields were doing the same for Reggie and Irene and little Tommy. For a brief moment, tears threatened to overwhelm her as she remembered, yet again, that she hadn't even been able to give Tommy his Christmas present in person.

'I'm so sorry, Ursula,' Beth was saying swiftly and her tone sounded sincere. 'I didn't mean to upset or embarrass you. I was just curious about how you came to fetch up in Grimsby of all places. Let's change the subject. How are you getting on at Oldroyd's, Shirley? What's the latest fashion in utility garments?'

The conversation moved away from Ursula and the girl seemed to relax. Soon she was laughing and, later, she joined in the games that the Kelsey family always played at Christmas. But for the rest of the day, Archie was aware that Beth was watching the girl closely and it was no surprise when they were alone later that evening when she said, 'Dad, what do you think of Ursula?'

'I'm not sure, love, but I can see you're not happy about her. What is it you suspect?'

'Nothing really.' Beth twisted a strand of her hair round the forefinger of her left hand – a sure sign that she was concerned about something. 'Her story is plausible, but – oh, I don't know – it's just a gut feeling, really. But it's the first time I've known Shirley to have a real friend so I don't want to spoil that.'

Archie didn't laugh; Beth's instincts had always been remarkable, even from childhood, and he wasn't about to ignore them now, so when she said, 'Just keep an eye on her, will you, Dad?', he agreed readily.

'I will, love, but all I'd say is, if she's working for the *Telegraph*, she must be all right. They'll have vetted her, no doubt about that.'

'Mm,' Beth said, but her tone sounded unconvinced.

A few days after Christmas, news filtered through that Hong Kong had surrendered to the Japanese. The news had been deliberately withheld until after the festivities.

'It's a good job we had our fun when we did,' Beth murmured as she hugged her family goodbye. 'Don't come to the station this time – please,' she begged. She knew – though she hoped none of her family guessed – that it might be a very long time before she saw any of them again.

Fourteen

It was not until March, 1942, that Beth was finally able to go to Scotland. The winter of 1941 and the early part of 1942 was viciously cold and Beth spent the first two months of the New Year kicking her heels and badgering Sybil Carpenter as to when the next stage of her training would begin.

'The weather has delayed things in Scotland – that's where you'll be going next. Just be patient, Beth. It'll happen soon enough, I promise, and then maybe you'll wish it hadn't.'

But Beth took no notice of Sybil's warnings; she was eager to complete her training and to be sent to France.

'You are amongst the first women we've recruited, you know,' Sybil tried to soothe Beth's impatience. 'We have a few women in France already, but not many, and we want to be sure everything is right before we send more. It's no good dropping you into the arms of a waiting German, now is it?'

Beth's common sense came to her rescue. 'Of course not,' she agreed meekly. 'I'm sorry, Miss Carpenter. It's just . . .'

'I know,' Sybil sympathized. 'You're keen and we like that, but that enthusiasm must not be allowed to cloud your judgement – or ours. Now, as soon as the next batch of recruits is to be sent to Scotland, I promise you, you will be one of them.'

Sybil Carpenter kept her promise and, early in March, Beth was given orders to travel. It seemed strange to be on a train, heading north and yet not going home so she was pleased to see one or two familiar faces from the training at Wanborough Manor.

'Am I glad to see you!' said Isobel Montgomery, who was nicknamed Monty, just like the army commander of the same name. It was a fact she invariably dined out on even though, in truth, she was no relation. She stowed her suitcase on the luggage rack above their heads and almost fell into the seat beside Beth. Monty was a 'jolly hockey sticks' type of girl, who had been privately educated and had been to finishing school in France. Yet there was no 'side' to her. Only her rather posh way of talking gave her background away. She had light brown hair and hazel eyes that were usually dancing with mischief. She was slim and energetic and always 'up for a laugh'. Really, Beth thought, they were two of a kind and it was natural that they had gravitated towards each other on the course. They had told each other a little about themselves – which perhaps they should not have done – and yet they instinctively knew that they could trust each other.

'And I'm glad to see you too, Monty. I thought there was going to be no one I knew. How're things? It seems like a lifetime ago now, but how was Christmas with your folks?'

Monty pulled a face. 'Awkward.' There was no need to say any more for Beth understood at once. 'You?'

'The same really. It was my dad. He's very sharp, and we're very close. I think he knew I was keeping something from him.' Beth sighed. She'd hated not being able to confide in her father, but she was sure, in his own way, that he understood. Perhaps he understood a little too much for comfort. But she knew she could trust him and rely on him not to say anything to anyone else – not even to her mother.

'Oh, look, there's Rob.' Isobel waved to a young man coming towards them. He grinned at them both and sat down on the opposite side of the carriage. Rob was a tall, handsome young man with brown hair, cut to regulation shortness at the moment, and dark eyes that crinkled when he smiled or laughed. He had a strong, determined jawline and white, even teeth.

'Hello, you two. OK?'

The girls both nodded.

'Phil will be here in a moment,' Rob said. 'He's just getting a newspaper. Ah, here he is.'

Phil was smaller than his friend with a slight build that even army training had not improved. His hair was mousey and his complexion rather pallid. But his appearance belied a wiry strength and Beth thought he could do rather well as an agent. Who would ever suspect someone who looked like a weakling? And his mastery of French was perfect.

The four of them travelled together, chatting or remaining in companionable silence as the mood took them. When they changed trains, the two young men gallantly helped the two young women, but Monty laughed and said in a low voice, 'You won't be able to play Sir Galahad for much longer. It'll be every man – or women – for themselves soon enough.'

Rob grinned at her. 'So make the most of it, why don't you?'

'Oh, don't worry,' Monty shot back, but she was laughing as she said it, 'I will.'

'What marvellous scenery,' Beth murmured, never taking her gaze from the view outside the train window as they passed the bleak grandeur of Rannoch Moor stretching to the hazy mountains beyond.

'It's cold though.' Monty shivered dramatically.

Rob, who was still sitting just across the aisle, leaned towards Monty and said softly, 'It'll be colder still when you're swimming in one of the lochs?'

Monty's face was a picture of horror. 'We won't have to do that, will we?'

Rob chuckled, enjoying her discomfort. 'It's what I've heard.' Then his expression sobered. 'Seriously, though. We are in for a rough time, you know.'

But Monty was determined not to be fazed. 'Oh, I'm tougher than I look.'

'I hope so,' Rob murmured.

The final part of the long journey took them through the glorious countryside on the west side of Scotland, ending at Arisaig House, a magnificent, but remote, stone building that would be their home for the next few weeks.

The atmosphere was now indeed deadly serious and strenuous. They tramped miles over the hills and glens, and were left in the cold and the darkness in the middle of nowhere to find their own way back to base. Beth surprised herself and her instructors too. Even in the FANY uniform she looked much younger than her twenty-three years and many wondered why she was there. But Beth had a secret weapon of her own; a sharp, receptive brain coupled with a photographic memory behind her pretty face. Everyone underestimated her. And her instinct was not to be ignored either. She was physically fit and had a determination unmatched by any of the other candidates. She handled weapons and explosives with care, but with confidence, and learned to shoot with the accuracy of a young woman brought up to the life of hunting, shooting and fishing.

'You've done this before,' said one of her instructors, grinning, and was amazed when Beth shook her head.

'I've never even held a gun before – of any kind – until I started training.'

'You're kidding me.' He gazed at her for a moment before asking, 'What part of Lincolnshire d'you come from, then?'

They had been allowed to speak English here, though amongst themselves in their off-duty time, the girls had decided to speak only French, especially now that they knew what they were being trained for.

'Oh crumbs, is it that obvious?'

The middle-aged sergeant, who'd been injured in the Great War and had volunteered to become an instructor at the outbreak of the Second World War, chuckled. 'Not to most people, duck, but after the last war, I trained to be a gamekeeper on an estate near Gainsborough. Then I ended up working for a laird up here in Scotland. I married a Scottish lassie, too. But when war broke out again' – his expression sobered – 'I had to volunteer to do my bit. Couldn't let all my comrades down who didn't make it back last time.'

Beth touched his arm, moved by his spirit. He'd had no need to volunteer again. He'd more than done his share the last time around. Then, trying to lighten the moment, she said, 'Well, I'm sorry you've recognized my accent – but I'm afraid I'm not going to tell you exactly where I'm from. Careless talk and all that.'

He nodded and murmured, 'Well done, lass.'

So, she thought, it had been yet another test to see if the friendly approach had made her homesick and loosened her tongue. Had he really recognized the

Lincolnshire dialect in her speech or had he studied her details and concocted the story? No doubt she'd never know.

The following day, the group of young women had to retrieve containers of arms and supplies that had fallen into the loch – just like Rob had warned them.

'I can't swim,' one girl wailed. 'They never asked us if we could swim.'

'Yes, they did,' another girl said. 'At least, they asked me.'

Beth saw the instructor shake his head and knew that the girl who couldn't swim would be on the next train home. Luckily, Beth was a strong swimmer, thanks to her father taking the whole family regularly to the swimming baths, to say nothing of trips to Cleethorpes' beach in the summer and swimming in the cold North Sea. At the thought of Archie, Beth's throat prickled and tears welled in her eyes. She dashed them away impatiently, waded into the freezing water and began to swim towards the package bobbing up and down in the ripples of the loch. Reaching it, she rested a moment, treading water and then, hooking her arm through the straps, she began to swim back towards the shore. Willing hands pulled her from the water and retrieved the package, whilst Beth lay gasping on the bank for a few moments.

'Is it cold?' Isobel asked.

'Freezing,' Beth muttered through chattering teeth. 'But you can do it, Monty. Go on.'

When they were back at their lodgings, warm and dry once more, Beth and Monty sat together drinking hot cocoa. Monty seemed to have the same determination as Beth and whilst they did not swap stories, there was empathy between them. Over the remaining two weeks, they watched out for each other, helped each other and quickly became firm friends.

'Obviously we're not supposed to tell each other much,' Beth said, when they were alone in the dining room one evening after dinner had finished and the other girls had disappeared, 'but I suppose it's all right to ask what you plan to do next?'

'By way of training, you mean?'

'Mm.'

'Nothing specific other than the parachute training we'll all have to do. That's somewhere near Manchester, isn't it? What about you?'

'I'd like to be a wireless operator.'

'Good for you.' Monty smiled. 'Hope you make it. You did brilliantly in the bit of Morse code training we did. I'm just not clever enough. I'll apply to be a courier, I think.'

Beth said nothing. She never bragged about her cleverness, but, privately, she believed that if she could pass as a native French speaker in only two years, learning to be a wireless operator would be a doddle. And besides, she had already proved that she was halfway there, thanks to her father's Morse code lessons. What would he say now, she thought, if he knew just how she was going to be putting his teaching to use? Perhaps, she thought wryly, he would regret having taught her.

'I don't expect they'll let us go out together, will they?' she murmured at last.

'I doubt it. The fewer people you know in the circuit you're assigned to, the better, and,' Monty added with a laugh, 'we know a bit too much about each other now I'd say.'

Again Beth said nothing, but she was thinking that she didn't know a thing about Monty, nor Monty about her. But she assumed Isobel was meaning that they knew each other's real names and that they'd trained together. Even that information could be dangerous if divulged to the wrong people.

'It's a shame, though,' Monty added with a sigh. 'I reckon we'd make a good team.'

Despite their disappointment that it was unlikely that they'd be sent abroad together, Beth and Monty stayed with each other through parachute training, though sadly Monty injured her ankle during the very last jump and was out of action for several weeks.

Beth went to Oxfordshire to train as a wireless operator. Rob was the only other person who'd been in Scotland with her who was also sent to Oxfordshire. Then it was back to London to the flat where they would stay until they were given a final briefing just before their departure for France. The days passed in the flat were tedious. Nothing seemed to be happening. They couldn't go home and couldn't write long, newsy letters. 'You'll have to be patient. You know we've got a special assignment for you,' Alan told Beth when she went to the offices in Baker Street. 'But things have got to be right the other end before we can send you in. We've just replaced the organizer out there, so we need a little time for him to get settled, make contacts and set everything up.'

So, Beth had to wait.

Fifteen

'Have you heard from Beth, then?' Lil asked as she popped into Edie's home for their morning cuppa together. It was a warm August morning and their back doors stood open to let in whatever bit of breeze there was.

Edie pulled a face. 'Only a measly postcard. It's on the mantelpiece there. You can read it, Lil. There's nowt private in it.' She sniffed. 'There's no room on the blessed thing for owt that the world and his wife can't see.'

Lil reached up and took down the card. 'It's posted in London. So, what's she doing there, d'you think?'

Edie shrugged. 'Your guess is as good as mine. Summat in the FANYs, I suppose. Though don't ask me what, 'cos I can't tell you. She didn't say much when she was home at Christmas and, of course, we've seen neither hide nor hair of her since. And that's more than seven months ago. I don't know what to make of it, I'm sure.'

'Mm,' Lil said thoughtfully as she replaced the card. 'I noticed she was unusually quiet about what she was up to. Not like Beth at all. She normally chatters nineteen to the dozen. Mind you,' she went on, smiling now, 'your Shirley made up for it. She's certainly coming out of her shell now. I think Ursula's good for her.'

'They certainly spend a lot of time together. Shirley's never at home these days.'

142

'That's good, isn't it, Edie? She looks a lot happier, I have to say.'

'Aye, I suppose so, but now and again I could use a bit of help about the place, 'specially when Archie's away. Some days I feel as if I'm run off me feet, what with the WVS and all the queuing we have to do.' She paused and then asked, 'Have you heard from Irene? I've not had a word from Reggie.'

'Yes, I had a letter last week. She's says they're all well.' Lil laughed. 'Reggie's a boy, Edie. You can't expect him to be much of a letter writer. Besides, from what Irene said, he's busy from morning till night helping out on the farm. She says he's developing into a big, strong lad. That must please you, surely?'

'Aye, it does,' Edie replied, but her tone was grudging, 'but I'm not there to see me own son growing up, am I? I just wish we could go and see them, though I suppose I'll just have to content myself that he's well and happy.'

'You've still got Shirley at home.'

Edie gave an unladylike snort, 'Aye, when she's here. And now she's talking about going into some sort of war work at the end of September when she's eighteen.'

'Eighteen. My, how time flies. Doesn't seem long since Irene and Beth were wheeling her about in the pram.'

'And Frank was teaching her to walk.' Edie sat down heavily at the table and poured out the tea as she added softly, 'They were all good with her, but poor Laurence couldn't cope with her crying. He'd sooner take Frank out and teach him to play football.'

The two friends were silent for a few moments, sipping their tea and remembering the past until Lil crashed her cup down into the saucer, her eyes lighting up, as she said, 'I know, we'll have a party for her. Eighteen's a bit of a milestone, Edie. We oughtn't to let it pass unnoticed. Let's give the lass a party, eh? We've about six weeks to plan it. That'll give us plenty of time to save up our rations.'

Edie smiled across the table at her friend. 'You're a good soul, Lil. A good friend. I don't know what I'd do without you.'

'Nor me, you, Edie. Now let's get our thinking caps on and, a bit nearer the time, you can write and tell Beth what we're planning. She'll not let the cat out of the bag. She's good at keeping secrets and I'm sure she'll come home if she can.'

'You're going the day after tomorrow,' Sybil Carpenter informed Beth when she visited the flat one evening in late September. 'It'll be a night drop, but I believe you were expecting that. We'll get you kitted out tomorrow.'

'Where am I going? Is it still to the Détanges' farm?'

'We'll tell you just before you take off,' Sybil said, smiling. Even at this late stage, everything was shrouded in secrecy.

Beth hardly slept that night. It seemed such a long time since she had first said she wanted to become an agent. The training had been long and arduous and even when that had been completed, they were still not ready to send her.

The next day seemed to drag. She packed her suitcase and then checked and double-checked that she had got everything and that all her belongings were what would belong to a young French girl. There couldn't be much; Leonie Moreau, which was to be her name from now on, had just lost everything in the bombing of her home in Boulogne-Billancourt, a suburb of Paris, which had been destroyed in March. Six hundred people had died so, sadly, it was feasible that a young girl would have lost all her family and her possessions too. This information had been provided by Alan, as the apartment where he, his family and Beth had lived had been bombed.

Sybil Carpenter arrived at the flat to give Beth her final briefing. 'There's only you going tonight, which is a shame in a way. It's always nice to have a bit of company even though you'll be on your own once you get there.'

'Not really,' Beth said. 'I already know Monsieur and Madame Détange. Well, a little, anyway – if that *is* where I'm going,' she added impishly.

'Yes, it is. To their farm in the Loire Valley near the village of St Michel-près-Beauvoir. The nearest town is, as you probably know, Beauvoir-sur-Loire. Locally, as you might imagine, they're just referred to as St Michel and Beauvoir. The agent we sent out recently is lodging above the *boulangerie* in Beauvoir. You're to act as wireless operator for him and for the local resistance group when they need to get in touch with London. The agent's code name is Bruce, by the way, and you'll have to be very careful about contacting him. The baker himself is trustworthy. He's a member of the local Resistance movement, which in rural areas is known as the Maquis, but his establishment is right opposite the town hall, which the Germans have commandeered for their headquarters in the district.'

Beth gasped and stared at her. 'Why there, of all places?'

'For the very fact that it *is* right under their noses. They wouldn't think an enemy agent – because that's what we are to them – would be foolish enough to do something like this.'

'Oh.' Beth blinked. She could see the logic, but thought it a dangerous ploy.

For a moment Sybil looked doubtful. 'I'm still not sure it's a good idea you going to people you know.' She sighed. 'But the powers that be seem to think it'll work. I hope it does for your sake – and theirs.'

'I'll make sure the Détanges are happy with the arrangements as soon as I get to the farm. If not, I'll move somewhere else.'

'If you have to do that, what about your cover story? A young girl wandering about occupied France is bound to arouse suspicion.'

Beth shrugged. 'Antoine will advise me, no doubt.' Antoine was the code name by which Emile Détange was now known.

Sybil smiled. 'Good girl,' she said, then added swiftly, 'Oh, I'm sorry. That sounded patronizing, but you really do look like a fifteen-year-old.'

Beth laughed with her, delighted that her disguise seemed to be working.

'Now, let's make sure you've got everything. Identity card, ration card,' Sybil said, handing each document to her. 'And a certificate of non-belonging to the Jewish race.'

Beth's eyes widened as she stared at her. 'What on earth is that for?'

Sybil sighed. 'There are dreadful tales coming out of Germany about how they are persecuting the Jews. It started a few years before the war. No doubt you heard of *Kristallnacht* – the night of the broken glass?' Beth nodded. 'Their businesses have been smashed,' Sybil went on, 'and they are forced to wear the Star of David.

There is no hiding place for them. We've already had a lot of Jewish refugees come to Britain, children especially, but a lot left it too late to get out and now they're trapped. Heaven alone knows what's happening to them, poor souls.'

'I – see,' Beth said slowly, but she didn't really. She'd heard rumours but she hadn't realized it had got as bad as that.

'And, of course,' Sybil went on, 'in the countries they are invading, the same thing is happening to the Jewish communities there. They're being herded into ghettos, so it's said.'

'Can't we do anything?'

'Win the war,' Sybil said promptly, 'and you're doing your bit to achieve that. Now,' she went on, 'we usually give our agents photographs of family and friends but since your home has been bombed in Boulogne-Billancourt and you've lost everything, we thought it best that you shouldn't carry anything like that. Have you memorized the address where you are supposed to have lived?'

Beth nodded. 'Yes, and I remember the street and the flat where we lived well.'

'We've decided to let you use the actual address where you lived with Alan and his family. The more truth that can be woven into a cover story, the easier it is for you to remember it.' Sybil was smiling as she added, 'I'm sorry, but we can't give you the lipstick we normally give to our women when they leave. You're too young!'

Beth laughed. 'That's all right. And I've been practising plaiting my hair. It's a few years since I did that!'

Already she was dressed like a French schoolgirl, with every item of clothing she was wearing being French made.

'And no cigarettes or perfume either, I'm afraid.' Sybil looked her up and down, checking for the slightest detail that would give her away. 'You'll do. You'll be met by members of the resistance group you'll be working with. They'll guide the plane in with lights and then help you with your parachute and the packages when you land. The code name of the circuit is Fisherman.' Sybil smiled. 'We thought that quite appropriate for you.'

Beth felt comforted; it seemed like a good omen, a link with home that would bring her good luck. 'It's a relatively new set-up,' Sybil went on. 'We sent a replacement male organizer out there two weeks ago – the first one only went out temporarily – but he desperately needs a wireless operator now. Antoine should be there to meet you when you land.' She frowned. 'This is the only part I'm doubtful about; the fact that you already know the people you're going to be with. You know him as Emile Détange, don't you? You could give so much away if you're caught.'

Beth nodded. 'I know, but Alan has told me that Madame and Monsieur Détange are to be known by their real names and that, if I'm questioned, I am to say that their son, Emile, is away fighting, but no one knows where. He advised me to think of Emile and Antoine as two entirely different people. That way, I'll find it easier.' Beth's stomach was churning, but whether from nerves or excitement she couldn't be sure. She just wanted to get on with it now, but Sybil was not finished with her instructions yet. 'Your suitcase wireless will be dropped at the same time as you. It'll be dark, of course, but you must retrieve it. Hopefully, though, there will be several willing hands to help you.'

Now Sybil held out her own hand in farewell. 'Time to go. Good luck.'

As Beth crossed the windy airfield towards the waiting plane, her nerves disappeared and all she felt was a tremendous excitement. At long last, she was on her way.

When Edie's letter arrived by a circuitous route on Sybil Carpenter's desk the morning after Beth's departure, it caused her an immediate problem that could not have been foreseen. A batch of handwritten postcards, completed by Beth before she had left, lay in the top drawer of Sybil's desk to be posted at regular intervals. But now, the letter from home required a different answer. Sybil frowned, her eyes scanning the letter regarding the proposed surprise family party for Beth's younger sister at the end of the month.

It'd make Shirley's day if you could get home, Beth, Mrs Kelsey had written.

Sybil picked up the receiver of the black telephone at her elbow. 'Alan,' she said into the mouthpiece after a few moments, 'your forger – d'you think he could do me a little favour . . . ?'

Sixteen

Beth landed with a bump in a dark field. She heard the thud of equipment and goods landing around her and then a rustle of movement from the trees at the edge of the field. A voice greeted her with the greeting, 'Red sky at night' and, giving the response, 'Shepherd's delight', she felt her arm grabbed and then she was being hustled away to the shelter of a copse. Once beneath its cover, a light was shone into her face and she put up her hand to shield her eyes.

'Good Lord!' said a familiar voice in French. 'It *is* you, Beth.'

'Well, yes, it is, but I'm Leonie now. And you're Antoine. Is that right?' Emile switched off the glaring light and a low chuckle came out of the darkness. 'Sadly, yes, because I'm in hiding with my compatriots. I can't live at home any more. It'd be too dangerous for my parents.'

'I don't want to bring danger to them either. Are you sure it's a good idea for me to live there?'

'My father's adamant that they want to do their bit, but I would ask you to leave at once if . . .'

He didn't need to finish his sentence. 'Of course I will,' Beth said swiftly.

'It's a good way to walk. We didn't dare have the drop take place anywhere near the farm.'

'Of course.'

150

'One of our guides – it's best you don't know his name – will take you there now. Please tell my parents that you have seen me and that I'm well.'

'I will,' she promised.

'I'll see them – and you – very soon. I come at night sometimes on a motorcycle we've – er – "borrowed" from the Germans. So don't have a fright when I turn up dressed in a German uniform, will you?'

The man who was to take her to the farm beckoned urgently.

She gave Emile a swift hug and whispered, 'It is good to see you again,' and then, following her guide, she was soon swallowed up in the darkness.

Arriving at the farm, Beth was enveloped in a bear hug by the big farmer, Raoul Détange. He was tall with grey hair and, despite the sadness and anxiety in his eyes, his smile was warm. 'It's good to see you again, but I wish it was in happier circumstances,' he said in his native tongue and Beth responded in French too. His wife Marthe smiled a welcome too, but her eyes were wary. She was small and stooped a little and her pure white hair was scraped back into a bun. She was dressed in a long black dress that reached almost to her ankles and a white apron. Once, Beth thought, she must have been plump, bustling about her work like any typical farmer's wife, but now she was thin and her face was gaunt, the skin hanging loosely beneath her jawline. What an awful effect the occupation of their country was having on these kind people, who only wanted to live out their lives in peace and harmony.

As soon as he saw that she was welcome at the farm, the man, who had brought her and whose name she didn't even know, disappeared into the blackness with a quick wave of farewell. Beth turned back to the elderly couple.

'Are you really sure you want me here? I'm so afraid it's putting you in danger,' Beth said, taking the elderly woman's wrinkled hands into hers.

'No more than we're in already with Emile hiding in the forest about sixty kilometres away. We know he's involved in acts of sabotage,' Raoul said, but far from sounding afraid, there was pride in his tone.

'Have you seen Simone and the children?' was all Marthe wanted to know.

Beth shook her head. 'I'm sorry, not recently, no. I've been—' She'd been about to say that she'd been in London and then in Scotland training, but she bit back the words. The less these good people knew about her, the better, so she ended lamely, '. . . away a lot.'

'Of course.' Raoul seemed to understand, though disappointment crossed Marthe's face.

'But I've seen Alan and I do know they're all safe and well.'

Marthe smiled thinly and nodded.

'And I must ask you to call me "Leonie". My name's Leonie Moreau now. Later, I'll explain the background story they've cooked up for me. It's quite easy.'

Once she was settled into the small, but neat, bedroom with its pretty curtains and patchwork bedspread, a small rug at the side of the bed and a blue and white patterned bowl and ewer on the washstand in the corner, Beth went back down the stairs.

Marthe was setting a meal on the table. 'It's not much,' she apologized. 'The Germans take everything we have and leave us very little.'

'Little more than a starvation diet,' Raoul said bitterly.

Beth looked startled. 'They come here?' she asked in a whisper, as if fearing they might already be at the door.

Marthe nodded, but it was Raoul who advised, 'The best way to hide, my dear, is in plain sight. Meet them, talk to them – just as we have to.'

'I didn't realize I'd have to do that,' Beth sighed. This seemed to be the way the British wanted some of their agents to act – in full view of the enemy, not skulking in hiding places. 'But you're absolutely right and it fits in with my background story.'

'Tell us.'

'My name is Leonie Moreau and I'm the daughter of a distant cousin of yours, Madame.' She chuckled. 'So distant, in fact, that you weren't even aware of my existence until I arrived on your doorstep to get away from the bombing at home.'

'And how are you supposed to have got here?' Raoul wanted to know.

Beth laughed. 'That's a good question. I borrowed some money and caught a series of trains. And I hitch-hiked some of the way.'

'And where is home?' Marthe asked, serving potatoes onto Beth's plate.

'Boulogne-Billancourt.'

Marthe looked up in surprise. 'Where you lived with Simone and Alan and the children?'

'Yes. We chose there because it's a place I know well, so I can be truthful about it if – if I'm ever questioned.' She saw Marthe and Raoul exchange a glance. 'What?' she asked, glancing from one to the other. 'What is it?'

'We haven't heard from Simone for some time now.

Emile has tried to find out about them, but—' She paused and asked again, 'Are they really all right?'

Beth smiled. 'They're all fine,' she said again. 'They're living just outside London.'

'But the bombing?' Marthe's eyes were wide with fear. 'And Simone? She hasn't been interned, has she?'

'Gracious, no. She's not an enemy. We're all on the same side. Besides, she's married to an Englishman, who's—'

She stopped suddenly, realizing that she shouldn't say any more. Alan's work was so secretive that even the slightest hint could be catastrophic. All she could do was to assure this lovely old couple that their family was safe and well, which she knew they were.

'So,' Raoul picked up her story again. 'Are we supposed to know any more about your family?'

Beth shook her head. 'No. You've never known them. The relationship goes back as far as your maternal grandparents, Madame, who'd lost touch with that branch of the family and you have never even heard of such a connection.'

'Won't they think that's suspicious?'

'I don't think so. When it gets down to generations of second and third cousins once or twice removed, I think we all get a bit vague. I certainly don't know some of my father's nephews and nieces and they're my first cousins.' She didn't mention her Aunty Jessie living two streets away. It was best that she forgot all about those at home, though the thought that she must do so saddened her.

'Very well, let's get this straight,' Raoul said. 'You are a very distant cousin who just turned up on the doorstep looking for somewhere to stay and work because your home has been bombed. Is that right?'

Beth nodded. 'You are the only relatives I have who live in the countryside and I worked out how I could get to you.'

'But how were you supposed to know about us?'

'My supposed grandmother was very interested in genealogy and used to reel off all the names of family members and where they lived when I was a little girl. And I remembered hearing about this farm.'

'And your grandmother? Who and where is she now?'

'My pretend grandmother? Oh, she died several years ago.'

'And your parents? Brothers and sisters?'

'All killed in the bombing. I was the only survivor.'

'And all this is made up?' Marthe was incredulous.

Beth nodded. 'But there's no need for you to worry about remembering any of it. All you've got to do is call me "Leonie". Leave the rest to me, if it becomes necessary.'

'Leonie, Leonie, Leonie,' Marthe murmured. 'I'll try.'

Raoul was glancing down at the clothes she was wearing. 'And how old are you, Leonie? That, at least, we ought to know.'

'I'm fifteen now and my birthday is the twenty-third of June, so next year I'll be sixteen.'

It had been decided to give Beth a totally new birth date.

'It's very easy,' Sybil had warned, 'if we use part of your true birth date, that you'll reel it off automatically. Far better that you learn a totally new one.'

So Beth must now remember that she'd been born in Boulogne-Billancourt on 23 June 1927.

'Good, good,' Raoul said, picking up the second of her two suitcases. It was much heavier than the one he'd already carried upstairs for her. He glanced at Beth. 'Is this what I think it is?'

Beth smiled. 'It's a wireless transmitter.'

'Then first thing tomorrow, we must hide it. I know just the place.'

Seventeen

The following morning after her arrival, Beth woke to the sounds of clattering hooves and the lowing of cows as they were herded into the milking shed. Even though it was early, sunlight streamed through the thin curtains and, despite only a few hours' sleep, Beth found she was wide awake and anxious to begin the day. Hiding the wireless transmitter was a priority. She dressed quickly, splashed her face and hands with cold water, hastily plaited her hair and went downstairs. There was no one in the kitchen, but bread, cheese and a glass of milk had been left on the table for her. Only a few minutes later, as she left the house, a dog came bounding towards her, his tongue lolling out.

'Hello, boy,' she said, holding out her hand in friendship to him. The animal was wary for a moment but then came towards her and stood in front of her, looking up at her as if assessing her. He was about two foot in height, with pointed, alert ears. His fawn-coloured coat was rough and wiry to the touch.

'Will I do, then?' she asked laughingly and, almost as if he were answering her, he gave a short bark, turned and seemed to lead her across the yard to the byre where she found Raoul and Marthe milking four cows. Beth hesitated near the doorway, not wanting to startle the animals, until Raoul should see her.

'Good morning,' he said, standing up from the low

157

milking stool and moving the pail of milk away from the cow. 'Did you sleep well?'

'Surprisingly well,' Beth laughed, 'after all the excitement.'

'I see you've met Jasper. He's our sheep dog and a very good one he is too.'

'What breed is he?'

Raoul laughed, a deep, rumbling sound that reminded her poignantly of her father. Sharply, Beth told herself that she must not think of home.

'You think he's a breed? I thought you'd think he was a mongrel. People make that mistake, but actually he's quite a rare breed. He's a Berger de Picard.' He nodded towards his dog. 'I can see he's taken to you. He doesn't act like that when the Germans come. I reckon he's got more sense than a lot of the folk round here. Now,' he went on, changing the subject abruptly, 'Do you know how to milk a cow?'

'I'm sorry – no.'

'Then you had better learn, if you are to help on the farm.'

'Shouldn't we hide the wireless first?'

Raoul chuckled – a deep, comforting sound. 'The Germans don't get up this early. We'll be safe for an hour or two.'

So, for the next hour, Beth learned how to milk.

'Very good,' Raoul said, smiling. 'Have you done this before?'

'No,' Beth said, stroking the rump of the cow she had just milked.

'Then you are a natural.'

Beth smiled, accepting the compliment graciously. She was by no means conceited, but she did seem to have a knack of picking things up quickly. She had been similarly praised during the paramilitary course in Scotland and had passed the Morse code and wireless operator's course with flying colours too. Her memory was faultless and would be a useful asset out here. She wouldn't need to carry a lot of written messages; it was all in her head.

'We don't like our agents carrying anything written down if it can be avoided,' Alan had warned on her last interview with him before boarding the plane to take her to France, 'Of course, you have to leave messages in the drop boxes but we have secret ways of writing those.'

Beth had nodded. She'd learned all about being able to write invisibly at training school.

'The only danger in remembering everything is if you get caught and interrogated. You could give away so much more.' Then he'd added with a smile, 'Just mind you don't get caught.'

And now she was here in France and the German army was just down the road and would even be visiting the farm. Raoul explained: 'Their headquarters for this district are in the town, but there are several officers billeted in our village.' He nodded in the direction of St Michel. 'Much to the disgust of most of the locals, I have to say, but' – he frowned – 'there are one or two who are a little too anxious to please our invaders. Collaborators!' He spat the last word out. 'Just be very careful, Leonie. Trust no one. And, like I told you last night, we get soldiers visiting here with their lorries to pick up supplies.'

'Do they pay you for it?'

Raoul laughed bitterly. 'Very little, if at all. They'd take everything we have and more, given the chance. And when the local Maquis commit an act of sabotage in the area, they take reprisals. They shot two men from the town last week, though so far no one has been harmed from St Michel – yet I suspect it's only a matter of time. For the moment, they are thinking of the supplies of food and accommodation the villagers can provide for them.'

Beth was shocked and yet it was what she had been told to expect. As they crossed the yard towards the farmhouse for a welcome mid-morning drink, she glanced around her at the beautiful countryside through which the River Loire meandered. It was quite flat around the farm and she was reminded of her home county. But she was suddenly aware that it was not as peaceful and innocent as it looked.

'Beth can't get home, Lil,' Edie told her with disappointment when Lil popped in on the morning of 30 September – the day of the party for Shirley's eighteenth birthday.

'Aw, that's a shame. But you're sure Archie's going to be here?'

'He's here now. He didn't get home until very late last night and he's still in bed.'

'What about Jessie and Harry?'

'Oh, they're coming. Have you invited your Norma?'

Lil laughed. 'No, I thought we'd give her a miss. Don't want a damper on the day and she and Shirley don't exactly hit it off, now do they?' She paused and then added, 'You've told Ursula, I suppose?'

'Oh yes, though I had a job to get her on her own. Shirley hardly leaves the girl's side. Right, now have we got everything ready?' Edie glanced around her front room, which had been swept and dusted with extra care for the occasion. Gifts were piled on the sideboard. 'I've been saving mine and Archie's sweet ration for the last three months for her. I just wish I could have got some pretty wrapping paper for her presents, but you can't get it now and newspaper doesn't quite look the same, does it, Lil?'

Lil smiled. 'Can't be helped, Edie, and it's what's inside that matters. I've given her some more scented soap. She seemed so pleased with what I gave her at Christmas.'

'She certainly was.' Edie glanced at her friend. 'More of yours that you've had stowed away?'

Lil pulled a comical face. 'You know me, Edie. Irene gives me expensive soap most Christmases and I never like to use it. Good old Wright's Coal Tar suits me, so I'm pleased for Shirley to have it. And Irene would understand.'

'I've knitted her a scarf and gloves from an old woolly I've pulled down. Now winter's coming and she walks to and from work every day.'

'No doubt Jessie will bring her something frivolous.' Lil smiled. She'd always been fond of Edie's gregarious sister.

'Oh, if there's anything "frivolous" still to be had in the shops, you can bet Jessie will hunt it down, but it'll balance Archie's sensible gift of National Savings Certificates.'

'I've made one of me trifles, Edie, and I've made a cake of sorts.' Lil grimaced. 'An eggless sponge. It's an "if-it" cake.'

Edie laughed. 'Aye, if it'll go round. I'll make the sandwiches last thing so they don't curl up. I've got spam and a tin of snoek.'

Lil laughed. 'I don't reckon anyone'll eat *that*, will they?'

'Actually, Archie quite likes it. Must be because it's fish.'

Lil turned to go. 'Right, I'll get back to me nets until this afternoon and then I'll get me glad rags on and come and help you set everything out.'

'Thanks, Lil.' Edie chuckled. 'She'd got a right mardy face on her this morning because I pretended I'd forgotten her birthday. I made out I had to be at the WVS early and was in a rush. I say, have you heard that Jessie wants you an' me to go out with her on the mobile canteen delivering meals to the folk manning the barrage balloon installations and the anti-aircraft batteries in the district?'

'Oh, that'll make a nice change, Edie. It'll get me away from Norma watching everything I do.'

'Now, Shirley'll be home just after six and Ursula said she could be here before that. I want a chorus of "Happy Birthday" when she walks in through the back door. That should put a smile on her face.'

Lil nodded, but said nothing. It wasn't an easy task, putting a smile on Shirley's face, but she was pleased that planning the party had kept Edie busy and occupied her thoughts; she wasn't dwelling quite so much on the absent members of her family.

Later that afternoon, the table was groaning under the weight of all the food Edie and Lil had managed to provide.

'We've been going short for weeks,' Edie said as she carried a plate of sandwiches through to the front room. The Morrison shelter had been covered with a snowy linen tablecloth that almost reached the floor, hiding what was really beneath it. Lil had laid out the knives, forks and spoons, plates, side plates, cups and saucers. 'And I know you have, an' all, Lil.'

'That's what friends are for, duck,' Lil said, as she set the sponge cake as a centrepiece on the table.

They stood back to admire their efforts. 'It's nearly as good a spread as we did for Frank and Irene's wedding.'

'We've done well, Edie, considering all the shortages.'

Edie chuckled. 'And with a nifty bit of improvisation here and there.'

At that moment, Archie appeared from upstairs where he'd been changing out of his work clothes and having a wash and brush-up in readiness for the party.

'By heck, girls, you've done a grand job there, but I reckon I just ought to sample . . .' He reached out towards a sandwich, but Edie smacked his hand. 'You keep your thieving fingers off, Archie Kelsey. Wait till everyone gets here and I want Shirley to see what we've been doing for her.'

They were all there, hiding in the front room, by the time Shirley arrived home from work. Even Jessie and Harry had managed to make it in time.

'Shush, everyone. That's her coming down the passage.'

They heard the back door open and then Shirley step into the scullery. There was a moment's silence before she called out, 'Mam?'

'Here, love,' Edie shouted. 'I'm in the front room.'

The door opened and everyone began to sing 'Happy Birthday' and Lil said later that the look on Shirley's face had been worth every bit of scrimping and saving she and Edie had done over the last few weeks. The girl had tears in her eyes; she wasn't used to being the centre of attention or having so much fuss made of her.

They all enjoyed the party and even gave in to Shirley's demand to play charades.

'But it's not Christmas,' Edie pleaded. 'We play charades at Christmas.'

'I know – but it is my eighteenth birthday, Mam.'

'All the more reason why we shouldn't be playing childish games,' Edie teased. Then she relented. 'Oh go on, then, just this once.'

Even Ursula joined in wholeheartedly, seeming to understand the rules of the game a little better now.

At the end of the evening, when their guests were starting to say 'we should be going', Shirley stood up and thanked everyone for coming. 'It's been a lovely party – I just wish Beth and the others could have been here too.' She hesitated and glanced warily at her mother, 'And there's something I have to tell you all and this seems like a good moment. As you probably realize, I had to register for war work because I was coming up to eighteen, but because I don't want to be drafted into something I don't want to do' – she pulled a face – 'factory work or something like that, I've volunteered for – for –' she paused again and glanced apologetically at Edie before ending with a rush, 'the ATS. I thought if it's good enough for the Prime Minister's daughter, then it's good enough for me.'

It took a few seconds for the news to sink in. The ATS was the Auxiliary Territorial Service, the women's branch of the British Army. Then Jessie was the first to clap her hands and say, 'Oh Shirley, well done you! That's marvellous.'

Archie was watching Edie's face. The last of her chicks to leave the nest. She would be completely on her own when he was at sea. And then he caught sight of Lil watching her friend too and he sighed inwardly with relief. Of course, there was always Lil. She'd be on hand whatever happened. Thank Goodness for Lil.

Her face expressionless, Edie got slowly to her feet and went towards Shirley. For one dreadful moment, the girl thought her mother was going to strike her across the face but, instead, Edie stood in front of her, just staring into Shirley's eyes. Then slowly, she nodded and began to smile. Without a word, she put her arms around her daughter and held her close.

Shirley hugged her in return.

'Oh Mam, I was so afraid you'd be angry, but I couldn't be the only one in the family not to do something important for the war effort, now could I? I've asked specifically if I can go into the anti-aircraft batteries. Serving selfish women with a new hat and listening to their grumbles about how their clothing coupons won't stretch far enough isn't quite my idea of helping my country. Although Oldroyd's have been very nice about it and have said I can have my old job back after the war. I mean, even Reggie – young as he is – is helping out on the land. And Beth must be doing something really worthwhile now she's in the FANYs.'

'I know, duck, I know,' Edie patted the girl's back and her voice was husky as she added, 'I can understand why you've done it, but just take good care of yourself, eh, and come home safe and sound. I'm proud of you.'

Now the tears ran down Shirley's face. It was the first time in her life that she could remember her mother ever saying those words to her.

Eighteen

Raoul stood in the centre of his yard and glanced around, narrowing his eyes against the bright light. He listened too. 'Mm,' he said at last. 'All seems quiet. Good. Leonie, fetch your wireless set and we'll hide it.'

When Leonie returned with the wireless set, Raoul took the heavy suitcase from her and led her out of the yard and into a meadow that sloped gently upwards away from the house. Jasper bounded ahead of them, stopping every now and again to sniff the ground. Halfway up the field, they walked down a dip in the land and up the other side and then on again up towards a small, tumbledown stone building at the edge of the field.

Raoul, puffing a little, explained. 'Years ago, we used this as a small barn for animal feed and occasionally as a shepherd's hut at lambing time, but now we bring them down into the sheds close to the farm when the ewes are due. It's better for them if the weather's cold' – he smiled – 'and it's certainly better for us. So, it's a bit rundown, but I think it'll serve your purpose.' He turned and gestured back towards the house and the farm buildings clustered around it. 'You must be aware that the Germans have their vehicles out all the time and whenever you are transmitting or receiving they can pick up your signals. They'd be most likely – and I'm counting on this – to drive into my yard first and then send out search parties. The beauty of this position, Leonie,' – Raoul used her name a lot and Beth realized this was to familiarize himself with it – 'is that you'll be able to see them from here and if they come towards you, they'll be hidden in the hollow for a few precious moments.'

He ducked his head as he stepped into the gloomy interior of the barn. The walls were crumbling and several large stones were loose. The floor was covered with dusty earth and a few bales of hay were stacked against the wall.

'When Antoine' – he even remembered to refer to his own son by his code name – 'told me you were coming and what you were going to be doing, I came up here and made a hidey hole behind some of these stones for your wireless. Now, tell me, can you see where it is?'

Beth let her eyes roam over the surface of the walls. She glanced down at the floor, but it looked as if no one had been in there for years.

'No,' she said at last. 'I can't.'

'You'll soon get to know where it is, but to start with, if you move the bales and then count six stones from the left-hand side of the doorway and four from the floor,' he said, demonstrating, 'and then pull out this stone . . . I can't mark it for you for obvious reasons. I've hollowed out what I hope is a big enough space to take the suitcase. Let's try it.'

It fitted perfectly and then Raoul showed her how to push the stone back in, and suggested that she should pick up a handful of dust from the floor and throw it against the stone so that it blended in with the rest of the wall and didn't look as if it had just been removed. She did as he bade her and, he was right, a cursory glance would reveal nothing, particularly as, coming in from the bright sunlight outside, the gloom would give additional cover. Then she moved the bales back into their position in front of it.

'And outside,' Raoul went on, 'I've left a small broken branch from the nearby hedge that you can sweep the floor with as you back out. Luckily, the doorway is hidden from anyone coming up the slope, so you can slip out and through the hedge. See, I'll show you.' He led the way to the hedge just behind the barn and demonstrated how she could part the branches carefully and slip through, the foliage springing back into place and concealing the gap. Now he pointed over the hedge. 'The ground slopes down from here and you'd be able to run down there and get some distance away from here before they saw you. I can't promise they won't catch up with you, but by following you down there, they'd hopefully be distracted from searching inside the barn too closely.'

'It's perfect, Uncle Raoul.'

He stared at her and then burst out laughing. 'I like the sound of that. I've never had a niece or a nephew.'

Beth laughed too but said very seriously, 'Well, just remember that you have now.'

'So, they've all gone now, Lil,' Edie said mournfully two days after Shirley's birthday party. 'She's been planning to join the ATS for some time, it seems, and she didn't tell anyone – not even us – until she was certain she'd been accepted.'

'You mean she's gone? Already?'

'Set off this morning in high excitement.'

'It's an adventure for her, duck. It'll do her the world of good.'

Edie sighed. 'You're right, of course, and she did promise she'll come as soon as she can get some leave. But until then, I'm on me own. Even Archie's gone back to sea.'

'We've got the WVS this afternoon, Edie.'

'I know, but it's the evenings when I feel it the most.'

Tactfully, Lil didn't remind her that she spent many evenings on her own. 'Come round to me. We can knit or sew together and listen to the wireless. There's Tommy Handley on tonight. You like him.'

'Aye, all right,' Edie said, but Lil could tell her heart wasn't in it.

'Are you going into town this morning?'

Edie shrugged. 'Hardly worth queuing for hours just for one, is it?'

'Now, now, Edie, you must look after yourself. Anyway, if you do, you could get me a few bits. I'm that busy with these camouflage nets – they're so much bigger than I'm used to doing.'

'I suppose so,' Edie murmured, but was hardly listening to her friend and Lil returned to her own home, pondering what she could do to help her neighbour.

Later that morning, Edie, dressed for shopping in town, went through the door that divided the two yards. Lil, with a long net hanging from the wall, was busy braiding. 'I thought I'd do this out here today, Edie. It's a lovely day and this one's almost too big for my wall indoors. It's a whopper. I reckon they must want it for covering a tank.'

Edie watched her for a few moments and then murmured, 'I suppose I could lend you a hand now and then, Lil. I can see there's a lot to do. That's if I can remember how to do it.'

'It's like riding a bike, Edie. You never forget.'

'Mm.' Edie was thoughtful, eying the net. 'Anyway, what do you want from town?'

'I've left a list on the table in the scullery, Edie, with my ration book and some money.'

'Right-o. I'll be off, then.'

As Edie turned away, Lil was smiling to herself. Her plan seemed to be working; she'd hoped that if she could make Edie think she was struggling to cope with the net making, her friend would offer help. Anything, Lil, thought to keep Edie occupied and stop her from brooding about her absent family.

When she returned from her shopping trip, Edie was tired and frustrated. 'Them queues are getting worse – I'm sure of it. They've banned the milling of white flour now, Lil, did you know? So we're stuck with the National wheatmeal loaf, whether we like it or not.'

'Come on in, Edie,' Lil soothed, ignoring the other woman's ranting. 'I've got us a bit of dinner ready and then we can be off to the WVS.'

'You shouldn't be feeding me, duck. Here, you have these sausages I managed to get. I got too many. It's going to take me a while to get used to buying for one.'

'All right, Edie, if you're sure. Tell you what, you keep 'em and cook dinner for us both tomorrow. I'll nip round to yours, eh?'

They'd always been willing to share everything, but they were both a bit more careful now, not wanting to encroach on each other's rations.

'Right you are,' Edie said and seemed suddenly a little more cheerful with the thought that she'd have someone to cook for the next day.

Lil had already changed out of the old clothes she wore to braid in. 'Right, let's have a bite to eat and then we can be off.'

Jessie was waiting for them at the door when they arrived. 'Ah, there you are. I'm glad you've come. There's so much to do. I was wondering if you can fit an extra day in? We could really use the help.' Her glance went from one to the other but rested on Edie's face.

'What d'you think, Lil?' Edie said.

'I'd love too, but I can't really spare any more time away from me nets.'

'Could you come on your own, Edie?' Jessie persisted.

'Well, I could do, I suppose, but I'd sooner come with Lil. We know each other's ways. We work so well together.'

Jessie laughed. 'I can't deny that. When the pair of you work together you get more than twice the amount done.'

'Tell you what,' Edie said, her face brighter and more animated than at any time since Shirley had made her announcement. 'What if I help you with your nets, Lil, and then we could both come here together?'

'I could give you half the money,' Lil ventured.

'I wouldn't hear of it,' Edie said firmly, some of her old spirit returning. 'I'm only suggesting it so you could still come here with me. Selfish woman that I am. Besides, I'd help you out anyway, Lil. What are friends for, eh?'

As Edie turned away and marched purposefully into the hall, Jessie winked at Lil. She had been in on Lil's plan to keep Edie occupied as much as possible.

'And what are you two up to?'

Jessie turned with wide-eyed innocence. 'Us, Norma? Why, nothing. Whatever made you think that? Come on, Lil, I'll show you and Edie what needs doing.'

'Aye, picking out the best jobs for your sister, I shouldn't wonder.'

'However did you guess?' Jessie turned her wonderful smile on the dour woman. 'But it's for your sister too, Norma.'

Now the woman couldn't think of a sarcastic reply.

Nineteen

With the occupation of their country had come the conscription of Frenchmen to provide forced labour for Germany. But many young men escaped to the forests and hills, particularly in the mountainous regions in Brittany and southern France, to avoid being sent away. Small resistance groups existed elsewhere where they could be sure of help from their families and friends and one such group had been set up by Emile and his friends in a large wooded area about sixty kilometres from his father's farm. They had been lucky to find two derelict cottages, once used by woodmen, they surmised, in the very middle of the forest where the trees and foliage were thickest, but they still posted lookouts at the edge of the trees day and night. So far, they had not been discovered and whilst it was very cold in the winter months – they dare not light fires very often – it was a discomfort the young men were prepared to bear; anything was better than being sent away.

Raoul Détange's farm lay in a region of the Loire Valley about sixty kilometres north-east of Bourges. Sadly, the whole area was within the German-occupied zone, but that was the very reason it was perfect for the SOE to send agents there. They had heard of Emile Détange and his band of men and had wanted to help for some time. They had sent an organizer and a wireless operator some months earlier and they had done valuable groundwork with Emile. Now the time was right for them to send their agents in to make the circuit fully operational. 'Bruce' had been parachuted in two weeks before Beth, but he desperately needed a wireless operator and someone who could act as a courier too. When Emile told him, on one of the rare occasions when they were able to meet, that his parents were willing – and ready – to help, 'Bruce' had travelled to Paris and had managed to make contact with a British agent there and get messages transmitted to London. They had informed him that they were sending someone very soon and that she would make contact as soon as she could. So 'Bruce' had to wait, holed up in his room above the bakery, watching the Germans in the building opposite and wondering if it really was such a good idea to be quite so close to the enemy.

'You'll be needing a bicycle, Leonie,' Raoul told her. He and Marthe used her name often as if to familiarize themselves with it. 'Come with me. I have an old one, which Marthe used to ride years ago. You can clean it up, though I don't know what state the tyres are in.'

Luckily, the tyres were reasonable but the frame was rusty, so Beth spent a whole day cleaning it. When she had finished and had blown up the tyres, she stood back to admire her handiwork.

'You've made a good job of that, Leonie,' Raoul told her, but she spread her hands for him to see the blisters.

'At a price,' she murmured.

'You will need a small hiding place on the bicycle. You won't be able to carry anything large, but you might have to leave messages somewhere for your contacts. Now, leave it with me and I'll see what I can do.'

An hour later, he called her out into the yard. He

was holding the bicycle with a satisfied smile on his face. 'See if you can find my hiding place.'

Beth searched all over the bicycle; the frame, the wheels, the handlebars, but she could see nothing. 'I give in,' she said at last. 'Show me.'

Raoul twisted the rubber covering from the end of the right-hand handlebar. 'It is hollow inside the metal. See? It is tight to pull this off, but that is good. It will not be easy to find it.'

'This is great, Uncle Raoul. Thank you.' She, too, was having to get used to calling the old couple 'uncle' and 'aunt'. 'And now I'd better go into town and see if I can find my contact.'

As she mounted her bicycle and pedalled out of the yard, Raoul watched her with worried eyes. 'Be careful, Leonie,' he called after her.

She raised her hand to wave and the bicycle wobbled dangerously.

'I'm fed up with being told I shouldn't visit Reggie. He doesn't write very often and I think that's only when someone stands over him and makes him. And I haven't heard much from Frank either. Maybe Irene could tell me a bit more. I need to go and see them, Lil.'

'I tell you what. When Archie comes home next time, why don't the three of us take a trip out to the farm to see the family? We'll have to start thinking about Christmas again soon and maybe this year we could persuade them to come home, even if it's only for a couple of nights. What do you think?'

Edie's eyes lit up. 'I think that's a great idea, Lil. I'll go into town in the morning when I go to do our shopping and ask about train times.'

When Archie arrived home later in the week, Edie greeted him with their plans. 'I've checked the timetable and we can catch an early train in the morning and one back to town at teatime. Archie, do say we can go – please.'

'Well . . .' Archie hesitated for a moment. He didn't want to upset the applecart and unsettle Reggie, but he could see how much it meant to his wife and he was sure Lil would be longing to see her family too. 'All right, love, we'll go. It'll have to be tomorrow because I sail again on the evening tide the day after.'

'Oh thank you, Archie,' Edie said, flinging her arms around him and giving him a resounding kiss.

Edie and Lil were like two children setting off on a day's outing. There hadn't been time to write to let Irene or Reggie know they were coming so Edie and Lil between them had packed food for the three of them for the day. 'I don't want to take advantage of the Schofields,' Edie had said firmly. 'Just because they live on a farm doesn't meant they can feed folks descending on them unannounced. It's shame the weather isn't better. We could have had a picnic in one of Mr Schofield's fields.'

Walking away from the halt at Fotherby, they walked down a long lane, Archie carrying the basket containing their dinner. Edie clutched a parcel of clothes for Reggie and Lil carried gifts for Irene and little Tommy.

'I hope these clothes I've got for him are big enough,' Lil said worriedly. 'I don't know how much Tommy'll have grown.'

They'd been walking for about half a mile when

Archie said, 'I reckon this is it. White Gates Farm, isn't it?'

'Yes, yes, this is it!' Edie said excitedly. 'Oh look, there's a young man sweeping the yard. He'll know where Reggie and the others are.'

'Edie, love,' Archie said quietly, 'that *is* Reggie.'

'Wha . . .?' Edie's mouth dropped open in astonishment. 'But he's too big, he's . . .'

But when the boy turned round she could see for herself that it was indeed her son. 'Oh my goodness, how he's grown. And look, there's little Tommy near the back door. Oh look, Lil, do look. See how well he's walking.'

'I'm looking, Edie,' Lil said, a catch in her voice. Reggie might have shot up, but their little grandson had altered so much, they could hardly recognize him. He was two years old and of course he was walking, but the two women hadn't stopped to think. They were still visualizing him as the tiny baby they had last seen.

Seeing them, Reggie flung down the brush and ran towards them, flinging himself against Archie. Then he stood back and his smile faded. He looked anxious. 'What is it?' he said. 'Is it bad news? Or – or have you come to fetch me back?'

'No, no, lad,' Archie said swiftly. 'We just wanted to come and see you, that's all.'

Reggie's features relaxed a little but there was still wariness in his eyes as if he wasn't quite sure whether or not he believed them. 'Oh, I see. You'd best come in, then, and meet Mrs Schofield. She'll make you a cup of tea.'

Archie held up the basket. 'We haven't come to encroach on her kindness. We've brought our own food.'

Edie stepped forward and hugged him to her, ruffling

177

his hair. 'But you could come home now, Reggie. The bombing's not so bad and we've got a Morrison shelter set up in the front room.'

Reggie shook his head. 'I'm not coming back, Mam. I like it here. I like helping Mr Schofield on the farm and I like the local school. There're several evacuees from Grimsby here and we're all good mates.'

'It's all right, son,' Archie said, putting his hand on the boy's shoulder. He could feel it shaking beneath his touch. 'It's just that your mam would like you home, 'specially now that Shirley's gone in the ATS, but we're not here to drag you back if you're really happy and the Schofields are willing for you to stay. You've got to think of them as well, you know.'

Edie's face was crestfallen at Archie's words and she shot him a look of reproach but she said nothing. Understanding how her friend felt, Lil squeezed her arm.

'Come on, Edie,' she said softly. 'Let's go and make a fuss of Tommy and find Irene.'

They left Archie talking to Reggie in the yard and went towards the toddler still standing in the doorway, clutching the frame. He looked up at the two women with a solemn face.

'Hello, ducky,' Lil said, bending down. 'We're your grandmas. Where's your mummy?'

He pointed to a door behind him just as they heard Irene's voice. 'Tommy, where are you, you little monkey? I can't take my eyes off you for a minute . . . Oh!'

Irene had appeared behind him, but she stopped and her eyes widened as she saw her mother and Edie. 'What are you doing here?'

Lil straightened up. 'We've just come to see you, Irene, that's all. Aren't you pleased to see us?'

'Oh – yes – of course. Of course, I am, but I wish you'd let us know. I'm in my old clothes and I could have dressed Tommy up a bit.' She scooped him up and turned away, carrying him into the kitchen and leaving the two women standing uncertainly near the back door, unsure what to do. Irene's head appeared around the inner door. 'Well, don't just stand there. Come in, now you're here.'

Edie and Lil glanced at each other. 'I don't feel exactly welcome, Lil, do you?'

Lil pressed her lips together as if she were holding back the tears and then said, 'Come on, let's go in. We've just caught them both on the hop, that's all. It'll be all right.'

They moved through a washhouse with a brick-built copper in one corner and a mangle standing nearby. The room was used as a general storeroom too. Thick coats and mackintoshes hung on a row of pegs, beneath which was a line of rubber boots of various sizes. Bags of coal were piled in another corner along with a heap of sticks and logs for fire-lighting. Buckets of pigswill were ready for feeding time and a large meal bin, which they guessed held foodstuff for the poultry, stood against the wall.

They entered the big farmhouse kitchen where a fire burned in the grate and the smell of freshly baking bread met them.

'My, this is a lovely kitchen, ain't it, Lil? Makes our sculleries look a bit tiny.'

At that moment, the farmer's wife came in by a door leading to the rest of the house. Although she was startled to see two strangers in her kitchen, she smiled a welcome as Irene made the introductions.

'This is Mrs Schofield, Mam. My mother and her friend, Mrs Kelsey. She's Reggie's mam.'

'I'm very pleased to meet you.' Mrs Schofield held out her hand. 'Please call me Ruth.'

'And we're Lil and Edie,' Lil said, pointing first at herself and then at Edie.

'Let me make you some tea. And there are fresh scones just out of the oven.'

'Well, we wouldn't say no to a cuppa, Mrs – Ruth, but we won't take your food. We've brought our dinner. Archie – that's my husband – is out in the yard talking to Reggie. He's got the basket.'

'There's no need, really. Of course, we have to abide by the regulations,' Ruth smiled, 'but there are things we can do on a farm that get round a lot of the rationing.'

'They keep four goats,' Irene said. 'Tommy's being raised on goat's milk and the cheese it makes is lovely.'

'I'll give you some to take back,' Ruth promised.

'That's very kind of you,' Edie said, feeling a little embarrassed now. 'But we only came to see the family. It seems so long since we saw them. I can't believe how Reggie's grown – I hardly knew him. I've brought him some clothes, but I don't know if they'll fit.'

'He's doing very well. He likes helping my husband and the two land girls we've got and he's doing very nicely at school.'

Edie frowned. 'He's not there today?'

'The local school is a bit overcrowded with all the evacuee children, so they do a rota system. Local children go in the morning and the evacuee children in the afternoon. Reggie'll go as usual this afternoon, unless, of course, you want him to stay off because you've come to see him.'

'No, no, we wouldn't want that. I never gave it a thought, if I'm honest, until just now that we've come on a school day.'

Ruth Schofield bustled about her kitchen, laying out cups and saucers and small plates. From her pantry she produced a wire tray of scones, still cooling from the oven, and thick yellow butter and strawberry jam and even a pot of cream.

'I know it's more like afternoon tea, but we'll call it elevenses,' she said, smiling.

Edie and Lil glanced at one another. They hadn't seen food like this since before the war. It outstripped the spam sandwiches made with the National loaf that they had brought with them.

'Please – help yourselves,' Ruth urged as she poured cups of strong tea for her visitors. 'Now, I'll just go out and bring your husband and Reggie in whilst you get acquainted with little Tommy.'

Irene sat down at the table beside her mother. 'Tommy, this is your grandma. In fact, they're both your grandmas.' She glanced up at them. 'We haven't decided what he's to call you both.'

'I'm Grannie,' Edie said promptly and then added, 'unless that's the name Lil prefers.'

'No, no, Edie, Grandma will be fine – or even Nanny.'

'Nanny would be easier for him to say whilst he's little, but then it would stick,' Irene said. 'Best we teach him "Grandma" and he can make up his own word. Now, are you going to your Grandma, Tommy?' She handed the little boy over to her mother, whose eyes filled with tears. It had been such a long time since she'd held him and in the time since then her arms had ached to hold him again.

Edie leaned forward to tickle his chin and the little

boy beamed at them both. The two women laughed delightedly. 'Well, at least he's pleased to see us, Lil,' Edie murmured.

They stayed until after Reggie had gone to school in the afternoon. Ruth, and her husband, Joe, when he and the two land girls came in for dinner, insisted that the visitors should share their meal. 'Your food won't be wasted,' Ruth assured them. 'You can eat it for your tea when you get home.'

'Well, if you're really sure,' Archie said, sitting down before a plate piled high with pork, apple sauce and stuffing and freshly picked vegetables.

'Everything on that plate,' Joe said, laughing, 'is off the farm.'

Archie chuckled as he picked up his knife and fork. 'I can see why Reggie doesn't want to come back to Grimsby.'

'Of course he's missing you all,' Ruth put in hurriedly. 'He talks about you all the time – but he really is better here, for the time being anyway. I'll try to get him to write to you a bit more, Edie,' she added, smiling fondly at the boy. 'But it's a struggle.'

'It's all right, Ruth. Just so long as I know he's all right.' Edie sighed heavily. 'I know I'm being selfish, but Shirley's gone into the ATS now, so there's no one at home when Archie's at sea. But at least you'll all come home eventually when the war's over.'

No one said anything and Edie didn't notice the look that passed between Reggie and Joe Schofield.

But Archie saw it and frowned.

*

By the time they left to walk up the lane towards the main road to catch the train, Edie had mixed feelings. They hadn't received the ecstatic welcome from either Reggie or Irene that she'd hoped for. Indeed, Irene had seemed on edge the whole time they were there. She'd talk to Lil about it tomorrow, Edie promised herself. See if she'd noticed it too. But Edie had seen Reggie's bedroom and was reassured that he had a nice little room at the back of the house on the same landing as Mr and Mrs Schofield and far enough away from Irene's bigger bedroom where she and Tommy slept so that no baby crying in the night would disturb him. She'd seen Irene's room too; a lovely, big, airy room with Tommy's cot in one corner.

'Mr Schofield fetched it down from their loft and cleaned it up for us,' Irene said. 'It's the one both their boys slept in.'

'They've got sons?' Lil asked.

Irene nodded and bit her lip. 'Yes – two. They're in the army. Abroad, Mrs Schofield thinks.'

'Just like Frank,' Edie murmured, feeling a sudden empathy for the woman who was doing her best to care for other people's families – their families – when she must be worried sick about her own boys.

'I know you both want them all home,' Archie said, as they walked along the lane, side by side. 'So do I, but you've got to admit they're better there until all this lot's over.'

The two women were silent.

'They're safe from the bombing and, by the look of it, being well fed. The Schofields – and those land army lasses too – seem nice and friendly; the girls must be company for Irene. And, by the sound of it, Reggie's made some friends at school.'

'I know all that, Archie,' Edie snapped, irritated with both Archie and herself; with Archie because she knew, deep down, that he was right, and with herself because she knew she was being selfish.

'It's – it's just that they're not at *home* where they should be.'

'I know, love, I know.' He crooked his arms, offering one to each of them. They linked arms and walked in step with each other. 'Let's hope it'll soon be over and then they'll all come back.'

He didn't mentioned Frank or Beth by name, but they were never far from their thoughts, and though he said no more, Archie was very much afraid that the war wasn't going to be over for some time to come.

Twenty

Beth pedalled through the village without anyone stopping her, but when she came to the outskirts of the town, it was a different matter. There was a road block with two German soldiers on guard beside it. Her heart felt as if it jumped inside her chest and then began to beat faster, but she kept her face straight, even managed to smile a little, though not too much, as she rode towards them. One of the soldiers stepped into the roadway and held up his hand, commanding her to stop. She applied her brakes and put her foot to the ground.

'Good afternoon,' she said in French.

The soldier barked at her in German, but it was quite easy for her to make out she didn't understand what he was saying because she didn't. Beth was fluent in the French language but she knew very little German.

Impatiently, the soldier snapped out the few words he knew in French. 'Papers.'

Beth fished out her identity card from her coat pocket and handed it to the young man, who didn't look any older than she was, though, she reminded herself, she was supposed to be only fifteen! Beth twisted one of her plaits nervously round her finger whilst the soldier looked at her papers.

'Where are you going?' he asked slowly.

Beth replied rapidly, so quickly that it was obvious

he did not understand her. The soldier on the opposite side of the road strolled across, a smirk on his face. In perfect French he said, 'My friend doesn't understand your language, Mademoiselle.' He turned to the other man. 'She said she is going into the town to buy bread.'

'Where does she live?' Now the conversation continued with one asking the questions in German and then the other translating his words into French.

'Détanges' Farm on the other side of the village.'

'Why does the farmer's wife not bake her own bread?'

'Because she has no flour.'

The first soldier grunted and thrust her papers back into her hands and waved impatiently for her to pass through the barrier. Beth rode on, breathing more easily with every yard she put between herself and the soldiers, but when she came to the town and found the bakery, directly opposite the German headquarters, as she had been warned, her hands began to shake a little. She leaned her bicycle against the side of the shop and went inside. There were three customers waiting to be served so she moved to the back of the short queue. At last she faced the baker across his counter. First she asked for the two loaves that Marthe really did need and then, glancing round to make sure that no one else had entered the shop, she gave the coded sentence.

'Have you any jam tarts today, Monsieur?'

The man kept his face expressionless but Beth had seen the brief startled look in his eyes.

'I may be able to find one for you, Mademoiselle. Will you wait here a moment?'

The baker, whose name Beth had learned from Raoul was Henri Lafarge, disappeared through a door at the back of his shop. He was gone some minutes and Beth began to grow nervous. Was something wrong? Did he not believe her or had she been betrayed already? After what seemed an interminable wait, Henri returned and, at the sight of the man following him through the door, Beth gasped and almost blurted out his name. Coming towards her, looking every bit as surprised as she was feeling, was the man with whom she'd travelled to Scotland and undergone rigorous training. Rob!

'Leonie, I presume?' Rob said, seeming to recover first and at once reminding her that they were not supposed to know each other. He held out his hand, just as if they were meeting for the first time. 'Bruce. Bruce Cordier. Please come through.' He led the way through the door and up the dark, narrow staircase to a room at the front of the building overlooking the street below and the Town Hall opposite. The room was shadowy, for the blinds were set so that Rob could see out but no one could see in. Once inside the room, he gave her a swift hug. 'I'm so glad to see you, and yet, I'm not. I could almost wish you had been a stranger.'

'I know what you mean, but we'll just have to do our best. Luckily, we didn't exchange much information about each other, did we?'

Rob shook his head. 'It's a good job they were so adamant about that. Now I can see why. Perhaps they knew – or at least thought – that there was a good chance some of us would bump into each other at some time.' He lowered his voice to a whisper. 'Have you heard about any of the others we trained with? Monty? Phil?'

Beth shook her head and then told him candidly, 'In a way, I'm glad it's you. At least we both know we've had the same rigorous training.'

'That's true, Leonie. I certainly know I can trust you.'

'And me you.' They smiled at each other and then Rob gestured around the room. 'Sorry about the gloom, but I leave the windows as they are all the time so as not to attract attention. I'm hoping it looks as if no one occupies this room.'

'What about at night?'

Rob shrugged. 'I have a small bedroom across the landing that overlooks the backyard, but mostly I'm in here keeping watch. I don't need to go out very much, but I like to see what they're up to.' He gave a nod towards the window.

'You don't go out at all?' Beth couldn't imagine anything worse than being cooped up in these two small rooms all the time. At least she had the freedom to be out even if she had to run the gauntlet of guards and patrols. 'What about food?'

'Henri keeps me well supplied. Well, as much as he is able, of course. I go out now and again – for a cycle ride into the countryside just to get a bit of exercise. But it's difficult to find a road where you're not going to get stopped.'

Beth grimaced. 'I know. I was stopped on my way into town this morning.'

He glanced at her, suddenly concerned. 'All right?'

Beth nodded. 'Fine, but it's a bit nerve-wracking the first time.'

Rob laughed wryly. 'Believe me, it doesn't get any easier however many times it happens.' He seemed to look at her properly for the first time. 'I must say, I approve of the disguise. You really look like a school-girl.'

'How have you been managing to get messages to Antoine?'

'With difficulty, because I daren't go to the farm. I

don't want to draw suspicion on the Détanges. They're being very courageous having you live with them. The fewer contacts we have, the better. That's why we're trying to set up a network of communication with each of us knowing only one or two people. And it's been even worse trying to get through to London. I've had to go to Paris and that's a nightmare and so risky too. You're not really sure who you can trust, you know. I've heard there might be a double agent working in the city and no one knows with whom his true allegiance lies.'

Beth pulled a face. 'So, what do you want me to do, Bruce?' Once more they were both trying hard to be as familiar with their code names now as they had been with their real names.

'Act as a courier between me and Antoine. I understand he visits the farm at night when it's safe?'

Beth nodded.

'And also communicate with London for us. You've got your wireless safely hidden?'

'Yes, we—' she began, but Rob held up his hand.

'Don't tell me. I don't want to know.'

Beth was quickly realizing just how secretive everything had to be for the safety of them all.

'How do I get messages to you?'

'We'll both use a drop box. There's a big oak tree between here and the village. It's on a stretch of road that's got a clear view all round so as long as you're careful, you shouldn't be seen. Not unless someone's got a pair of binoculars trained on you and that's a million-to-one chance. I've made a hollow in the back of it. Just leave any messages there. And I'll leave you mine either for Antoine or for you to transmit. By the way, I presume you've no lemons for writing the notes invisibly. What about trying onion juice or milk?'

Beth laughed. 'I'll experiment to see what works the best.'

'Or there's vinegar,' Rob went on, trying to remember all the liquids they'd used on the training course. 'But now you'd better go. You've been here quite a time for just buying bread.'

With the two loaves sticking conspicuously out of the basket on the front of her bicycle, Beth left the town. This time the two soldiers nodded and smiled at her and waved her straight through. She smiled back rather shyly as she hoped a young French girl would do – not flirtatious or over friendly, but just enough to prove she wasn't hostile. It was such a difficult and potentially dangerous line to tread!

She didn't breathe easily until she had reached the farm. On the way, she had spotted the oak tree on the road between the town and the village that Rob had told her about. She hadn't stopped to investigate it, but at least now she knew exactly where it was.

'Oh, you do look smart, Shirley,' Edie said, holding out her arms in welcome. It was two weeks since their trip to White Gates Farm and Archie was back at sea. Though they'd enjoyed seeing the family, it had unsettled Edie even more. She was mortified to see how much Reggie was growing up without her and both she and Lil were missing such important years in Tommy's life. They hadn't been there to see him cut his first tooth, take his first faltering step and to hear his first words. She knew Archie was right – the youngsters were safer in the countryside – but the moments of loneliness wouldn't go away. Although she spent most of her waking hours with Lil, it was night time, when she went to bed, knowing that she was completely alone in the house, that accentuated her solitude. But it was the one thing she couldn't talk to Lil about. Poor Lil had been alone in her house every night since Irene had gone to the country. She could talk to Lil about everything else under the sun, but not this one thing. It made Edie feel even more isolated than ever.

But now Shirley was home, even if only for a few days, and Edie welcomed her with open arms.

The girl's eyes were shining and she looked more – now what was it? Edie wondered – yes, alive, than she'd ever seen her. Her hair, cut short now, curled out from beneath her cap. When she removed the cap, she explained: 'I've had a light perm, Mam. What do you think?'

'It looks lovely and it shines so.'

Shirley took off her jacket and hung it carefully over the back of a chair. 'One of the girls on camp showed me how she rinses her hair with vinegar. It lessens the grease in it. That's why mine always looked so drab and lifeless.'

'Have you made some friends, then?'

'Yes, I suppose so. One or two, but they're all a friendly bunch. There's a whole gang of us that stick together.'

'I'm glad.'

'How's Ursula? Has she popped in now and again like she promised?'

'Oh yes. She's called in once or twice when she knows your dad's at sea and I'm likely to be on my own, though me and Lil spend a lot of our time together.'

Shirley laughed. 'As if you haven't always.'

Edie had the grace to smile and say, 'Well, that's true. I don't know what I'd do without your Aunty Lil.'

'I know, Mam,' Shirley said softly. 'I know.'

Edie glanced at her. She was suddenly seeing a much nicer side to her youngest daughter. Perhaps being in one of the services, feeling she was 'doing her bit' and meeting new people – even making some friends – was giving Shirley a new confidence and consequently honing her into a nicer person. Living amongst a group of young women, Shirley would soon be sat on from a great height if she trotted out one of her sarcastic remarks.

'So, how long have you got?'

Shirley chuckled. 'Right question, Mam.'

'Eh? What d'you mean?'

'The girls were saying that when you go home on leave, everyone asks you, "When are you going back?", almost as if they want you gone again. But if they ask, like you did, it sounds as if they really want you home but just want to know, to make the most of the time you have. See?'

'Yes, I do. I must remember that when Frank comes home on leave.'

Shirley's eyes widened. 'Have you heard from him?'

Edie shook her head. 'Only indirectly, through Lil. Irene hears from him, of course, but he never was much of a letter writer. I – I don't expect him to write to me.'

'Well, he should. He ought to write to his mam, even if it's only now and again. I fully intend to write to you every week. D'you know where he is now?'

'Abroad, we think. Irene has to write to a BFPO address.'

'Oh yes, British forces posted overseas. I didn't know what it stood for until recently. If he is abroad, Mam, that'll be why he can't get back home. Oh, they'll get leave, but it might not be long enough for them to get back to England.'

Edie was silent for a moment before asking quietly, 'Are you likely to be sent abroad?'

Shirley shrugged and avoided her mother's gaze. 'I really don't know yet, Mam, I've only just completed basic training.' She glanced at the mantelpiece where Edie put all the recent letters for Archie to see when he came home. She could see that there were three of her letters there. 'Any news from Beth?'

'Only those stupid postcards and we haven't had one at all since your birthday party when she couldn't come home.'

'Mm,' Shirley said thoughtfully as she took down the last two cards from Beth and scrutinized them. The writing on them certainly looked like Beth's, but there was something strange about the last one that had arrived – the one that had told them she would be unable to come home for the birthday party. For a moment, Shirley couldn't think what it was and then she realized. It was the way Beth had ended her message. Usually she put: '*Lots of Love to Everyone – Stay safe*'. The first part was there, but the last two words were missing. Would Beth have forgotten to write what had become a kind of talisman to the whole family? It was a ritual which had gained the status of a superstition. Thoughtfully, Shirley replaced the cards on the mantelpiece.

Twenty-One

The first time the German vehicles visited the farm after Beth's arrival, she was cleaning out the pigsty in one of the farm buildings at the side of the crew yard. Over her shoulder she saw a large open-topped German staff car swing into the farmyard carrying a driver and an officer sitting in the back. She felt her heart quicken, but she carried on with her task. Behind the first vehicle came a truck painted in camouflage colours and carrying two soldiers with the German rank equivalent of the British Army's private. As the officer got out of the car and strode towards her, she brushed the slurry towards the drain with a strong sweeping action. He stopped a few yards from her and smiled. In perfect French, though she noticed he kept the German form of address, he said, 'I had better be careful not to get in your way, Fräulein.'

She glanced up at him, her heart thumping so loudly in her chest now that she thought he must hear it.

'Good morning,' she managed to say politely, though she couldn't stop her voice from sounding cool. No doubt he was used to it for he smiled sardonically and gave a little bow. 'My name is Major Kurt Hartmann. We have come to collect supplies. I have not seen you here before.' The statement invited an answer.

Beth met his steady gaze. He was undoubtedly a handsome man with a strong, firm jaw line, piercingly blue eyes and fair hair that showed just below his peaked cap. His uniform was immaculate and his polished boots glinted in the wintry sunlight.

Beth smiled at him. It wasn't so hard if you ignored the uniform he was wearing and everything it represented, she told herself.

'Then I will fetch Monsieur Détange.' She dropped the brush she had been wielding.

'What is your name, Fräulein?' he called after her.

'Leonie,' she said over her shoulder, crossing her fingers that both Monsieur and Madame Détange would remember it.

'A pretty name,' the officer murmured, watching her trim figure in the working clothes of a farm labourer as she walked away from him and disappeared into the house, 'for a pretty Fräulein.'

Raoul Détange appeared and nodded briefly to the major. 'It's all ready for you in the barn,' he said, as he crossed the yard. The major clicked his fingers and the two soldiers, who looked extraordinarily young, Beth thought as she watched from the kitchen window, clambered down from the truck and hurried to obey.

Major Hartmann became a frequent visitor to the farm, always on the pretext of collecting food and supplies for his troops from the reluctant farmer, but as soon as he alighted from his vehicle, he looked around for Beth.

'You want to keep out of his way,' Raoul warned her after one visit when the German officer had seemed particularly friendly, smiling and bowing courteously towards her and trying to engage her in conversation.

'I wish I could,' Beth said grimly, 'but don't you think it would look even more suspicious if I'm missing *every* time he comes? I mean, if he sends his men to look for

195

me, they might find things I really don't want them to find.' She was thinking of the radio hidden in the little barn in the fields.

'I see your point, but be careful, Leonie.'

'I will,' Beth said solemnly, knowing that the kindly farmer only had her interests at heart. 'Besides, I'm supposed to be only fifteen.'

Raoul snorted. 'Huh! That won't bother the likes of him.'

The next time Major Hartmann arrived, Beth hid in her bedroom.

'He asked where you were,' Raoul told her worriedly. 'He's getting far too interested in you for my peace of mind.'

'I'll be careful, Uncle.'

So, on the following visit, she made sure she spoke to the major.

'I missed you last time, Fräulein,' he said, touching his cap in a mock salute.

'Oh, I'm sorry,' she said cheerfully, leaning on the sharp-tined pitchfork she was carrying. 'I must have been out in the fields.'

'The farmer – he is good to you? You seem to work very hard.'

'Uncle Raoul?' She widened her eyes, as if in surprise. 'Oh yes, he's wonderful. And Aunt Marthe too. I don't know what I'd have done if I hadn't been able to come here after we . . .'

She stopped and dropped her gaze to the floor as if embarrassed to continue.

'After what, Fräulein?'

Beth bit her lip, pretending that she was reluctant to tell him. 'After –' she whispered, 'after we were bombed.'

There was a pause before the major said, 'I'm sorry.'

Beth was surprised; he sounded as if he really meant it.

'The war is a dreadful thing,' he went on, softly. 'It separates people who might otherwise have become friends.' He was gazing at her intently as he said, strangely hesitantly, 'Would – would you do me the honour of allowing me to take you out to dinner?'

Beth's heart quickened. This is what she – and Raoul – had been afraid of. She blinked, feigning surprise. Then she smiled and simpered as she believed a girl of her supposed age might have done. 'Oh Major, I'm flattered, but I couldn't. I'm only fifteen, you see, and – and . . .'

The major frowned. 'You look a little older than that.'

'Do I?' Beth said eagerly, as if delighted. She remembered that at that age she had always been in a hurry to grow up. Then she feigned a pout. 'I wish I was, then I could join up and . . .' She stopped, pretending to be appalled at what she had been about to say.

He smiled ruefully. 'Then it looks, Fräulein, as if we are destined never to become friends. It's a shame, because I would have liked that – very much.'

He saluted her once more, turned and strode back to the car. But he did not, Beth noticed especially, use the Heil Hitler salute. She frowned as she watched him go. Was that the last time she would see him? She rather thought that it was not. Though he had acted like a true gentleman, she had seen the look in his eyes; a look that said he liked her, that he was attracted to her and that he would not give up the pursuit whatever her age might be.

He came again three days later. Beth tried to disappear but the truck swept into the yard before she could escape from the barn into the house. Luckily, Raoul was with her. 'Stay with me,' she urged. She'd confided in the older man what had happened. She hadn't wanted to tell him – hadn't wanted to worry him – but she'd felt she had to be honest with him. The safety of them all lay in them being completely open with each other.

'I wish Emile was here,' Raoul muttered.

'I don't,' Beth whispered back. 'And it's Antoine now.'

Raoul grunted. 'How am I expected to remember to call my own son by a different name? It's all so ridiculous.'

'I know,' Beth soothed. 'But it's to protect us all. If he was caught using his own name, it would lead them straight to you and Aunt Marthe.' She saw Raoul shudder at the thought. 'Anyone who works underground must have an alias. Even me.' She grinned and, as Major Hartmann came towards them, whispered, 'You're doing very well – just don't forget I'm Leonie.'

But it seemed that this time it was not Beth whom the major had come to see, though his glance flickered towards her and he gave her a brief nod. At that moment several German soldiers jumped from the rear of the vehicle and began to run to different parts of the yard, into the buildings and even into the back door of the farmhouse.

'I have had reports that a wireless signal has been picked up in this area,' Major Hartmann told them calmly. 'My men have been ordered to conduct a search. You will cooperate.'

It was an order, not a question. Raoul, clenching his

hands, clearly felt helpless and Beth's heart was beating rapidly. But, bravely, she decided it was time to put her acting skills to the test. Twisting one of her plaits around her finger, she stepped a little closer to Kurt Hartmann, but not close enough to appear suggestive. She attempted to play the innocent, asking the sort of questions that a puzzled, guiltless fifteen-year-old might pose.

'What are you looking for?' Behind her, she could feel Raoul's fear, but she smiled up at Kurt.

'A wireless,' he said, a little impatiently.

'Like you can listen to music and that?' Before he could answer she turned to Raoul. 'We haven't got a wireless, have we, Uncle?' She turned back to face the officer again. 'We had one in Boulogne-Billancourt. But we lost it.'

Kurt frowned. 'You said,' he said shortly. 'In the bombing.'

'I miss it. I used to love listening to the music.'

'It's not that sort of wireless,' Kurt said. 'It's a wireless transmitter for sending and receiving messages.'

Beth blinked at him. 'Who to?'

'The enemy.'

Beth laughed. 'Why would any of us want to send messages to you?'

'Not us, you silly girl. To *our* enemies. The British – the Free French.'

'Oh!' Beth pretended to be taking this in. Then she nodded as if beginning to understand. 'Yes, I see what you mean. But – but what sort of messages?'

Kurt shrugged. 'About British airmen getting back home if they have parachuted out of a damaged aircraft, about dropping supplies – arms mostly.'

Beth gasped and widened her eyes. 'Are they doing that?'

Kurt stared at her for a moment and she could see that he was wondering if she really was that stupid. He gave a swift nod as his troops appeared from the house and the outbuildings and gathered in the yard once more.

'Nothing, Major,' one young soldier reported.

'Very well.' As the soldiers climbed back into the lorry, Kurt said softly, 'We know there is a circuit operating in this area and we mean to find it.' Now he stared directly at Raoul. 'Where is your son, Herr Détange?'

'My – son?' For a moment the older man hesitated and Beth was so afraid he was going to say something careless. But Raoul shrugged and murmured, 'I only wish I knew, Major Hartmann.' And he dropped his head as if mourning the possible loss of his son.

'I see,' Kurt Hartmann said and added, as he turned away, 'Well, if you do hear anything from him, it would be better for you, your wife and Leonie here, if you were to tell us.'

As the lorry drew out of the yard, Beth heaved a sigh, but it was not one of relief. 'We must get word to Antoine,' she said.

'He'll be here tonight, no doubt with a message he wants you to send.'

'They missed finding the wireless, thank goodness. But perhaps I'd better move it.'

'No, no, leave it where it is. It's in the best place.'

'But we were told to move to different places when we transmit. That way it's harder for them to pick up the signals. They already know there's one around here somewhere. I just want to protect you and Aunt Marthe.'

Raoul put his hand on her slim shoulder and his voice was none too steady as he said, 'You're a brave girl, Leonie. A very brave girl. But you mustn't worry about us. We both knew what we were getting into from the very start when we offered to help. We've just got to carry on until we've driven these – these bastards from our land and you can go back to your family.'

Beth said nothing as a moment of homesickness threatened to overwhelm her. She was very afraid it was going to be a long time before that could happen.

Twenty-Two

When Jessie heard that not one of Edie's family – or Lil's, for that matter – were coming home for the fourth Christmas of the war, she insisted that they should all celebrate at her home. 'You do it every year, Edie, it's time you had a break.'

'Me and Lil do it together, Jessie. It's no trouble, really.'

'Well, me and Harry want you to come to us this year. Lil, too, of course. And,' she laughed, 'we'll even ask Norma, though I have my doubts that she'll come if it's me doing the asking.'

'What about Ursula? Shirley's friend? She's been coming to us at Christmas and Easter. Poor lass is all alone. Shirley said the woman she lodges with is a real misery and always disappears to relatives at holiday times, leaving Ursula on her own.'

'Of course she can come. The more the merrier.'

And so for the first time in her married life, Edie didn't spend Christmas in her own home. Just to Lil, for she didn't want to upset Jessie, she said, 'I'm all at sixes and sevens. I'm so used to us planning Christmas together, I just don't know what to do with myself.'

'There're two things you can do, Edie,' Lil said firmly. 'For a start, you can help me get this net finished before Christmas and then we can put some extra hours in at the Centre.'

Jessie had spared no expense in order to do everything that rationing and shortages would allow to feed her guests.

'Oh, you've got it looking lovely, Jessie,' Edie enthused as she gazed around Jessie's front room. A bright fire burned in the grate – Jessie and Harry must have gone without fires for a while to save the coal for today, Edie thought. Paper chains were looped across the room whilst white-painted pine cones nestled in amongst an arrangement of holly branches. Jessie had even managed to find a small piece of mistletoe. Edie's glance took in the table, laid with Jessie's best china, glassware and table decorations. 'Oh, do look, Lil. However have you managed to get that holly looking as if it's got frost on its leaves, Jessie?'

'It was a Ministry of Food suggestion, would you believe? If you dip the greenery in a strong solution of Epsom salts, when it dries, it looks just like frost.'

'How imaginative,' Lil murmured, marvelling once more at Jessie's ingenuity. Not only was Edie's sister always to able to 'make something out of nothing' in clothes, but she could also conjure up all sorts of handicrafts and she was inventive too. Instead of a bowl of fruit on the sideboard, there were carrots, beetroot and parsley making a colourful display that could still be eaten.

'You're so clever, Jessie,' Lil said sincerely and though Jessie brushed aside the compliment, the pink tinge to her cheeks told them that she was gratified by their praise.

'And what do you all want to do this afternoon?' Jessie said as she served the Christmas pudding. 'At least we won't *have* to play charades.' They all laughed except Edie; she would have loved to have been forced to play charades because it would have meant that at least one of her family was home.

'I reckon me and Archie will stay here in front of this nice fire and have a bit of a sleep,' Harry said. 'What do you say, Archie?'

'Sounds like a good idea to me, Harry.'

Christmas dinner had been served in Jessie's front room, using their Morrison shelter as a table, just as Edie did. Jessie had lit an inviting fire in the grate and the two men planned to sit in the two armchairs beside it and talk and doze the afternoon away.

'And you girls can have a good old gossip without us getting in the way.'

The meal over, the women cleared away and the guests insisted that they should do the washing-up in Jessie's scullery. 'You've done enough,' they assured her. 'That was a lovely meal.'

'I really liked the pudding, Jessie,' Lil said. 'It tasted a bit different to the one we make, didn't it, Edie? Would you give me the recipe, Jessie?'

'I'd like it too,' Norma put in. 'Because next year, you must all come to me.'

'Next year!' Edie exclaimed and added determinedly, 'Oh, the war will be over by then, Norma, and everyone will be home.'

At White Gates Farm, the table groaned under the weight of food that Mrs Schofield had cleverly amassed. She hadn't broken any of the regulations but on a farm there were always ways to skirt the rationing. The two land army girls had gone home for three days but Ruth and Joe's generosity had extended to including three airmen from the nearby RAF camp who couldn't get to their homes during the leave allowed. The company of the young men enlivened the day. They played board games with Reggie and Irene and entertained Tommy. One of them, a married man with a son almost the same age as Tommy, couldn't get enough of the little chap. They'd brought chocolate for him and Reggie and tobacco for Joe Schofield. And into Ruth's grateful hands they'd loaded some rationed foodstuffs that the farm didn't produce.

As Christmas Day drew to a close, everyone declared it had been one of their happiest ever and Ruth retired to her bed, weary but elated that she had been able to give all those who were far from their loved ones a good day; a day to remember.

Irene went to bed with the image in her mind of a handsome, dark-haired young pilot, who reminded her poignantly of Frank, dandling her son on his knee.

On the farm in France, it was a very different scene around the kitchen table. The Germans had taken almost everything that was edible for their Christmas feasting leaving the Détanges with scarcely enough to eat, never mind celebrating the festive season.

'Emile – I mean Antoine – won't come,' Raoul said softly. 'He believes it's a very dangerous time to visit. That's when the Germans might spring a surprise search, knowing that it's a vulnerable time for families when they might feel compelled to come home.'

Surreptitiously, Marthe wiped her eyes but she smiled bravely. 'But we have our niece staying with us, Raoul. We have family here.'

Beth touched the older woman's hand in a gesture of gratitude for she, too, was missing not only her own family dreadfully, but also the handsome Frenchman too. Over the weeks they had been working together under dangerous circumstances and had become very close. Emile's dark brown eyes looked into hers, his expression not guarded like Kurt's, for he knew her real age. Beth knew that Emile was falling in love with her, and she with him, but also that the daily danger they lived in kept him from declaring his feelings for her. Those similar feelings that, unfortunately, Kurt Hartmann did not have to hide.

Three nights after New Year's Day, Beth woke suddenly in the middle of the night to the droning of a British bomber overhead, its engine sounding damaged; the aircraft was in trouble. At once, she threw back the covers and began to dress hurriedly, pulling on trousers and thick jumpers. For a moment she thought the plane had flown on, but then there was a terrific crash that rattled the windows. She hurried to look out and, in one of Raoul's meadows, she saw flames leaping into the air. She winced. If there were any crew still on board, they would not have survived such an inferno. But she must go to see. Perhaps the crew had bailed out and were somewhere nearby needing help. She opened her bedroom door and crept downstairs to find both Raoul and Marthe already in the kitchen. The farmer was already dressed and pulling on his sturdy boots. His wife, with a shawl thrown over her nightgown, hurried between her pantry and the table, spreading out what bit of food they had left, rousing the range fire to wakefulness and setting the kettle to boil. It looked to Beth as if they'd fallen swiftly into a

well-rehearsed routine, but it was the first time something like this had happened since her arrival.

'What do we do?' Beth whispered as if already she
feared the Germans might be listening. Surely they could
not have missed hearing such a noise; they would be
here soon.

'We go and see if we can find any survivors.'

'What about the Germans?'

Raoul shrugged, almost nonchalantly. 'If they come,
they come. But if we can get to the airmen first . . .'
He stood up, 'Come on. Let's go.'

Jasper was already standing at the back door, his
pink tongue lolling, his eyes bright and expectant. He
knew he had work to do and when Raoul opened the
back door, he raced out into the night.

'I didn't see any parachutes, but then the plane was
almost overhead by the time I woke up,' Beth said softly
as they hurried after the dog.

'Don't worry,' Raoul said, sounding surprisingly
calm. 'If there's anyone out there – at least within a
reasonable distance – Jasper will find them.'

They walked through the blackness, the land lit inter-
mittently by a fitful moon. They had walked through
one field and into the next, a ploughed field awaiting
its spring wheat, when they heard a soft bark. Even
Jasper, it seemed, understood the need for quiet.

'Where is he? I can't see him.'

'This way,' Raoul murmured, unerring in his sense
of direction.

Again, another bark, nearer this time and, within
minutes, they saw a dark shape on the ground with
Jasper standing guard. A parachute billowed out from
the still form of the airman. Beth fell to her knees beside
him.

'What – where . . . ?' the young man began, disorientated by his fall. He was speaking in English.

'It's all right. We're French. We're here to help you. Are you hurt?'

'I – don't know,' he said again in English, but he seemed to have understood her question even though she had spoken to him in French. She dare not give away her true nationality yet, if at all. He tried to sit up, but the parachute cords still pulled at him.

'Get it off him,' Raoul instructed, 'and I'll bury it.'

Beth wondered why Raoul had grabbed a spade from outside the back door as they'd left the house. Now she understood. It was as if it had been standing there in readiness. Perhaps it had, for the farmer seemed confident in his actions. He'd done this before, Beth was sure.

The airman, recovering swiftly now, released his parachute and sat up.

'Can you stand?' Beth asked as she hooked her arm under his and helped him up. 'All right?'

'I – think so. Doesn't seem to be anything broken. I was just winded, I think.' He looked around him. 'Where are the others?'

'I don't know. You're the first Jasper has found.' She looked down at the dog. 'Go find, Jasper,' she told him. 'Good dog.' And the animal raced off once more.

'How many of you are there?'

'There – there should be seven, but I think I might have been the last to get out. I came out third.' He lifted his gaze towards the burning aircraft, its flames still lighting the night sky. 'Poor sods.'

'Come, lean on me. I'll take you back to the farmhouse.'

'Are you sure? It could mean trouble for you.'

'We'll take that risk.' She would like to have taken him to the little barn to hide him, but there was something already far more important – even than a British airman – hidden there. Somewhere on the farm would have to do for tonight.

Another figure came stumbling through the darkness towards them, carrying his parachute.

'Lewis – you OK?' a voice came out of the gloom.

'Yeah. I seem to be. Where's Jimmy?'

'Dunno. What shall I do with this?'

'Give it to me.' Beth could see Raoul still digging in the softened earth in one corner of the field. 'My uncle is burying them.'

'What's she say?' the newcomer asked his companion.

'Give her the parachute. Her uncle is going to bury them.'

'Are they going to help us?' she heard the airman, whose name she didn't yet know, ask as she took the bundle of white silk and hurried away.

'I reckon,' Lewis replied and there was no mistaking the fervent hope in his tone.

As Raoul and Beth pushed the two chutes into the deep hole he had dug, Beth whispered. 'There's another one somewhere. They're talking about someone called Jimmy. They think three got out of the plane. The rest . . .' She couldn't bring herself to say the words but Raoul understood.

'We must hurry. That crash will have alerted someone in the village, no doubt.'

It was a close shave. Jasper had found the third airman – Jimmy – who was also miraculously unhurt, all three parachutes were buried and the five of them and the dog returned to the farmhouse.

'We can't stay here,' Lewis protested, as Raoul

ushered them inside and offered them the bread and cheese and a cup of weak coffee which Marthe had prepared. In their absence, she had dressed. 'We don't want to bring trouble on you.' He understood French, but still spoke in English himself.

'Bring the food,' Raoul said. 'I will take you to my pigsty. We've built a hiding place in the roof. You can get up to it by a ladder, which I must then remove. I regret the smell will not be pleasant, but you should be safe there. The Germans are fastidious.' He chuckled. 'They don't like to get their shiny boots dirty.'

The three airmen, whose names Beth now knew to be Lewis, Jimmy and Geoff, were safely in the loft and Raoul had just returned, locked the door and turned down the lamp, when they heard the vehicles roar into the yard.

'Quick! Upstairs. Get back into your night things and into bed. You, too, Marthe.'

'What about you?'

'I shall stay down here until you've had time, then I will open the door – if they knock, that is, which I'm sure—'

He had not finished his sentence before a loud banging on the door began and a voice shouted, '*Raus. Raus.* Out. Out. Open up.'

'Hurry.'

'But you're dressed. Won't they—?'

'Go, Marthe, please.'

Whilst Beth and Marthe hurried upstairs, Raoul took off his jacket, his shoes and socks and loosened his shirt, so that it looked as if he'd just pulled some clothes on when he'd heard the commotion. In her room, Beth stripped and put on her nightdress. Then she folded the clothes she'd been wearing neatly over the chair beside her narrow bed. Now she could hear that Raoul had opened the back door and the soldiers were rushing into the house. Beth slipped into bed and turned on her side, her face away from the door, as the soldiers came pounding up the stairs.

Twenty-Three

Archie lay in bed with his eyes wide open staring into the darkness as he listened to the bombers coming back from a raid in the early light of morning. One, two, three, he counted, and then he could no longer distinguish the engines of individual aircraft as several flew in together. Edie lay beside him, fast asleep, undisturbed and untroubled by the noise overhead. He wondered where they'd been and had they all come back. He doubted it – there weren't many bombing raids that took place where all the aircraft came back safely. And then, as the sounds died away, his thoughts turned – as they nearly always did – to Frank and Beth, and now to Shirley too. He missed them every bit as much as his wife did and he worried about them, for perhaps he understood, even more than their mother did, just what danger they might all be in. He believed Shirley was still in England, but he knew Frank was abroad. And Beth – well, he didn't even know where she was.

Tomorrow he would have to go back to sea. He never said anything to Edie – or to anyone, for that matter – but he was more fearful every time he put out to sea now. He'd been lucky so far, he knew, but just how long would that luck hold out?

*

The German soldiers ran riot through the farmhouse, crashing into all the rooms, upturning the beds, pulling furniture away from the walls. They did the same in the barns, tipping over bins full of valuable animal feed, oblivious – or uncaring – of the damage they were causing. They found ladders and climbed into the hayloft, but – thankfully – not one of them thought to look above the pigsty. For a frightening half-hour, they held Raoul, Marthe and Beth in the kitchen at gunpoint whilst they searched the property. Beth considered that a fifteen-year-old would be so terrified that she would cling to Marthe and weep. Marthe wept too, but her tears were real and not put on as were Beth's. Inside, the highly trained agent was seething. She was frightened – of course she was – but her fear was for the farmer and his wife and the three airman. If they were found . . .

At last the soldiers gave up their search and reported to their superior – this time not Major Hartmann – that they could find nothing, not even a trace, of British fugitives.

Questioned, Raoul lifted his shoulders in a Gallic shrug. 'I heard the aircraft crash and saw the fire.'

'You didn't go out to see if you could help them?'

Again, a shrug. 'Who could have survived that?' It was a reasonable comment and though the officer stared at him for a moment, he then turned away, seemingly satisfied. 'You would do well not to even think of aiding the enemy. You could be shot.'

Marthe let out a wail and buried her face in Beth's shoulder.

Emile arrived late into the night, but Beth had stayed up, waiting for him, for she guessed he would come if he could. She had insisted that his parents went to bed, promising she would call them if he came. He hugged

213

her swiftly and then held her shoulders at arm's length, gazing into her eyes. 'You are all right? Maman and Papa too?'

'We're fine, but there are three British airmen hiding above your father's pigsty.'

Emile smiled. 'I helped him construct the hideout. He's used it once or twice before you came. Can you send a message to London at once to request they send a light aircraft as soon as they can? I don't want my parents in any more danger than they already are, so I have the map references for a suitable field some distance from here belonging to another farmer who keeps out of the way when a drop is being made and will deny all knowledge if questioned. But he is a loyal Frenchman and on our side.'

'I'll go now,' Beth said at once.

'I'll come with you.'

Hand in hand – her hand felt so good clasped in his – they crept through the darkness, listening intently to the slightest sound. An owl swooped low over their heads, startling them, but they pressed on. Outside the small barn they paused and glanced around. There was no sound, no lights anywhere.

'Right,' Emile said softly, 'I'll stay out here whilst you send the message about the airmen. You know what to say, but keep it as brief as you can.'

In the pitch black of the interior of the barn, Beth lit the candle she had brought and set it on a stone that jutted out from the wall. Then she removed the wireless from its hiding place, setting up the aerial. The tapping out of the Morse code message echoed loudly in the stillness. Surely, she thought worriedly, it could be heard fields away, but she carried on. Her message sent, they waited half an hour, standing outside with their arms around each other.

'Oh Beth,' Emile murmured, forgetting for once to use her codename, 'when all this is over—'

At that moment, the wireless set began to bleep. You certainly pick your moment, London, Beth thought wryly and eased herself out of his warm embrace to step back into the barn. The answer was that arrangements would be made and they would send a coded message on the night the Lysander would arrive over the normal wireless airwaves amongst the personal messages that were broadcast from the BBC. The message would say, 'Aunt Matilda has gone home on the 2 o'clock train'. This would give the local resistance group – Emile's men – the expected time of arrival. The number 'two' would be changed to whatever time the aircraft would be due. Despite the fact that Beth had told Kurt Hartmann that her uncle did not have a wireless set, Raoul kept one hidden beneath the floorboards in his bedroom; something else the searching soldiers had not uncovered.

Beth stowed the transmitter behind the stones and removed the candle. 'I'll come back in the morning and make sure everything looks undisturbed. And now we'd better go and wake your parents. Your mother would never forgive me if they missed your visit.'

An hour or so later, as they said their goodbyes at the gate, Beth whispered, 'I will take any message to the dropping point in the oak tree just outside the village.'

'If there are Germans about, go on into the town to see Bruce, but only if there is no other way. Henri Lafarge is trustworthy, but the less you are seen in town making contact with Bruce, the better.' Emile held her close for a moment and kissed her forehead. Releasing her swiftly, he turned away and was immediately lost in the darkness. She could not even watch him go, but the feel of his lips still tingled on her forehead.

'1943 already, Lil, and still no end to the war,' Edie said disconsolately as they walked together to the WVS a few days after New Year. They had celebrated – if that could be the right word in such circumstances – the turning of the year very quietly, just the three of them in Lil's house.

'I know, duck, but let's hope this year will bring an end to it all, eh?'

'I can't see it myself. I talked to Archie about it before he went back this morning. He isn't hopeful.'

'I've had a letter from Irene. She's heard from Frank and though he doesn't give much away, she reckons he's in North Africa.'

'Africa? Whatever is he doing there?'

'Perhaps he was part of the British Eighth army that triumphed over Rommel two months ago. Now wouldn't that be something if your Frank had been part of that?'

'Is he all right?' Edie was hungry for this kind news – news of her family and of Frank's safety. She didn't really care what battles he'd been in, just so long as he'd come through them unscathed.

'He's fine. Very cheerful and asking her to send photos of Tommy. The little chap won't know him when he gets back and your Frank is so worried he won't take to him.'

''Course he will. Frank's his daddy. How could he not take to him?'

Lil pulled a face. 'It's going to be very difficult for them all to settle back into ordinary life once it's all over, you know, Edie.'

'Why? I should think they'd be only too glad to get back home to their families. I know I can't wait to get 'em all back under my roof. Oh look, there's Ursula. I wonder what she's doing out this time of the day? You'd think she'd be at work, wouldn't you?'

'She's freelance, isn't she? I mean, she doesn't actually work for anyone sitting in an office, does she? She'll be out looking for a story, I've no doubt.'

'Ursula, Ursula, duck,' Edie raised her voice. The girl looked round, startled for a moment, but when she saw the two women she knew, her face relaxed into a smile.

'You didn't come round on New Year's Eve. Are you all right?'

Ursula nodded. 'I didn't like to. You have all been so good to me even now that Shirley is away. It was kind of Mr and Mrs Charlton to invite me for Christmas Day and I feel so embarrassed because I have not enough money to buy you something for all your kindness.'

'Now, don't you worry about that, duck. We're only too glad to have you with us. I don't like to think of anyone being on their own, especially at Christmas. Have you heard from your own folks?'

Suddenly, Ursula's smile faded and her face took on a closed expression. 'No – I – I don't hear from them. Letters are difficult to and from – Switzerland.'

'Are they?' Edie asked innocently. 'I wonder why. I thought Switzerland was neutral.'

'It is, but perhaps mail has to come through occupied areas – I don't know. I just know I don't hear from them.'

'Then I'm sorry for you. There's nothing worse than

217

not hearing from your family – and I should know because I haven't heard from Beth for weeks now. Still,' she said, trying to put a brave face on it, 'Lil's heard from Irene and, through her, indirectly from Frank. Shirley writes every week, bless her –'

Lil hid her smile. Shirley was rising in her mother's estimation every day because she wrote regularly and came home whenever she could.

Shirley was having a whale of a time. It seemed totally inappropriate to Lil that someone should be actually enjoying the war and yet Shirley was doing so. She had been drafted to become part of a mixed team on an anti-aircraft battery somewhere. They suspected she was in London, but Shirley was being very secretive.

'I can't tell you where I am, Mam,' she'd put in her last letter. '"Careless Talk" and all that.'

'– And I know from Irene that Reggie's all right. Tell you what, Ursula,' Edie added impetuously, 'we'll go to the pictures tonight the three of us – my treat – and afterwards you can come and have a bit of supper with me and Lil. How does that sound?'

'Thank you – I'd like that. You're very kind.'

They enjoyed the two films, but when the Pathé news came on, Lil felt Ursula, sitting between them, move uncomfortably. She glanced at the girl's face, illuminated by the light from the screen. Ursula was absorbed in the news with a small smile on her mouth. Lil glanced back at the flickering scenes; she didn't feel like smiling for the news was bleak. The Germans now occupied the whole of France, having taken over control of Southern France the previous November. The Vichy Government still existed but they had very little power now, if any. The euphoria of Montgomery's victory at El Alamein at the end of October, when the church bells had rung out in celebration for the first time in over two years, already seemed a long time ago.

If only we could get some good news, Lil thought disconsolately, it would lift all our spirits and help us to carry on.

Twenty-Four

'I've had another letter from Irene,' Lil said coming in through Edie's back door the morning after their trip to the cinema. She was holding the single sheet of paper in her hand. 'It's Frank . . .'

Edie turned frightened eyes towards her friend. Her heart felt as if it missed a beat and then began to pound. 'What?' she whispered. 'Tell me, Lil.'

'He's been injured, but it's not serious.'

'Are you sure?'

Lil nodded. 'He's been hit in the leg.'

Reassured now that her son's life was not in imminent danger, Edie asked, 'Then he's coming home?'

Lil shook her head sadly. 'No, it's not even bad enough for that. Not what they used to call in the last war "a Blighty wound". No, he's being treated out there.'

'Huh!' Her anger flaring suddenly, Edie banged the saucepan she was holding down on to the draining board with a thud that made Lil jump. 'They might at least send him home, even if it's only for a few weeks. I can look after him far better than any hospital out there.'

'You would think they'd send them back, wouldn't you, if only to give them more space for new casualties? But no, he's got to stay out there.'

'I bet Irene's upset, isn't she?'

220

Lil didn't answer immediately but glanced down at the letter again. 'I expect so,' she murmured.

'Can we send him a food parcel?' Edie had recovered her composure and was now turning her mind to practical matters. 'I've got some tinned fruit saved up from before the war. I could send that.'

Lil was amused by, but completely understood, Edie's need to feed her injured son, to send him a tasty titbit. It was what mothers did, she thought.

It was three days before the awaited message regarding the pick up of the British airmen was received in France. Personal messages were broadcast by the BBC in London on *Radio Londres*; programmes operated by the Free French to their countrymen who were under Nazi occupation. And it was also a means of sending coded messages to the French Resistance. Although the Germans had forbidden the French people to listen to the service, many still did so in secret. Though the enemy were aware of this happening, they had no way of knowing which were genuine messages sent by separated families and which were the messages being passed to the Resistance. Beth wrote the time on a scrap of paper in onion juice and got out her bicycle from the shed. Whilst they waited impatiently for news, the three airmen had been fed and allowed out into the yard for fresh air and exercise whilst Raoul and Beth kept watch. How fortunate it was that Raoul's farm had good views all around. Anyone approaching could be seen for some distance.

She cycled along the lane from the farm and through the village, waving to the one or two people she had met before; Monsieur Cavalier, the butcher, whom Raoul had warned her might be a collaborator, Monsieur Duval, the blacksmith, who most certainly was not. He hated the invaders of his country with a passion and made no secret of it. That in itself was dangerous and the circuit had reluctantly decided that they could not trust him, but only for the fact that he was so outspoken. And then she saw the local priest, Father Monnier, walking down the road, his long cassock flapping in the breeze. The clergyman was an enigma. He hid behind his calling and no one was sure on which side his loyalties lay. The resistance group wished they knew, for his church could have been very useful as a hiding place although Raoul had remarked sagely, 'That's the first place they'd look.' And he had been proved right. On four occasions – including this most recent event – the church had been searched from crypt to the rafters. Beth nodded to each of them in turn but cycled on, taking the road out of the village towards the town four miles away.

Approaching the oak tree at the side of the road, she saw that a German road block had been set up close by. It hadn't been there the last time she had come this way. She suspected that the Germans moved these frequently. Now, she would not be able to use the hollow in the tree, but would have to ride on to the town to find Rob.

Beth cycled up to the barrier across the road and braked. Her hands were trembling but she kept them firmly gripping the handlebars, the right-hand one of which held the important message. Although the writing was not visible to the naked eye, a piece of paper pushed into the hollow handlebar would still look suspicious. She could be arrested straightaway. Steeling herself not to glance down at it, she smiled at the soldier walking towards her. He was not one of those she'd seen before. Dressed in a short, tight schoolgirl dress and coat, hoping that it looked as if she was growing out of them, ankle socks and shoes that had seen better days, and with her hair in two plaits, she hoped she still looked the part of a young girl.

He spoke to her in German but, quite truthfully, Beth lifted her shoulders and shook her head in a gesture to say that she did not understand what he was saying. Impatiently, the soldier pretended to scribble on his hand, indicating that he wanted to see her papers. Producing them, she waited, holding her breath, whilst he scrutinized them. He glanced up and said something else in German. She caught the word which she knew meant 'school' but she didn't want to give the impression that she understood anything he was saying so she frowned and shrugged again. Perhaps he was asking her why she was not in school. Irritated, he thrust her papers at her and waved her on, signalling to his companion on duty at the road block that he should raise the barrier and let her pass.

Once more, Beth leaned her bicycle against the wall of the bakery and glanced around her. There was no one near enough to see her quickly remove the piece of paper from the handlebar and then enter the shop. Monsieur Lafarge greeted her with a smile and gestured with his head towards the back room and the stairs to the upper floor. She climbed the dark, narrow staircase and knocked on a door on the landing, tapping out 'L' for Leonie in Morse code. The door was unlocked and opened at once. No one else knew their prearranged signal.

'Trouble?' Rob asked, for he knew that she would only visit him if the usual channels of communication to the circuit were blocked for some reason. Beth nodded and swiftly explained, ending, 'The plane is coming in at two-thirty tomorrow morning. We have to get a message to Antoine somehow. It's no good waiting to see if he comes to the farm tonight. He might not come, and besides, even if he did, it'd be too late to organize everything.'

'Leave it with me,' Rob said. 'I'll make sure he gets it.'

'Do be careful. We'll make sure the airmen are ready. They've been very patient, hiding above a smelly pigsty. Now, I'd better get back and I'll take something from Monsieur's bakery and put it in my bicycle basket. No doubt the Germans will still be there when I get back. Oh, can you destroy this for me?' She handed him the slip of paper, which she had intended leaving in the hollow of the tree. Rob struck a match and burned it in the empty grate. As she left, he hugged her swiftly, murmuring, 'Stay safe.' The saying reminded her poignantly for a moment of the way she had always signed off her letters to her family. The memory brought a lump to her throat. She turned away quickly before he should see the tears in her eyes.

At last, Lil got her wish; there was some better news. On the very last day of January, the Germans surrendered in Stalingrad and over the next weeks the Russians began to push the invaders from their territory. And in Africa there were continued successes.

'I reckon the tide's turning, Edie,' Lil said optimistically. 'What does Archie think?'

'I don't know. We don't talk about the war much when he's home. He seems very preoccupied just now. I expect he's worried about them all – just like I am.'

Lil said nothing but privately she was thinking that life at sea must be even tougher for Archie than normal. Hadn't Edie thought of that? But it seemed her friend was so wrapped up in her concerns for her children that Archie was taking second place in her mind.

On Tuesday, 18 May, Lil rushed out of her back door, crashed open the door between the two backyards, threaded her way through Edie's lines of washing and almost launched herself into Edie's scullery. 'Edie! Edie! Have you heard? Oh, isn't it marvellous news?'

The scullery was empty, the living room too. The whole house was silent. Lil's excitement at being able to bring some good news for a change was thwarted. Then she heard footsteps overhead. Edie must be upstairs making her bed. Lil went to the foot of the stairs. 'Edie? Edie? You there?'

'Yes, Lil, come up, duck. You can give me a hand with this bed, save me keep running round and back again to tuck it all in.'

Lil, chuckling softly, climbed the stairs and went into Edie's bedroom. As she stood at one side of the bed and began to pull the sheets and blankets into place, she said again, 'Have you heard the news?'

'How could I, Lil? You know Archie's away and I . . .'

'. . . don't listen to the news,' they both said in chorus and Edie had the grace to smile. 'So, what's happened? Nothing awful, 'cos I can tell by your face.'

'A squadron of Lancasters bombed the dams in the Ruhr and Eder valleys in Germany. I bet they went from Scampton. Anyway, it's been a huge success, they say, and should halt the German war production for months. It could shorten the war, Edie, and maybe the Allies are already planning the invasion of Europe. Think of that

– our lads landing back in France and all the other countries under enemy occupation.'

'That is good news, Lil. I reckon when we've finished making this bed, we deserve a cup of tea to celebrate!'

Twenty-Five

In France, there didn't seem to be any hope of liberation yet. Beth continued her chores on the farm and her clandestine work whenever she was needed. She rode around the countryside on her bicycle unhindered for the most part; it seemed that the sentries recognized the young girl and waved her through their road blocks often without even stopping her. If only they knew, she thought to herself as she carried yet another message received from London. Often she carried very dangerous messages about sabotage that London wanted carried out. If she thought it was safe, she would deliver this type of message to Rob in person; she was more afraid of being caught with an incriminating piece of paper than of being questioned as to why she was visiting the town. She always had a plausible excuse. She began, too, to visit other shops so that her visits to the baker were not so obvious. Sometimes, she even went into the town when there was no message to deliver or receive, just to divert any suspicion.

But Emile – and Rob agreed with him – would not allow her to go with them on sabotage missions. 'You're far too valuable as a wireless operator and courier, Leonie. We can't afford to lose you.' And besides, he wanted to add, *I* couldn't bear to lose you. There was so much he wanted to say to her, but he couldn't. Not in the middle of a war when both their lives were in constant danger. And so Beth had to be content to play the role assigned to her. And it was an important one, she knew. If she were caught, London would have to send out another wireless operator and it could take weeks for someone new to learn the ropes. In the meantime, the valuable work of the Fisherman circuit would be seriously disrupted if not destroyed.

The only real worry that Beth had at the moment was the frequent visits from Kurt and his men. But the weeks passed safely into months and spring turned into the summer of 1943. There were no more sudden raids searching for allied airmen and, ostensibly, the Germans' visits were, of course, to collect food, but Kurt's continuing presence worried Raoul. 'He never came so often before you arrived here,' he told Beth. 'He just used to send his men.'

'Oh dear,' Beth said worriedly. 'Ought I to leave?'

Raoul shook his head. 'No, that would make him all the more suspicious.'

'You think he's suspicious?'

Raoul gave a low chuckle. 'Actually, no, I don't. He's taken a liking to you. It's obvious and that's why he keeps coming here.'

Beth sighed. 'I know. But what can I do? I've tried telling him I'm only fifteen – well, I'll be sixteen at the end of this month, according to the date we used as my birthdate – but it doesn't seem to have done what I wanted; kept him away.'

Raoul lifted his big shoulders. 'Better he comes to see you because he's attracted to you than . . .' He left the words unsaid. His glance searched her face. 'You're a very pretty girl. I can tell that Em – I mean, Antoine – likes you too. Don't tell me you haven't noticed?'

Beth blushed prettily and dropped her gaze. 'Well, yes, at least – I – I hope so.'

Raoul's face clouded and for a brief moment he looked unutterably sad. 'When it's all over – I hope . . .' His voice cracked and he could say no more, but he covered her hand with his, his grasp warm and strong and comforting.

And so, each time the vehicles belonging to the German army came roaring into the farmyard, Beth felt a jolt of fear and not only now at the thought of being discovered as an agent. If she had any warning from the sound of their engines coming down the lane, she would try to be elsewhere other than in the yard. She would hurry upstairs in the house, or into the fields, running and running in the opposite direction to the little barn in the field to put distance between herself and Major Hartmann. But it was not always possible to be absent; it would become obvious if she did it too often.

So sometimes she stayed and faced him, smiling when he climbed out of the car and strode towards her. There was no denying, Beth thought objectively, that he was a very handsome man – if only he hadn't been in the wrong uniform!

He stood before her, giving a polite little bow. 'Fräulein! I am pleased to see you today. You've been missing the last two times I called.'

'Yes, I'm sorry.' She smiled brightly at him. 'How are you, Major?'

He stepped a little closer. 'Kurt – please – when there is no one to hear.'

His men were busy loading supplies onto the lorry and Raoul was watching them morosely.

'Are you still sure that you won't allow me to take you to dinner? We could go into the town if you are afraid the villagers would think badly of you. I know how it is for you young girls. You'd be thought a collaborator' – he smiled – 'or, worse, a spy for your country's enemy.'

Beth stared at him, her heart thudding. Then she managed to laugh a tinkling, silly girlish sound. 'Me? A spy? Oh, now that would be fun, wouldn't it?' She put her head coquettishly on one side. Then she pretended to sigh. 'But I'm not clever enough.'

'I'm sure that's not true,' he said softly and stared at her for a moment as if trying to make up his mind about something. 'Perhaps,' he said slowly, 'there is a way you can help us – me, that is.'

Beth felt a quiver of fear, but she kept her eyes wide in a mystified stare. 'Really, Major? How?'

He stepped even closer, towering above her, but his nearness was not threatening, it was rather as if he were about to take her into his confidence. 'You could tell me of anything that happens in this area.'

'I don't understand,' she said innocently. 'What sort of thing?'

'If you hear of any enemy aircraft dropping things?'

Beth frowned. 'What sort of things?'

'Supplies. People.'

'*People?* Why would they drop people?' She bit her lip, wondering if she were pushing the dumb act a little too far. She saw him watching her as if trying to decide if she really was as naïve – or stupid – as she was making out. She decided to act as if she had realized what he might be talking about. 'Oh, soldiers, you mean?'

'Possibly. More likely it would be agents.'

Now perhaps she could pretend once more not to understand. 'What for? What do they do?'

Patiently, he explained. 'The French have formed

resistance groups and the British are aiding them by sending weapons and ammunition and people – men and women – as secret agents to send radio messages back to England.'

Beth's face brightened. 'Oh – is that why you were searching Uncle's buildings? You thought one of these agents might be here?'

'Precisely.'

She shrugged. 'Well, there's no one here except Uncle and Aunt and the lad from the village who comes to work on the farm when we're extra busy. And me, of course,' she ended with a winning smile. She hoped she was acting the part of a naïve, perhaps rather simple, fifteen-year-old girl who would be flattered by the attentions of a handsome German officer.

Suddenly, he asked her sharply, 'Do you know where their son is? Emile Détange?'

She might have been thrown off guard by his sudden question, but the role-play in her training had been excellent. 'Always,' their instructor had warned them, 'be on your guard for the unexpected question that will catch you out. Don't answer too quickly. Take a moment to think . . .'

Beth frowned. 'My cousin? He's not here.'

'Do you know where he is? Does he visit? Has he been here at all since you arrived?'

Now, he snapped out the questions, no longer the friendly occupier of her country trying to appease her or even perhaps paying court to her. As she believed a young girl would have reacted at the sharpness in his tone, Beth stepped back and tears filled her eyes. The ability to weep at will had saved her from many a hiding in her childhood and even a caning at school. And all the games of charades at Christmas at Shirley's

231

insistence, when Beth had had the family in stitches with her impersonations, had honed her talents. Now, once again and in a far more desperate situation, her acting skills came to her rescue. She hoped Major Hartmann could not read her thoughts as the image of Emile's face, of him creeping through the darkness to bring messages to her, of his gentle kiss on her forehead in the seclusion of the barn, flitted through her mind.

'I – no – I've not seen him. I don't know where he is.'

'Do your aunt and uncle know?' His tone was still firm – he wanted answers – but he spoke a little less harshly now.

She bit her lip as the tears slipped down her cheeks. She shook her head. 'I don't think so. Aunt Marthe cries all the time.'

'I'm sorry, Fräulein, I didn't mean to make you cry.' He stepped closer and put his arms around her, drawing her against his chest, her cheek resting against his uniform.

And that was how Raoul saw them as he stepped out of the barn.

Later, she was able to explain to Raoul and Marthe everything that had been said. 'And I think he knows about the British airmen. Just as he was leaving he said, "If you hear any light aircraft landing nearby, be sure to let me know." He must know that such aircraft only land if they're picking someone up.'

There had been two more airmen who had hidden above Raoul's pigsty for two nights until a Lysander had flown in to rescue them. Again, the pick-up had been arranged through Beth, but this time there had been no need to involve Rob. The tree trunk had been unguarded.

'Let's hope they got away safely the other night as they were supposed to,' Raoul murmured.

'And Emile?' Marthe whispered, her mind on her son rather than on the airmen. Her eyes were fearful, her fingers to her lips. 'He asked about Emile? By name?'

Beth nodded.

'Well, he would, wouldn't he?' Raoul said reasonably. 'He'll know we've got a son and he'll know his name. It's natural he should ask about him. Just so long as he doesn't start asking us about "Antoine".'

Twenty-Six

Edie wasn't dealing very well with being on her own for days – even weeks – at a time. She counted the days now to Archie coming home from the sea more than she ever had done in their married life. Always – until now – she had had the family to keep her busy, too busy sometimes, but Edie, a born homemaker and mother, had revelled in it. Even when she had gone to bed exhausted, it had been what she always called a healthy tiredness. 'I'm not ill,' she would say to Lil, 'because there's a good reason why I'm weary.' Then she'd smile and add, 'but I wouldn't have it any other way.'

But now was a different matter; she was alone and very lonely. 'If it wasn't for you, Lil, I don't know what I'd do,' she'd say a dozen times during the weeks when Archie was away. Lil tried to keep her friend busy, but it wasn't always easy to think of things they could do. Any pleasure the two women had had in shopping was now gone; it was an unending chore coping with the rationing and the shortage of goods that weren't on ration. And the queues just seemed to grow longer, often with disappointment in the end. 'That's another two hours wasted,' Edie would grumble as they trudged home from the town, their shopping bags hardly any heavier than when they had set out.

'Have you heard from Shirley?' Lil asked.

'She writes every week – never misses.' Her tone hardened as she added, 'That's more than I can say for Beth. Only one postcard in months, Lil. I wonder about that girl, really I do.'

'I expect she's busy, Edie. If she's involved in nursing now, maybe she's even been sent abroad.'

'She'd have let us know if that had happened.' Edie paused and there was uncertainty in her tone as she added, 'Wouldn't she?'

'Of course, she would, duck,' Lil tried to reassure her, and then steered the subject away from Edie's children. But that was easier said than done. Edie was still going through them – one by one – in her mind. 'Frank's on the mend. I actually got a letter from him yesterday.'

'I expect he's had more time whilst he's been laid up.'

'He's going back on light duties next week, he said.'

'That's good.'

'Is it?' Edie said mournfully. 'I'm not so sure 'cos it might mean he'll be back in the thick of the fighting again soon.'

Lil bit her lip, unable to argue with Edie's logic.

'We could take a trip out to the farm again – just the two of us – or we could ask Ursula if she'd like to come with us. Or Jessie.'

Edie pulled a face. 'Archie said he thought it best to stay away. I don't think we were ever so welcome last time.'

'Oh, I'm sure we were. It was just that we arrived unexpectedly. This time we could plan it and write and tell them.'

'I suppose so.' Edie seemed strangely reluctant and, for once, her friend couldn't understand why. The truth was that Edie didn't want to see her young son happy and well settled in the countryside. She knew it was selfish of her, but it hurt and the cut had gone even deeper when he hadn't even seemed pleased to see them. All that had worried him was that they had come to fetch him home. Perhaps it was better, as Archie had suggested, to stay away until the end of the war. But then, Edie promised herself, he would come home. She'd make sure of that.

'I wish we could go to Cleethorpes beach like we did with the kids in summer before the war.' She sighed heavily. 'I used to like a walk along the sands this time of year, even when it was crowded.'

'I like the beach best in winter,' Lil said, 'when we've got it all to ourselves, even though it's a bit chilly. Still, there'll be none of that until the war's over. I've heard there are rolls of barbed wire all along the beach and you can't get near the sand, ne'er mind the sea. There'll be no holidaymakers this year.'

'Do you remember, Lil, taking all the kids to see the illuminations in Cleethorpes the year they were put up? We all went, even Jessie and Harry. Reggie was only three and I don't reckon he'll remember much about it, but the others do.'

'I remember,' Lil murmured, 'and the crowds in summer, flocking in by train. You could hardly move on the prom.'

Recalling the happy times the two families had shared only made Edie even more maudlin.

'We could go to the park,' Lil suggested, trying to get her friend's mind away from happier memories, 'it'd be nice to see all the vegetables they're growing there now as part of the Dig For Victory.'

Posters were being displayed all over the country

exhorting householders to use every bit of available space to grow their own vegetables. Lil had even planted potatoes in the earth covering her Anderson shelter.

But Edie was listless. 'I suppose so,' was her disinterested reply, 'but I'm not sure I want to see it now. Have they taken the lovely ornamental entrance gates away yet for the war effort, like they were threatening?'

'I don't know, Edie. But let's go anyway.'

'They might set us on digging,' Edie said, with a sudden flash of her old humour.

'I wouldn't mind if they did,' Lil laughed. 'It'd be a change from making nets.'

Emile sneaked into the house under cover of darkness. After greeting his parents he gave Beth a swift, brotherly hug. Quickly they told him about the day's events and his face sobered. 'You will have to be careful, Leonie.'

Now, they were all using her cover name all the time; the more they came to think of her by that name, the safer it would be. Now, too, they always called Emile by his Maquis name – Antoine – though his mother still found it difficult. Emile sat down at the table whilst Marthe laid a meal out for him and wrapped more food in a bundle for him to take back to his compatriots hiding in the forest.

'This is what you need to transmit tonight. We are hiding two British airmen who were shot down two nights ago and have managed to evade the Germans and find us. We need them to be picked up as soon as possible and we also need more ammunition.'

'And I need some more radio valves,' Beth murmured,

committing to memory the list that Emile was reeling off.

Before leaving, he went with Beth to the barn in the fields. 'I think this is as safe a place as any, you know. I wouldn't worry about moving it. If they do find it here – as long as it's not whilst you're actually transmitting – you can deny all knowledge of it.'

Beth laughed softly. 'And you think they'd believe that?'

'Probably not,' Emile was forced to agree with a sigh.

'The most dangerous time is when I *am* transmitting. That's when they can pick up the signals.' She paused and then added, 'Antoine – I'm so worried about your parents. Do you really think I should be staying with them? I mean, it's one thing if I get caught, but quite another if they—'

Emile moved towards her in the darkness and she felt his arms slip around her, his lips against her hair. 'They know exactly what they're doing. Believe me, if my father was a younger man and didn't have the farm to run, he'd be out there in the woods with me.'

'But your poor mother. If they were arrested . . .'

'I know, I know,' he whispered. 'But she's tougher than she looks. Just you' – she felt his lips brush her forehead – 'look after yourself.'

And then, almost before she had realized it, he was gone, slipping like a wraith into the darkness.

It was easier – and safer – transmitting at night. There was always the danger that if the Germans did arrive unexpectedly, her absence from the farmhouse in the middle of the night would be difficult to explain. But from the barn she could see even the smallest light coming towards her and, in the stillness of the night, voices and sounds could be heard more clearly and Beth felt it was a risk worth taking. Each time she left the tumbledown building, she peered out cautiously to make sure no one – not even locals – were watching. Then she covered the traces of her visits, scattering dust over the floor to hide her footprints.

She was pleased with the hiding place; she didn't envy those agents in towns or cities where, every minute of the day, they might be discovered or betrayed. Here, Raoul was a respected member of the local community and no one would suspect the burly farmer of harbouring a secret agent. If anything, he was thought to be collaborating just a little too much with the enemy. But most of his neighbours could sympathize; they were in the same position and were obliged to succumb to their invaders' demands or suffer untold consequences. To protect themselves and their families – especially their loved ones – they had to cooperate, even though it hurt their pride to do so.

But some of them did wonder where exactly young Emile Détange had gone. One or two guessed; their sons had also mysteriously left home, bidding a fond farewell, but refusing to say where they were going or what they were going to do. Many had gone away to avoid being sent to Germany to work or even to fight on the Eastern front for the Germans. Many a father envied their son's bravery and many a mother wept with fear.

And Marthe was one of those mothers.

Edie lay alone in the Morrison shelter in her front room listening to the enemy bombers droning overhead. And then the bombing began. At first it was some distance away, but then the planes came nearer and nearer until they sounded as though they were directly overhead. She heard the whine of a falling bomb and then there was a terrific crash, so close that she felt the whole house shake. She screamed, sure that the building was going to fall on top of her.

'Lil! Lil!' she cried, wishing that she had gone into her neighbour's Anderson or that Lil was here beside her. 'Why didn't I get her round here when it started?' she whimpered. More bombs fell, not so close now, but still they were falling on the town.

At last, after what seemed an age, the noise died away and eventually the All Clear sounded. Edie crawled out of the shelter and struggled to the back door. She flung it open and staggered to the gate in the fence.

'Lil! Lil, are you all right?'

'I'm here, Edie. A bit shaken but—' Before she could say any more, Lil found herself enveloped in a bear hug.

'Oh thank God, you're all right. Lil, in future we stay together. I'll come into yours or you into mine. Even when Archie's home. I'm not going through another night like that again, not knowing what's happened to you.'

'I'm all right, duck, honest. Come on, let's get inside and get the kettle on.'

'I must have a look outside first, Lil. I reckon there was at least one bomb fell in our street. I hope Jessie's all right.'

'Come on, we'll go together.'

They emerged from Lil's front door to see a flurry of activity further down the long street.

'It's not near Jessie's. It's the other end.'

'There she is, though, look. Handing out drinks to the rescuers from the mobile canteen. And there's Norma alongside her.' Edie laughed wryly. 'Strange bedfellows this war's caused, Lil.'

'Aye, well, they get along when they're helping others, I'll say that for them.'

'Come on, Lil, we'd better go down and see if we can help.'

Though it was early morning and they hadn't had any breakfast, the two women were fully dressed. 'I'm not being caught in me nightie when there's a raid,' Edie had declared, 'in case I have to be dug out.'

But their help was not needed. 'You go home, Edie love,' Jessie said. 'There's plenty of us here and you look as if you've had a rough night of it yourselves.'

So the two women sat in Lil's living room, drinking tea and trying to calm their nerves.

'It was bad enough, Edie,' Lil said, 'but I reckon those things they're calling butterfly bombs which they dropped on us a month ago were awful weapons. They were sneaky.'

'Anti-personnel bombs, Archie said they're called. They don't go off on landing but wait until someone touches them.'

'Evil, I call it. It's as if they're aiming them at kids, 'cos they'll know youngsters can't resist collecting bits of shrapnel and that.'

'That's why Archie won't hear of Reggie coming home yet,' Edie said dolefully. 'He says he might get in with the kids running riot. We've always let our youngsters play out in the street, but Harry's been telling him that bomb sites are a favourite playground for the local kids now. Them that haven't gone away, that is.' There was a wistful note in her voice as if she almost wished her Reggie was at home to run riot.

'Sorry, Edie, but I agree with him,' Lil said, bravely ignoring Edie's baleful glare.

Edie sighed. 'I know you're both right, but . . .' She bit her lip to stop herself repeating the never-ending lament: I just want them home.

Twenty-Seven

'Jessie and Harry will come to us this year,' Edie declared at the beginning of November, the traditional time when she and Lil started to think about planning for Christmas. 'It was nice last year, I won't deny it, and good of them to cater for all of us, but I don't mind telling you, Lil, it wasn't the same as being here. Norma's not said any more about us going to her, has she?'

Mentally, Edie crossed her fingers. Norma's dismal house was the last place she wanted to spend Christmas.

And it seemed Lil felt the same. 'No – thank goodness. We're like two peas in a pod, you and me, Edie. We like things done our way.'

Edie had the grace to laugh along with her. 'And we like to be in our own home, don't we? But what about Norma? She's welcome to come here, Lil.'

Lil pulled a face but said, 'I'll ask her. Will Shirley get home, d'you think?'

'She doesn't know yet, but she doesn't think so. She says a lot of her friends have younger brothers and sisters at home who they want to see and because she hasn't – I very much doubt that Reggie will come, d'you? – she thought she ought to volunteer to stay there. She says they'll have a merry time of it, anyway, but it's not like being with family.'

Lil was obliged to agree that it was unlikely. She chuckled. 'No doubt she'll get them all playing charades.'

'I shouldn't wonder. Anyway, Archie will be home, so there'll be six of us. It's not a bad number, but there'll be no young ones to liven us up.'

'Oh, your Jessie will do that, duck, don't you worry. And you could ask Ursula.'

'Mm.' Edie was thoughtful. 'I haven't seen her lately. She doesn't call round so much now Shirley's not here.'

'Maybe she's made some other friends.' Lil paused and then sighed. 'I just wish little Tommy could be home for Christmas, but Irene is adamant they're staying put.'

'One thing we know is that Christmas 1943 is going to be the toughest yet, Lil,' Edie moaned.

'It's to be expected. I know the war's only been going four years, but it's the fifth Christmas and the shortages are really biting now. Do you think Mr Schofield will bring us a bird or two?'

'I do hope so, though we mustn't expect it, Lil. But just in case he does, I've got the presents ready for him to take back to the family. I've knitted Reggie a scarf to keep him warm when he's out in the fields from an old fisherman's woolly of Archie's. There was plenty of wool in it for me to make a muffler for Tommy too and a little knitted waistcoat.'

Lil chuckled. 'I'm not surprised. Archie's a big feller. I've not had a lot of time to make owt, but I've managed to pick up a few bits and pieces through the year that I've put on one side. And I've got a calendar to send to Irene. She can mark off the days to them coming home. Let's hope it'll be this year, Edie.'

'Amen to that, Lil.'

*

Joe Schofield arrived once again on Edie's front doorstep on Christmas Eve bearing a goose and two rabbits.

'Things aren't easy, missis, not even in the countryside now. The longer this war's going on, the harder it's getting even for us. Any road up, we killed a pig a fortnight ago and I've brought you some sausages and brawn. I'm just sorry there's no turkey or chickens for you.'

Edie almost snatched the food out of his hands before she remembered her manners and invited the big man in. 'It's wonderful, Mr Schofield . . .'

'Joe, missis, please.'

'Joe, then. I don't know how to thank you.'

Joe shrugged. ''Tis the least we can do. Besides, we've got your family. It's a poor exchange, we know that, but we do love having them and we're trying to do our best so's they're not so homesick at Christmas. The missis is planning quite a party. She's invited a few RAF lads from the nearby camp again – those that live too far away to get home. So I reckon we'll be making merry and it'll be nice for the youngsters.'

'That sounds lovely,' Edie said, but she couldn't help feeling a pang of envy that strangers would have her family with them at Christmas and she would not.

As they all sat round Edie's table on Christmas Day, the conversation passed from one topic to another, but always seemed to come back to the one that was upper-most in everyone's mind; the war and its consequences for them all.

Shirley had managed to wangle a seventy-two-hour pass at the last minute and had arrived home very late on Christmas Eve. There hadn't been much time for conversation the previous evening, so Edie asked now, 'Did you have a long way to travel?'

'Now, Mam, you know I can't tell you things like that.'

'Oh, surely,' Ursula, sitting beside her, said, 'you can tell your own family?'

Shirley laughed. 'But you might put it in the paper. You might decide to write a feature on how a local girl has joined the ATS and what she's doing. And then you'd get me arrested.'

Ursula turned a bright pink as she said in a hurt tone, 'I would never do that. I would never do anything that could harm you or your family. You are my friend.'

'I was only teasing, Ursula. Don't take on so. But seriously, we do have to be very careful, so I find it's best to say nothing and then I know I haven't let the cat out of the bag.'

Ursula frowned. 'Cat? What is this cat?'

'It's just a saying, duck,' Edie said. 'It means to let out a secret.'

'Oh. I see. Sometimes, I do not understand your quaint sayings.'

'I'd like to make a toast,' Harry said, trying to alleviate the awkward moment. 'Raise your glasses, ladies and gentlemen, because I believe 1944 is the year when something momentous is going to happen that will bring an end to the war. Oh, I'm not saying it'll happen just like that –' he snapped his fingers – 'but, to follow on from Mr Churchill's words after the victory at El Alamein, when he said it was perhaps the end of the beginning, well, this year, I believe, it really could be the beginning of the end.'

'I'll drink to that, Harry,' Archie said. 'We all will.'

Eagerly, they raised their glasses and drank to Harry's hopes.

As he put down his glass, Archie glanced across the table at Ursula. The girl had not drunk the toast with the rest of them, had not even raised her glass to her lips. Instead, she sat with her eyes downcast, twisting the wine glass round and round in her fingers, just watching the swirling red liquid.

When Emile visited the farm in the middle of the night four days into the New Year, he had grave news. He came on the motorcycle, which he left some distance away from the farm, but he was still dressed in a German uniform. 'I rode straight through a road block on the way here, shouting at them to open it up quickly because I was on urgent business for the Führer.' He laughed. 'That name is like an "open sesame" even here in the middle of France.' Then his expression sobered. 'But I've been incredibly lucky not to have been stopped before now, especially as I've come to tell you that we think one of our group – Julien – has been arrested.'

They were all sitting in the kitchen in their night-clothes, apart from Emile, of course. Marthe roused the fire and made a hot drink.

Raoul raised his eyebrows. 'Julien Lafarge? The son of the baker in the town?'

Grimly, Emile nodded. 'He went home for the New Year. We warned him not to go, but he feels the cold more than the rest of us. He wanted just a few nights in the warmth of his own bed and to see his parents, of course.' He shrugged helplessly. 'And now . . .'

'Do you know for certain?'

'We're almost sure. Bruce heard the commotion in

the middle of the night of New Year's Day. They broke the shop window and forced their way upstairs to the living quarters.'

'What about Bruce?' Beth gasped. 'Is he safe?'

'For the moment. Thankfully, they were only concerned with Julien and, once they found him, didn't think to search the whole house. They didn't even arrest Henri and his wife.'

'Why ever not?'

Emile smiled wryly. 'Henri supplies them with bread and cakes. The Germans aren't fools. Besides, they'd got the man they wanted.'

'Is Bruce still there? Above the shop?'

'Yes, but he's getting ready to leave. I can't tell you where he's going because I don't know. Perhaps you could find out, Leonie? We shall have to be even more careful about having too many contacts. I used to meet with Bruce now and again, but I daren't any more. You'll have to act as courier for us and you must only have Bruce and me as your contacts.'

Beth nodded, twisting her hair around her finger. She felt so sorry for the brave young man, Julien, and for his family, but she was also very anxious for Rob. If he were arrested . . .

'I'll see what I can find out,' she promised.

'Be careful,' Emile whispered, as he kissed her cheek in farewell.

The following morning, as Beth cycled through the village, she could feel a change in the atmosphere. The bad news had travelled fast. There were only one or two people out. Most, it seemed, were clinging to what they thought was the safety of their homes. But the enemy was no respecter of property. They would gain entry by force if they wished. And those who had ventured out, hurried along with their heads bowed as if trying not to attract attention to themselves. Someone from their nearest town had been betrayed, they were sure of it. But by whom, no one knew, and now they all felt vulnerable. Who would be the next to be questioned?

Beth rode along with her head held high and hummed a little tune. She was a sixteen-year-old girl now, who worked on a farm for her uncle and knew nothing about any resistance group. Two road blocks barred her way to the town this morning and there was an unmistakable excitement amongst the guards. They were laughing and joking with each other and, though Beth could not understand very much of what they were saying, she caught the words 'Maquis' and 'arrested' and knew that they were jubilant about Julien's capture.

Beth shuddered for the poor young man.

Henri Lafarge was still behind his shop counter, serving his customers. His face was set in a bland expression, but Beth could see the anguish deep in his eyes. He was terrified for his son. When the shop emptied, Henri gestured upstairs.

'He's up there, collecting the last of his things. Go up, but this is the last time. I want him gone – and you too. I don't want you to visit my shop again.'

Beth nodded, upset by the brusqueness of the man's tone, but she knew it was nothing personal. It was fear – not only for Julien, but also for himself and his wife; they were all at risk.

Beth tapped out the code and Rob opened the door cautiously, closing it swiftly when she had stepped inside. 'You've heard?'

'Only that he's been arrested. Monsieur Lafarge looks awful; his face is grey and the look in his eyes is just terrible, poor man.'

'I know. He's asked me to leave, but I was going anyway. Obviously.'

'Am I permitted to know where?'

'Of course. You'll have to know. About a mile out of town on the road towards Paris, there's a tumbledown cottage in the middle of a small wood that doesn't look as if it's been lived in for years. But best of all, there's a cellar and the entrance to it isn't very noticeable. Besides, I don't think the Germans would search the wood unless they had a reason. I think I'll be fairly safe there.' He smiled wryly. 'As safe as any of us are anywhere.'

'But it'll be awfully cold, won't it?'

'No more so than where Antoine and his compatriots are living. They've got—'

'Don't tell me,' Beth said swiftly. 'I don't want to know. How did you find the cottage?'

'I've been cycling around the local countryside, looking for somewhere suitable in case I ever had to leave here quickly. And now I have to.'

'Let me help you.'

'No, Leonie. Thank you, but we mustn't be seen together. You go home now and I'll be in touch as soon as I can. We'll use the oak tree for a while longer and then I think I'll have to find another drop box. Oh, and can you tell London about Julien?'

Beth nodded and then hugged him swiftly. 'Take care,' she murmured. 'Stay safe.'

As she left, Beth paused in the shop and faced Henri squarely. 'Monsieur Lafarge, I'm so sorry about Julien, but if I stop coming here so abruptly, it will seem strange.

Besides, Madame Détange will still need me to buy bread from you sometimes.'

The poor man ran his hands distractedly through his hair. 'Of course, you are right. I'm sorry. I'm not thinking straight.' He glanced at her with frightened eyes. 'But Bruce is going, isn't he?'

'Oh yes, and he'll only come back here if he really has to.'

Henri nodded. 'Thank you,' he said huskily.

Twenty-Eight

'It's the very devil, in't it, Lil? I don't know where my children are. Oh, I know where Reggie is. He's safe, I suppose, even though I don't like him being away. Shirley won't say where she is even though she must still be in this country. We don't really know where Frank is. Beth seems to have dropped off the face of the earth and I – I don't even know where my poor Laurence is buried.' Her voice broke on the final words and she dabbed at her eyes with the corner of her apron. Lil put her arms around her. It wasn't often that Edie wallowed in self-pity, but on the rare occasions when she did, Lil was always there to comfort her.

'Shirley'll be fine, duck. She's really enjoying herself and it's brought her out of her shell. This war's been a blessing in disguise for your Shirley. She looks great and she's got so much more self-confidence. I'd never have believed it, if I hadn't seen it with my own eyes. And as for Frank, well, I know he's in danger but he's got a lot of mates around him. I'm sure he's going to come through. We've got to believe that, Edie.' She paused, but because the two friends were always honest with one another, she was forced to acknowledge, 'It's your Beth I'm most worried about, if I'm honest. It's just not like her not to write at all. Even the postcards were better than nothing.'

'I know,' Edie wailed, for once giving way to tears.

'And I can't talk to Archie about it. If you so much as mention her name, his face closes up. But I think, secretly, he's worried sick. She was always his favourite.'

'Oh now, don't say that, Edie. Archie loves all his kids just the same.'

'Well, yes, I know that, but there was this special sort of bond between the two of them. It was before you came to live next door, so you won't remember, but he was at home when she was born and he was the first to hold her. I reckon it was something he's never forgotten.'

'Well, I suggest you do try and talk to Archie the next time he's home. Let him know you're feeling just as worried as he is. It might help both of you.'

The beginning of 1944 brought a feeling of expectancy. Like Harry had said, it seemed that people felt, if not actually knew, that this year could be a turning point.

The staff car carrying Kurt and his driver roared into the farmyard, a covered lorry following. It was not the usual truck that came to collect food. Raoul paused as he crossed the yard towards the byre and frowned anxiously. 'What's he doing here?' he muttered to himself. 'It's not the day for collecting anything.'

Beth had gone to the little tumbledown barn to broadcast to London. This was not a good time to have the Germans visit. And when the cover on the back of the lorry was flung back and ten or more soldiers jumped down and began to run in all directions around the yard, searching the outbuildings and even heading towards the farmhouse, Raoul felt his heart leap in alarm. But he managed to maintain a look of puzzlement on his face as Kurt strode towards him. The officer gave a polite little bow, though his face was serious as he said, 'I am sorry for this intrusion, Herr Détange, but my orders are to take the girl back for questioning.'

Raoul swallowed the fear that rose in his throat. 'Questioning? Leonie? Whatever can you want with her? She's only a young girl. If it hadn't been for the war, she'd probably still have been at school.'

Kurt gave a thin smile. 'So we are led to believe, but we have received some information that leads us to think that she may not be all that she seems. Where is she?'

Raoul waved his hand vaguely. 'Somewhere around. I'm not sure where. I don't keep watch on her all the time. She's a good little worker.'

'So, you don't know what she's doing' – he emphasized the final words – 'all the time?'

Raoul faced the man squarely, but his heart was racing and his legs were trembling. 'No, I don't.' He didn't want to be disloyal to Beth – to betray her – but he had others to think of; Marthe, Emile and all the resistance workers who were with his son.

Kurt was issuing orders. 'Search everywhere. All the buildings and then the fields.' He turned back again to the farmer. 'Or is she out cycling?'

Raoul shrugged, managing to stop himself from glancing towards the shed where Beth kept the bicycle she used. He wanted to go to Marthe, wanted to comfort her and, most of all, he wanted somehow to warn Beth. But he couldn't; he couldn't move. His legs wouldn't work and, for a brief moment, he thought he was going to pass out. He passed a hand across his forehead as he watched the soldiers searching his farm and listened to their shouts.

Oh, Beth, run, run.

In the little stone barn in the fields, set close to the sheltering hedge yet with a good view of the slope leading up to it from the farm, Beth finished her transmission and removed her earphones.

It was then that she heard the shouting and looked out of the small opening in the wall to see a line of soldiers, spread out across the width of the field, walking slowly up the slope towards her. And they were carrying guns.

Swiftly, as she had practised so many times, Beth packed the wireless back into its suitcase, pushed it into the hole in the wall and replaced the bricks. She glanced out of the window space again. There was still time to pick up a handful of dust from the floor and spread it over the brickwork so that the hiding place was not easily noticeable. Then she pulled the bales of hay into place and picked up the besom from the corner and whisked it backwards and forwards across the floor, moving to the door as she did so. Flinging the brush into the far corner, she left the shack, squeezed through the hole in the hedge and ran down the slope. Now she was out of sight of the searching soldiers. She slowed her pace. Taking deep breaths, she told herself: Act normally. They'll glance into the shack but you've left no trace that anyone's been there. She looked around her; where was the farm sheepdog who'd followed her up the field? There he was, happily sniffing the hedgerows.

'Jasper,' she called. 'Here, boy.'

She whistled shrilly and the dog looked up, his tongue lolling, then he bounded towards her. She patted his head and pulled gently on his silky ears. 'Now, boy,' she whispered. 'You've got to look after me. Let's play, eh?'

She pulled the ball, chewed with constant wear, that she always carried from her pocket. Jasper gave an excited bark, but she was no longer afraid of the soldiers finding her; in fact, the sound might draw them away from searching in the barn too thoroughly. She threw the ball as far as she could and Jasper raced after it. She laughed aloud and clapped her hands, but out of the corner of her eyes she saw the first soldiers pushing their way through the hedge.

The ball firmly gripped in his strong teeth, the dog was racing back to her to drop it at her feet. Panting heavily, he looked up at her with his soft brown eyes as the soldiers came towards her, pointing their guns at her.

Jasper bared his teeth and growled and one of the soldiers levelled his gun towards the dog.

'No, no, don't. Please don't. He won't hurt you.'

She put her hand on the dog's head and soothed him. The animal looked up at her and she was sure there was a question in his eyes. 'It's all right, boy,' she murmured.

'*Raus*,' the nearest soldier to her said and gestured with the barrel of his gun that she should walk up the field. Beth shrugged, but, deliberately, she turned to her right and began to walk to the gate at the far side of the grass field and away from the barn.

'This way,' another soldier said gruffly in poor French. Beth turned her winning smile on him and said slowly, 'This is the quickest way back to the farmyard.'

And without waiting for him to argue, she set off with Jasper trotting obediently at her side, though her shoulders were tense with fear. At any moment she expected to be shot in the back.

When she arrived in the yard, she avoided meeting Raoul's anxious glance and, smiling, she went straight towards Kurt. 'Hello, Major Hartmann. Have you come for supplies?'

Kurt did not return her smile. Instead, he said abruptly. 'Get into the car, Fräulein, if you please.'

Beth feigned puzzlement, although now she had guessed why he was here.

She shrugged and did as he asked. He climbed into the back seat beside her and his driver started up the engine. She had no time even to say goodbye to Raoul and Marthe. The only one to utter a sound was Jasper, who barked frantically and struggled to chase after the car as it swung out of the gate and roared up the lane. But Raoul held onto him. He knew that the soldiers would not hesitate to shoot his dog.

'It's all right, boy,' he murmured, but in his heart he knew it was anything but 'all right'.

He went into the farmhouse to find his wife waiting for him, tears streaming down her wrinkled cheeks, her apron to her eyes. 'What will happen to her?'

'I don't know,' Raoul said flatly, 'but I fear the worst if – if they torture her. I don't think she'll hold out.' They stared at each other until Marthe whispered hoarsely, 'What about Emile? Can we warn him?'

'Antoine,' he corrected her gently. 'And yes, you're right. Somehow, we must get word to him.'

'But how? You have no idea where he is, have you?' Raoul shook his head.

'And don't trust that lot in the village,' Marthe said,

with sudden strength in her tone. 'I think it's one of them that's said something to the Germans about Leonie. We'll just have to wait until Em— I mean Antoine – comes here again.' It was hard for a mother to rename her only son.

'But he's only just been here – last night – with the message that she was to send this morning.'

'Do you think she got it sent before they found her? It doesn't look as if they found the wireless.'

'We can only hope she got through, because if she did, there should be a drop in a couple of nights and a Lysander to pick up two airmen.'

'And do you know where that is to be?'

Again Raoul shook his head. 'They change it each time. But I might hear the planes coming and I can go out and look.'

Fear shot across Marthe's eyes, but she said nothing. She would not stop Raoul going out after curfew if it was to warn her son, even though she feared for them both. They were all in this fight together and whatever it took, she would help them rid her beloved France of the invaders.

Twenty-Nine

Kurt took her to the town, where the Germans had established their headquarters for the area. Through his shop doorway, Henri Lafarge saw the vehicles roar up to the building across the street and his heart constricted. He still had no idea what had happened to his son. It had been four weeks now since Julien's arrest and he'd heard nothing. Henri believed his son had been taken somewhere else, though where, he didn't know. The soldiers who still came into his shop to buy bread and cakes, when there were any, were pleasant enough and he and his wife had never been questioned. He wondered if Julien, whose codename was Edouard, had been so badly treated that he had broken down under interrogation and had betrayed Leonie.

Henri shuddered. He hoped not; he wouldn't want to think his son had done such a thing, however badly beaten he had been. His mind shied away from imagining what Julien might be suffering. He was amazed that he and his wife had not been arrested too. Apparently, the Germans didn't think to suspect the polite, helpful man they saw most days when buying bread! And yet they knew full well he was Julien's father.

The man stood in his shop doorway. The window, smashed on the night of Julien's arrest, had been boarded up. Henri could no longer display his wares in the window. Not that there was very much to put on show nowadays, he thought morosely. Then he saw Rob cycling down the street and he stepped back into the shadows of his shop, hoping that the agent was not paying him a visit. But Rob leaned his bicycle against the wall, just as Beth had done so many times, and stepped into the shop.

'Bonjour, Monsieur. A loaf, if you please.'

Henri stepped behind his counter, picked up a loaf and then leaned towards Rob. 'She's been arrested.'

Rob, sorting out some change from his pocket, stopped and slowly looked up to meet the other man's gaze. 'Who?'

'The girl who used to come to see you. Leonie.'

The colour drained from Rob's face. 'When?'

'Major Hartmann brought her in about an hour ago.'

Rob was thoughtful for a moment, his mind working quickly.

'I'm going to cycle out to the farm. Perhaps Monsieur Détange will be able to tell me more.'

'You won't get back before the curfew.'

'Don't worry about me. I may stay at the farm or try to get word to Antoine.'

'How much does she know? Many people?'

Rob shook his head. 'Only you and me and Antoine and, of course, the Détanges, where she's staying, but she doesn't know where Antoine is hiding out. He deliberately always visits the farm.'

'But she knows all the messages she's sent – map references and such.'

Rob sighed. 'True.' There was despair and defeat in his tone. He could see the whole circuit, which had been so carefully built up and which had lasted a surprisingly long time in occupied territory, being torn apart with men – and women – being arrested, tortured and possibly shot. He glanced out of the window. Only the sentry posted at the entrance to the building opposite was about. Now was a good time for him to leave whilst there was no doubt great excitement inside that they had a suspect to interrogate. Poor Beth.

Rob handed over the money and picked up the loaf. 'Thank you, Monsieur. I will not come back here again. You are already in danger because of your son's arrest and even more so now, I think.' As he turned to leave, he murmured, '*Bonne chance.*'

'You've brought the girl?'

Two Gestapo officers had arrived from Paris the previous day and had demanded that any suspects in the area should be rounded up for questioning. Beth's name had been suggested – though not by Kurt – and so he had had no choice but to arrest her.

Heinrich Schulze, the senior Gestapo officer, narrowed his pale eyes behind his rimless spectacles. He was a small, thin man with a gaunt face and a cruel mouth. 'And the farmer and his wife? You should have brought them too.'

Kurt said nothing.

Schulze shrugged. 'No matter – for the moment. No doubt she will implicate them under interrogation.'

Kurt frowned and said, 'I'm sure she is innocent. She is only a young girl – nothing more than a schoolgirl.'

'I shall be the judge of that, Hartmann. We shall soon know when she is interrogated.'

Kurt hesitated. He wanted to say more, to try to convince the Gestapo officer that they should go easy on the girl.

'I have watched her closely for months, whenever

we have collected supplies from the farm. And we have searched the farm on two separate occasions and found nothing.'

Schulze's eyes narrowed. 'But you have still not located the place where someone is transmitting – despite, as you say, having searched that area. You will search again, Major Hartmann, whilst we have the girl, and more thoroughly – much more thoroughly.'

Kurt was far from happy. He had been obeying orders in bringing Leonie to their headquarters, but he had hoped that he would be the one to question her and that, after a brief interview, he could return her to the farm. But now that Schulze had taken over, he was afraid for the girl. The Gestapo officer was known for his brutality. He got results, certainly, but his methods were inhuman. Kurt wished fervently that there was some way in which he could help Leonie, but he felt powerless. But then, surprisingly, Schulze gave him an opening.

'Search the farm again and let the old man know that if he cooperates – if he tells you all he knows – it will go better for the girl.'

Kurt left the man's office, eager to return to the farm in the hope that he could find something out that would mean Leonie was innocent. He didn't believe – didn't want to believe – that Leonie could be his enemy. True, over the past few months since he had made the suggestion, she hadn't passed any useful information to him, but that could be because she really didn't know anything. Kurt clung to that hope as he got back in the car and instructed his driver to take him back to the farm. Behind him, the lorry, laden once more with armed soldiers, followed him.

*

'Bring her to my office,' Schulze instructed one of his cohorts. 'We'll see if she's as innocent as Hartmann would like to think.' The older man had seen the look in Kurt's eyes when he was pleading the girl's cause and guessed that the young officer had formed some sort of attachment to her. He sighed. It happened in wartime, of course, when the occupying forces lived amongst the local community, but it was not something he condoned, though he had heard that in some countries German soldiers had been actively encouraged to consort with suitable young women.

Beth was ushered into the office and made to stand in front of the desk. She looked very afraid and, this time, it was not all an act. The man in front of her was everyone's picture of a tough, ruthless Gestapo officer.

'Name?' he snapped.

Over the next few minutes, Beth answered his questions about herself, telling him the cover story that had been learned and rehearsed so well and played out every day. Mentally, she crossed her fingers, hoping that Raoul and Marthe would remember what they were supposed to say. They, too, had rehearsed often during the time that Beth had been with them for she was sure that at some point they would be questioned. They had all prepared for this day, hoping it would never happen and yet being ready for it if and when it did. And now it *was* happening – at least to Beth.

Schulze leaned his elbows on his desk and linked his fingers, staring at her with cold eyes. 'I expect,' he said slowly, 'that all this nonsense you have told me is your cover story. You have been well trained by your superiors in London, I grant you that. Major Buckmaster, is it not, who is charge of F Section?'

Beth stared at him, hoping her surprise at his

263

knowledge did not show on her face. She frowned. Had someone talked? Had he tortured someone from another group to give him such information? Unless, of course, Julien . . .

'I don't know what you are talking about.'

'I think you do. Did you train in Scotland too?'

'I didn't "train" anywhere. I came here to my uncle's farm when my home was bombed and my parents were killed. I told you.'

The man smiled thinly and without any humour reaching his eyes, which remained cold and hard. 'So you did,' he said sarcastically. And then his smile faded. 'But now you had better start telling me the truth. Let's start with their son – Emile Détange. Where is he?'

Beth shrugged. 'I have no idea. I haven't seen him since I arrived. He's away fighting in the war.'

'And on which side do you suppose he is fighting, eh?'

Beth blinked. This was one question she had not foreseen, but she decided to state the obvious. 'For the Free French, I would think, wouldn't you?'

'You mean he's in England?'

'We don't know where he is.'

'You would do better to answer my questions, girl. I have no wish to hurt you but, if I have to, I will.'

'Hurt me?' Beth decided to play the little girl act. 'Why?'

'Because I want the truth.'

'I have told you the truth, I came from Boulogne-Billancourt—' she began again.

'Yes, yes, I know all that, but I don't believe you. I think you are a British Agent dropped by parachute. Have you been carrying messages on your bicycle? Because I know you have been cycling around the countryside, into the village and, occasionally, into the town.

'Only to fetch something for my uncle or aunt.'

'And why would your aunt want you to buy bread from the baker across the street? Doesn't a farmer's wife always bake her own bread?'

'Not when all her flour and yeast have been' – Beth licked her lips, knowing she was being very daring, knowing she might be making the man even more incensed – 'taken.'

His face darkened and a muscle in his temple throbbed visibly, but he could not deny that the farmer's foodstuffs had been raided by his own men. It took a lot to feed all the men in this area and they took freely from the locals and especially from the farms.

There was a long silence in the room and then, with ominous quiet, Schulze said, 'Since you will not co-operate, Krueger here' – he gestured towards a sharp-featured man in Gestapo uniform – 'will have to persuade you . . .'

Thirty

When Raoul saw the car sweep in through the gate again, his heart lifted in relief only to plummet again when he saw that Beth was not in the car. Then the lorry turned in at the gate, halted and the armed soldiers spilled once more into his yard and began yet another search. Watching from the kitchen window, Raoul squeezed his wife's arm gently and whispered. 'Remember the story, Marthe, and her name is Leonie. Her life might depend upon us.' Then he left the house and went out into the yard.

'Major Hartmann,' Raoul asked, 'what exactly is it you hope to find?'

'A wireless set or perhaps British airmen waiting to be picked up.'

Raoul waved his arm encompassing his house and buildings. 'Then search away to your heart's content. You will find nothing and no one here.' Luckily, at the moment, it was true, unless, of course, they decided to search the fields and came across the derelict barn.

Kurt moved closer. 'Schulze is interrogating Leonie. You know what that means, don't you?'

Raoul shook his head sorrowfully.

'He – he' – even Kurt shuddered at the thought of what might, already, be happening to her – 'is a brutal man. Oh, he doesn't do the dirty work himself – he has his minions to do that – but he will order her to be – to be persuaded to talk.'

'But there is nothing Leonie' – deliberately, Raoul used her name, more to remind himself than anything else; he prayed silently that Marthe would be strong enough, that fear would not let her forget the cover story – 'can tell you.'

Kurt stepped closer to him, so close that Raoul could feel the man's breath on his face.

'But what about you, Monsieur? If you tell me the truth, it will go easier – a lot easier – for the girl. In fact, I may be able to get her released immediately.'

For one brief, dangerous moment, Raoul hesitated. But he was careful to keep his face blank. Nothing of the turmoil inside his mind showed on his face. He was terrified for Beth. He had become very fond of the pretty, laughing girl, but he knew that if he were to utter one word of the truth, all their lives would be in danger. Marthe's, Emile's, his own and countless others who worked in the resistance group, to say nothing of the two airmen waiting to be picked up if Beth had managed to send the message. Fortunately, this time they had not come to the farm but were in hiding somewhere with Emile. And, Raoul told himself, Beth had volunteered for this dangerous work. She had known full well what to expect and had done it all the same. He was filled with admiration for her bravery and yet he was also very afraid. But he, too, summoned up his courage as he faced Major Hartmann.

'She is my wife's niece, Major, who has come to stay with us because she has lost her home and the rest of her family. I cannot believe you think she is capable of . . .' He shrugged as if the whole idea was beyond his comprehension. 'Well, I'm not sure what you are thinking.'

'*I* don't think anything,' Kurt said, 'but the Gestapo

believe she could be a British agent and I'm afraid that's what counts.'

Grimly, Raoul nodded and, his tone laced with sarcasm, added, 'And you are only obeying orders.'

'Of course,' Kurt said.

There was a long pause whilst the two men stared at each other, like two boxers at the start of a contest, but it was the German who looked away at last with a sigh. 'Very well, if you are determined to be obstinate, there's nothing more I can do. I was only trying to help Leonie.'

Raoul remained very still, his face impassive, but his heart was beating faster than normal as the major glanced towards the house. 'Perhaps,' he said softly, 'your wife would be more co-operative.'

Fear sliced through Raoul like a knife, but from a reserve of strength and courage that even he hadn't known he possessed, he managed to say, 'You can talk to her, of course. Please come in. No doubt she will make you something to eat whilst' – he glanced around at the soldiers tearing his farm apart once more; even now they were clomping through the farmhouse with their heavy boots – 'your soldiers finish their searching.'

Kurt hesitated a brief moment. The elderly man was surprisingly calm. Was he a very good actor or did he really have nothing to fear? Kurt wanted to believe the latter. He wanted – more than anything – to believe in Leonie's innocence.

To Raoul's surprise, Kurt was surprisingly calm and almost gentle with Marthe, keeping the conversation light and talking to her just as a guest in her kitchen might do. Perhaps, Raoul thought shrewdly, the man thought the soft approach would work better with the frightened woman. Marthe could not hide her fear like her husband could, but Raoul hoped that the officer would think her anxiety was natural when enemy soldiers were tramping through her house and flinging her possessions everywhere.

'Your niece? She is the child of your sister or brother?'

Marthe shook her head and for a brief moment, Raoul saw the look of triumph light the officer's eyes. But Marthe spoke surprisingly calmly though Raoul could see her hands were shaking. 'No,' she said and Raoul held his breath, 'it goes back a generation further. I was an only child.' This Raoul knew to be the truth and the advice when concocting a cover story was always to use the truth when possible. Marthe managed to smile at the German as she pushed a plate containing two small portions of bread and cheese towards him. 'Please help yourself, Major.' Then she sat down on the opposite side of the table and went on. 'We had lost touch with that side of my family – until Leonie appeared – but according to her, we have the same grandparents on my mother's side.

'And you believe her?'

Marthe looked at him squarely now. 'Oh yes, she knew so much about the family. I doubt she could have found all that out.'

Careful, Marthe, Raoul was thinking. Marthe was feeling more confident now, but even that frightened Raoul. Don't say *too* much, he was willing her.

'And she's lost all her immediate family?'

'So it seems.'

'Where did she live?' His tone had sharpened a little.

'In Boulogne-Billancourt.'

'Yes – yes, I know that, but where – exactly?'

Marthe shrugged. 'I have no idea. Like I say, we'd lost touch. I just know her home was bombed.'

'If all her family were killed,' Kurt asked reasonably enough, 'why wasn't she hurt?'

'She wasn't at home when it happened.'

'Ah.'

After a few more minutes, Kurt left the house, signalled to his soldiers that they were done here, got into his car and was driven away.

Raoul put his arms around his wife, who was still shaking. 'You did very well, my love, but you do realize they will be back, don't you? Maybe again and again.'

Against his chest she nodded, but clung to him, gaining strength from him.

They were still standing like that, comforting each other, when a soft knock came at the back door.

Marthe looked up. 'Emile?' she whispered. Raoul smiled and stroked her hair. 'Antoine,' he reminded her gently. 'I don't think so – not in daylight – but I'll see.'

He opened the door to a stranger, for he didn't know Rob, so tight was the security followed by the circuit.

Rob glanced over his shoulder before saying, 'May I come in?'

'Of course, but just give me a moment.' Raoul turned away and went back into the kitchen but left the back door open.

'Marthe, there's a stranger asking to come in,' he whispered. 'Be careful what you say. He may be working for the Germans.' He returned to the door and invited Rob into the kitchen.

'You are our second visitor of the day. We have just had the Germans searching our farm. What they hope to find, I have no idea. Marthe, please give the gentleman a cup of coffee. Well, it's not really coffee,' Raoul added with a grimace. 'It's a mixture made from chicory. Once, Monsieur,' he added sadly, 'I could have offered you wine. But not any more. *They* have taken it all. Now, how can I help you?'

'My name is Bruce and I am Leonie's contact.'

Rob sat down at the table and began to drink the hot liquid thirstily. 'I saw the Germans here, so I've been hiding in your field until they left. I know Leonie's been taken to their headquarters in Beauvoir and I need to get a message to Antoine urgently.'

'I'm sorry. I don't know who you're talking about. Yes, Leonie lives here with us. She is my wife's niece, but I don't know anyone called Antoine.'

For a moment Rob stared at them and then nodded slowly and sighed. 'Of course, you are quite right to be cautious. I could be working for the Germans. I am not, but I don't know how to convince you.'

'We live in dangerous times, Monsieur, and we don't know who to trust and who not to,' Raoul said. 'Even people in the village and in the town, whom I thought I knew – counted some of them as friends before the war – are no longer to be trusted. We keep ourselves to ourselves. Luckily, living on a farm, we can almost be self-sufficient, even though,' he added bitterly, 'the Germans take most of our food.'

'Please don't worry any more about it,' Rob said, standing up. 'Thank you for the coffee.'

From the back door of the farmhouse, Raoul and Marthe watched the young man retrieve his battered bicycle from behind a hedge and pedal away in the opposite direction to the village and the town.

'You know, Marthe, he could have been genuine, but I couldn't take the risk.'

'It's strange he didn't ask any more questions. I think if he'd been German he would have pushed a bit harder.'

'Mm,' Raoul pondered, feeling guilty now that he

hadn't helped the young man. 'And another thing – his French was perfect but he spoke it like the British do, not like the Germans. Ah well, better to be safe than sorry.'

Raoul closed the door on what he hoped would be the last visitor of the day.

Thirty-One

Krueger took Beth to a small cell-like room, deep in the cellars of the Town Hall where the Germans had made their headquarters. They were quite alone – no one was there to witness whatever was to take place. And Beth knew, by the satisfied smirk on the man's face, that something unpleasant was surely going to happen.

'Sit,' he commanded. Beth was trembling as she sat in the single chair in the centre of the room under a bright light.

In broken English the man said, 'You will tell me the names of the circuit you belong to or I will be obliged to hurt you.'

Beth frowned, shook her head and shrugged. Krueger repeated his request in German and this time, Beth genuinely did not understand him. At last he spoke in very poor French to which she replied in French. 'I don't know what you or the other man are talking about. I've told you who I am, where I'm from and how I came to live with my uncle and aunt.'

He struck her across the left side of her face so swiftly that she was unprepared for the blow, which knocked her off her chair. 'You will answer my questions.'

Still playing the part of a young girl, Beth began to cry, though now her tears were real. The side of her face was still stinging and she wondered if he had broken her jaw.

He stopped and dragged her upright and pushed her back into the chair. 'We've seen you riding around the countryside on your bicycle. You must be carrying messages.'

'No, no, I'm not. I go to the village and the town on errands for my aunt.'

'You should have everything you need on the farm. There should be no need for you to go anywhere – unless it is to act as a courier.'

At least, she thought, he doesn't think I'm the wireless operator. Bravely, and perhaps foolishly, she said, 'Supplying the Germans takes all our resources. We run short of necessities sometimes.'

The retort earned her another blow across the face but this time she was prepared for it.

'I don't believe you and I think you could be the one transmitting from this area. We know there is someone.'

Beth's heart sank, but now she decided she could play the dumb schoolgirl. 'I don't know what you mean. Major Hartmann asked me the same thing, but I don't understand. What sort of wireless is it? Uncle hasn't got a wireless.'

'Don't play the stupid girl with me, because I think you are older than you are pretending to be. Eighteen or nineteen at least. You must be, to have been trained and sent out here.'

Beth's tears flowed faster, her acting powers coming to her aid, but it seemed Krueger was not to be convinced. He squatted down in front of her, so that his cold eyes were on a level with hers. 'You will tell me what I want to know or else you will suffer great pain and then you *will* tell me.' He licked his lips almost as if he was hoping she would still refuse. He was clearly savouring the thought of torturing her.

Beth shook her head, the tears running down her face. 'I don't know anything.'

He stood up again, towering over her. 'Take off your shoes and those ridiculous childish socks.' As she obeyed, Krueger pulled a pair of pliers from his pocket. Again, he squatted in front of her and took hold of her left foot. 'You have one last chance.'

Beth stared at him but said nothing.

Krueger pushed the pliers beneath the nail of her big toe and pulled.

In the offices above, Kurt heard her screams and shuddered.

When Beth came to – she had fainted at the excruciating pain – she found she was still in the little cell lying on a filthy mattress on the floor with a rough blanket thrown over her. But she was alone. Three nails had been pulled from her left foot and her toes were bleeding, the pain throbbing through her whole being. She sat up and buried her head in her knees. She had not been given any water either to drink or to bathe her injured foot. She had no idea how long she'd been unconscious or what time it was now. All she could think about was, had she said anything? Had she given anything away? Were the Germans at this moment scouring the countryside to find Emile and his compatriots? And what about Monsieur and Madame Détange? Were they safe or had she in her agony – for agony it had certainly been – betrayed them? And had they found the wireless? She glanced around the small cell searching for her shoes, in the heel of one of them was secreted the cyanide pill.

It saddened her to think that she would have to end

her life in this filthy cell. She would never feel Emile's arms around her again or hear his voice; she would never go home to Grimsby, to smell the sea and watch for her father's ship coming home or see the members of her family ever again. But she had volunteered for this dangerous game and if it meant the saving of others, the Détanges, Emile and all those in the circuit, then she must . . .

But her shoes were missing.

Now, as terror flooded through her, the door opened and Krueger entered. He stood a moment gazing down at her. 'You are a very foolish girl to resist. It will only result in yet more pain if you do not tell us what we want to know.'

Beth breathed a sigh of relief. It sounded as if she had given nothing away. But what if . . .?

He crossed the floor and pulled her upright. 'Come, he has more questions for you.' He half dragged, half carried her up the steps and along corridors to Schulze's office. She thought she saw a glimpse of Kurt in one of the rooms they passed by, though in her suffering she could not be sure of anything, but her resolve remained strong. She must say nothing.

'Sit down, Leonie.' Schulze's voice was almost kind. 'I am sorry we have had to treat you this way, but we now have proof that you are some kind of agent. We have found the cyanide pill in the heel of your shoe. So, now it would be better for you if you talk.' He leaned forward, resting his arms on his desk as he said quietly, but menacingly, 'Krueger can be even more cruel than he already has been and now we know you are not telling us the truth.' He spread his hands in a helpless gesture as if the decision was totally out of his hands and in hers.

Despite the dreadful pain, Beth was still able to think clearly, to rationalize. She would bluff it out to the end, to the *very* end.

'Now, shall we begin?' Schulze said smoothly.

Beth stared at him, meeting his steely gaze with a calmness that she certainly wasn't feeling inside. But she said nothing. She could no longer deny the presence of the pill hidden in her shoe and its implications. She could no longer deny being some kind of agent, but now she would say nothing. Whatever they did to her she would not speak.

After several minutes of questioning, Schulze shook his head, pretending sadness. 'I am disappointed in you, Fräulein.' He glanced up at Krueger waiting near the door. 'You had better try again, and – if this fails' – he looked back at Beth – 'we will have no alternative but to put you against a wall and shoot you as a spy.'

Beth shivered, but still she said nothing.

Krueger's treatment of her over the next few hours was brutal. He whipped her naked back, leaving inflamed wheals on her skin. He pulled out the remaining two toenails on her left foot and he subjected her to the 'water treatment', taking her almost to the point of drowning.

But in all that time, though she screamed in pain and gasped for breath, still she said nothing.

At last she was left alone in the cell, bleeding and sore and aching in every part of her tortured body. She lay curled up on the mattress, exhausted but unable to sleep for the pain.

She guessed it must be night now, for no one came near her. She had been given water, which she'd drunk thirstily, and food which she did not touch. She feared some kind of drug that would make her talk. She had to risk drinking the water for her throat was parched.

Through a haze of weariness, she heard the door open quietly and someone step into the room. She braced herself to be dragged from the floor, but someone was bending over her and whispering.

'Leonie, it's me. Kurt. I've come to help you. I must get you out of here. They are going to kill you if you do not talk.'

She wanted to say, 'They'll kill me anyway', but she had vowed to remain silent. This could be another of their insidious tricks; getting someone she knew to work on her with kindness.

'Can you stand?' Kurt held out his hand and helped her to her feet. 'We must be very quiet. Not a sound. I have a car outside in the backyard, but we have to get past the sentry. If we are stopped, I shall say I have orders to take you to Bourges for further questioning. You understand?'

Dully, Leonie nodded. No doubt the torture would be even more ruthless wherever he was taking her.

In the dim light from the lamp he had brought, he glanced down and saw her bleeding foot. 'You poor girl,' he murmured and picked her up in his arms, carrying her out of the cell, up the stairs and along corridors to the courtyard at the back of the huge building. A sentry was posted outside the door. He stared at the major for a moment, but did not challenge his superior as Kurt placed Beth tenderly in the back seat of his staff car and then got into the driver's seat himself. As he started the engine, the sentry stepped forward.

'Would you like me to wake your driver, Major Hartmann?'

Kurt shook his head. 'No, let the man sleep. This is something I must do myself. Orders, you understand.'

'Of course.' The man stepped back and saluted, 'Heil Hitler!'

'Heil Hitler,' Kurt murmured half-heartedly as the car began to move.

In the back seat Beth rested her head against the leather upholstery and closed her eyes. Wherever he was taking her, she had no strength left to resist.

They travelled for some distance and then, through her semi-conscious state, she felt the car stop and heard him turn off the engine. She was aware of Kurt getting out of the car and walking a short distance and then banging on a door. Somewhere close by, a dog began to bark. After several minutes, the door opened and she heard him say, 'I have brought Leonie back. You must get her away from here – into hiding – at once. When they find out she has gone, they will scour the countryside for they have proved she is an agent. They found a suicide pill in her shoe but she has refused to talk, hence the brutality inflicted upon her.'

And then relief and amazement flooded through her as she heard Raoul's voice. 'Bring her in.'

She felt herself lifted and carried into the farmhouse and set gently in Raoul's chair at the side of the range.

'*Mon Dieu!*' the older man exclaimed. 'What have they done to her?'

'They are vicious thugs. I want you to know I have had no part in this. I believed in her innocence and I thought they would just question her and believe her too. It seems I was wrong – on both counts. I think, Monsieur,' his voice cracked a little, 'I have allowed my heart to rule my head.' Now he turned from Raoul and looked down at Beth. 'I don't know how much you and

279

your wife are involved, but you should expect a visit. Very soon.'

'We are not involved. We didn't know any of this. We believed that she was my wife's niece.' If Leonie could stand such torture, then he would do no less, though he feared for Marthe.

The two men regarded each other solemnly and Raoul could see that the younger man did not believe him. 'Even so,' Kurt said slowly, 'I fear you would not be believed. Perhaps you and your wife, too, should go into hiding, if you can.'

Raoul shrugged. 'I have my farm to run. Your men need to be fed.' Perhaps, he was thinking, he could get Marthe to go away, but he doubted it. If the Germans thought about it, they would lose so much by leaving the farm unattended. Perhaps that would save them both. But not Leonie. They must get her away as soon as possible. Thank goodness Emile had chosen this very night to visit. He was upstairs at this very moment. He had hidden in the attic when they heard Kurt's knocking.

'Perhaps you are right. I will see what I can do, but don't count on it.' Kurt smiled wryly. 'I rather think I am going to be in some trouble myself after this night's work.'

Raoul was sure of it as he led the way to the back door and stood watching as the German officer climbed back into his car and drove away. Raoul believed that was the last time they would ever see Major Kurt Hartmann.

The sound of the car's engine faded into the night and, after a few minutes of complete silence save for the soft hooting of an owl, Raoul closed the back door and went back to Beth. She was lying hunched in his chair, her face deathly white, her eyes closed. He shook his head sadly and went to tell Emile that it was safe to come down. Marthe was waiting anxiously at the bedroom door, a shawl around her shoulders. Swiftly, Raoul explained what had happened.

Marthe gave a soft cry and covered her mouth with a trembling hand. 'I must go to her.'

Whilst Marthe gently bathed Beth's wounds and bandaged her foot, which was still oozing blood, Raoul and Emile discussed in soft voices what could be done. 'I knew she'd been taken. Bruce told me. He risked everything by coming to our hideout.'

'So he was genuine. He came here, but I didn't know what to think.'

Emile, his gaze never leaving Beth's face, nodded. 'He was – is – working with us but you weren't to know. You did the right thing, Papa.'

It had been a long time since Raoul had heard his son utter his name and a lump rose in his throat. He put his hand on the younger man's shoulder and squeezed it. And he watched his son as he stood looking down at Beth. There was such a mixture of conflicting emotions on Emile's face; anger against the perpetrators of such heinous treatment, anxiety at what might still happen to all of them, and love – yes, love – for this courageous girl.

At last, Emile dragged his gaze away from Beth as he said, 'I'll take her with me.'

'But she can't walk.'

'Then I'll carry her as far as the motorcycle,' Emile said fiercely, then, more gently, he added, 'but what are you and Maman going to do?'

Before Raoul could answer, Marthe said determinedly, 'Stay here, of course. What else should we do? If we flee, we shall look guilty. If we stay, they might believe us that we were ignorant of what Leonie was doing.'

'They might question you.'

'Huh!' Marthe gave an unladylike snort. 'They think too much of their bellies to risk losing the provider of their food.'

'There are other farms,' Emile said, playing the Devil's advocate.

'Not as good as ours,' Marthe declared vehemently.

The two men smiled at each other, surprised at Marthe's display of determination. She had always been such a gentle, reserved woman, but it seemed she possessed an inner strength that had not needed to show itself before this desperate hour.

'We'll be all right,' Raoul said. 'You just take care of this poor girl here.'

'I will.'

'What do you want me to do about the wireless?'

Emile thought for a brief moment before saying, 'Leave it where it is for the moment. If they come back and search more thoroughly, they may find it, but if they do, then they might believe that you genuinely knew nothing about what Leonie was doing. If you move it, it propounds your involvement.'

Raoul nodded.

'If nothing happens for a few days, I will bring two armed men with me one night and retrieve it.'

Again, Raoul nodded.

Emile turned and clasped his father's hands and then embraced his mother. His voice was husky as he said, 'You realize I may not be able to visit for some time. They may well be watching the farm from now on.'

The three of them stood together for a moment before Marthe, ever practical, said, 'Food. You must have some food before you go', and she began to hurry towards her larder, but Emile put up his hand. 'No time, Maman. I daren't risk staying here any longer and there's a long way to go.'

His parents had no idea where Emile and his compatriots were hiding or how far away it was. It was better that they did not know.

'What about taking my wheelbarrow? We can put blankets in the bottom to make it softer for her,' Raoul suggested, but Emile shook his head. 'No, I must take nothing that could lead them back here if they catch us. Now, we must go.'

Beth roused sufficiently to understand that Emile was taking her away. Through swollen lips, she whispered her thanks to the elderly couple. Emile picked her up tenderly, but she winced and let out a little cry of pain.

'I'm sorry, my darling,' Emile murmured against her hair, and hearing his endearment his parents glanced at each other. In better times, how happy they would be to hear such words, but now . . .

Thirty-Two

'She'd have been better off stopping at home instead of gallivanting off to join the FANYs. She could have found herself a nice young feller, got married and had a barrowload of bairns of her own by now. Where can she be, Lil? We've not had word from her for ages. Not even so much as a postcard now. I'm worried sick, I don't mind telling you. It's not like Beth at all. Now, if it had been Shirley who'd gone off and never bothered to write home, I could have understood it, yet she writes regular as clockwork every week. And long, newsy letters too, just like the ones you'd *expect* to get from Beth.'

'What about Reggie? Does he write?'

Edie pulled a face. 'Now and again, but you know what lads are like and, when he does, it's all about how wonderful Mr and Mrs Schofield are.'

'That's better than him writing to say how miserable he is, isn't it?'

'I suppose,' Edie said, fretfully. 'Yes, of course it is. I'm being selfish, I know I am, and there's only you I can talk to like this, Lil. I can't even say this sort of thing to Archie, but you understand, don't you? I just want them all back *home*.'

'I know, Edie, I know, and so do I, but we've just got to be patient. We're not alone in this, you know.'

'Of course, I know, Lil. I've already lost one son and

you think I don't know? Oh, I'm sorry, I shouldn't snap at you of all people, but I'm so worried about all of them, to say nothing of Archie out at sea. It's always been dangerous work – fishing – but it's even worse now.'

Lil knew that only too well, but she said nothing and changed the subject. 'Have you got your floors done, Edie? Friday's your floor day, isn't it? Like me.'

'Aye, I'd done 'em all by eight o'clock this morning, Lil. I'd nowt else to do.'

'Right, then, we'll go down to the WVS this afternoon, if you've nothing else on. I'm sure they could use an extra half a day from the two of us. There's still a lot of folks who've been bombed out needing help. Jessie said the other day they were expecting a delivery of clothing. That will need sorting out, if nowt else.'

Emile carried Beth for miles, over rough terrain and up and down hills, stopping every so often to rest and to listen for any sounds that might indicate a search party scouring the countryside for the missing prisoner. Perhaps, with luck, her escape would not be discovered until the morning. But what, Emile, wondered, would happen to the German officer who had helped her?

He carried her away from the Loire valley where the river flowed serenely on, unaware of the conflict close to its shores. As dawn spread across the fields, Emile reached a safe house a good distance away from his father's farm. Still there was a long way to go. Luckily, he had left his motorcycle here the previous night and walked the rest of the way to see his parents. Some instinct had made him be extra cautious. Leaving Beth with the parents of one of the members of the resistance group, he roared off on his machine, coming at last to the wooded area. He negotiated the curving paths through the forest to where he and his friends had their hideout. They'd been fortunate in finding two deserted woodmen's cottages, in the very middle of the wood, which they used as their base.

Swiftly, he explained what had happened and said, 'Pierre, she is with your parents but we must get her away as quickly as possible. The Germans will be scouring the countryside. They know she is an agent, but I don't know what she has told them, if anything.'

Pierre looked anxious. 'You're going to bring her here?'

'Where else can I take her?'

'But if she has told them anything . . .'

'There's nothing she could tell them that could endanger us. She doesn't know where our hideout is.'

An older man touched Pierre's arm. 'She is a brave woman, Pierre, who has done much to help us. We can do no less than come to her aid now. Perhaps we can get a message to London somehow and they can pick her up.'

Pierre capitulated at once. 'I'm sorry, Antoine of course we must help her. I – I am just so afraid for our organization. It has worked so well – until now.'

'Thanks to Leonie,' Emile said softly and Pierre muttered, 'Yes, you're right. I'm sorry.'

Emile touched the man's shoulder and said, 'Would you drive the truck for me?' He smiled. 'You understand its temperamental ways much better than I do.'

When the young men had taken to the forest, Pierre's father had given them an old truck to take with them. Pierre was a good mechanic and he kept it in reasonable repair, but because of its age and the difficulty in getting new parts for it, it was unreliable. They set out, Pierre driving the noisy vehicle and two men sitting in the back armed with shotguns.

'If we're caught,' Pierre muttered, 'we're done for.'

Emile's face was grim and he remained silent, for he knew that his friend was right. But when the three men with Emile saw the injuries inflicted on Beth, their resolve hardened and they forgot all about any concern for their own safety.

'They will pay for this,' Pierre murmured. 'One day, we will make them pay.'

'I agree, my friend, but for the moment we must get her to safety.'

Luckily, there were two doctors amongst their number, Jewish men who had fled for their lives. Now, they cared for the resistance fighters and the Allied airmen who'd been shot down as well as rescuing their fellow Jews and sending them down the escape route whenever they could. Now the two young men tended Beth.

'You say the Germans have discovered she's an agent?'

Emile nodded bleakly. 'They found the cyanide pill hidden in the heel of her shoe.'

'Do you think she told them anything?'

'The German who took her back to the farm told my parents she had said nothing.'

'And you trust him?' the doctor asked sarcastically.

Emile pulled a wry face.'

'Have you heard from Bruce?'

'Not since he came here to tell us about Leonie.' Still Emile referred to her by her code name. It was safest that his men should know her only by that name.

'If she has given anything away, it'll be him they look

for first and then probably you, Antoine.' Even here, they all used each other's code names.

'The only information she could have given them was about my parents, of course, but the Germans already knew she was living there and they'd naturally suspect them. And Bruce, who was her contact in the town, Monsieur Lafarge and his bakery, where Bruce lodged, and the drop box in the tree. And me.'

'And, of course,' added Gaston, the elder of the two doctors, 'the map references for our dropping zones.'

'If she could remember them, yes, I suppose so.' Emile sighed. 'Well, we'll soon know one way or another.'

The members of the resistance group hiding in the woodland, twenty-three in all, kept watch for the next two days, curtailing their activities until they were sure that Beth had given nothing away. Her recovery was slow and painful but the doctors assured Emile that no lasting damage had been done.

'There's nothing broken,' Gaston told him, 'though she's badly bruised from head to foot. The worst injury is where they've pulled all the toenails from her left foot. That must have been agony.'

'Has she said much yet?'

Gaston shook his head. 'Manny' – he referred to the other doctor – 'and I decided to give her a sedative to help her sleep and keep her free from pain for a while.'

'But we need to know if—' he began, but Gaston interrupted ominously, 'You'll know soon enough, my friend.'

After two days, Emile and the others began to feel that perhaps they were safe. Four nights after he had brought Beth away from the farm, he went back accompanied by two members of the group armed with rifles. Carefully, they approached the farm and tapped on the back door. It was opened in only a few moments; Raoul must have been waiting for them.

'Has anything happened?'

The old man shook his head. 'Not as far as the Germans are concerned. They've not even been back here. But I have an airman above the pigsty. Two nights ago, I heard a plane in the distance that sounded as if it was in trouble. When I went outside I saw a white parachute in the moonlight. Jasper found him.' Raoul sighed. 'He was the only one to get out. The plane crashed some miles away, so I don't think they thought to look for anyone here.'

'That was a bit dangerous, Papa, when the farm might be searched any minute.'

Raoul shrugged with a typical Gallic gesture. 'What could I do? He was lost and very afraid.'

'We've come for the wireless set, but I've no wireless operator now. Leonie's not well enough yet. Besides, we don't want her transmitting from our hideout. Their detection equipment would soon track us down.'

'The man who came here – Bruce, was it? – could he transmit from here if you leave it for a little longer?'

Emile pondered the problem. He'd wanted to remove the wireless set, to get rid of any evidence that would implicate his parents, but there was the airman to think of now.

'I'm surprised they've not found it,' he murmured.

'They nearly did one day when Leonie was transmitting, but she saw them and led them away. They were so busy chasing her that they didn't think to check the barn. That was the same day they arrested her.'

'If you're sure you want to take the risk, Papa, I'll get a message to him. Tell him to come here.'

Raoul nodded. 'I'll show him where the wireless is – if

he can operate it, that is – then he can come and go as he needs to. He won't even need to come to the farm each time and we can deny all knowledge if he's caught.'

'Won't you and Maman come with me? You'd be much safer. You've done enough already and I fear for Maman – for both of you.'

Raoul shook his head. 'If that lovely girl can take that sort of punishment and not say a word, then we can do no less.' He smiled fondly. 'Your mother is showing a courage that not even I knew she possessed. No, don't worry about us, my son, just take care of yourself – and Leonie.'

Rob came to the farm the following day. 'I am a trained wireless operator,' he told the farmer and his wife as he sat in their kitchen. He was about to tell them that he and Beth had trained together and then he stopped himself. The less anyone knew, the better, as recent events had proved. They were all now sure that Beth had given no information away, though she had suffered terribly for her bravery. Rob, however, had other news from the town.

'The German officer who helped Leonie escape has been arrested. He will be court martialled and most likely shot by firing squad as a traitor to his country.'

'How did they find out it was him?'

'Apparently, there was a sentry on duty when he took Leonie out to his car behind the Town Hall. He didn't question it at the time and they didn't find out she was missing until the next morning, which gave you time to get her to safety. But when the hullaballoo started, the sentry realized that Major Hartmann had not been acting under orders and he told his superiors what he knew. So, Hartmann most certainly saved her life at the expense of his own.'

Quietly, Raoul said, 'I think he was in love with her. That's why he did it.'

'Poor man,' Marthe murmured. 'I've always believed that the ordinary German people don't want to be at war any more than we do. It's just the Nazis.'

'I'm sure you're right, Madame,' Rob agreed as he got up. 'And now, Monsieur, if you will show me where the wireless set is hidden, I won't need to come to the farm any more. It would be safer.'

Raoul led him up the field with Jasper at his heels. The dog was restless, looking around him as if searching for something or someone.

'I think he's missing Leonie,' Raoul said. 'We all are.'

Rob said nothing, but he was thinking about the merry, clever girl he had known through training and more recently here as his wireless operator and courier and now she was lying hurt, viciously beaten by ruthless men. His resolve to continue the fight strengthened.

He sent a brief message to London identifying himself and stating that he was taking over from Leonie, who had been arrested and tortured, but was now safe. No message came back immediately and Rob knew that the authorities would be trying to verify if he was genuine. If she had spent some time in German hands, they would think that perhaps her wireless transmitter had been captured and that the message came from a German posing as an operator. Careful checks would have to be made before London would trust him.

And the British pilot would just have to put up with the smell of Raoul's pigs for a while longer.

Thirty-Three

Beth's injuries healed, though she still limped as it would take some time for the toenails on her left foot to grow again.

'I need to get back to work, Emile. I can't just stay out here doing nothing. I'm a burden on you all.'

Emile put his arm around her shoulders. There was so much he would have liked to say to her, but they were in the middle of a war and living as fugitives and it was neither the time nor the place. However, there seemed to be an understanding between them even without the words being spoken. They sat close together when eating and if it was deemed safe to light a fire at night, they sat in front of it, the flickering flames lighting their faces as they glanced at each other often.

'You're not a burden on any of us. Besides,' he grinned impishly, 'being the only woman here, it's taken for granted that you'll help with the cooking.'

Beth chuckled. Despite what she had done, her role as a woman and a woman's duties were not in doubt! Then her smile faded. 'Maybe I ought to go back to England – next time there's a pick-up.'

Emile's arm tightened around her shoulders. 'Don't you dare. I want you here – with me, where I can keep my eye on you. If you go back, they'll only send you out again as soon as they think you're fit and goodness knows where they might send you then. Besides, you're doing a grand job here. Bruce is itching for you to be well enough to take over the wireless operations again. He's finding it very tough and dangerous to keep going out to the farm every time to send and receive messages.'

'But I can't go back to the farm, can I? It wouldn't be safe.'

Emile shook his head. 'No, it wouldn't. Papa told me only last night when I risked a quick visit to the farm, that he and Maman had been taken into the town for questioning, but allowed home again after a couple of hours.' He laughed wryly. 'I think the Germans realized that their supplies would be seriously depleted if they arrested either of them.'

'Thank goodness,' Beth said with heartfelt relief. She had been so worried about the old couple.

'I've been talking the matter over with the others and we think we've found a solution. On the opposite side of this wood there's a bit of higher ground and we think you could transmit from there. It would be a bit of a trek, but I don't think the Germans bring their detection equipment anywhere near there. What do you think?'

'If they did suspect, though, wouldn't it bring all of you into danger? I wouldn't want that.'

'We're all aware of that, but it's more important for us to be in contact with London. We're already getting short of equipment, ammunition and explosives, though luckily food is no problem. The farmers near here are all partisans.'

So it was arranged. Emile fetched the wireless set from the barn one night and the following day it was hidden in one of the old cottages. 'It'll have to be carried there and back each time, but we'll do that for you and

293

we'll always have at least two of the group come with you to keep a look out whilst you're working.'

The new system worked well and soon Beth was back in touch with London. Supplies were dropped and pick-ups arranged quickly and successfully. If it was possible to be happy in such dire times, then Beth believed herself to be just that. She felt comparatively safe now, even safer than she had done living with the Détanges where visits from the enemy were always a probability. But now, even though living rough, she felt a contentment she had not expected.

And she was truthful enough to acknowledge that it all had to do with being close to Emile.

Archie was home from sea for a few days, but he was restless.

'There's summat up, Edie. I can feel it. I don't know what it is, but I'm on edge and I don't know why.'

Edie glanced at him. This was not like Archie at all. A more placid, rational man you couldn't meet.

'I expect they're planning an invasion.'

'Who?' Archie's tone was unusually sharp.

'The Allies, of course. Who did you think I meant? Not Hitler now. He made a mess of things when he didn't push for it in 1940, but turned his attention to Russia. Thank God he did' – her gratitude was heartfelt and sincere – 'else I don't know where we'd all have been by now.'

Archie smiled and teased, 'So you do take a bit of notice of the news, then?'

Edie sniffed. 'Hard not to when you're at home and even when you're away' – there was no need for her to remind Archie that she deliberately never listened to news bulletins when he was at sea – 'Lil's always popping round to give me the latest. She should have been a reporter for the paper. She's always first with a juicy bit of gossip. And now, whenever she calls in to say hello, Ursula always wants to know what we've heard and it all has to be gone through again.'

'Does she now?' Archie murmured and frowned.

'Well, I can't stand here gossiping all day, Archie Kelsey. This ironing won't do itself and if you want clean clothes to go back to sea, you'd better get out me way. I've got to get it all done today if you're sailing tomorrow.' Edie never forgot the superstitions that might help to keep her beloved Archie safe.

'Right then, I'm off down the pub. Harry might be there. He often pops in at lunch times now when Jessie's busy. He reckons she's hardly ever at home.'

Edie looked up sharply. 'Is he grumbling? Because if he is—'

'No, no, not at all,' Archie reassured her swiftly. 'Not Harry. You know Harry – he never complains about owt. I reckon in his eyes your Jessie can do no wrong.'

'He's a good husband, I'll say that for him.' Edie glanced up and smiled. 'We've been lucky – me and Jessie – to find such lovely men to marry us.' She kissed him soundly before turning back to her irons heating on the hob. 'It's just a shame,' she murmured, 'that poor Jessie and Harry didn't have children. They'd have made lovely parents.'

'You know,' Archie said as he put on his jacket, 'I'm surprised they've never adopted. There're plenty of poor kids out there who need a loving home.'

'Aye, and there'll be a lot more when this lot's over. The bombing will have left orphans. Archie,' she stood up quickly, 'we could—'

'Now, now, Edie love, I know you're feeling lonely just now, but you'll have plenty to do once they all get home after the war.'

Edie smiled good-naturedly. 'Perhaps you're right, if only it would hurry up and happen.'

'Besides, we might be thought too old now, love.'

'I don't think Jessie would be, though. I might suggest it to her.'

'Go carefully, then. It's a touchy subject.'

'You could have a quiet word with Harry.'

Archie shook his head and put up his hand, palm outwards as if fending off her suggestion. 'Oh no. Men don't talk about things like that. Well, we don't, any road up. We leave that to you womenfolk.'

On 6 June, 1944, the hoped-for invasion of Europe began. It was a long, long day and the whole country waited, half in fear, half in hope, until news came through at last that the Allies had a foothold once more on French soil.

'We can't fail now, can we?' Lil said anxiously to Edie. 'Surely we can't lose now.'

Edie was smiling. 'Course we can't. It's like Harry said when he made that toast at Christmas – this really could be the beginning of the end.'

'Oh I hope so, I do hope so.' Lil murmured and then pondered, 'I wonder where Frank is, Edie. D'you think he's there?'

Edie's face fell. 'I reckon – if he's had the chance – yes, he'll be in the thick of it. If nothing else, he'll want to get back into France to avenge his brother's death when we were driven out. I just hope he – he keeps safe.'

Lil nodded, her throat too full to speak for a moment. She looked upon Frank as her own son and always had done, even before he became her son-in-law. She didn't dare to imagine what would happen to Irene if Frank didn't come back. She didn't want the same life for her daughter as she had had. She patted Edie's arm and turned away, managing to say huskily, 'I've shopping to do. I've got your list, Edie. I'll see what I can queue for today.'

In France, Emile, his compatriots and Beth had been busy. Beth now had her wireless working again and had been able to receive and transmit vital messages in preparation for the planned invasion. And Bruce, miraculously undiscovered, had been a vital link. The group had carried out sabotage, blowing up railway lines, bridges, German ammunition dumps and generally irritating the enemy and slowing down the resistance to the Allies, who would now, ironically, be classed as the invaders – but invaders who were this time welcomed by the French people.

'There'll be reprisals,' Raoul warned Emile on one of his night visits to his parents' farm. 'They've already shot four men from the town.'

'Is Bruce still safe?'

Raoul nodded. 'He came here yesterday. He told us about it.'

Emile frowned. 'We ought to think about getting him out of there. If he were to be arrested now, it would be certain death for him after probably being put through hell first.'

'He could come here,' Raoul said, but Emile shook his head. 'No, you and Maman have done enough.

297

You're still hiding British airmen when necessary and that's dangerous enough.'

'I wish Leonie could come back to us. We miss her.'

Emile smiled. 'I know, but it would be very unsafe for her and for you too. Besides, she's doing a grand job with us. We've even got her doing the cooking.'

The three of them laughed as Marthe said fondly, 'Well, give her our love and – both of you – take care.'

Thirty-Four

During the weeks following D-Day, Edie broke her own rule. It had nothing to do with any superstition; it was just a decision. She read the newspapers, both local and national, and readily discussed the news with Lil. Once converted, she became the most avid newspaper reader of them all. She even listened to the news bulletins on the wireless, something she had vowed she would never do when Archie was away. Now that the tide of the war was turning in favour of the Allies, she couldn't get enough of the up-to-the-minute news. Towards the end of August, she went through the door in the fence and straight into Lil's scullery.

'You there, Lil? I've got a bit of news for you. They'll soon be home now. All the family will soon be home. Paris has been liberated and Montgomery is pushing from the north and General Patton from further south. Surely, it can't be long before the whole of France is free, can it?'

'I don't expect so, duck.' Lil was smiling at her friend and joining in her happiness. Maybe she, too, could start to look forward to Irene and Tommy coming back; she hadn't dared to before now.

'Eee, wait till Archie sees this. He'll be home late tonight. I can't wait to tell him.'

*

Beth woke in the hayloft to a scuffling sound. Since the Allies had arrived and the Loire valley and all its towns and villages had been liberated bit by bit, she had been back at the Détanges' farm. Now, she, Emile and all the others could emerge from their hiding place to be reunited with their family and friends. But all was not quite as they'd expected or hoped. There was much bitterness and locals were seeking out anyone they thought had been a collaborator. Everyone suspected their neighbours, their friends and even members of their own family. And so Beth was hiding in Raoul's hayloft, just in case someone should come looking for her.

'It'll soon be over,' Raoul tried to reassure her. 'They're just going a bit mad at the moment. Just lie low for a day or two. They'll soon have better things to think about.'

And so Beth was spending her days – and her nights – in the hayloft with Raoul bringing food to her. She woke at the slightest sound, listening intently even through the darkness.

It's only rats, she thought now, and turned over sleepily in her warm burrow in the hay. But then she heard someone quietly ascending the ladder. She lay still, hoping she was completely hidden in the dark corner, yet the early morning light was now filtering through the opening in the loft. It could hardly be called a window, for there was no glass, but it was the shape and size of one; the place where, for the past three days, she had watched the yard and the lane leading to the farm for any unwelcome visitors. The wireless, still needed to send messages, was hidden behind the boarding in the opposite corner to where she was lying. Her heart began to thud. Had they come for her? Was this really it? Was this to be her ignominious end after all that she had endured and already survived? Were the very people she had helped to save now to turn on her in their ignorance of the true part she had played in their deliverance?

A soft voice came out of the half-light. 'Beth?' It took only a second for her to recognize the voice. She pushed her way out of the hay and sat up. 'Emile. Oh, Emile . . .' And she stretched her arms wide to him. His arms were about her, his lips warm and sweet on her mouth as he lay beside her.

'Where have you been?' she whispered between kisses. 'I've been so worried.'

After he had brought her back to the farm, he had disappeared and she'd had no idea where he'd gone.

'My darling,' he murmured.

She pulled at the buttons on his shirt, her need for him surging through her. They struggled out of their clothes and then clung together, kissing and caressing, all else forgotten in the release of a mutual passion that had, for so long, been denied.

'Oh my love,' he said, as he buried his face in her neck. 'I'll never let you out of my sight again. I promise you.'

His lovemaking was tender and yet there was a desperate need that he could no longer hide. He had loved this girl for so long – perhaps even from the time he had first known her in happier times when they'd been so young and carefree and innocent. Then had come the war and the danger, and that love had had to be denied. And yet, she had known of his feelings and had adored him in return. But now, the war was at an end and the future was theirs.

They lay together cosy and safe in the warm hay.

'Beth,' he said, daring now to use her real name. 'Will you – please – marry me, my darling?'

Beth giggled deliciously. Her fears were forgotten. Nothing and no one could hurt her now that Emile was by her side. 'I think I'd better, don't you?'

He wrapped his arms around her and held her close as they whispered and laughed together, planning their hopes for the future.

Between kisses, he said, 'I heard a funny story yesterday from Rob. He said I was to be sure to tell you.'

'Mm,' Beth murmured, sleepily. She had no need of amusement; she had everything she wanted right here beside her.

'It was about a woman agent who was captured and sent to a prison camp to await execution, but then they found out that she was related to Montgomery.'

At once Beth was wide awake. 'Good Heavens! Monty! Isobel Montgomery – it's got to be.' She sat up. 'Oh Emile – is she . . . ? Did they . . . ?'

'She's safe and well. Evidently, her captors didn't dare to execute her. In fact, as the Allies advanced, a German officer actually drove her to them, hoping that it would save his miserable neck.'

Beth laughed. 'Oh, that's priceless. Good old Monty. After it's all over I must—' she began, but it was then that they heard the shouts of a band of villagers coming down the lane towards the farm.

Emile peered out of the window. 'They're coming.'

Beth stifled a sob. After everything that had happened, after she had come through it all and should now be safe, and now that they were free to declare their love, was she to lose her life at the hands of the very people she had helped?

'Stay here,' he whispered as he grasped her hand briefly.

'I'll try to stop them coming up here. Get right into the corner and I'll move these bales in front of you. Quickly now.' She clung to him for a moment and then did as he asked.

'I love you, Beth,' he whispered as she heard him move to the ladder and climb down. Then she heard a scrape and a thud as he moved the ladder away from the loft opening to try – in a vain attempt she was sure – to lure the searchers away from where she was hiding.

Emile stepped out of the barn door as the gang of men entered the farm gateway. For a moment, the man in the front – obviously the self-appointed leader – stopped and stared at him. Emile faced him squarely, his arms folded.

'Emile – you're back,' the man said unnecessarily.

'As you see,' Emile answered shortly. 'What brings you here, Maurice Arnaud?' As if I didn't know, he thought bitterly.

'The girl. We want the girl. She's a collaborator and you know what we do to them.'

From D-Day, Edie followed the news avidly and visits to the cinema were now just an excuse to see the Pathé news too. By the middle of the month, De Gaulle was back in France visiting the liberated areas and towards the end of August, he entered Paris and the people of the city celebrated with him.

'It's been bad enough here, Lil, but I can't imagine what it must have been like to have your country occupied.'

'It doesn't bear thinking about, Edie, but they'll soon be free now. The Allied armies are advancing rapidly across the whole of France now, so the papers say.'

'I wonder where Frank is, Lil,' Edie murmured, but she dare not even speak Beth's name so deep was her anxiety for her daughter.

But just when they thought the tide had really turned in favour of the Allies, Germany unleashed a new and deadly weapon; the V-1 rockets or doodlebugs, as they became called. By July, parents were sending their children out of the cities yet again.

'Did you hear them going over us yesterday, Lil? Archie reckons they're not aimed at us though. They're on their way to the cities, Sheffield, most likely.'

'The reprisals will start, Edie. The Germans took drastic revenge on ordinary civilians – whole villages sometimes – for any German officers killed by the French Resistance, and now I expect they'll think it's payback time. D'you know, I can find it in my heart to feel sorry for the German women and children. I shouldn't think they ever wanted a war any more than we did, but they're going to take the brunt of the retaliation when the Allies get there.'

'Aye, you're a more forgiving soul than I am, Lil.' Edie smiled. 'There ought to be more folk in the world like you.'

'Well, somebody ought to put a stop to it. If they go on playing tit-for-tat, it'll never be over.'

Thirty-Five

Emile suppressed a shudder as he faced Maurice and the men ranged behind him. He knew only too well what was happening right now to girls and women who had fraternized with the enemy. They were being humiliated and ostracized – or worse. Sometimes, whole families were being punished for collaborating during the dark and difficult days of occupation.

'She was not a collaborator – far from it. She—' Whatever he had been going to say was cut off as Maurice barked an order.

'Hold him.' Two burly men ran forward, caught hold of Emile and held him fast. Though he struggled, in his weakened state after months of living rough in the woods, he was no match for them. 'Search everywhere. Even the house. I know she was living with the Détanges. What I don't know is, whether or not they're collaborators too,' the man said in his deep, rumbling voice.

'No, no,' Emile shouted. 'They're not. You know they're not, Maurice.'

The big man turned on him. 'I know you're not, Emile. We all know you've worked with the Resistance since the early days. But are you sure about your parents? Can anyone be sure of their neighbours or even of their family any more?' There was a bitter note in the man's voice as his cohorts searched the farmhouse and the outbuildings.

Stay hidden, Beth, Emile prayed silently. He twisted his head to see his elderly parents being hustled out of the house and into the yard. His mother was shaking, his father angry and struggling against the men who held him.

'Monsieur,' Maurice turned to him. 'We suspect you and your wife were collaborators.'

Raoul spat on the ground at the man's feet. 'How dare you?' he boomed. 'When my son risked his life every day for the likes of you to stay safely in your homes? I didn't see you living in the woods, Maurice Arnaud, or your family going short.'

Maurice clenched his fists and took a step towards Raoul, but then he stopped and contented himself with a glare filled with loathing, saying only between gritted teeth, 'I'll not hit an old man and, for the sake of your son, you'll not be harmed, even though you supplied the enemy with food.' His glance included Marthe, still being held by one of his men.

Raoul glanced around the surly villagers. 'But tell me – all of you – didn't you do what the occupying forces told you to do – to save your lives? What good would it have done to deny them food? They'd have taken it anyway and likely killed us too. We did *not* collaborate, but we had no choice.'

'Yes, you did,' one of the men holding Marthe said. 'I'd have sooner burned my farm to the ground than let them have my crops and livestock.'

Raoul, still being held fast, twisted to look at him. 'Ah yes. François, the shoemaker. Don't try to tell me you never mended a German's boot.' The man's glance dropped to the ground. 'And you, Lucas, the blacksmith, did you never shoe a German horse? And you, Victor, did they not buy meat from your butchery?'

'I always kept enough back for the villagers,' the man protested. 'They were always fed first.'

'Never mind all that now,' Maurice snapped. 'We all did what we had to do, we accept that now, and there'll be no reprisals against you, Raoul. But tell me, where is the girl?'

Raoul answered swiftly. 'Gone.'

Maurice's lip curled. 'To her *friends* in Germany, no doubt. Well, let me tell you, the officer who helped her escape has been shot by his own people for helping her.'

'Maurice,' Emile now spoke quietly. 'She worked with us – she was one of us – sent from England as an agent. She was the wireless operator and at times a courier for our circuit. She kept us in touch with London. It was she who radioed when we needed a drop or to get escapees out. And she sent the messages that sent us arms.'

They all knew that the Resistance movement had been active here and several of the villagers had helped airmen to find the route home.

For a brief moment, Maurice looked uncertain.

'What about the time Julien Lafarge was betrayed? He was arrested and tortured before being shot and then five men from our village were shot in reprisals for having helped two British airmen. Are you saying that girl had nothing to do with all that?'

'I am,' Emile said calmly.

'Then who did betray him? It wasn't one of us' – Maurice gestured with his hand towards the group of men ranged around him – 'so who?'

Emile shrugged. 'I don't know, but I think the "safe" house where the airmen stayed in the village sometimes was no longer safe. That's where they were found.'

'You think the British airmen betrayed Julien?'

'No, I don't. Not for a minute. I think it was just bad luck that the Germans raided that particular house. Whether or not they had a tip-off, I don't know.'

'The airmen were questioned,' Victor put in. 'Henri Lafarge saw one of them brought out from the German headquarters across the road from his shop when they were being taken back to a prison camp. He'd been badly beaten – he could hardly walk. The German soldiers had to drag him to the lorry. They flung him in the back. Brutes, they were.'

'And you think you're any less of a brute, because I know exactly what you're planning to do if you find that poor girl,' Raoul said.

Some of the group had peeled away and were wandering into the outbuildings and even into the farmhouse. With a supreme effort, Emile kept his gaze firmly fixed on Maurice's face; he didn't want to give away any hint as to where Beth was hiding.

There was a moment's pause whilst some of the men shuffled their feet and murmured to each other, their uneasy glance coming back to Maurice. And then came the shout that Emile had dreaded to hear. 'She's here. In the hayloft. We've got her.'

Emile met Maurice's accusing gaze squarely, but he kept silent. Two men appeared out of the barn dragging Beth between them.

'Fetch a chair from the kitchen,' Maurice barked. 'And tie her to it. Philippe' – he beckoned the village barber – 'get your scissors ready.'

Emile struggled again, but he was held fast.

'You barbarians,' Raoul shouted. 'She's no more a collaborator than you are, Maurice Arnaud. Let her go.'

Maurice spun round and shook his fist in Raoul's

face. 'Hold your tongue, Détange, else the same will happen to your wife for having sheltered her.' Raoul glared at him and then his wrinkled face fell into lines of disappointment and sadness. 'You don't know what you're doing, Maurice,' he said softly now. 'Yes, we helped her, we sheltered her, but she was working with us, for us. If you don't believe me, look at her feet. There's the proof.'

'Take no notice of him, Maurice,' Philippe said, brandishing his scissors as Beth, her eyes wide and frightened, was tied to one of Marthe's kitchen chairs. With an expression of fiendish delight, Philippe grasped a handful of Beth's hair and hacked at its roots. Her dark locks fluttered to the ground and were blown away by the wind. Beth bit down hard on her bottom lip and kept her gaze fixed on Emile's face. She could see tears in his eyes; this brave man who had suffered countless dangers was shedding tears over the loss of her hair. The sight of his acute distress was almost the undoing of her. The image of his smile, of the love in his eyes even though it had never been spoken of between them, had kept up her courage during her time of captivity, but to see him now – and he was weeping openly – was harder to bear than the indignity she was suffering.

When Philippe had cut away as much of her hair as he could with his scissors, he drew a razor from his pocket and without soap or water ran it over her head, leaving small cuts and scrapes on her scalp. Then, with a cruel smile, he stood back to admire his handiwork.

'And what would your German lover think of you now, eh?' he smirked.

Slowly, Beth turned her face towards him, gathered a globule of spittle in her mouth and spat at his feet. Incensed, the man drew back his hand and struck her across the face with such force that she fell sideways, only the restraints kept her from falling off the chair to the ground.

With a roar, Raoul pulled himself free and strode across the yard. He knelt beside her and cradled her head on his shoulder. He glanced up at Maurice and then bent and untied the laces of Beth's shoes. As he slipped them off her feet, the men drew closer and saw for themselves where her toenails on her left foot had been wrenched out.

For a brief moment, Maurice looked shame-faced, but then he muttered, 'That's no proof. They could have done that to her to cover the truth.'

'You think so, eh?' Raoul said bitterly. 'Well, let me tell you, Emile is right. The English sent this girl over here as a wireless operator. Her cover was here, working on my farm. She has risked her life and this is the thanks you give her.' As Beth began to come round, he stood up. 'Release my wife and Emile and get off my land. You're not welcome here any more, Arnaud. Nor any of you.' He waved his arm to encompass them all.

As the men, muttering amongst themselves, turned away, Emile untied the bonds fastening Beth to the chair and tenderly carried her into the farmhouse. Now that they were out of earshot, her courage failed and she clung to Emile, sobbing against his shoulder whilst Raoul tried to comfort Marthe. She, too, was weeping inconsolably. 'Oh Leonie, poor Leonie. Look what they've done to her. The brutes! How could they do that after all she's been through?' It was difficult after all the months of using Beth's cover name to call her anything else. It would take time for the fear of being in daily danger to lessen. And it would be a long time before the memory of Beth's humiliation – and hurt – suffered at the hands of both the enemy and, now, their own people would be erased.

Emile held her close and kissed her shorn head trying to show her by his loving action that what had happened made no difference to his feelings for her.

'You must go home,' he murmured. 'I'll get you home.'

But, with her face buried in his chest, she shook her head. 'I can't. I can't go home looking like this. I can't *ever* go home.'

Thirty-Six

May 1945

'It's looking like it's finally over, then. We're all just waiting for an official announcement from the Prime Minister, but plans for the celebrations are starting already.'

'That's all very well,' Edie frowned, 'but when are they all coming home? That's what I want to know.'

'I expect Irene and Tommy will be the first to come back. There's no need for them to stay in the countryside any longer, is there? I can't wait to see our Tommy. Fancy, he's going to school already, so Irene said in her last letter. And your Reggie will have grown too. He'll be school-leaving age now, won't he? You can hardly credit it, can you?'

'It's been a long time,' Edie sighed. 'I just wish we'd been able to see them more often, but it was always difficult, wasn't it, even though they were only a few miles away?'

Lil said nothing. The war had made it even harder for her to eke out her earnings; she hadn't been able to afford many jaunts into the countryside.

'But I'll tell you summat, Lil. I'm not letting our Reggie go to sea. It'll be over my dead body if he does.'

'What about Frank? D'you reckon he'll go back to sea when he does get home?'

312

Edie shrugged. 'I expect so. It's all he knows.' She paused, remembering the quarrel with Archie. 'If he can find owt, that is.'

They were silent for a few moments, each lost in their own thoughts about the changes that were to take place soon.

'So,' Edie said at last, 'when can we take down the blackout and start trying to get back to normal?'

'Normal?' Lil murmured. 'What's that?'

'Well, y'know, before all this started. Get back to how we was before.'

Lil eyed her friend sorrowfully as she said softly, 'Edie, duck, we'll never get back to how things were before the war.'

Edie placed her cup gently back onto its saucer and met her friend's gaze. 'Then,' she said, resolutely, 'we'll just have to make a new life, won't we?'

'Edie – I've had a letter from Irene. They're coming home on Tuesday.'

'Aw, Lil, that's grand. What about Reggie? Is he coming an' all?'

Lil bit her lip. 'She doesn't say, Edie. Sorry.' Suddenly, Lil seemed ill at ease. 'I'll have to go, duck. I'm going into town to do a bit of shopping. Owt you want?'

'Don't think so, Lil. I'll have to go myself tomorrow.'

'Ta-ra, then.' Lil scuttled away and it wasn't until she closed her own back door behind her and leaned against it, closing her eyes for a moment, that she let out a sigh of relief. She had indeed had a letter from her daughter but she hadn't taken it with her to Edie's in case her friend expected to be allowed to read it. When the rare letters came from Frank to Edie, or, even rarer, the postcards from Beth, Edie had always let Lil read them. And she, in turn, had always shared her letters from Irene with Edie, but today she couldn't show her friend this particular letter. There was news of Reggie but Lil didn't want to be the one to tell his mother.

'I've had a letter an' all,' Edie said on the Monday evening when Lil came round for tea. The two women often shared tea together when Archie was away. 'From Reggie. He definitely doesn't want to come home. He wants to stay in the country. Did you know?' There was accusation in her tone.

'No – yes, I –' Lil was suddenly flustered, but she couldn't carry on a deliberate lie. There'd never been any secrets between the two friends, not in all the years they'd known each other. She sighed heavily. 'Irene mentioned it in her letter, but I didn't tell you then because I thought mebbe she'd got it wrong – or he'd change his mind.'

Edie sniffed but said nothing, though her tone was a little stiff when she said, 'Well, evidently he hasn't. He's so taken up with the farming way of life that he wants to stay there.'

'At least he won't be wanting to go to sea, Edie,' Lil said with surprising craftiness.

Edie wrinkled her forehead and, mollified a little, she said, 'That's true, Lil. I hadn't looked at it like that. But – not to want to come home to us – I can't understand that.'

'He's not so far away. It's not as if they went into Derbyshire like Mrs Griffin's children. When things get easier, you an' Archie'll be able to go and see him and he'll come home every so often, surely.'

'I – dunno.' Edie was clearly still upset to think that her youngest son didn't want to come back home. She'd lost one already; Laurence was never coming back. She couldn't bear to think that she'd lose another.

'Still, there's Frank,' Edie went on, making a supreme effort to cheer up. 'He'll be home soon and then him and Irene can find a little house somewhere near. We'll be able to see little Tommy every day. He'll want to come to see both his grannies, now won't he?'

Lil nodded, but she was chewing her lip nervously. It had to be said. 'They say that our lads won't get home immediately. 'Specially, those that went in a bit later on in the war like – like Frank.'

Edie stared at her for a moment before saying flatly, 'Oh.' She turned away, muttering to herself so that Lil hardly heard. 'But at least he *will* come home.'

Lil cleared her throat, trying to change the subject. 'When's Archie due in? Will he be here before Tuesday?'

Tuesday loomed large in Lil's world. It would be so good to have Irene and Tommy home again and to have company in the house, even if only until Frank came home and the little family wanted to set up in their own home. At least she'd have them with her for a few weeks, maybe even months.

'No, he's not due back until the middle of next week. Still,' Edie turned back towards her friend with a smile, her good humour restored, 'it'll be nice for you an' me to have Irene and little Tommy to ourselves for a bit, won't it? And Shirley'll be home any day. In her letter last week, she said she'd got leave soon.'

Lil nodded, relieved that Edie was once again seeing the positive side of things.

At that moment Edie's back door opened with a rattle and Jessie breezed in, 'Right,' she said, without any

315

kind of formal greeting, 'are we organizing a street party tomorrow, then? Like we did for the coronation in thirty-seven? It's what our street does best.'

Edie and Lil, sitting at the table with a cup of tea in front of them, looked up at her in amazement. It was late – even by Jessie's standards – to be paying calls. Tea, which Edie and Lil often shared when Archie was away, was over.

'Party? What sort of party? It's nobody's birthday, is it?'

'No, but the war's over. VE day's set for tomorrow and Mr Churchill's going to speak to the nation.'

Lil frowned. 'Are you sure, Jessie? I just listened to the six o'clock news and they said that the Prime Minister won't be broadcasting tonight.'

'That's right, but he will be tomorrow afternoon at three o'clock. They've just interrupted programmes to say that tomorrow will be VE day – Victory in Europe. Several folks must have heard it too,' she waved her hand airily towards the street, 'as I came up; they're outside now hanging out the flags, stringing bunting across the street and decorating their front windows. So, what about it?'

Edie and Lil glanced at each other. 'I don't see why not,' Edie said, a slow smile spreading across her face. 'It looks as if we've got summat to celebrate now. And Irene and Tommy are due tomorrow, an' all. We'd best get our thinking caps on, Lil, to see what food we can contribute.'

'I baked this morning ready for Irene and Tommy coming home so I can spare some cakes,' Lil pulled a wry face, 'though they're only wartime recipes, I'm afraid.'

Edie laughed. 'So did I, so we can rustle up quite a bit between us. And I can make some Spam sandwiches.'

'And I'll make a jelly or two.'

'I haven't had time to bake, but I'll let you have whatever I can.' Jessie smiled archly. 'I've been busy organizing this for the last four days ever since we knew the war was really going to be over. I'm very sorry I didn't come and tell you sooner. Now, I've got to go and see a man about some trestle tables.' She stood up to leave. 'And I'll get Harry to go up into the loft tonight. I'm sure we've got a flag up there somewhere.'

'We've got some bunting in our loft,' Edie said. 'Tell Harry to come round early tomorrow morning and he can fetch it down.'

As she turned to go, Jessie said over her shoulder, 'Oh, and by the way, get your best frocks on. The Mayor's agreed to come and hand out a threepenny bit to every child.'

Edie and Lil gaped at her as Jessie wiggled her fingers in farewell and left the way she had come in. They heard her high heels tapping down the passage before either of them spoke.

'Right,' Edie said with renewed vigour. 'Let's get started, Lil. We'll give the kids in the street the best party they'll ever remember. Poor scraps haven't had any fun for years. Some won't even remember a time before this country was at war. Tommy certainly won't. He weren't even born then. Let's hope him and his mam get here before it's all over.' She sniffed. 'Even if Reggie thinks he's too good to come back to our humble home.'

Early the next morning, the street was bustling with folks hanging out yet more flags and bunting and every house had some sort of decoration in its front windows. Someone dragged a piano out of their front room onto the pavement and a motley collection of instruments from mouth organs to accordions appeared in readiness to make a merry, jubilant noise. Every household contributed what they could and by early afternoon, a veritable mountain of food appeared on the assorted collection of tables that had been placed in a long line down the centre of the street. Each household provided chairs and tablecloths and the excitement amongst the children grew to fever pitch until they were running up and down, shouting and laughing as if they had been let out of prison. And, indeed, to them, and to the adults too, that was exactly what it felt like. Finally, they were all released from the constraints of wartime; from shortages – though rationing would continue for several months, perhaps even years – from the blackout and from the fear of bombing raids. Everyone was out on the street.

In the middle of the morning, Shirley arrived to an ecstatic welcome from her mother. 'Oh Shirley, you're the first one home. Welcome back, love.'

'Don't get too excited, Mam, I've only come on leave. I've to go back tomorrow night.'

Edie's face fell. 'Oh, I thought you'd be coming home for good.'

Shirley grinned. 'We've to get demobbed, just like Frank, and it won't be for a while yet. And besides –' suddenly, she hesitated – 'I'm thinking of staying on in the forces in some way, Mam. I've really taken to the life. I really don't want to go back to being just a shop girl.'

Edie stared at her. 'Not come home? Oh Shirley, not you an' all. Please say you don't mean it. And there's nothing wrong with working in a shop, let me tell you.'

'You'll have Frank back, Mam, and Beth and, of course, Reggie.'

'That's just it, Shirley.' Edie wiped her eyes with the corner of her apron. 'Reggie's not coming home. He wants to stay with the Schofields. Look,' she reached for the letter propped behind the photograph of Laurence on the mantelpiece, 'see for yourself.'

Shirley read the letter with a frown. 'But he's not old enough to make such a decision, Mam. You can *make* him come back.'

'Well, yes, I suppose so.' Edie was doubtful. 'But can you imagine your dad agreeing to that? He's always been adamant that we should let our kids do what they want in life.'

Shirley shrugged. 'When Reggie's older, yes, but not yet, surely. Anyway,' she said, folding the letter and replacing it on the mantelpiece for Archie to read when he came home, 'it's not my worry, thank goodness. Now, I'd better go and find Ursula and see if she's coming to this party.'

'I haven't seen her lately,' Edie said. 'To be honest, I don't even know if she's still here.'

'I'll go and see.'

Shirley found her friend in her room. She looked thin and pale and, at first, was reluctant to open the door.

'What's up, Ursula? Are you ill?'

'No – yes – I've had a cold,' she said lamely.

'Then it'll do you good to come out and celebrate with the rest of us.'

'I don't want to join in. People think I have a strange accent. They might think I'm German. It'd be best if I stay here.'

'Don't be silly, Ursula,' Shirley reassured her. 'If they were going to think that, you'd have heard it long before now.'

Ursula remained silent. She did not tell her friend

that there had been several times when her nationality – and her loyalty – had been questioned. She'd even been taken to the police station on two different occasions when neighbours of her landlady had reported that there was a 'woman with a funny accent' living in their street. She had managed to answer the questions satisfactorily, but she could still see the doubt in the officers' eyes.

'Mam won't let anyone say a word against you, Ursula, and nor will I. Just stop worrying and looking so anxious or folk will start to think there's summat fishy. Get your coat 'cos you're coming with me.'

Out in the street, Shirley linked her arm through Ursula's and made her sit at one of the tables just outside her own home. 'Now have some of Aunty Lil's "if-it" cake and for Heaven's sake, *smile*. This is supposed to be a celebration.'

There weren't many men present, just a few fishermen who were not at sea, dock workers, those engaged in reserved occupations, men too old and boys too young to have gone to war. And, although the Home Guard stand-down had taken place the previous December when they had become an inactive reserve unit, today several of their number still proudly wore their uniform, knowing that it would now be inevitable that they would soon cease to exist altogether. When the dancing began, no man present was left a wallflower. Even young boys, much to their disgust, were press-ganged into dancing with their mothers or aunts, but they drew the line at dancing with girls of their own age. Girls were soppy, was the general opinion amongst boys until they reached a certain age when their interest changed.

'Harry's never been so popular,' Jessie laughed, taking a breather to stand beside Edie and Lil. 'Ah, there's the photographer from the *Telegraph*. I must get the children lined up for a photo with their paper hats on.'

'Where've all those come from?' Edie said, staring at the children running riot, but each child was sporting a colourful paper hat.

'Oh, I made them,' Jessie said, airily. 'Now, where's the Mayor gone? He ought to be in the centre of the picture.' And she dashed away again.

Edie and Lil laughed together.

'I just don't know where your sister gets her energy from, Edie. She must have been making all those hats for weeks. And she always looks so smart too. Look at her today in her costume, high heels and her own patriotic hat. How clever she is. Who else would have thought of shaping a Union Jack scarf into a hat? She puts the rest of us to shame in our pinnies and sensible shoes.'

Edie's smile faded. 'I reckon it's because she's got no kids, you know. It was a bitter disappointment to both her and Harry and she's always been the same. Keeps herself that busy, she hasn't time to brood.'

'Aye, I know, I know,' Lil said softly, and she did. The long years of widowhood had often been lonely and burdensome. What Lil would have done without the friend now standing at her side, she didn't know.

Even Norma had made a grudging appearance, standing outside her sister's house and viewing the proceedings with her lips pursed in disapproval. 'I expect this racket will go on half the night. It's the same down my street,' she was heard to grumble, but no one was taking any notice of her. The war was over; there was peace at last and their menfolk would be coming home. Demobilization would take months, maybe even a year or two before everyone was home, but at least they would be coming back. So many would not and even on this day of ecstatic celebration, Edie was not the only one to spare a quiet thought for her lost boy. But she kept her sadness to herself, plastered a wide smile on her face and joined in the singing in a raucous voice.

And then at three o'clock the sound of Big Ben came over the wirelesses. The windows were flung open and Mr Churchill's voice echoed down the street, telling everyone that the war was finally over, that the representative of the German High Command and Government, General Jodl, had signed the act of unconditional surrender and that the people might allow themselves 'a brief period of rejoicing'. Although he sounded a note of caution, warning that there were still tough days ahead, because Japan still fought on, no one took any notice as cars and vans hooted and the people, waving flags and sporting home-made rosettes in red, white and blue, laughed and cheered and joined hands with strangers to dance. Not even the drizzly weather could dampen their spirits.

The merrymaking had no sign of abating when, by late afternoon, Edie and Lil fetched chairs from their houses and set them on the pavement outside Edie's front door watching the end of the street where they hoped Irene and Tommy would appear.

'I reckon your Norma's right. This lot's going to go on half the night.'

Lil chuckled. 'All night, probably, Edie. Jessie said Harry's trying to organize fireworks for later. And as long as Terry keeps playing that piano, they'll keep dancing.'

'Aye, well, let 'em, I say. The youngsters haven't had much fun for years. If I was twenty years younger, I'd be in amongst 'em myself.' Then she glanced down the street again. 'Mebbe we should have gone to the station to meet Irene, Lil. She might have a lot of luggage.'

'She said not to, Edie. Said she'd manage.'

Edie laughed – a deep, infectious chuckle. 'Always Miss Independent, your Irene. Ah, now is this her?' Edie squinted down the street. Both women stood up, eager to welcome Irene and Tommy home. 'Naw, can't be. It's a lass pushing a pram.'

But as the young woman drew nearer with a young boy walking beside the pram, Lil said, 'It *is* her.' For a brief moment she felt a stab of fear. What on earth . . . ? But then she smiled. 'It's the one she took with her, Edie. Tommy was only tiny – remember? I 'spect she's bringing it back and using it to carry her luggage.'

They were silent for a moment, staring down the street until Edie said harshly, 'Mebbe so, Lil, but I don't reckon I've ever heard a suitcase make a noise like that.'

Quite clearly now, echoing down the length of the street, were the wails of a young baby and the noise was coming from the pram which Irene was pushing.

Thirty-Seven

The young woman, with blond hair drawn back from her face into waves and curls to her shoulders, was dressed in a short-sleeved print floral dress. She faltered and stopped a few feet from her mother and Edie, her blue eyes troubled and apprehensive. Tommy, now four and a half, clung to the pram handle and leaned against his mother's skirt. He stared at the two older women as if he didn't recognize either of them. Perhaps he didn't for he'd hardly seen either of them since he'd left Grimsby.

'Mam?' Irene said hesitantly. Briefly, her glance took in her mother-in-law. 'Aunty Edie.'

Lil felt faint and clutched at the chair to steady herself. She just continued to stare at her daughter, opening and shutting her mouth though no words would come. It was Edie who said, bluntly, 'What's all this, Irene? Is it yours?'

Irene bit her lip and flushed scarlet. There was no need for her to answer; her reaction told them the truth. Edie turned on her heel, went into her house and slammed the door so hard that Lil flinched.

After a moment's pause, whilst both Irene and Tommy waited, the little boy staring up at his grandmother with soulful brown eyes, Lil said flatly, 'You'd better come in.' She held out her hand to Tommy, though she made no move to hug her daughter. And she didn't even glance into the pram.

Inside the house, with the door firmly closed against prying neighbours – even Edie – Lil faced Irene. 'Now – you'd better explain yourself, my girl.'

Lil had so looked forward to her daughter and grandson coming home and now it looked as if it was all going to be spoiled.

'Aren't I welcome, Mam?' Irene asked in a husky voice. 'Because if not, then I'll go back to Mr and Mrs Schofield.'

'And do they think this' – Lil waved her hand towards the pram and the still crying infant – 'is your husband's?'

Irene bit her lip and shook her head. 'Look, Mam. She's yelling because she's hungry. Let me feed her and put her down and then we – we can talk.'

'Oh aye. And what makes you think I want to talk? Mebbe I want to put you straight back on the train and send you packing. That's what I ought to do.' And silently she added to herself – it's what I'll have to do if I want to stay friends with Edie.

Irene lifted her head and stared back at her mother with a defiance in her eyes that Lil had never seen before. Irene had always been biddable, a good little girl, though Lil remembered she could be stubborn if the mood took her. But now . . .

Lil sighed and relented. 'Feed it, then, if you must, and then we'll decide what's to be done.'

'It's a she, Mam. And her name's Marie.'

Irene bent and picked the yelling child out of the pram. Now, Lil could see that the baby was about three or four months old with fair, downy hair and though, at the moment, she was red-faced with crying, she could see that the baby was a pretty little thing.

Irene sat down in the easy chair beside the fireplace and unbuttoned her blouse.

Shocked, Lil waved her hand towards Tommy and said, 'You don't let him see, do you?'

For the first time since she'd arrived home, Irene smiled. 'He's used to it. Besides, he's seen all sorts in the country, haven't you, love?'

Lil bit her lip and then said firmly, 'Come with me, Tommy, and I'll get you summat to eat. You must be hungry, an' all.'

As she led her grandson into the scullery, peace reigned as the baby began to suck noisily at Irene's breast. Normally, such a sight and sound would have filled Lil with joy, but now the sight of the little girl horrified her.

Oh, Irene what have you done? And where will it all end?

'There, lovey,' Lil said gently to the young solemn-faced little boy. 'You eat that up.'

Tommy gazed up at her and in his piping voice he said, 'You're my grandma, aren't you?'

'Yes, I am.'

He frowned. 'You came to the farm, didn't you?' Lil nodded, her throat too full to speak. She had been so happy to see Irene and Tommy well settled in the countryside. The Schofields had seemed such nice people, but had they stood by whilst *this* had happened and done nothing, said nothing?

'Your daughter and her little boy will be fine with us, ducks,' Ruth had said. 'Don't you worry about them. We'll look after them. In fact, you'd be welcome to come here too, if you can.'

Sorrowfully – how she wished she could have said 'yes' – Lil had shaken her head.

'I can't – I'm doing war work. I don't think I'd be allowed.'

'That's a shame,' the kindly woman had said, 'but you're welcome to visit them any time.'

But it hadn't been possible for Lil to travel even the relatively short distance to the village near Louth many times during the years that her family had been there. She had contented herself with Irene's newsy letters. At least, Lil realized now with a shock, they'd been full of news and everything that she and Tommy had been doing when they'd first arrived. She even remembered snippets of the letters word for word for she'd poured over them so many times.

> *The Schofields have got two sons,* Irene had written, *but they're in the army and their parents are missing them like crazy. So, Mr and Mrs S are making a big fuss of Tommy. He's getting quite spoiled. They've got two land army girls working on the farm and Mrs S is quite happy for me to help out on the farm too and she doesn't mind baby-sitting occasionally when we go to a dance in the village . . .*

Two sons, Lil remembered. Was it one of them who had fathered Irene's bastard? Lil shuddered at the dreadful word, for that was what that poor bairn was – or was she? Lil wasn't sure what the law was if a married woman gave birth to a child who wasn't her husband's. She wondered what Irene had put on the birth certificate. Maybe she'd had the sauce to put Frank's name. Edie would be incensed if that were the case.

As if she wasn't mad enough now, Lil thought sadly.

Tommy was eating his meal neatly, using his knife and fork correctly. He's been well trained, Lil thought.

'Did you go to the village school, Tommy?'

The boy swallowed the mouthful before replying. 'Yes, Grandma. I like it there. I shouldn't really have gone before I'm five, but they let me start early. Just for half a day. Will I have to go to school here now?' The little boy was well-mannered and articulate for his age.

'I – I expect so.' Lil faltered. 'Unless, of course . . .' Her voice trailed away as a sudden thought struck her.

Maybe it would be best if they went back to the farm. Were Mr and Mrs Schofield prepared to have them back because one of their sons *was* the baby girl's father?

'Did you – um – see Mr and Mrs Schofield's sons much?'

'No. They never came home.'

'Not all the time you were there?'

Tommy shook his head as he set his knife and fork neatly side by side on the empty plate. 'May I have some pudding, please, Grandma?'

'Oh – I'm sorry, I haven't made any pudding.'

Tommy pouted for a moment. 'Mrs Schofield *always* made pudding.'

'I'm sorry. I'll be sure to make one tomorrow.' That's if, she thought to herself, you're still here.

As Lil stood up and began to clear away Tommy's plate, Irene opened the door into the scullery. 'She's asleep now. I've put her back in her pram just until we decide . . .'

'Then Tommy'd better go outside and play.'

Irene drew in a sharp breath. 'He's not going out into the street. Not yet. Not until . . .'

'Then he can go into the backyard. Tommy,' she turned to the boy, 'if you go into the washhouse, you'll find a ball near the mangle. It's one I kept here for Reggie to play with when I looked after him.' There was a catch in Lil's voice at the memory. 'You can have a kick-about.'

'Isn't there anyone I can play with? At the farm I played with Alfie, who lived at the end of the lane.'

Lil sighed. She could see there were going to be a lot of comparisons made between life here in the town and on the farm. And none of them favourable to us, Lil thought. Perhaps it would be better all round if they did go back. And yet her heart wrenched at the thought of losing her daughter, grandson and – it had to be said – her granddaughter for good. She loved her daughter devotedly, even though at this moment she was angry and disappointed in her. Yet Irene was still her flesh and blood as were Tommy and the baby.

Lil had a granddaughter! The realization came as a shock.

It was what they'd all wanted; a little girl alongside Tommy. Frank especially had always wanted a little girl, he'd said. But not this way – not like this! He wouldn't want this one and his mother had already made her feelings very plain. If Irene stayed here, then Lil's friendship with Edie was over. And if the little family went back to the country, then Lil would be alone for the rest of her life with nothing to look forward to except fleeting and infrequent visits to the farm when she could save the money for the fare. It was a heart-breaking decision she would have to make but, even though she loved Edie as a dear friend, family would always come first, as indeed it would with Edie. Lil couldn't blame her for taking her son's side, as 'sides' there'd surely be. And what would Archie say when he came home from his latest trip? Lil shuddered. The whole family would be against her; indeed, soon the whole street might ostracize them, for Edie was a force to be reckoned with in the neighbourhood. She'd turn everyone against her former friend.

Sensing the tension between the two women, Tommy slipped down from his chair and went out of the back door, closing it quietly behind him. Slowly, Lil turned to look at her daughter.

Thirty-Eight

'Whose is it?' Lil asked bluntly unable to hold back the question any longer the moment Tommy was out of earshot.

The stubborn look Lil remembered so well came over Irene's face. 'I'm not telling you that, Mam. I don't want anyone making trouble.'

'Why? Is he married?' Lil almost spat the words out in her growing disgust. She no longer knew her own daughter. She would never have thought that Irene could do something like this. Archie had always called her 'a good little lass'. Well, he wouldn't think so now.

Irene closed her eyes. 'Don't ask, Mam. Please don't ask any more.'

'I take it he is, then. And he's not going to stand by you? 'Spect he's gone back to his wife, has he? After a nice little fling that leaves you holding the baby. Literally. Oh,' she snorted contemptuously, 'men have it so easy. Just have their fun and walk away without a backward glance—'

'He's dead, Mam,' Irene blurted out, unable to bear her mother's tirade any longer. 'He's not coming back to anyone.'

Horrified, Lil's mouth dropped open as she stared at Irene, whose eyes filled with easy tears.

'Well, I'm sorry for the young feller,' Lil said stiffly. 'I wouldn't wish anyone any harm. And I feel sorry for the Schofields. They must have been devastated.' Even though Tommy had indicated that they'd never been home, Lil believed the little boy had got it wrong.

Irene frowned. 'The Schofields? Why would they be devastated?'

'Losing their son, of course.'

'Their son?' Irene stared at her mother and then she laughed wryly as she understood just what Lil was implying. 'Oh, no, Marie's father's not one of the Schofields' boys. As far as we know, they're still both fine and itching to come home as soon as their turn for demob comes up.'

'Oh!' Lil was startled by this revelation. 'Then who—?'

Irene sighed. 'Mam, I told you I'm not telling you his name. I won't ever tell anyone because I don't want to cause trouble for his poor family. But I'll just tell you this and it's all I'm going to tell anyone. He was a bomber pilot and he was killed on a raid.'

'Do his family know, I mean—?'

'I've said, no more, Mam,' Irene snapped. She made as if to get up but Lil put out her hand to stop her.

'All right, all right, I won't ask any more.' Heavily, she added, 'It won't make any difference anyway. I just thought that he – or they – might stand by you in some way, but . . .' Her voice faded away as the last vestige of that hope died. But she still had another question. 'You said the Schofields would have you back to live with them? Why, if the child's not their son's?'

Irene's mouth was tight and there was a trace of accusation in her tone as she said, 'They're good people. They understand how lonely I was. How – how I was missing Frank – afraid he might never come back. It was wrong, I know that, and I'm not making any excuses, but it's what happens in war. I'm not the only one.'

'And that makes it better, does it?' Lil muttered.

'No, but just remember, I could have had her adopted and said nothing to anyone. The Schofields would have kept my secret, but I could hardly have sworn a four-year-old little boy to secrecy, could I? It'd've come out somehow, sometime. Better to face the music. And there was Reggie too. He knew and he'd have told his mother, I don't doubt. Besides,' her eyes softened, 'Marie's a dear little thing. I couldn't bear to give her up.'

'So the Schofields knew him, did they?'

'Just stop digging, Mam, 'cos you're not getting to know any more either from me or from them.'

Lil could see that she was going to be told nothing more so all she said now was, 'So, what are you going to do?'

Irene gave a wan smile and Lil could see the sadness in her eyes. She was putting on an act of defiance, but Lil knew her daughter – she hadn't changed so much – and Irene wasn't feeling as brave inside as she'd like everyone to think.

'Unless you turn us all out here and now, I'm going to stay here until Frank gets home and tell him the truth and let him decide.'

Lil's mouth dropped open at the audacity of her decision. 'Well, I reckon you'll find Edie has summat to say about that long before Frank has a chance to get home.'

Edie was sitting at her table, a cup of tea growing cold in front of her as she stared out of the window over-looking the backyard. The door into the yard from the passageway running between two houses banged and Shirley's shadow passed the living-room window overlooking the backyard. The back door opened with a flourish and closed with another crash. Everyone knew when Shirley arrived home. There was a moment's pause whilst she took off her shoes in the scullery and then padded on stockinged feet into the living room.

'Ursula's gone home. She says she's got a cold and isn't feeling well, but I reckon it's because she feels awkward.' Shirley laughed. 'She thinks folks don't like her accent. I told her, if they'd been going to object, they'd have done it months ago.'

Suddenly, a shaft of fear struck her as Shirley realized her mother was sitting, just staring into space as if . . . There was no sign of an evening meal being prepared, though, after all they had eaten at the party, that was reasonable enough. But there was something strange about her mother's attitude. Her face was a mask, her shoulders slumped. The girl caught her breath and sat down, suddenly quiet, in a chair opposite Edie. 'Mam?' she whispered. 'What is it? What's happened? Is it – is it Dad?' Despite not being actively involved in the war, Archie was in constant danger fishing in the North Sea. 'Or – or our Frank?'

Edie blinked, brought out of her reverie. 'It's Frank, at least . . .'

'Oh no, no!' Shirley cried, shocked. 'But the war's over. Surely he's not got killed *now* at the very last minute?'

'No, no, duck,' Edie said hastily, 'it's nothing like that. He's fine as far as I know, though,' she added bitterly, 'I reckon there's someone he'll want to kill when he does get home.'

'Mam, you're talking in riddles. Just tell me what's

happened? Oh, I know,' she went on, making up her own stories. 'It's our Beth. She's got herself in the family way, has she? That's why we haven't heard from her in months.' She laughed gleefully. 'By heck, Dad'll have a ducky fit if his precious Beth's got herself into trouble.'

'It's not Beth,' Edie said flatly. 'It's Irene.'

'What do you mean, "It's Irene"? What about her?'

'She's come home today – this afternoon – pushing a pram up the street as bold as brass – with a little babby in it.'

Shirley's mouth dropped open. 'Never! Not Irene!' She paused, blinking as the enormity of what her mother was saying hit her with full force. 'My God! What's our Frank going to say?' She paused and then added vehemently, 'Or do!'

Edie's mouth was grim. 'Divorce her, probably, the little trollop. Eee, Shirley, how could she do it? To Frank? To all of us?'

Shirley was silent for a moment. There weren't many people in the world that she truly liked, but Irene had been one of them. Though it was she and her older sister, Beth, who were best friends, they'd both been kind to Shirley and had often included her on their outings, even though she was younger than they were. They hadn't had to do it, but they'd never made her feel left out. They'd always taken her 'down dock' to meet Archie when he came ashore and involved her in raiding his sea bag for the treats that were always there. And they'd never missed taking her into town on their shopping sprees when Archie was 'king for a day' down Freeman Street. No, of all the family, Beth and Irene had shown the awkward young girl the most kindness and understanding. But now, since she'd joined the ATS, Shirley had found her niche. She'd made friends – real friends – of her own. Though she'd felt closer to her mother when she'd been the only one left at home, she'd been honest enough with herself to know that, once the others came back after the war, the focus of attention would move away from her again. When Frank, Beth and Reggie were all back, Shirley would hardly be noticed – or missed. So, she had taken the decision to make her own life and it had been the right move for she was happier and more self-confident than she'd ever been. Her plainness at the side of her prettier, cleverer sister wasn't so noticeable when she was smartly dressed in her uniform. But now a different sort of tragedy had hit their family and perhaps, after all, her mother would need her now.

'Well, Mam,' Shirley said at last, 'it's not often I'm shocked, but I have to say I am this time. I'd never have thought it of Irene.' She caught her mother's gaze and held it saying softly, 'Whatever is poor Aunty Lil going to do?'

'Aye,' Edie said gruffly, 'that's what I'd like to know.'

Slyly, Shirley added, 'What would you do if it had been Beth who'd come home with a babby in her arms?'

Edie shook her head. 'I don't know, duck. I really don't, but I do know what I'm going to do about that 'un.' She jerked her thumb towards the wall that divided the two houses. 'I aren't having owt to do with her. And I'll tell our Frank not to, either, when he does get home.'

At that moment, through the thin wall, they heard the wails of a hungry child.

For the rest of that day and the whole of the following day, neither Edie nor Shirley went next door. It was probably the longest time that the two older women had gone without at least speaking over the fence as they hung out their washing or having a cup of tea or a meal together in one of their houses. Lil didn't know whether to be sorry or relieved that Edie hadn't come round.

The next morning, as Shirley was getting ready to return to camp at the end of her short leave, Edie said, 'I've decided to go and see Reggie and see if I can persuade him to come home. Like you said, Shirley, he's not old enough to make that sort of a decision.'

Shirley smirked, 'And to find out more about Irene's bastard.'

Edie smiled grimly and said sarcastically, 'However did you guess?'

'I wish I could come with you, but I've got to get back. Just you be sure you write and tell me what happens, Mam. With both of them.'

'No, no, you run along, duck. I'll write and tell you all about it. I promise.'

Shirley kissed her mother goodbye, doubting very much whether Edie would tell her anything. Still, she thought, as she hefted her kitbag onto her shoulder and set off up the street without a glance towards Lil's house, she knew enough now to write and tell Frank what was waiting for him when he got home. She'd write to Beth, too, if only she knew where she was.

Edie was kneeling on the hearth black-leading the range. Although she had a modern cooker standing in the scullery, she still took pride in the shining appearance of the fireplace in the living room. Every Friday she would wash the ornaments and dust the photographs standing on the mantelpiece and polish the two brass candlesticks, standing at each end. She stood up, wincing a little as her knees protested for a moment. She removed everything from the mantelpiece, washed the top and then each item. She paused for a moment, holding the photograph of Laurence, his handsome face smiling up at her from its frame.

'What would you think to all these goings-on, eh?' she murmured and then, with a sigh, she replaced it tenderly in the centre. Next came the fender and the brass companion set with its poker, hearth-brush, tongs and tiny shovel, and then the toasting fork. It had always been Beth's job to make hot buttered toast for all the family for Sunday tea. Edie polished them all lovingly with Brasso and, last of all, the heavy black iron kettle would be cleaned and set back on the fire for the inevitable cup of tea that, by this time, Edie felt she had earned.

Usually, Lil would come in about now and they'd sit and chat, but, this morning, there would be no Lil.

Later that morning, despite her worries, Edie enjoyed the train journey. Much as she loved the town of Grimsby and its people – and she really did – it was good to get out into the open countryside, to see the animals grazing, the gently rolling fields of the Wolds with the crops growing in the early summer sunshine. And best of all, it was so good to know that England was now free and at peace once more. No more bombing, no more blackouts and soon, hopefully, no more rationing. If only all her family would come home. Frank was safe, but what a welcome home he would get now! Her heart ached for the sadness that awaited him. After all he'd done to help fight a war to preserve freedom and make a better life for his little family, for

Irene to betray him in such a way, well, Edie couldn't countenance it. And she certainly couldn't forgive the girl. What would happen? She couldn't begin to guess. She tried to turn her mind away from that particular trouble; today – more than anything – she hoped to persuade Reggie to come back home. And yet, she was honest enough to admit that, once she got to the Schofields, the temptation to ask about Irene would be too great.

But there was one more of her brood about whom she hardly dared to think: Beth. What had happened to Beth? She was so alone in her fears for her elder daughter. She couldn't talk to Archie about it; she didn't want him to be any more worried than he already was. Beth was the apple of his eye – always had been – and if something had happened to her, she didn't think her poor Archie would ever get over it. Well, you don't get over losing a child, she admonished herself sharply, just as she'd never get over Laurence's death. You just get on with it. And she hadn't felt able to confide in Lil, either, though she'd wanted to often enough. The postcards had continued to arrive, albeit infrequently, so she must be all right, mustn't she? Though recently, she reminded herself, they had stopped altogether.

Out at sea, Archie was thinking about Beth too. It was peaceful out here, he mused. The life was hard, the conditions often cold, wet and uncomfortable, but it was the only life he knew and, all in all, it was a good life, even though there'd been the added dangers recently. He still had his regular crew, mostly older, seasoned men – even more so now that all the youngsters had gone off to war. Problems from home seemed very far away when he was at sea, yet even here he could not leave behind his concerns about Beth.

He'd never confided his anxieties to any other member of his family, though had Laurence or even Frank been at home, he might have taken one of them into his confidence. But Laurence was gone and Frank had not been home for years.

It had been the postcards that had first made him suspicious. He knew they brought Edie comfort and she seemed to believe their authenticity, but to Archie there was something odd. At first, they'd arrived with a strange regularity. Though Beth was bright and outgoing and very organized, he doubted that even she would have written on the same day every month and then the frequency had lessened and he'd been very sceptical that the last few cards had even been written by her. Oh, the handwriting was hers – or if not hers, then an excellent forgery – but it was the wording that troubled him – or rather the lack of it. In her earlier cards she had always mentioned a member of the family, or referred to Irene and her nephew, Tommy.

'*Sorry you can't write back to me,*' she'd written in one early missive. '*But I'm moving about so much with the work I'm doing, letters would probably never reach me.*'

And then the postcards had started and recently the way she signed off was different. Her usual '*Stay safe*' message to them all was missing.

And that had been when Archie had really started to worry.

Thirty-Nine

Lost in her thoughts, Edie almost missed Fotherby Halt where she had to alight. Hastily, she gathered up her coat and handbag. Leaving the platform, she passed through the gate and walked eastwards down the long lane at the end of which was White Gates Farm. She came to the farmyard gate and paused for a moment, catching her breath. Hens scratched in the dirt and ducks and geese waddled about the yard, squawking. Three geese came towards her, menacingly, it seemed. She liked to see the countryside but she didn't think she could ever feel a real part of it. She was a townie.

Ruth Schofield appeared at the back door of the farmhouse and then hurried across the yard, shooing the birds away. They protested loudly, but obeyed, far more frightened of the farmer's wife than she was of them.

'Better than a guard dog, they are.' Ruth smiled. 'Come in, my dear. Reggie's not here at the moment. He's out in the fields with Mr Schofield and the land girls.' She grimaced as she pulled open the gate in invitation. 'I 'spect we'll be losing them soon now. Still, it's wonderful news it's all over, isn't it?'

Edie nodded and stepped through the gate and into the yard.

'Come along into the house and I'll make us a nice cup of tea.'

Edie beamed. 'They're the most welcome words I've heard all day.'

Minutes later, seated across the kitchen table from the farmer's wife, between mouthfuls of home-made shortbread, Edie asked, 'Is Reggie all right, Mrs Schofield?'

'Ruth, dear,' the woman reminded Edie gently. But then a wary look crossed her face as she added, 'He's fine, but I can guess why you've come to see him.'

'I got a letter from him,' Edie blurted out, 'telling me that he wants to stay here – that he doesn't want to come home. Why?'

'He's happy here – oh that sounds awful,' Ruth said swiftly. 'What I mean is, he wants to make working on the land his job. He says the only thing back in Grimsby would be fishing and he doesn't want to go to sea.'

Edie felt the relief flood through her. At least she and her son were agreed on that. 'But I want him home,' she said, as tears filled her eyes. She brushed them aside, embarrassed by a show of weakness in front of this comparative stranger.

'I know you do,' Ruth said gently, 'but he's taken to the life so well here. He's got a real love for the land – an instinct. He'll make a wonderful farmer in years to come. Joe thinks the world of him and,' her face fell into sorrowful lines, 'to tell you the truth, Edie, we're not even sure our own two sons want to take over the farm when we're too old to manage it any more. We're only tenant farmers, mind, we don't own it, so it's not as if there's an inheritance as such, but we'd still like to think that the land we've toiled over will be in good hands.'

'But they're both all right – your boys?' Edie asked hesitantly. 'I mean – they're coming home?'

'Oh yes, yes. We've been lucky – we know that.' Ruth bit her lip. She knew that Edie had lost her eldest son. In that moment, she felt the twinge of guilt of a mother whose sons had survived.

Edie sighed heavily. She'd always vowed she'd never rule her children's lives – not once they were grown-up. But, to her, Reggie was still a boy. Could he really be expected – or trusted – to make such an important decision? And what would Archie say? She smiled inwardly. She knew exactly what her husband would say.

'Let the boy have his way – if that's what he wants. It'll be a hard life, but a good one for him. But it's a sight better than fishing, love.'

Archie loved the sea and his way of life. It was what he had been brought up to know, for his father had been a trawlerman too, and Archie had wanted no other job, but he was not blind to the many dangers; dangers which had got even worse over the six years of war. No, Archie wouldn't want to stop Reggie doing what he wanted.

'So, you want him to stay with you? Live here, like?'

'We do, Edie,' Ruth said promptly. 'And I promise you we'll look after him. And we'll make sure he comes to see his family regularly. Joe will be going into Grimsby more often now and he can bring Reggie with him.'

Edie forced a smile, but could not trust herself to speak as she was obliged to accept the inevitable.

It wasn't long before they heard noises in the yard and four people came into the kitchen that was at once alive with chatter and laughter. And amongst it all was Reggie.

'Hello, Mam, what're you doing here?' He grinned and then, seeing her expression, his smile faded. 'Ah, I bet I know why you've come. Well, I aren't coming home.'

Edie stared at her son; she hardly recognized him. He had grown so much. He was tall and thin, yet his shoulders were broadening, already giving promise of the strong, well-built man he would one day be. His brown hair still curled, though it was cut shorter now. His face and hands were tanned with working outdoors in all weathers, but his cheeky grin was still the same until overshadowed by the mutinous look he now wore.

'Sit down, Reggie,' Ruth said, getting up from the table and bustling about her kitchen. 'And talk to your mam.'

Now his face took on a little boy's appealing look. 'Mam, I love it here. I love the land and the work' – he grimaced comically – 'even though it's hard sometimes. Besides, I *can't* come home, Mam. Mr Schofield needs help. Now the war's over, the land girls'll be going home. He'll have no one.'

'He'll have his sons back.' Edie couldn't quite hide the edge of bitterness in her tone. The Schofields were lucky; both their sons were coming home and now it seemed they wanted to keep one of hers too.

'Tell you what,' Reggie said, his eyes lighting up. 'Why don't you and Dad come and have a holiday here on the farm at harvest time?'

Ruth Schofield took up the plea. 'The Government have warned folks not to flock to the seaside all at once, so the farmers around here are advertising for Harvest Holidays for town and city folks to come and have a working break.'

Edie laughed, though her laugh was a little strained. 'We *are* at the seaside. We don't need to go there.'

Ruth laughed too, 'Of course you are. How silly of

me. But perhaps you'd like a few days in the country-side.'

'Helping with the harvest, you mean?'

'Only if you wanted to. We'd be pleased to have Reggie's family any time. We've plenty of room.'

'But you want him to stay?' Edie repeated her earlier question in front of Reggie. 'You want him to live with you?'

'It's what he wants, Edie.'

'But you've not tried to persuade him to come home, have you?'

'Well,' Ruth glanced uncomfortably at Reggie, 'no – I must admit, we haven't.'

'Mam, please see it from my point of view. And,' Reggie added craftily, 'you don't really want me to go to sea, do you? And what else would I do if I came back to Grimsby?'

'They'll stop the ten-and-six-a-week they've been paying you.' It was Edie's last shot across Ruth's bows. She saw the woman and Reggie glance at each other.

'We know that,' the farmer's wife said softly. 'It's not about the money. Besides, we'll be paying him to work for us.'

'They've been paying me already, Mam, for what I've done after school and at weekends.'

Edie felt herself beaten. If only Archie were here. She'd know what to do then. She would have been guided by his common sense and reasoning. Edie was honest enough with herself to know that her argument stemmed from her overwhelming desire to have all her chicks back under her roof. But it seemed now that that was never going to be possible.

'I'll see what your dad says when he's next home,' was all Edie would promise. 'We'll both come out to see you. We might be able to borrow your Uncle Harry's car. It's been laid up all the war but he's taken it to the garage to have it put into working order again. Aunty Jessie says they're waiting for a new battery for it and new tyres and they're hard to come by at the moment.'

The Kelseys had never owned a car, but Harry and Jessie had bought a second-hand Morris 6 painted green and black in 1935.

'It's a nice motor, Harry,' Archie had said, as he stood looking at it, 'but you'd do best not to be seen driving it around Grimsby.'

'Eh? Why ever not?'

'Fishermen don't like the colour green. Edie knows better than to buy a green dress. The only green that ever gets into our house is vegetables. I thought you'd have known that, Harry, working on the docks.'

'Oh lor'! Yes, I do, but, to be honest, I was that delighted getting such a bargain, I never thought about it. Mebbe that's why it was so cheap. I'll get it painted over.' Harry had been as good as his word. He would never want to bring ill-luck on Archie and his fellow fishermen and so the car had been repainted a maroon colour. But for the duration of the war, it had stood idly in the narrow alleyway behind their house.

Now Edie murmured, 'I was just counting the days until you all come home, that's all.'

Reggie, who had every faith that his dad would agree with him and would be the one to persuade his mother to agree too, touched her hand and said huskily, 'I know, Mam, I know.'

They were both thinking of the one who could never come back.

'Are you sure, Reggie, really sure that this is what you want?' She was still clinging to a last vestige of hope, even though in her heart she knew it was in vain. And she knew for certain when she saw the light in his eyes.

'It is, Mam, I promise you.'

She nodded, the lump in her throat almost choking her as she said, 'Then so be it. We'll say no more about it now, but, you understand, your dad will have to agree.'

Reggie nodded, his eyes shining. He had no fear of his dad doing anything else.

But there was still plenty that Edie had to say to Ruth, though this time it was not about her son. For the twenty minutes or so whilst the farmer and his workers drank tea and ate a fruit pasty as their 'elevenses', Edie held her tongue. She wanted to be alone with Ruth once more before she broached the delicate subject of her daughter-in-law.

She watched the easy rapport between Joe Schofield – a big, quiet man, with a firm handshake and gentle eyes – and his workers. The two land army girls were quite sweet with Reggie, teasing him as they might a younger brother – in fact, they reminded Edie heartachingly of the way Beth and her brothers had been together when they'd all been at home. Shirley, though, she thought sadly, had always been the odd one out, but Edie realized now it had been the young girl's own fault; she had never joined in the family banter, holding herself aloof and always looking slightly disapproving. But now, there was hope even for Shirley. She, too, seemed to have found her niche in life, even though, to Edie's chagrin, it would keep her away from home as well. And here, the two girls and Reggie – and even Joe and Ruth – were just like a family. Reggie would miss these two lasses when they went home. But, as the conversation went on, Edie gleaned that one of the girls – Pearl, with dark hair and brown eyes – was also thinking of staying on.

'She's found herself a boyfriend on the next farm,' her companion, Eve, with red curls and dancing green eyes, said.

Edie nodded and smiled. Perhaps, she was thinking, it was Pearl she ought to be talking to about Irene.

When Joe rose to go out, the three workers got up at once.

'You stay here, lad, and talk to your mam. We can manage for an hour or so.'

'No, no,' Edie said at once. 'I wouldn't want to keep him from his work.' She stood up and clasped the embarrassed boy to her ample bosom before saying firmly, 'Off you go, but don't forget where we live now, will you?'

'We'll see he comes home often to see you,' Joe said in his deep voice. 'Things should get easier now.'

Edie was touched that the man referred to the house in Grimsby as Reggie's home, but she knew in her heart that this was no longer so; the farm was where the boy wanted to be and these good people would parent him from now on.

She nodded and forced a smile, though, for a moment, she was unable to speak.

When they'd all gone out, chattering and laughing together, Ruth busied herself at her sink to wash up the cups, saucers and plates that had been used. Automatically, Edie stood up and reached for a tea towel.

'Ruth, there's summat else I want to ask you.'

'I thought there might be,' the woman said softly, setting a cup carefully on the wooden draining board for Edie to pick up to dry.

'About Irene.'

Ruth sighed as if she had been dreading the inevitable question. She'd known that Edie's visit wouldn't only be about Reggie.

'D'you know who the father of her baby is?' Edie asked bluntly.

Ruth's slight hesitation before she answered spoke volumes. 'Not – really.'

'But you can guess? Am I right?'

Ruth bit her lip but was obliged to nod.

Edie felt guilty at interrogating this nice little woman who was so good to Reggie, and yet, she had to know. 'So?'

'The girls – Pearl, Eve and Irene – used to go to the village dance on a Saturday night. Reggie went too sometimes, but me and Joe used to look after Tommy. We didn't see any harm in it, Edie.' Ruth turned towards her with pleading eyes. 'We wanted the young ones to have a bit of fun – oh, I know, maybe Irene shouldn't have gone,' she added swiftly, as she saw Edie open her mouth to make some retort. Ruth hurried on, not giving Edie a chance to speak. 'But she worked so hard on the farm alongside the others, we thought she deserved a night out once a week and she was missing her husband so much—'

'Was she now?' Edie muttered sarcastically.

'There's a bomber station not far from here,' Ruth went on, 'and the lads from there used to come to the village dance if they weren't flying. Of course, there was a bit of rivalry between the local farmhands and the RAF boys in their smart uniforms. Caused a bit of ill feeling now and again, I think, when they'd all had a bit to drink. But the local bobby was very good. He was usually around on a Saturday night to stop any quarrels getting out of hand. But one night there was a bit of a fisticuffs between Pearl's boyfriend and one of the airmen. Evidently, this RAF lad was getting a bit too friendly with Pearl, if you know what I mean.'

Oh aye, Edie thought wryly, I know exactly what you mean, but she didn't interrupt this time; she didn't want to stop Ruth, who seemed to be a long time coming to the point.

'Well, it seems your Irene—'

She's not 'my' Irene, Edie wanted to shout. Not any more. And I doubt she'll be Frank's when he gets home. But she bit her lip and remained silent.

'– stepped in and broke up the fight. Ken – that's the RAF lad – had a cut and a black eye and Irene administered first aid.' Ruth smiled. 'All the girls went on a first-aid training course in the village hall one night a week.

Another night in the week when Irene had left her son in Ruth's care! Not that Edie thought that a problem; she liked this woman and would have trusted her own children with her. With a jolt, she realized that that was exactly what she was going to do; leave her Reggie to be looked after by Ruth. But now, she wondered, just how many nights a week Irene had left Tommy to go out dancing or . . . she shied away from the picture that came into her mind.

'Irene patched him up and they got talking and' – she sighed – 'well, you can guess the rest. They were both lonely. Irene's husband was far away and she didn't even know if he was ever going to come back. And Ken – well, he was facing danger and possible death every time he went up in his bomber, wasn't he?'

'Did he ever come here – to the farm? Did you meet him?'

'A group of the lads from the station used to come

350

now and again and, yes, he was one of them. Especially at festive times – like Christmas and Easter – when they couldn't get leave to go home or it was too far for them to travel in the given time. But I promise you, Edie,' Ruth turned troubled eyes to her, 'I had no idea things were getting out of hand. I feel so guilty now that we encouraged her to go out and have fun. If I'd thought for one moment . . .' Ruth picked up the corner of her apron and wiped her eyes.

Edie was touched by how upset Ruth was over something that was hardly her concern and certainly not her fault. She had opened her home and, it seemed, her heart to strangers in dangerous times. She'd looked after them all and tried to do her best for them and this was how Irene had repaid the kindly woman by bringing shame to her door. Edie was moved to put her arms around Ruth. 'It's not your fault, love. You're not responsible in any way. Irene is. And the feller, of course.'

Edie patted her back and released her and they both sat down at the table again.

'Do you know much about him?'

Ruth shook her head. 'Only that he got killed on a bombing raid just before Irene found out she was carrying a child.'

'Killed!' For a moment, Edie was stunned. This was something she hadn't thought of. She'd imagined meeting up with him somewhere and giving him a piece of her mind. It took her a moment to recover before she said hoarsely, 'So – he didn't know, then? She didn't have a chance to tell him?'

Ruth shook her head.

'Do you think,' Edie asked slowly, 'it would have made any difference if he had known?'

'How – how d'you mean?'

'Would he have stood by her? Married her?'

Ruth gasped. 'But – but she's married. I mean, your boy's coming home, isn't he?'

'Thank God, yes, but I don't reckon he'll want to take on someone else's kid. I reckon he'll divorce her.'

Ruth stared at her for a moment and then glanced away, mouthing a silent 'Oh'.

'So,' Edie said grimly, 'the little madam's come home to see if my Frank'll be daft enough to forgive her and take on a cuckoo in the nest, has she?'

'If that's how you see it, Edie,' Ruth said, her tone a little stiff now. 'But I told Irene before she left that if things didn't work out for her and her kiddies back home, then she was welcome back here.'

'Well, she'd be coming without Tommy, I can tell you that now. Tommy'll stay with his dad – with us. You'll not take any more of my family from me.'

Ruth blanched and her mouth trembled. Edie could have bitten her tongue off. 'I'm sorry,' she said swiftly, but the damage had been done, the words had been spoken and could not be unsaid.

Ruth waved her hand and shook her head. 'I can understand how you must feel and, to be honest, we wouldn't have suggested them coming back here except that we felt so guilty it happened whilst she was under our roof and – and' – she avoided Edie's eyes – 'Irene said she thought that that was what would happen. She wasn't even sure if her own mother would have her back.' Now she glanced at Edie. 'She's your best friend, isn't she?'

Edie sniffed. 'She was, but we haven't spoken since the day Irene arrived home.'

'That's a shame.'

Edie didn't answer.

Forty

As Edie waited for the train, carefully carrying a basket laden with eggs, butter and cheese from the farm, her thoughts were in turmoil. Ruth had hit a raw nerve when speaking about Lil. Edie was missing her old friend more than she would ever have believed possible. Ever since the day that Lil and Tom had moved into the house next door that was only a wall's thickness from Edie's home, the two women had been close friends. Each of them having a baby of a similar age had brought the women together as perhaps nothing else could have done. When Tom was lost at sea, Edie became Lil's rock and she, in turn, was there to help Edie at the births of both Shirley and Reggie.

Edie sighed as she heaved herself onto the train and found a seat. She hardly saw the countryside passing by the window; her thoughts were turned inwards. What was the right thing to do? Should she go round to make peace with Lil and then they could face this problem together? But the thought made her shudder. Though she longed to see her grandson Tommy, she didn't want to see Irene and she certainly didn't want to clap eyes on the little bastard in their midst.

But there was no doubting the fact that she was missing her dear friend.

As Edie alighted and left the station, she thought, I'll wait until Archie gets back from sea. He'll know what's best. She sighed again. It had been the story of her life: waiting for Archie to come home from the sea before she could make any momentous decision that affected the family. The only time she'd had to decide something really important had been when she'd sent Reggie away to the countryside with Irene and Tommy. There, she thought, it always comes back to bloody Irene!

Irene was sitting near the window of the front bedroom overlooking the street below. Lil – though still unsure of the future – had, for the moment, insisted that her daughter should have the bigger bedroom for herself and the baby. Having just fed Marie, Irene had buttoned her blouse and moved closer to the window, watching the comings and goings on the street below. The house was silent. Lil had taken Tommy into the town to buy him some new shoes and even the restless baby was quiet for the moment, replete and sleepy in her arms.

Irene saw Edie coming along the street, carrying the heavy basket, her expression like thunder. Irene's hopes died in that moment. Whatever her husband would feel, the woman walking along the street below was never going to allow her son to forgive his wife. As Edie crossed the road towards her home and disappeared from Irene's view, the young woman tensed, holding her breath as she waited for a knock on their door. But no knock came and Irene breathed a sigh that she wasn't quite sure was relief or disappointment.

She laid the baby in the battered cot, which she and Lil had struggled to get down from the attic room. Normally, Lil would have enlisted Edie's help – and certainly Archie's, if he'd been at home – but this time . . .

The baby slept soundly and Irene, exhausted by loss of sleep the night before – Marie had been particularly fractious – lay on her own bed. But sleep eluded her even now for her thoughts were troubled. Of course, she hadn't meant it to happen. She loved Frank; she still did and she always would. But stuck in the countryside – which she'd hated – miles from family and friends, she'd been lonely and bored. She did her share of the chores in the house and around the farm – she wasn't an idle girl – but she missed being able to dress up, wear a little make-up and high heels, going into town and having her hair done or going to the cinema. She longed for a girly chat with Beth as they got ready together in Irene's bedroom for an evening out. She missed town life, the life she was used to and, most of all, she hungered for Frank's arms around her and his kiss. Of course, she'd got Tommy and young Reggie with her. He was like a younger brother, but it wasn't the same as having Beth – or even Shirley – here. Besides, Reggie was growing to love the country life. She could see it in his face every day. He actually revelled in being out in all weathers, working in the fields or tending the animals. Young as he was, he worked as hard as any man and certainly as hard as the land army girls, Pearl and Eve. Irene smiled wryly as she thought about those girls. They had been the saving of her sanity and yet the reason for her fall from grace too. For a while, they'd been friendly enough but they hadn't included her in their evenings out. To them, she was a staid, married woman with a young child, whilst they were young and fancy-free. But one night, when the two girls were getting ready together in the bedroom they shared, Irene had offered to do their hair for them.

'I've done my own and my friend's for years,' she said, as she combed Pearl's hair into the latest style.

'Who's your friend?' Pearl said.

'Beth,' Irene said and there was no escaping the wistfulness in her tone. 'And there was her younger sister, Shirley, too. We often took her out with us. We've lived next door to each other all our lives. We've grown up together.'

'Is she still at home? Back in Grimsby?' Pearl wanted to know.

Irene bit her lip and easy tears filled her eyes as she shook her head. 'She's gone to London.'

'London? Crickey, that's about the most dangerous place she could be, isn't it?'

'Tell us about Beth,' Eve said kindly, sensing that Irene needed someone of a similar age to talk to. She doted on her baby boy – that was plain for all to see – and Reggie was a link with home, but they were neither of them great conversationalists. And Ruth, though she was a kindly, motherly woman, was not interested in fashion and hairstyles. Eve doubted she ever had been.

So, Irene told them all about her life, ending, 'I miss my husband and me mam, of course, but me and Beth had something very special. We really are like sisters, better than some, actually. Well, I suppose she is my sister in a way now.'

'How come?' Eve asked.

'I married her brother, Frank.'

Pearl pulled a comical face. 'Then you're lucky. Me and my sister fight like cat and dog. Always have done. My mam used to have to step in between us when we were little.' She grinned as she met Irene's gaze in the mirror. 'And not so little, too, if I'm honest. I have to say, I'm not missing having my hair pulled out by its roots.'

'Why don't you come out with us?' Eve said suddenly. 'I'm sure Mrs Schofield would look after little Tommy for you. She adores him. I reckon he reminds her of her own boys. And Reggie too. She'll mind them both, I'm sure. He's no trouble.'

'She must be worried sick about her lads,' Pearl murmured.

Irene bit her lip. 'Oh, I don't know if I ought to.'

'Your Frank wouldn't mind, would he? He trusts you, doesn't he?'

Irene nodded.

'Then do come.'

'Well, if you're sure, I'll ask her, and if she says yes, I'll come out with you to the dance in the village on Saturday night.'

Eve squeezed her arm. 'Of course we're sure. We'd love to have you with us. And there are some very handsome RAF lads from the camp that's not far away. Oh sorry,' she giggled, 'you're a married woman.'

'You can always look,' Pearl teased.

'But you mustn't touch,' Eve added and dissolved into helpless laughter.

And so that is how the Saturday evenings out to the dancing at the YMCA hut in the village had started for Irene. For the first few weeks it had been innocent enough, but then she'd met Ken Forbes.

She'd danced with several of the other RAF lads – a different partner for every dance so that no one got too close or started to take liberties. Not that they'd tried, she reminded herself; they'd all been perfect gentlemen. And there were several of the village 'elders' always present to keep an eye on their local girls and the policeman usually called in just before closing time to make sure everyone behaved. But then, one week, there was a new face on the bus that arrived from the RAF camp. A tall, slim young pilot officer with short curly blond hair and merry blue eyes. He'd stood by the bar at the end of the hut with his pals, his eyes raking the room. Irene had watched him covertly, but his glance had settled on Pearl and he'd made a beeline for her and asked her to dance. They'd only been dancing a few moments, when Mick, a local farmer's son, had tapped the RAF officer on the shoulder. Even above the music, Irene heard him say, 'She's my girl.'

Irene had seen the newcomer shake his head and his arm tighten around Pearl's waist. Incensed, Mick grabbed the young man's shoulder and twisted him round, wrenching his arms away from Pearl. Before anyone could intervene, Mick had aimed a punch at the officer's face. Pearl had screamed but it was too late – the young RAF officer was on the floor, his hand to his eye. Irene had jumped up and rushed across the room, anxious to break up the fight.

'Now, now.' The local bobby stepped in, too, before any more blows could be thrown. 'I think you'd better leave – both of you – but I'd get that eye seen to, young feller, afore your commanding officer catches sight of it.' He turned to the local farmhand. 'And you, Mick, should know better. These lads are a long way from home and he wasn't doing any harm. Now, shake hands with our guest and take your young lady home.'

Morosely, the two young men shook hands, but as Mick turned towards Pearl, she stood with her hands on her hips and glared at him, her face red with anger. 'Well, if you think you can call me "your girl" any longer after that display, you can think again.'

'Aw, Pearl . . .' Mick began to plead, but it was no use. Pearl stalked off to the cloakroom to fetch her coat and called to Eve and Irene. 'Come on, you two, I've had enough for tonight.'

But Eve was wrapped in the arms of one of the RAF lads and had no intention of leaving early.

'Irene, are you coming?'

But Irene's gaze was on the RAF officer, trying to stem the blood flowing from the cut above his eye.

'I'll – er – wait for Eve. You go, if you want to.'

'Suit yourself,' Pearl snapped and went out into the night.

Irene walked towards the injured young man and said, 'Come on, let's get you patched up. There's a first-aid box in the little kitchen at the back.'

And that had been the start of it. When she'd bathed his face and put sticking plaster over the small cut, they'd sat together for the rest of that evening until the dance came to an end just before midnight.

'I don't think it will leave a scar,' she told him, thinking that it would be such a shame for his handsome face to be marred.

He'd made light of the injury, but added, 'I'm sorry it happened. I wouldn't want to upset the locals. I'll have to apologize if I see him again. It was my fault. Please tell your friend I'm sorry. It won't happen again, I promise.' He looked so contrite, his apology genuine.

'I'll talk to Pearl – see if I can get her to forgive Mick.'

'I wish I'd seen you first, because if I had, I'd have made a beeline for you.'

As the master of ceremonies – a rather grand name for the young man who organized the weekly village hop – announced that the next dance would be the last, the young RAF officer held out his hand to Irene. 'Pilot Officer Ken Forbes at your service.' He smiled ruefully. 'Although I rather think it was the other way round, but now we've been properly introduced, please will you dance with me?'

How could she possibly have refused such a request?

After that first night, Ken had been a regular visitor to the village dances. He had apologized to Mick, and Pearl had been persuaded to forgive the local boy and their romance was back on track. Irene thought that, secretly, Pearl had been rather flattered to have two good-looking young men fighting over her. The RAF lads arrived on transport from the camp, but one or two would stay later than the time the lorry left to take them back. And soon, Ken was one of those who stayed behind, insisting on walking Irene back to the farm. The second time he'd walked her home, he'd shyly put his arm around her waist. 'It's pitch-black tonight. I don't want you falling over in those high heels.'

Maybe she should have stopped it there and then, but it was so good to feel a man's arm around her again.

The third time, he had drawn her into a field behind the shelter of a haystack and kissed her gently. 'You know I'm falling in love with you, Irene, don't you?'

'Oh Ken, you can't – you mustn't.'

'Because I might be killed at any minute, you mean?' he'd whispered sadly.

'No, no, I don't mean that. You know I don't. And – and I'm becoming fond of you. Too fond. But you know I'm married, don't you?'

Irene had always worn her wedding ring; she'd not tried to hide the fact.

'I thought perhaps your husband had – you know.'

'Frank's away in the army. He's been gone for years – I think he's abroad – but as far as I know, he's all right.'

'I see.' There was a pause before Ken had asked softly, 'But we can still be friends, can't we? You'll still come to the dances and let me walk you home, won't you?'

Irene hesitated. She really liked Ken. She felt a thrill of excitement when she saw him walking in through the door; her knees actually trembled. It was something she'd never experienced before. Perhaps that was because she'd known Frank all her life. Maybe Aunty Edie had had a point when she'd said they'd been too much like brother and sister; there had never been that first ecstasy of falling in love.

But now she knew what it felt like.

Forty-One

As Edie opened her back door, she was surprised to see Shirley at the sink. 'What are you doing here? I thought you'd gone back this morning.'

'I decided to see if I could get an extra day or two on compassionate grounds. So I rang my superior officer and she granted me another two days.' Shirley grimaced and said sarcastically, 'Generous, aren't they? Anyway, Dad's back tonight and I want to hear what he thinks of all this. And how did you get on with Reggie? I'm surprised he's not with you.'

Edie set the basket carefully on the table as she said flatly, 'He really doesn't want to come back. That's another thing your dad will have to decide.'

But now Shirley's attention was taken up with the contents of the basket as she said gleefully, 'Oooo, what have we got in here?' Already she was reaching out to unpack the goodies.

Edie tapped her daughter's hand lightly and, for the first time in days, she smiled. 'Now, now, keep your mitts off. Mrs Schofield gave me some eggs, cheese and butter.'

'Real eggs?' Shirley's eyes widened. 'My, that was good of her.' Then she smirked. 'Unless, of course, it was payment for Reggie.'

Edie frowned as she said sharply, 'He's worth a darn sight more than a few eggs to me.'

Shirley sat down at the table, still eying the basket. 'You goin' to share it with them?' She tossed her head towards next door.

'Certainly not.'

Shirley paused before saying craftily, 'You would have done – before.'

'Well, I aren't now,' Edie snapped. Then she looked guilty and murmured, 'Although it's a shame to deprive Tommy just because . . .'

'Invite him round for tea, then. No reason why we can't see him. It's not his fault, is it?'

'No – poor little scrap. He must be wondering why his gran and Aunty Shirley don't want to see him.'

'There's no need to speak to either Aunty Lil – or *her*. He plays out in the backyard. You can catch him some time and ask him round.'

'That's a good idea, duck. I'll do that.' Edie glanced at the clock on the mantelpiece. 'Mebbe tomorrow, eh? It's getting late now and my feet are killing me.' She sat down heavily in one of the armchairs near the range.

'You sit there, Mam. I'll get the tea on.'

Edie blinked and glanced up at the girl as she rose to go into the scullery. 'What are you wanting to borrow, bein' so helpful all of a sudden?'

'Nothing,' Shirley said airily, but her mother knew there was something she was not telling her. Edie knew her daughter too well to be deceived.

When they'd finished the cheese omelette that Shirley had made with the fresh eggs and cheese and she'd poured her mother a cup of tea, Edie sat back, burped gently and patted her chest. 'That was nice but I reckon I'll suffer for it.'

'We've not been used to decent food for so long,' Shirley said, pushing the cup and saucer towards her mother. 'But surely, now the war's over, things'll get back to normal, won't they?'

'Not straight away. Me an' Lil were only saying' – the words came automatically before she'd stopped to think – 'we reckon rationing will continue for a while yet.'

There was silence between them, but Shirley was drumming her fingertips on the table.

'So, out with it then, miss. What have you been up to?'

For a moment Shirley hesitated and then said bluntly, 'I've written to our Frank and told him.'

Edie stared at her daughter. 'You shouldn't have done that. You should have waited till—'

'He got home? I don't think so, Mam. He's got a right to know what that little trollop's been up to.'

Edie leaned across the table as she said slowly, 'And what if he doesn't come home at all now? What if he stays away because *you*'ve interfered in summat that's not your business?'

Shocked, Shirley stared back. 'It *is* our business and,' she repeated firmly, without a hint of apology in her tone, 'he's a *right* to know.'

'But if he doesn't come home,' Edie said menacingly, 'if I lose another one of me family, I'll blame you.'

Shirley's mouth twisted. 'Oh, I get it. You and your precious boys! You don't really care that I'm not coming back here permanently, do you?' She sprang to her feet. 'I don't reckon you even care that much whether Beth comes home or not, do you?' She paused and then shouted. '*Do you?*'

'Of course I care about you and Beth,' Edie said wearily, but they were both uncomfortably aware that her tone lacked conviction.

*

'What's this I hear?'

Lil had opened the front door in answer to the urgent knocking, fearful of what would greet her. When she'd seen who her visitor was, her mouth had dropped open.

'Norma. Good heavens! What are you doing here? Is something wrong?'

Norma stepped across the threshold without waiting for an invitation. 'Don't let's discuss private matters in view of the whole street, though I expect they all know. Bad news travels fast and there're a lot of nosy parkers in this street. You should have moved back home like I wanted you to when Tom died.'

Lil didn't answer. At the time, their mother had still been alive and had become a querulous, demanding woman, disappointed and bitter with her lot; traits that would only worsen as she grew older. Lil had known that the real reason her sister had wanted her to move in there had been because she had wanted help to look after the family. But Lil – with Edie's support at the time – had resisted and a frostiness had developed between the sisters as a result. They had never been close. Norma resented the fact that Lil had 'escaped' from the unhappy home life by marrying Tom, leaving her to cope with their quarrelling parents and younger siblings. Lil had shuddered – and she did so again now – at the thought of what life would have been like 'back home' after an all-too-brief glimpse of real happiness with Tom.

'It's not fair,' Norma had complained at the time. 'I've not had the chances you've had.' Indeed she had not. Norma had never been a pretty child and had grown into a plain-looking young woman who didn't even try to make the best of herself. She'd sneered at the girls of her own age who tried to keep up as best they could with the latest fashions, the new hairstyles and experimenting with cosmetics.

'What's the use?' she'd grumbled. 'There aren't enough men to go round.' The observation was true; the Great War had taken a whole generation of young men and left many girls facing the future as spinsters. And if truth be known, Norma had been – and probably still was – jealous of her prettier sister, Lily.

So Lil had not moved back home but had clung to the little house her husband had found and the remnants of the life she and Tom had dreamed of.

Back then, she thought sadly, she had had Edie's strength and support.

'So,' Norma said now, marching through the narrow hallway to the living room. 'Is it true?' She flung open the door and then paused on the threshold, her hand still on the door knob as her disapproving gaze came to rest on Irene sitting in front of the fire with the baby girl on her lap. 'Ah, I see that it is.'

Lil sighed as she closed the front door and went through to the scullery, pushing past her sister and muttering. 'I'll make us some tea.'

'Tea won't solve this little how d'ya do,' Norma snapped, drawing off her gloves and sitting down at the table.

Norma was now a middle-aged, plump woman, with lines of bitterness etched deeply into her face. Fine red veins marked her round cheeks and her hair, showing premature signs of grey, was drawn back into a bun at the nape of her neck. Her long black coat and her manly shoes were the same ones she'd worn for years; Irene couldn't remember ever seeing her in anything else. Her disapproving glance raked over her niece and the child, but Irene met her gaze squarely. This was the one person whose criticism didn't affect her; she didn't care tuppence for her aunt's censure.

'Aunty Norma.' Irene forced a smile. 'How nice.'

Norma snorted. 'Nice? Is that what you call it?'

As Lil came back carrying a tray of cups and saucers, Norma turned on her. 'You'd do best to pack her off back to the countryside. Her and both her brats. We've never had scandal in the family.'

Lil placed the tray on the table carefully, resisting the urge to pick up a cup and throw it at her sister. 'Oh,' she said, with surprising calmness, considering her inner turmoil, 'Are you sure, Norma, with an alcoholic father and a whining mother? It was hardly a secret down our street, now was it?'

'Father was not an alcoholic. How dare you say such a thing!'

'He spent more time in the local pub than he did at home, Norma, or has he become the perfect father now he's gone?'

Norma wriggled her shoulders. 'You shouldn't speak ill of the dead, Lil. 'Tain't seemly.'

Lil pushed the tea towards Norma. 'I've no sugar,' she said shortly without a word of apology.

'I no longer take sugar in my tea,' Norma said loftily. 'I haven't done since the beginning of the war.'

'Who has?' Lil muttered and sat down on the other side of the table to drink her own tea.

'So,' Norma said again, 'What are we going to do about it?'

Lil glanced at her but it was Irene who spoke up. 'I'm staying here until Frank gets home and then we'll see.'

Norma laughed, but there was no humour in the sound. 'Oh, we'll see then all right. He'll throw you out on your ear, that's what Frank Kelsey will do, my girl.' She turned towards Lil and jerked her head towards the wall between the two houses. 'And what's she got to say about it? Plenty, I shouldn't wonder.'

Again, it was Irene who spoke up. 'Aunty Edie is upset. Naturally. But it's Frank who has to decide. It's up to him.' Irene got up. 'And now, if you'll excuse me, I'll take my little bastard upstairs out of your sight.'

'Well!' Norma exclaimed. 'I never did. I'm appalled, Lil, I really am. I never thought to hear such language coming from a member of our family. She's nothing but a common whore and you'd do best to rid yourself of her and her brat if you want to be able to hold your head up ever again in this community.'

'I'll do no such thing,' Lil said hotly, seeming to be able to stand up to Norma far better than she could to Edie. The difference was that she minded what Edie thought. It mattered to her, whilst she couldn't have cared less about Norma's bigoted opinions. 'Like Irene said, we're waiting for Frank to come home.'

Norma smiled nastily as she asked, 'Are you sure he'll come home at all now?'

To this, Lil had no answer.

Forty-Two

As the dock tower came into view, Archie felt the familiar rising excitement and yet, over the war years, there was always a tinge of fear too. Safely home from another trip, he'd soon see Edie and hear the latest news of the rest of the family. But he never knew if that news would be good or bad; he'd never forget his homecoming when Frank had been waiting on the dockside in June 1940 just after Dunkirk. He'd seen his son as his ship nosed its way to its berth and he'd known at once that something was very wrong. When they'd been children, they'd often been there waiting for him, but recently no one had come to meet him.

Ever since that day he'd anxiously scanned the quay-side, looking for any member of the family, and when he couldn't see anyone, he'd breathed a sigh of relief and turned his attention to off-loading his catch and doing all the necessary tasks at the end of a trip.

But this time, Shirley was waiting. He felt his heart contract. Was Edie ill? Or was it Frank? Had something happened to Frank in the very last moments of the conflict? That would be ironic and so hard to bear. Or – no, no, NO – not his Beth. And the very fact that it was Shirley standing there when she should have been away with the ATS added to his anxiety. He wanted to rush ashore, to clatter down the gangway as soon as it was in place, but he could not. He was the skipper and by his own rules he was always the last one to leave. Whatever it was – and he was sure by now that it was bad news of some kind – it would have to wait. When at last he left the ship, it was to find Shirley shivering on the quayside in the cold wind that blew in from the North Sea, even in May.

At once he put his arm around her. 'What is it, love?' he asked at once. 'Cos I know it's summat by you being here.'

'Oh Dad!' For a moment Shirley clung to him, comforted by his presence. Archie had always shown her love and understanding, though she had the sneaking feeling that Beth was really his favourite. But he never let it show and perhaps it was her own insecurity that led her to even think such a thing. Whenever he brought Beth a present, there was always a similar one for Shirley. When he took Beth out, Shirley went too, and yet it was a feeling that Shirley could never quite suppress. Perhaps it was just in the merest of glances when there seemed to be an empathy passing between Archie and Beth that never happened between Shirley and her father. She had never – quite – been able to quell a prickle of jealousy whenever they were together, even when she was there too and included in everything that was happening. It had always been the same until at the age of sixteen Beth went to work for the Forsters and then to live in France as a nursemaid to their children. It had been such an adventure for a young girl, even though neither Edie nor Archie had wholly approved. Yet Beth had shown such a spirited determination that in the end they had agreed to her going.

'What's happened? Archie prompted, feeling more anxious – if that were possible – with each passing second.

'It's Irene,' Shirley blurted out at last. 'She's come home.'

Archie frowned. 'Well, of course she has, but—'

'She's got a baby.'

Archie blinked. 'Eh?' For a brief moment, he was confused and then, from the look on Shirley's face, he understood.

'Oh!'

'Yes, it's "oh!" all right. Large as life and bold as brass, she comes waltzing down the street – on VE day when there was a street party going on, mind you, and all the neighbours were gawping.' Now there was no holding back; Shirley was in full flow. 'And Aunty Lil' – old habits died hard and Shirley could think of no other way to refer to their neighbour – 'has taken her in. She's there with Tommy and her little bastard.'

A hardened seaman though he was, Archie had never liked to hear his family use coarse language, especially his girls. He winced, but, for once, said nothing. They began to walk slowly away from the docks towards home, Archie still with his arm around Shirley's shoulders, she leaning into his side for comfort and reassurance. 'Mam's not speaking to Aunty Lil and—'

Archie was so shocked that he stopped walking and turned to look down into Shirley's face. 'Not speaking to Lil? Why ever not? It's hardly Lil's fault, is it?'

'No, but she's taken her in.'

'Of course she has, Irene's her daughter!' He frowned down at her. 'Would you expect us to cast you out if you got into trouble, lass?'

'This is different,' Shirley said stubbornly. 'She's married. To our Frank.'

'Aye, aye, she is.' They walked on for some distance

371

until, at the end of the street where they lived, Shirley said in a small voice now, 'There's something else, Dad.'

He sighed heavily. 'Go on.'

'Mam's mad at me.'

'Why?'

'Because – because I've written to Frank and told him.'

Archie's voice was sorrowful rather than angry. 'Aw, lass, you shouldn't have done that. Best keep out of it and let Irene and Frank sort it out between them.'

'But he has a right to know,' Shirley persisted. 'Just think what a shock it'd be for him to come home and find all that out when he got here all excited at seeing her and Tommy and then being greeted with *that*.'

Archie said nothing more as they arrived at the passage leading to their backyard. For a moment he hesitated, asking in a low voice, 'Any news of Beth?'

Shirley shook her head, pressing her lips together. Archie sighed again before opening the back door into the scullery and shouting his usual greeting, 'Here I am, Edie love. Home again safe and sound.'

Edie did not come to him, meeting him with a kiss and a swift hug that told him she was so relieved and glad to see him. Instead, she was waiting for him in the living room. Admittedly, as always, the kettle was singing on the hob, the table was laid for tea and an appetizing smell was coming from the oven, but things were different. There was a tension in the air that never usually pervaded their home.

'So,' she said as he came in. 'You've heard, then? Madam here couldn't wait to impart a juicy bit of gossip.' She turned resentful eyes on Shirley. 'I wonder you don't take out an advert in the *Telegraph*. Tell the whole world, why don't you? Get Ursula to write a piece about it.'

'I'll just change me clothes, Edie love,' Archie said calmly, kissing her cheek. 'And then we'll talk about it over tea.'

'No, we won't.' She jerked her head towards the shared wall between their house and Lil's. 'Tommy's coming in for his tea. He wants to see his granddad.'

Archie smiled. 'Good. What about the others? Are they coming an' all?'

Edie glared at him. 'Are you mad, Archie Kelsey? 'Cos you must be, if you think I'm having that whore in my house ever again.'

Archie turned away and climbed the stairs with heavy footsteps.

The news itself had come as a shock but his wife's reaction to it was far worse than he could ever have imagined. To think she wasn't even speaking to Lil. He couldn't believe it.

'Now then, Tommy lad. How are you? My, you've grown.'

Archie picked up his grandson and swung him round, but the four-year-old didn't squeal with delight as he had done when Archie had seen him at the farm. Instead he clung on to Archie's shoulders and looked almost scared of being tossed into the air. Sensing the young boy's discomfort, Archie set him gently on the ground. Tommy looked up at him with huge eyes, dark and solemn. His brown hair was thick and wavy. He was so like Frank that Archie's heart felt as if it turned over. But Frank was safe, he reminded himself, he was coming home. But to what?

The four of them sat around the table but the conversation was stilted and awkward. Edie found she couldn't think of anything to talk about to the young boy; the problem of his mother was uppermost in her mind. Shirley tried, but her gaiety was forced and false. Only Archie was able to speak naturally.

'Did you like living in the countryside, lad? I expect you find it strange to be back in the town.'

Tommy regarded his grandfather with a serious gaze. 'Mam said we lived in the town before, but I can't remember it.'

Archie blinked but then realized. Tommy had been a babe in arms when he'd left. Of course he had no recollection of living in Grimsby, of living in the house next door. Perhaps he couldn't even remember . . .

As if reading her father's mind, Shirley said, 'Then you can't remember your daddy?'

Tommy's glance fell to his plate as he pushed the food on it around with his fork. He shook his head.

'Eat up,' Edie admonished. 'We can't afford to waste food. Not in this house,' she added, wondering if, living on the farm, the boy hadn't been brought up to understand the shortages that everyone else was suffering. Or maybe, she thought bitterly, his mother's mind had been on other things.

'I'll take him back,' Archie said, rising from the table when they'd all finished.

'No need for you to go round,' Edie snapped. 'He can go through the yard gate. You can watch him into the house from there.'

For as long as any of them could remember, the communal door in the wooden fence between the two houses had always been left open like an invitation for the members of both households to mingle freely. And

374

they had; until now. But since the day that Irene had returned home, the door had been firmly shut and Edie was determined that it would stay that way.

But Archie had other ideas and he was, after all, the man of the house.

'I'll take him in, Edie,' he said firmly in a tone that brooked no argument from her or anyone else.

Taking Tommy by the hand, Archie led him out of their back door, turned to the left and lifted the latch. He paused, glancing down at the child. 'OK, Tommy lad?'

The boy nodded, but he didn't look all right. He looked as if he was expecting trouble between his mam and his granddad even though, at his tender age, it was unlikely he understood the cause of it. Archie squeezed his hand but couldn't think of anything to say in comfort. He knocked on Lil's back door and, as they always had, he opened it without waiting for it to be answered and stepped inside. 'Lil, love, you home?'

There was no one in the back scullery, and moving into the living room he found Irene sitting beside the fire, the baby in her lap. She glanced up, her eyes widening. 'Oh, Uncle Archie, I didn't expect—' Her glance went to her son with a frown. 'Is he all right?'

'As nine pence,' Archie said cheerfully. 'You run along upstairs and play, Tommy, while I have a chat with your mam. And come round for your tea again, won't you?'

Fear flitted across Irene's face, but she knew there was no getting out of it and she gave a brief nod to her son. She would have to face her father-in-law sooner or later, so she might as well get it over with. The door closed behind Tommy and they heard his feet tramping up the stairs.

'Your mam out, is she?'

Irene nodded and looked down at the baby gurgling happily. Archie, too, looked at the child, taking in her bright blue eyes and fair curly hair. As far as Archie could tell – he wasn't very good in such matters – the little girl resembled her mother. That could be a good thing, he mused, but he didn't voice his thoughts.

'She's a pretty little thing,' he murmured, not quite sure how to open the conversation that was going to be painful for both of them.

Tears spilled down Irene's face. 'Oh Uncle Archie, I'm so sorry. I wouldn't have hurt Frank – all of you – for the world, but . . .' She lapsed into silence.

'But it happened. Look, lass, I'm not going to interrogate you. In fact, I don't really want to know the whys and wherefores.'

'Aunty Edie does,' Irene blurted out.

A wry smile twitched his mouth. 'Aye, well, your Aunty Edie would. But I'm not here for that. I just need to know what you want to happen now?'

Irene wiped away her tears with the back of her hand. 'I don't think what I want will come into it, do you? It's – it's what Frank will want that matters. And – if he does what his mother says – he'll have nowt to do with me.'

Archie was silent for a moment, struggling with his conscience. The last thing he wanted to be was disloyal to his wife and yet there were things that had to be said. At last he said quietly, 'It'll be up to Frank. He's a man now. He's been through a war and none of us know how that might have altered him. Not one of us – not even his mam, though she might think she can guess how he'll take the news or what he'll do.'

Irene's voice trembled as she said, 'There was a piece in Mr Schofield's paper a few weeks ago about a soldier who came home on leave to find his wife had had a baby that – that wasn't his.' She bit her lip. 'He – he killed them both.' Instinctively, her arm tightened round her child and she stroked Marie's downy hair.

'Frank wouldn't do that, love. The worst that can happen is that he'll want no more to do with you – that he'll want a divorce.'

Irene flinched but she nodded sadly and said huskily, 'I know.'

'If that turns out to be the case, what would you do? Live here with your mam?'

'I'm not sure she wants me here really. Oh, she wants Tommy. I suppose you all do. I expect that Frank will want to keep Tommy.' Her mouth trembled again and easy tears filled her eyes.

'And what about you and – and the bairn?' He didn't even know the child's name, though he could guess it was a girl by the pink jacket she was wearing.

'We can go back to the farm. Mrs Schofield will have us back, but – but I don't want to go without Tommy. I want to be near him, at least, even if – even if . . .' There was a pause before she added hesitantly, 'I suppose I ought to write and tell Frank.'

Grim-faced, Archie said, 'No, need, love. Shirley's already done that.'

Despite what she had done and the trouble it was causing, the look of horror that crossed Irene's face tore at Archie's heartstrings.

Forty-Three

'I hope you're not thinking of trying to persuade our Frank to forgive the little trollop?' was Edie's greeting as Archie stepped into their house once more.

'I'm not going to try to persuade him one way or the other, love, and neither should you.'

Edie snorted. 'Well, I don't want owt to do with her. She's ruined Frank's life – and after all he's been through – torn this family apart and wrecked my friendship with her mam. And if' – she wagged her forefinger in Archie's face – 'it means that our lad will leave home then – then – well, I don't know what I'll do. I'll likely kill her and her little bastard.'

Shirley, who had been listening to the heated exchange between her parents, said slyly, 'Unless Frank gets there first.'

'There's to be no more talk like that,' Archie boomed, suddenly angry. He was usually a mild-tempered man. He didn't drink to excess, didn't smoke much and loved his family above all else. He rarely raised his voice and he had never once lifted a hand in anger to any of his children. Chastisement had always been left to Edie, though all five of his offspring had always been aware when he disapproved.

Both Edie and Shirley blinked, knowing that, for once, they had pushed him too far. Seeing their shocked faces he calmed down at once. 'We'll sort it all out when Frank gets back. I expect' – he glanced at Shirley – 'when he gets your letter, he'll apply for compassionate leave.'

'But he'll be coming home for good, won't he?' Edie said. 'He'll be demobbed.'

Archie sighed as he sat down in his easy chair by the fire. 'I really don't know, love. All I know is they're demobbed by a kind of rota. It depends on the date they went in as to when they come out. Frank didn't go in until towards the end of '40, so he's not going to be home yet, is he? But let's just leave it until he does get back, eh? There's nowt more we can do till then.'

'And,' Edie raged, as if she laid the blame for everything on Irene's head, 'Reggie's not coming home.' She flung the letter their youngest son had written into Archie's lap. Archie glanced up at her and then slowly picked up the letter and began to read it. 'He prefers to make his life with strangers rather than with his own family.' There was a catch in Edie's voice and Archie realized at once just how much all this was upsetting his wife. She'd wanted all her little chicks back in the nest, but it wasn't going to happen.

'It'll be a better life for him than the sea, Edie love.'

'I know that,' she snapped. 'I'm not a fool. And', she added grudgingly, 'they are nice people – the Schofields – even if they haven't kept a proper eye on her.' She jerked her head towards the house next door.

Archie sighed. 'Irene's a grown woman. She—'

'They encouraged her to go out and have *fun*. Fun, indeed! Out till all hours of the night with the land army girls, I shouldn't wonder. But she was a married woman with a young son and a husband at war facing God alone knew what dangers. Do we really want our Reggie living in a household like that? And their own two sons will be coming back. What'll happen then, eh? They'll put Reggie out on his ear, that's what.'

Archie frowned, puzzled. 'How do you know all this?'

Edie wriggled her plump shoulders.

'She went out to White Gates Farm to see Reggie,' Shirley said. 'To bring him home, but he wouldn't come.'

'It wasn't quite like that,' Edie said. 'When I got there I could see how happy he is. He's grown – filled out. You'd hardly recognize him, Archie.' There was nostalgia and longing in her tone as she added softly, 'He's almost a man now. He's grown up without us.'

'Then don't you think,' he said gently, 'we should allow him to make a man's decision about his own future? I know you want all your family back home again, love, but it's not going to happen. The war's changed us all and nothing's going to be the same as it was before. We've got to build a new life, not hanker after the old one.'

Edie sat down heavily in the chair on the opposite side of the fireplace, for the moment defeated in the face of her husband's common sense and fairness.

'Tell you what,' Archie went on, 'we'll go out to the farm together the next time I'm home and I can see for myself how the land lies.' He smiled at his unintentional pun, then his expression sobered again as he added, 'But as for the other business, let's leave things as they are for now, eh?'

He picked up the evening paper, signalling that, as far as he was concerned, the discussion was at an end.

Shirley and her mother glanced at each other. They had no intention of leaving things as they were.

The matter was not spoken of between them again for the rest of Archie's time ashore, yet it lay heavily between them and caused a tension in the home that had never before been known in the Kelsey household. For the first time in his life, Archie went back to sea with relief. And yet he left once more with a deep anxiety in his heart. Still there had been no word from Beth. And now the war was really over, surely that didn't look good.

As soon as she knew Archie's ship had safely left the dock at the end of his brief time ashore, Edie banged loudly on the communicating door between the backyards.

'Lil – Lil! You there? I want a word.'

There was a long pause before Lil appeared and hesitantly approached the fence. The summons had held none of Edie's usually friendly tone. No 'Get the kettle on, duck' as had been their normal greeting when visiting, as it had been most mornings for years. But now, Edie hadn't even come into her neighbour's yard, never mind her home.

'Edie?' Lil said, her voice trembling, as she opened the door.

'I want you to tell that trollop of a daughter of yours – if you're still owning her as your daughter and let me tell you I wouldn't if she was mine – to get herself and her bastard back to the farm. Them folks encouraged her to go out dancing – and drinking an' all, I shouldn't wonder. Well, they can look after them. But Tommy stays here. He's to come and live with us. And if she's out the way, then maybe my Frank will come home.'

Lil stared at Edie with frightened eyes. 'Is that what Archie's said?'

Edie had never been one to tell lies. She'd always

believed in the saying "tell the truth and shame the devil", but for once she was very tempted. She drew in a deep breath, about to say that yes, that was what she and Archie had agreed, but the words stuck in her throat. She gave an exasperated sigh, angry with herself as she was forced to admit, 'No, it's what *I* say. She's a bad mother and I won't have my grandson living under her influence any longer. It's what Frank would want.'

'You've heard from him?'

Reluctantly, Edie admitted that they had not, but she insisted, 'It'll be what he does want though. I know my son. He'll get shot of her once he's home so she might as well go back now and save him the bother. The Schofields have said they'll have her back.'

'How d'you know that?'

'Because I went to see them. I wanted to find out what had gone on.' She omitted to tell Lil that she'd also gone to see her own son and had been obliged to agree to him staying there – at least for the time being. But she wasn't going to let that matter drop either, whatever Archie said.

In spite of herself, Lil moved closer to the fence. 'Did – did they tell you anything? Irene won't say a word. She – she won't even tell me the father's name.'

'Some airman from a nearby station. The lads used to go dancing in the village on a Saturday night and your trollop of a daughter decided she'd go out with the land army girls, who, let me tell you, were young, free and single.'

'What about Tommy? Who looked after him?' Lil asked.

Edie snorted contemptuously. 'The Schofields. They encouraged her to go. "Have a bit of fun", they said. Well, look where that bit of fun has landed us all.'

'The airman?' Lil asked tentatively. 'Irene told me that much but—'

'He's dead.'

'Yes, she told me that too, but that's all. I don't know any – any details.'

'He was killed on a raid just before she found out she was pregnant, so that's why she's come crawling back here hoping our Frank'll be daft enough to forgive her.'

'Do – do you know his name – the airman's?'

Edie sniffed. 'Ken something, I think Ruth said, but she didn't tell me his surname.' She eyed Lil speculatively. 'Oh, I know what you're thinking. That his family might be prepared to take on the child.' She laughed mockingly. 'Do you reckon they'd be daft enough to believe every little whore that turns up on their doorstep claiming their son's the father of her bastard? Well, I wouldn't and I don't expect they would either. Not if they'd any sense.'

Lil's face had turned bright red. She dropped her gaze and turned away, her shoulders hunched, any hope of her long friendship with Edie being able to survive this scandal now crushed. She returned inside and closed her back door, leaning against it for a moment and closing her eyes. Then she took a deep breath, plastered a smile on her face and went into the living room.

'What did she want?' Irene asked at once.

'She wants you to go back to the farm but to leave Tommy here. With them.'

Irene's mouth tightened. 'I'm going nowhere until Frank's got home. We'll see what he says first. If he wants me to go, then I will. But I'm not leaving Tommy. Not with Frank and certainly not with them. Whatever happens, Tommy stays with me.'

Lil bit her lip, undecided whether she should tell Irene everything that Edie had said. But then, she thought, the time for all these secrets was over. 'She's been out to see the Schofields.'

Irene stared at her mother for a moment, her mind working busily. 'The nosy old cow. What did she tell you?'

'Only what you've already told me, but she did find out that his first name was Ken.' Cautiously, Lil asked, 'What about his parents? Have you been in touch with them? I mean, might they—?'

Reading her mother's mind, Irene cut off the suggestion before it could even be voiced. 'No, I haven't. I don't even know where they live. Besides, I wouldn't let them have her even if they wanted her. Marie's mine and that's an end of it.'

Lil turned away. Sadly, she thought, that was far from the end of it.

Forty-Four

Three days later, Edie rapped loudly on the fence, once more. 'Lil – *Lil*.'

The woman appeared at her back door, drying her hands on a rough towel. 'Just doing a bit of washing.'

'On a Thursday?' Edie was incredulous. Washday was always on a Monday.

'There's a lot of washing with a—' Lil stopped, embarrassed as Edie's mouth hardened. Then she asked harshly, with more spirit in her tone than Edie could ever remember hearing from her erstwhile friend, 'What d'you want?'

'I want you to tell that trollop of a daughter of yours to get herself and her bastard back to the countryside.' Edie waved a letter in Lil's face. 'Frank's written to say he's not coming home. See what that little trollop has done. But if she's out of the way, then maybe my boy will come back.'

Shirley had gone back, but a letter had come in answer to the one she had written and Edie had had no compunction in opening it.

Lil, thinner than ever with the worry and upset her daughter's homecoming had caused, blinked in the face of Edie's wrath. 'What – what do you mean?'

'He's written to say,' Edie emphasized every word as if explaining to a child, 'that he's not coming home. He won't get demobbed yet because he didn't go in at the beginning and though he could get compassionate leave, he doesn't want to. All because of *her*. I've lost Laurence, Reggie doesn't want to come back, Shirley's stopping on in the ATS and God knows what's happened to Beth. And now this. Frank's not coming either because of her.'

'Oh Edie.' Lil was almost in tears. She desperately wanted to put her arms around Edie as – in happier times – she would have done instantly. But now there was this awful chasm between them that she feared would never be bridged. She was so afraid that their friendship was shattered for ever. And right now, she didn't know what else to say; there was nothing she *could* say, for she was all too well aware that the fault for this latest disappointment for Edie did indeed lie with Irene.

'So you tell her, Lil, to go back out of the way, but she can leave Tommy with us.'

Lil stared at her for a brief moment before snapping, 'She's going nowhere. Her and the bairns – both of 'em – are staying put.' With that she turned her back on Edie and returned to her dolly tub, thumping the clothes with the posser with a viciousness she hadn't known was in her nature.

The rift between the former friends deepened.

With no one at home now, when Archie was at sea, and the WVS work dwindling, Edie hardly knew how to fill the long, lonely days. She missed Lil more than she'd ever admit and the noise of the crying infant next door only fuelled her anger. Even Tommy did not come into her house unless his granddad fetched him and Edie couldn't even bring herself to ask Lil to let him visit her when Archie was away. She counted the days and the hours until Archie would come home again, something she had never needed to do before. But now the days stretched endlessly and his time at home was all too brief.

Archie had no intention of keeping his distance from his grandson and if that meant he had to see Irene – and even her baby – then so be it. As soon as he was home again, the next morning after breakfast, he said casually, 'I'm just off next door.'

He turned towards the back door, ignoring Edie's glare. He could, of course, have said he was off to the pub – his wife would have thought nothing of that – but Archie had never lied to Edie and he wasn't going to start now. He might have hidden things from her – like the time he went to Dunkirk – but he would never deliberately lie to her.

'Hello, Lil love,' he said cheerfully when she opened the back door to him, her eyes wide with surprise and worry.

'What's happened?'

'Nowt that I know of, love. Can I come in?'

'Oh – yes – of course.' She pulled the door wider and her small scullery was at once filled with his bulky presence.

'I thought young Tommy might like a walk to the docks to see the ships. He wasn't old enough before they went away and it's high time he knew what his dad and his granddad did – and his other granddad, an' all,' he added swiftly, anxious not to miss out the man after whom Tommy had been named.

Lil smiled weakly. 'That's good of you, Archie. He doesn't get out much. We don't let him play in the street. The other lads – you know.'

Archie frowned. 'Being bullied, is he?'

Lil nodded and then smiled wanly. 'Mind you, that girl your Shirley's pally with saw them one afternoon and sorted the little tykes out, but, of course, she's not always around.'

Archie frowned. 'Ursula, you mean?' Something was still troubling him about Ursula, but he couldn't really put his finger on it. 'Anyway,' he went on, pushing thoughts of the girl out of his mind, 'D'you reckon he'd like a walk out?'

'I'm sure he would. Tommy – Tommy,' she called, 'your granddad's here. He's come to take you out.'

The boy jumped up from the table where he'd been drawing and hurled himself at Archie, wrapping his arms around his granddad's legs. His delight at seeing Archie was undeniable, but Irene, sitting near the hearth with the baby on her lap, looked unsure.

Patting the boy on the head so that he loosened his limpet hold, Archie moved closer to look down at the infant. 'Irene, love, how are you?' he murmured, but his gaze was on the little girl chortling in her mother's lap and kicking with sturdy limbs. 'She's a pretty little mite, isn't she?' he murmured. 'She looks strong and healthy.'

'Aunty Edie said Frank's not coming home because – because of me. Is that true?'

Archie sighed. 'Well, I know he's not coming home yet, love, but whether it's all to do with' – he gestured towards the baby – 'I couldn't really say.'

'Aunty Edie can,' Irene said bitterly. 'She's adamant that it's me who's caused another member of her family not to come back.'

'Has he written to you?' Archie asked gently.

Irene pressed her lips together and shook her head,

not trusting herself to speak. After a moment, when she had composed herself, she said, 'If he'd just come home and talk to me, then we could sort it out even if – even if he wants me to leave.' She glanced up again at Archie. 'But I want you to understand, Uncle Archie, that I'll fight to keep Tommy. Whatever Aunty Edie thinks, he'll stay with me.'

'Aye well, a little lad of his age should be with his mother, but . . .' Archie sighed and stopped. He understood both sides of the argument; that was his trouble and he really couldn't decide which one to take. Instead, he chose to ignore the whole problem for the moment. Nothing could be done until Frank came home and made the decision; it was all up to Frank and if he wasn't coming back at the moment, they'd all have to just bide their time and wait and see. In the meantime, he could help out with young Tommy. 'Come on, then, lad, let's you and me go and have a look if my ship's all right.'

By the time Archie brought the boy back home, Tommy's eyes were wide with wonder and he chattered with excitement. 'Granddad took me all over his ship. I saw the engine room and the fishing nets and oh – everything! And we saw Aunty Shirley's friend, didn't we, Granddad?'

Ursula had been on the dockside again, this time talking to a scruffy, bearded fellow, who was gesticulating wildly with his hands. She had seemed to be pleading with him, but her entreaties were being met with an obvious refusal. Archie watched as the man turned away. She followed him and caught hold of his arm but he shook her off and quickened his pace away from her. She was left standing, just staring after him, her shoulders slumped. Then, as she turned, she caught sight of Archie and Tommy. For a moment she seemed disconcerted, but then Archie noticed her straighten her shoulders, force a smile on her face and walk deliberately towards them.

'Hello, love,' Archie said, though he couldn't prevent a wariness creeping into his tone, even though he tried hard to keep it friendly and non-judgmental.

'I was trying to get a story,' Ursula began to explain quickly, her voice high-pitched. 'There's – there's a trawler late back and I wanted to know about it, but he wouldn't tell me anything.'

Archie frowned, suddenly anxious. If there was a trawler missing, then he certainly wanted to know about it. 'Which ship? Do you know?'

Ursula shrugged. 'No.'

'Then I'll find out. Come on, Tommy, we'll go to the dock office and—'

'Oh no, please don't trouble yourself.' She caught hold of his arm as if to prevent him. 'It's – it's not important.'

He stared at her for a moment. 'Of course it's important. If a ship's late in, it might be in trouble. This has nothing to do with you writing about it for the paper. *I* need to know and I need to know now.'

Her hand dropped from his arm and he was sure that a look of fear crossed her eyes. 'I see,' she said and her voice was flat, devoid of emotion.

'You can come with us if you like,' he said more gently.

She shook her head. 'No, no, I must – get back – to the newspaper – tell them I couldn't find anything out.'

'I'll let you know,' he promised as he moved away, anxious to get to the dock office.

She pushed her hands deep into the pockets of her

raincoat and nodded. He strode away, Tommy taking little running steps to keep up with the man's long strides. When Archie glanced back a few moments later, the girl had disappeared.

'There's no ship missing, Archie,' Jack Reeves told him.

'Are you sure?'

'Positive. Everyone who's supposed to be back has docked. What made you think a ship was missing?'

'Oh – just some girl. She reckoned one of the trawlers was late. She must have got it wrong.'

Jack smiled knowingly and arched his eyebrows. 'D'you mean that girl who's always hanging round the docks? Ursula somebody?'

'Aye, that's her. Do you know owt about her?'

Jack shrugged. 'Not really, Archie. We just all assumed she was – you know . . .'

Archie blinked. 'I hope you're wrong there, Jack. She's a friend of my daughter's. She told us she worked for the *Telegraph* and that she was just looking for news stories.'

'Did she now?' Jack murmured, a thoughtful frown on his face.

Archie, too, was puzzled and, as he listened to his grandson's lively chatter as they walked home, he determined to question Shirley more about her friend the next time she came home on leave.

He sighed. It was difficult – it always had been – being away at sea so much. He hadn't been able to keep his eye on his family as they were growing up. Edie had done a wonderful job on her own for much of the time, but just now and then he realized, with sadness, that a father's hand had been needed on occasions. And he hadn't been there. He just hoped his daughter hadn't been getting into bad company. Still, Shirley was safely away now. The ATS was sorting her out. Even he could see that she was a much happier – and nicer – person. Though he was still a little cross with her that she'd interfered in this business between Irene and Frank. But then, he argued with himself, perhaps it was better that Frank knew now. At least he would have some thinking time before he did come home. Archie was unsure as to what Shirley's true motive had been. Once, it would have been purely out of spite, but now – he wasn't so sure.

If only, he thought, Beth had been here. She would have brought a calming influence to all of them. With each day that passed, Archie grew more anxious about Beth and he was sure it was the same for Edie, though they never spoke about it. The only person he felt able to confide in was Harry when they met for a drink in the pub.

'Haven't you heard a word from her, not even now it's all over?' Harry was incredulous when Archie told him of his worries.

Archie shook his head, not trusting himself to speak for the moment, so big was the lump in his throat.

'Surely she should be coming home by now,' Harry said, voicing Archie's innermost fears. 'I mean, she's not in the forces like Frank, is she? He'll not get demobbed until he's told, but Beth ought to be free to come home.'

'I think she joined the FANYs. That's what she told us, anyway.'

Harry frowned. 'That's nursing, isn't it?'

'So I believe.'

'Oh – well, then – she might be abroad, I suppose.'

'Mm.'

Harry glanced at Archie. 'You sound doubtful.'

'No – no, not about that, Harry, it's just that—' He hesitated.

'Come on, man, spit it out.'

Archie sighed, looking down into his beer and twisting the glass round and round. 'It's just that I've heard whispers – rumours, you know – that the FANYs were sometimes used as a cover for – for women agents.'

Harry gaped at him. 'The sort that were dropped into occupied Europe to help the local resistance groups?' Rumours had circulated amongst the fishing fraternity, who, in other parts of the country, especially on the south coast, had sometimes been used to take agents to French shores.

Archie nodded and the two men were silent for several minutes.

'She always did crave excitement, did our Beth,' Archie murmured at last.

'Those postcards you got,' Harry said slowly, as if thinking aloud. 'Where did they come from?'

'London. Always London.'

'And never a letter?'

Archie shook his head.

Now, it was Harry who said thoughtfully, 'Mm.' And after yet another pause, he added quietly, 'Odd that, knowing your Beth. Always the chatty one, the one with all the news.'

This time, Archie could think of nothing to say, but his anxiety deepened. Come back to us, Beth, he prayed silently. Wherever you are, stay safe and just come home to us.

Forty-Five

Whilst Edie waited with growing impatience – and deepening disappointment – for even just one or two members of her family to come home, life went on. In July, the country went to the polls and when the results came out at the end of the month, Edie was appalled.

'I can't believe it,' she said, staring at the newspaper in front of her. 'They've thrown poor old Churchill out. He won the war for us, but they've thrown him out. How terribly hurt he must be. I can't understand it.'

'Well, I can, love,' Archie said in his deep voice. 'I think the country feels the need for a change and Labour is promising all sorts of reforms, including public owner-ship of power industries and inland transport. And then there's education –' Archie was warming to his theme now – 'they're planning to raise the school-leaving age to sixteen and provide further education for adults, but I think the best promise they're making is a National Health Service where everyone – rich or poor – will have the right to medical treatment. Mind you, Edie, what I think would be perfect would be a labour govern-ment with Churchill as Prime Minister, but that's never going to happen.'

'You don't mean to tell me that you voted labour, Archie Kelsey?' Edie accused him.

A little shame-faced, Archie admitted, 'Actually, I did.'

'Well, I'm surprised at you.'

'So, you voted Tory, did you?'

'Of course. We always have, haven't we?' She paused and then added, a little grumpily, 'I wish you'd said. I needn't have trudged all the way to the polling station. We've only cancelled out each other's vote. I wouldn't have bothered if I'd known.'

Archie wrinkled his brow. 'Sorry, love. I never looked at it that way.'

'But what made you vote for *them*?'

'Because they seem to stand for the working class – the likes of us. And, if nothing else, I like the sound of the health service they're proposing. It's high time everyone got decent care if they're ill, not just because they can afford to pay for it.'

Edie blinked. She took little interest in politics and, if truth be known, she'd only ever voted Tory because she knew that's what Archie did. Now she was being forced to think for herself and whilst she understood Archie's desire for a better world for their children and grandchildren – grandchild, she corrected herself – because that other little brat was nothing to do with their family, she couldn't forget Mr Churchill's brave, rallying speeches all through the terrifying days of the war and especially when Britain stood alone. If it hadn't been for him, she was sure that they'd all be living under Nazi rule by this time. Folks seemed to have forgotten all that. She sighed heavily, no doubt everyone wanted to put the past six years behind them – just like she did – and move forward, as Churchill himself had said, into 'broad, sunlit uplands'. But why hadn't they believed that he could be the one to help them to do that?

Edie shook the newspaper in exasperation. 'Well, I don't understand it. But I'm not going to argue with you, Archie.' Silently, she thought that there were other things she could argue with him about far more easily than politics.

'We'll have to wait and see if this new government keeps their promises.' He sat down in his chair by the fire and took up the newspaper, which Edie had cast aside now.

Edie was restless. War work at the WVS centre had all but ceased, there was no one at home whenever Archie was at sea and she still couldn't bring herself to speak to Lil.

'Could we go and see Reggie before you have to go back?'

Archie glanced up. 'I don't see why not, love. I'll ask Harry if I can borrow his car. In fact, I'll nip round now and ask him. I sail tomorrow evening, so if we're going, we'll have to set off early.' He heaved himself out of his chair, reached for his cap from behind the door and left the house.

Harry was only too pleased to lend Archie his car, especially when Archie promised to fill it up with petrol when he returned, the basic petrol ration for civilians having been restored at the beginning of June.

They set off the following morning, both in high spirits at the thought of seeing Reggie, but the visit was not a success. Reggie was out in the fields all day helping with the harvest and though he dashed home at dinner time, he spoke to them through mouthfuls of food and then rushed out again.

'Mr Schofield can't manage them 'osses without me, I'll have to go.'

'All right, lad, you run along,' Archie said, but Edie pursed her lips, angry and hurt that their son couldn't spare them even a few more minutes.

And there was an uncomfortable atmosphere between Ruth and Edie. The farmer's wife was pleasant enough and generous, giving them dinner and loading them with eggs, cheese and butter to take home, but Edie could not forget, nor forgive, the woman who she believed had not only enticed Reggie away from his parents but had also had encouraged Irene to go out dancing. And look where that had led!

Irene thought a lot about Ken Forbes during the weeks and months she waited for Frank to come home. She was desperately sorry that she had hurt her husband and all his family – to say nothing of her own mother, who had had such hardships to bear already in her life. They didn't deserve this, none of them did. And yet, she could not totally regret her time with Ken. He was not to blame for their brief affair; he'd been a single man with no wife to go home to and he'd been lonely too, just like Irene, amidst the madness and unreality of life during wartime. He had been such a handsome, kind man who had made her feel loved and wanted and he had helped her to forget, even if only for a few blissful moments, how much she missed her husband. And it was Frank whom she truly loved. And then there was Marie. She was a little darling with bright, golden curls and a winning smile that could melt your heart. But the child couldn't melt Edie Kelsey's, though she was fast winding her way into her Grandma Lil's. And Uncle Archie – now there was a kindly man. He'd never once reproached her, even though she had betrayed his son. He still came and took Tommy out with him every time he was at home from sea and he never failed to smile down at Marie.

If Frank was half as understanding as his father, then perhaps – but she hardly dared to hope. Edie would be sure to have her say. None of her family had ever stood up to Edie Kelsey.

Grimsby fishermen were out on strike early in August, complaining bitterly that the foreign trawlers landing their catches in the docks were driving down the price of fish, and the value of some of the local fishermen's catches was half what it should have been.

'I'll have you at home for a bit, then,' Edie said, gleefully. She would even go without Archie's pay if it meant him being ashore for as long as the strike lasted.

'You most certainly will not,' Archie replied heatedly. 'I don't believe in strikes – though I do agree they've got a point. But I shall do my job. As long as the man who owns my trawler wants me to go to sea, I shall go.'

So Archie ran the gauntlet of the pickets and put to sea as usual, but always minding, on his return, that he was first in the line of trawlers waiting to dock on the high tide.

In the middle of August, there were more celebrations for VJ Day – Victory over Japan – and now the whole world was at peace. But this time, although the street celebrated again as it had for VE day, there was no revelry in either Edie's house or Lil's. They stayed behind closed doors.

Archie, home for three days from the sea, disappeared to the pub, meeting Harry for a drink. 'Thank God it's *all* over now, Harry,' he said.

'I'll drink to that, Archie.'

They sat in companionable silence for several minutes before Harry said softly. 'Any news?'

Archie sighed heavily. 'No more'n you already know. Nothing from Frank and not a word from Beth. I really . . .' He paused and swallowed hard before adding, 'I'm really afraid now that something's happened to her, but I daren't say owt to Edie.'

'Wouldn't you have heard something by now from the authorities if . . . ?'

Archie shrugged. 'Perhaps not if she's been involved in something top secret abroad.'

'Ah,' Harry said, understanding at once. That had been his thought too.

Archie sighed, 'Anyway, all this other business seems to have taken Edie's mind off Beth a bit and with Reggie staying on the farm . . .'

'It'll be a much better life for the lad, Archie.'

'I know that and I've sided with him, but that doesn't go down well with Edie. Oh, I can see her point, Harry, don't get me wrong, but I've always advocated letting our kids do what they want with their lives, and that doesn't sit easily with her. She thinks she knows what's best for them.'

'She just wants them at home, Archie. You can't blame a mother for that.' There was a note of wistfulness in his tone that Archie couldn't fail to notice.

'I don't,' he said gently, with unspoken understanding, 'but you have to let the young ones fly the nest some time.'

'I agree. The trouble is that Edie's been forced into parting with hers by the war far earlier than she would have done normally. Especially Reggie.'

'You're right, Harry. But it's been the same for everyone. Thousands of families have lost loved ones, have been separated for years and,' he smiled wryly, 'I've no doubt a great many are at this moment being faced with the same sort of shock that we've had with Irene. The war's ruined – or certainly altered – a lot of lives.'

A noisy group of revellers congaed past the open door of the pub, singing, 'The war is over, the lads are coming home . . .' to the traditional music played to the dance.

Archie and Harry exchanged a smile. 'I'd best be getting back. I don't want to leave Edie on her own for too long. She's not out merrymaking today.'

Harry chuckled. 'But Jessie's in the thick of it. The bunting and the Union Jack hat she made are on full display once more. And Terry is playing his piano at the end of the street. I think I'll stay here a bit longer, if you don't mind. I might have a quiet game of dominoes with old Charlie over there in the corner. It'd save me getting roped into the dancing because of the shortage of men. Mind you don't get dragged into it, Archie.'

'They'd have a job. My dancing days are over – if there ever were any.'

He stood up, shook Harry's hand and made his way home, but it was with leaden feet and an even heavier heart.

Forty-Six

'Are you having a party for little Tommy? He'll be five next Wednesday, won't he?' Jessie asked.

Edie pulled a face and sighed. 'I really don't know what's happening. Usually, we would have done summat together but now—'

'Oh for Heaven's sake, Edie, surely you can put your differences with Lil and Irene aside for one day. What about that little lad? Think of him. He hasn't a clue what's going on. It's his *birthday* and a very important one at that. He'll start school here in the same week, won't he?'

Edie shuddered at the thought. 'I expect so,' she said tightly. 'But that won't be a very happy experience for him, will it?'

Jessie blinked. 'No worse than for anyone else.'

Edie glared at her sister. 'You think not? He'll be bullied for sure when the other kids find out about his whore of a mother.'

Broadminded though Jessie was, she winced at Edie's description of Irene. 'Well, I reckon we should have a little party here for him. Maybe on another day. When will Archie be home? He'd not want to miss it.'

'Thursday.'

'There you are, then. We can give the little lad another party on either the Friday or the Saturday, because Archie certainly won't sail on a Friday, now will he?'

Edie laughed wryly. 'No, he won't.'

'Saturday'd be best for us and then Harry can come as well.'

'All right,' Edie agreed reluctantly, but for once her heart wasn't really in the planning of a party. The last one she'd helped to organize – for VE day – had ended in disaster.

Irene had enrolled Tommy in the local primary school, but she was anxious. Several children from their street went there and she was sure word would soon spread like the proverbial wildfire. Tommy would be bullied, she was sure.

He'd been at school less than two weeks before it happened. Irene felt helpless, but aid came from an unexpected quarter. Shirley, home on leave, arrived at Lil's back door, holding Tommy by the hand. Ursula stood a little uncertainly behind her. Irene was the one to open the door and for the first time since her homecoming, the two former friends and sisters-in-law faced each other.

'He's got a bloody nose, Irene, but we've sorted them out. I don't think it'll happen again. But mebbe you ought to meet him out of school rather than let him walk home on his own. He's only just five.'

Irene avoided meeting Shirley's gaze and bit her lip. 'Thank you,' she said huskily as she reached out to grasp Tommy's arm and pull him into the house. 'Thank you – both of you.' Then she closed the door.

As they walked through the backyards, Shirley muttered. 'I expect she doesn't want to go out much. Afraid of the stares and the whispers. But she ought to look out for Tommy more.'

Inside her own home, Shirley told her mother. 'We

saw Tommy on our way home. He was being bullied by some kids in the street.'

'Eh?' Edie turned anxious eyes towards Shirley. 'Who was it? Them little buggers at the end of the street?' She started towards the back door as if she would go this very instant to protect her grandson.

'It's all right. We put a stop to it, Mam. In fact,' Shirley grinned, 'Ursula was a real star. She gave the two lads a clip round the ear and they ran off.'

Ursula laughed. 'I happen to know them. They live next door to where I have lodgings. They'll be worried I'll tell their mothers.'

Edie nodded absently, her mind returning to her grandson. 'Is Tommy all right?'

Shirley pulled a face. 'More or less. They'd ripped his pullover and thrown his satchel in a puddle and he'd got a bloody nose.'

'Poor little scrap.' Edie muttered. 'None of it's his fault, yet he has to bear the bullying and the cruel taunts about his mother, I bet.'

Ursula glanced at Shirley, but said nothing. She knew all about Irene and the trouble she had brought on the family.

It was Lil, who, on hearing what had happened, decided that she would be the one to take Tommy to and from school each day.

'You've enough to do, Mam. I – I ought to go,' Irene said hesitantly.

'It's only ten minutes' walk. And it'll do me good to get away from me work for a bit. Besides, me grandson's safety comes first.'

After a week of taking and fetching Tommy, Lil was surprised by a loud summons from Edie, banging on the door between their yards. 'Lil? You there, Lil?'

Lil approached the other side of the fence with trepidation. Now what? Was Frank back? Was this the day fateful decisions would be made?

'What is it?'

Without preamble, Edie said, 'I've seen you taking and fetching Tommy every day because that little trollop daren't show her face, I expect. But I can fetch him home each afternoon, if you like, and then he can have his tea with me.'

Lil hesitated for a moment before saying, 'That's very kind of you, Edie—'

'It's not kindness, Lil,' Edie said harshly. 'I want to see me grandson an' I won't stand by and see him bullied because of *her*.' She turned away without another word, entered her back door and slammed it behind her, leaving Lil staring after her.

And so they fell into a kind of routine, but it was an uneasy one of mutual help. Both sides of the feud, for that was what it had become, were at least united on one point; Tommy's wellbeing was paramount.

When Archie was at home, he took his turn in meeting Tommy out of school, and the big man's presence was a warning to the would-be bullies. Once the nastiness had stopped, to everyone's relief, Tommy seemed to settle in well at the school. It would be a shame now, Archie thought, if he had to be uprooted and sent back to the country; new school, new classmates. Another upheaval for the little lad.

Edie was sunk in gloom, not even the thought that the war was finally over could raise her spirits.

'It says here,' Archie said, jabbing at his newspaper, 'that they're increasing the rate at which servicemen are

404

demobilized. A million men by December, they reckon.' He glanced up at Edie. 'That might include Frank, love.'

But Edie was not to be comforted. 'Mebbe,' she murmured disconsolately. 'But will he come home even then?'

'He'll have to sometime,' Archie muttered. 'He might as well get it over with.' He paused and then asked, 'Have you written to him?' He held his breath, waiting for the answer that he was sure was coming.

'I certainly have,' Edie said grimly, 'and I've told him exactly what I think. Frank will listen to me. He'll know I'm right. He wants to get shut of the little trollop and fight her – in court, if necessary – for custody of Tommy.' Edie met his gaze. 'He can live with us. They both can and, if necessary, we'll move.'

'Move? Whatever for?'

Edie jerked her head in the direction of Lil's home. 'To get away from them, of course.'

'But – but what about Lil? You and Lil?'

'There is no "me an' Lil" any more, Archie. I don't want owt to do with Lil Horton ever again.'

If there was any greater shock to be had than those Archie had suffered already, then this was it. He'd never dreamed he'd hear such words from Edie's lips.

As the first Christmas since the war had ended approached, Archie had one more trip to sea, but he had had no chance to speak to Shirley as he'd intended to do; she had had no more leave. Before he left, he said to Edie, 'When you write to Shirley, Edie love, just ask her a bit more about Ursula, will you? I'm not sure about this girl she's been keeping company with. She's still hanging around the docks, talking to unsavoury characters. I've seen her there several times. I've just got an uncomfortable feeling about her and I don't want Shirley getting in with someone – unsuitable. That's all.'

Edie glared at him. The relationship between husband and wife was strained. It had been ever since Irene had arrived home and it was something that had never happened before in the whole of their married life. But Edie was adamant in her withdrawal from Lil and her family – apart from Tommy, of course – and she knew that Archie still went round next door, still talked to both Lil and Irene. He'd had the cheek to come back one day and say what a pretty little thing the baby was. That, as far as Edie was concerned, had been the last straw.

'Are you saying I haven't looked after me own daughter, Archie Kelsey? After all these years of bringing up your children when you've hardly been here. Oh, it's all very well to come home every few weeks and spoil 'em rotten. King for a Day, aren't you, down Freeman Street, when you've money in your pocket?'

'Edie love, I meant no such thing and you know it. It's just this Ursula. She was on the docks again when I took Tommy down to see the ships after school yesterday. She was talking to a right scruffy character. And I'd seen her with him before. That time when she told me there was a trawler late back – and there wasn't. That was funny for a start.'

'She's a reporter for the newspaper, for heaven's sake. She's got to go all over the place to find news.

'Is she employed by the *Telegraph*?'

'Well – not exactly. She writes bits and pieces for them from what Shirley said. A freelance, she calls herself.'

'There you are, then, even the folks at the paper have

got doubts about her, else they'd have taken her on, wouldn't they?'

'Maybe – maybe not. Newspapers use freelances regularly, don't they?'

'Quite possibly, and I'm also sure they'll verify anything a freelance sends in, but that still doesn't answer my doubts about exactly who and what she is.'

'What do you mean, "what she is"? You make it sound as if she's a – as if she's a –' For once, even Edie was lost for words.

'I don't really know what I'm saying, love. It's just that I've got this feeling that something's not quite right.'

Edie laughed sarcastically. 'And I thought it was women who were supposed to have intuition.'

Archie smiled weakly. 'Aye, well, fishermen have too, you know.'

'No – you're a superstitious lot. That's what you are.'

Now Archie's smile broadened. 'And one of 'em is not going to sea on a quarrel.' He held out his arms. 'Come on, love, don't let's argue. Give us a kiss.'

Edie submitted to his kiss, but she couldn't summon up the usual warmth or bring herself to say 'Take care' as she always had.

Before he'd reached the end of the street on his way to the docks, Edie was regretting her coolness towards him.

In Shirley's next letter, she wrote, *I've been really lucky and got over a week off at Christmas and New Year and I was wondering if Ursula can come to us for Christmas, Mam? She's no family here and the old misery she lodges with is going to her daughter's in Lincoln. Ursula will be on her own.*

Edie wrote back at once. *She can, as far as I'm concerned, though she'll have to share her rations with us. But I'd better tell you that your dad isn't too sure about her. And besides, won't she be going home to Switzerland soon?*

A week later, Shirley wrote, *I really don't know Ursula's plans – perhaps she'll tell us at Christmas. But I do know she wants to stay and do a series of articles about all the folks coming home after the war. You know, servicemen and women, evacuees – everybody.*

'Well,' Edie said aloud to the empty room as she folded Shirley's letter and put it on the mantelpiece behind Laurence's photograph. 'It won't be any good her coming to this house for *that*, will it?'

The queues for food seemed just as long as they had during the wartime, but now people groused about it more.

'I thought the war was supposed to be over,' Jessie grumbled as she and Edie stood in a queue outside the butcher's shop before going on to the WVS together. Lil no longer helped out as their war efforts at the centre were winding down.

'So they say,' Edie murmured, 'but I haven't noticed much difference yet. No one's coming home.'

Jessie glanced at her, but said nothing. She knew all about how not one of Edie's family was coming back to live at home and she felt sorry for her sister. She knew, too, all about the heartache Irene had brought upon the family and how Edie and Lil were no longer on speaking terms, though Jessie was shrewd enough to know that the blame for that lay at Edie's door. In

Jessie's mind, Lil needed her friend more than ever at this moment.

'Have you heard anything from Beth?'

Edie pursed her lips and shook her head. 'Not a word.'

Jessie squeezed her sister's arm as they shuffled further up the queue. 'She'll come back,' Jessie said. But Edie wasn't sure. If she'd still been alive, surely by now Beth would have made contact. And yet, wouldn't the authorities have let them know if she had been killed, just as they had about Laurence? It was a mystery.

Jessie bit her lip and asked tentatively, 'Have you spoken to Lil yet?'

Again Edie shook her head.

'Well, you should, Edie. You've been friends for more years than I can count and it's not her fault her daughter's a little trollop.'

'Isn't it?'

Jessie cast a sly glance at her sister. Jessie had never been one to hold her tongue when there was something to be said and she wasn't going to start now. 'You can't be held responsible for what your kids do when they grow up, duck. Just be thankful that – so far – neither of your girls have got themselves in the family way.'

'I hope I've brought them up to know what's right and wrong,' Edie said primly.

'That's not the point.' Jessie paused for a brief moment before saying harshly. 'It's in the breed, Edie, isn't it?'

Edie stared at her. It was the first time she could ever remember her sister referring to the fact that Edie herself had had a shotgun wedding.

'Jessie, how could you?' Edie said reproachfully, but Jessie only shrugged. 'It's a fact, though. And you know

409

me, I only speak the truth, even though it might hurt sometimes.'

She was right, but Edie was shocked that her own sister could fling it back into her face at a time like this. And Jessie was not finished yet. 'You've maybe brought your daughters up to be perfect because of what happened to you. But you want to watch your Shirley.'

'What d'you mean?'

'Mrs Doughty at the WVS was telling me that her hubby had seen Shirley hanging around the docks with that friend of hers when she was home on leave the last time.'

'Ursula works for the *Telegraph*.' Edie went on to make the same excuse to Jessie as she had to Archie. 'She's looking for stories and I expect Shirley was just helping her. That's all.'

Jessie pursed her lips and cast a disbelieving glance at Edie. 'If you say so, Edie. If you say so. Come on, we're next in line – if there's anything left by now.'

When Edie arrived home she felt unsettled. Jessie's reference to her past and the advice that she should make up her quarrel with Lil, to say nothing of her warning about Shirley, had disturbed Edie. There was no doubt she missed her friend dreadfully, but her own rigid moral code – no doubt born out of her own mistake – could not and would not condone what Irene had done. She had been unfaithful to Frank, had cuckolded him, and Edie could not forgive her for that. She sighed heavily as she unpacked her shopping, such as it was, and asked herself if she was really being unfair to Lil as Jessie had stated so bluntly. But this was different, this wasn't just a young lass getting herself into trouble and marrying the father of her child as she and Archie had done. They'd been engaged, planning to get married anyway. It just happened that the wedding had to be brought forward a little, that was all. This was totally different, she told herself. This was infidelity of monstrous proportions. But was Lil to blame? At the moment, Edie couldn't answer her own question.

And then there was Shirley. Archie had expressed doubts about Ursula and now Jessie had done the same. Whatever was she going to do about Shirley?

Forty-Seven

There was no pleasure in wrapping presents this year, nor hanging up the home-made paper chains and decorating the small artificial tree they'd had for years and which was looking sadly dilapidated. Edie made the Christmas puddings and a cake but her heart was not in it. And worse still, she was having to do it all herself this year. There was no Lil to share the planning and the preparation with. And there'd be no Lil and her family round Edie's table on Christmas Day, though Edie hoped Tommy would be allowed to come round at some point, maybe for tea.

Archie's ship was due to dock two days before Christmas Eve on the evening high tide, but when the following morning dawned and he had still not come breezing in the back door, calling a greeting as he always did, Edie began to worry. By the time Shirley arrived home on leave just after midday, Edie was pacing the hearth trying to decide whether or not she should go to the fish docks to find out for herself what was happening. How she wished she could have gone next door to share her worries with Lil. But the gulf between them held her back. Besides, Irene and her little bastard were still there and she certainly didn't want to run into them. But she would have loved to have felt Lil's arms around her and been able to pour out her fears to her understanding friend. And no one knew better than Lil what it was like to wait for hours for news of a husband missing out at sea. And then, in Lil's case, it had been the very worst news.

'The trains were packed,' Shirley grumbled. 'I reckon because the war's over they're letting as many home on leave as they can this Christmas. And, of course, there're lots of them being demobbed as well.' She sat down in her father's chair, eased off her shoes and rubbed her feet. 'I feel as if I've been on my feet for hours and then, when I got here, there's some kind of flap on. The newspaper seller at the station was shouting about a trawler being lost at sea.'

At Edie's startled gasp, Shirley looked up and then glanced round the room as if only just realizing that her father had not arrived home. Her eyes widening, she looked up at her mother as she asked hesitantly, 'Dad?'

Edie pressed her fingers to her lips and shook her head wordlessly.

'Right,' Shirley said, with renewed vigour. 'We'll go down to the dock and find out what's going on.'

'They'd – have let us know, if – if—'

'Of course, they would, Mam, but we'll go anyway. Come on, get your coat.'

Edie was usually the strong, determined one, but for once, she seemed to have gone to pieces.

'We – we had words just before he left,' she blurted out, the guilt washing over her like a tidal wave.

Shirley looked at her in surprise. 'You and Dad quarrelled? But you *never* part on a quarrel. It's a rule in this house.' She gave a wry laugh. 'It's almost a *law*.'

'I know,' Edie said, distraught with anxiety.

'What about?' Shirley asked bluntly and then added beneath her breath, 'As if I didn't know.'

'*Her.*' Edie's tone was harsh as she gestured to the house next door. 'Look what trouble she's caused.'

Once, Shirley would have leaped at the unexpected chance to drive the wedge between her mother and Lil even deeper. Since their friendship had deteriorated so swiftly, Shirley had felt closer to her mother than ever before and even though she was away from home, Edie seemed to confide in Shirley more in their regular exchange of letters. But a change had come over the young woman; she was leading her own life now, was more self-confident and had made friends, the bitterness she felt about her place within the family still rankled a little, but now she could put it behind her and move forward with her own life.

'She's split this family apart,' Edie was saying, 'And if owt's happened to your dad, I'll blame her an' all. I've never – in all the time we've been married – parted on harsh words. And it's all her fault that we did.'

Shirley made no comment, but reached for her mother's coat on the peg behind the door. 'Come on, we'll go and see what we can find out.'

For a cold winter's afternoon the dockside was surprisingly busy. 'Looks like summat's up,' Edie murmured, squinting through the gloom for the sight of anyone she knew; anyone who might know something.

'Well, well, well, look who's over there.'

'Who?' Edie asked sharply, but she couldn't see anyone she knew.

'Over there. Standing in the shadows.' Shirley's sharper eyes had spotted someone she knew. 'It's Ursula.'

'Where?'

Shirley pointed and following the line of her daughter's gaze, Edie murmured, 'Mebbe your dad was right about her. What's she doing hanging about on the dock-side on a day like this?'

'She'll be here to get a story,' Shirley said. 'Come on, let's go across. She might know something.'

'They won't tell a reporter before they tell the families – if – if there's anything to tell.' Tears smarted in Edie's eyes; already she was fearing the worst.

'Oh, you'd be surprised what Ursula can find out. Come on.'

As they drew close to where she was standing, Shirley called out to her. 'Ursula.'

The girl jumped visibly, then she seemed to relax when she realized who was calling her name. 'Oh – Shirley. And Mrs Kelsey.'

'Have you heard any news? My dad should have docked yesterday and Mam's worried sick it's his trawler that's missing.'

'There are two late back,' Ursula said. 'And it seems they've lost radio contact with both of them.'

'Oh no!' Edie breathed.

It was what had happened the night Lil's husband, Tom, had been missing.

'You there, Lil?'

Lil heard the knocking on her front door and hurried to open it. To her surprise, it was Jessie standing there. 'Can I come in? It's arctic out here.'

'Oh, yes, yes, of course.' Lil was flustered by Jessie's unexpected arrival on her doorstep. As she closed the door and replaced the draught excluder she asked. 'What is it? Is something wrong?'

'Haven't you heard? There are two trawlers late back and one of them's Archie's.'

Lil's fingers fluttered to cover her mouth as she gasped, 'No, oh no!'

'Edie didn't come to tell you, then?'

Mutely, Lil shook her head as tears filled her eyes. She should have been there for her friend, should have been there to comfort and console her, but it seemed the chasm was too wide and deep for Edie to turn to her even in her greatest trouble. The realization cut Lil profoundly and she dropped her head as the tears flowed down her cheeks.

'Come on, Lil. I'll make you a cuppa.' It was just the sort of thing that Edie would have said – had said so many times – that Lil's tears flowed even faster.

Lil had always been a little in awe of Edie's sister. Jessie was strong-minded and outspoken – even more so than Edie, and she was bad enough when she was in the mood. But Jessie strode through life carrying all before her, not suffering fools at all, never mind 'gladly', as the saying went. She had been the proverbial tower of strength in the WVS and Lil wondered what Jessie would do now that the war was over. No doubt she'd find some other worthy cause to organize. Maybe she would stay on and build up the peacetime work of the local WVS. But, for the moment, Lil was thankful to let Jessie take over and make tea for them both.

'Where's your Irene? Would she like a cup?'

'She – she's upstairs. Putting Tommy to bed.'

'Ah, bless him. He's growing into a grand little chap. I saw him last week round at Edie's.' Jessie met Lil's gaze as she handed her a steaming cup of tea and sat down with her own. 'Now, tell me about this baby. What's gone on, Lil?'

Lil sighed and shrugged helplessly. 'Irene won't tell me much. Edie found out more than I have.'

'Edie!' Jessie was startled. 'I thought she wasn't speaking to any of you – apart from Tommy, of course.'

'She isn't – well, not really, but she comes and shouts at me over the fence now and then. She's blaming us for the fact that none of her family are coming home.' Lil sighed. 'I suppose – in all fairness – it is Irene's fault that Frank's decided to stay away at the moment, but we can hardly be blamed for Reggie and certainly not for Beth.'

'Ah yes, Beth. None of us know what's happened to her, now do we?'

Lil's head shot up as she stared at Jessie. 'What – what do you mean?'

Jessie shrugged. 'Scarcely a word from her for months. Not even since the war ended.' She cast a sly glance at Lil before she said bluntly, 'I reckon she might have got herself into trouble and daren't come home. Her dad idolizes her. He'd be so disappointed and her mam would half kill her.' She sniffed. 'Though I expect Shirley'd be cock-a-hoop to think the idol had fallen from her perch.'

'They'd stand by her,' Lil murmured. 'It's what you do.'

Jessie eyed Lil speculatively. 'You're standing by Irene, then?'

Lil nodded. 'She's my flesh and blood. She's all I've got. Her and Tommy and – and Marie.'

'Can I see her?' Jessie asked in what, for her, was an unusually gentle tone. Whenever a baby had been born into the family, the childless Jessie had become wistful and it seemed that the unexpected – and unwelcome – arrival of Irene's baby girl was not going to be an exception.

'Of course.' Lil jumped up. 'I'll fetch her down.'

'Don't wake her if she's sleeping.'

'Well, she might be now. You come upstairs, then.'

'All right.' Jessie set her cup down and stood up to follow Lil.

She's a strange one, Lil was thinking as she led the way upstairs and into the front bedroom where Irene and her two children slept. Jessie was a good-looking woman, tall and slim, with shoulder-length brown hair and dark eyes. She always dressed smartly. Clever with her sewing machine and needle and thread, she'd turned pre-war clothes into fashionable garments by shortening skirts and copying the latest styles from magazines. She always wore a jaunty hat and, in winter, a fur stole around her shoulders over a tailored costume. She was outspoken to the point of blunt rudeness on occasions and though most of the time she used big words where simpler ones would have done, when she was angry or 'on her high horse' about something as Edie had always described it, she was quite capable of peppering her language with swear words. Jessie was a strange mixture, but Lil had always liked her even if she had been a little in awe of her. She'd certainly admired her strength of character.

But tonight Jessie was gentleness personified as she leaned over the side of the cot that had served all Edie's children and Tommy's early weeks too. It was strange, Lil thought irrationally, that Edie hadn't demanded the cot be returned to her. Perhaps she hadn't stopped to think the 'the little bastard' might be sleeping in it, Lil thought wryly.

'She's a pretty little thing,' Jessie murmured as she gazed at the sleeping child in the dim light from the night-light on the mantelpiece. 'Lovely blond hair and such long eyelashes.' Then she straightened up and turned to look at Irene hovering in the shadows on the far side of the bedroom.

'Oh, Irene love,' Jessie said, with a surprising note of sadness in her tone. 'Whatever is Frank going to say?'

Forty-Eight

It was a long evening for all of them. When midnight came and went and there was still no news, Shirley at last persuaded her mother to return home. 'We can't do any good here, Mam. They'll let us know if they hear anything.'

'I'll be staying,' Ursula said. 'I'll come at once if . . .'

Edie was cold, chilled through, and it wasn't all because of the winter's night. Her heart felt as if it was frozen. But she allowed Shirley to lead her home as one might have done a bewildered child.

'I'll make cocoa and then you're going to bed.'

'No, no, I can't do that, Shirley. Really, I can't. I'll sit here in the chair near the fire, but you go up.'

'No, no, I wasn't going anyway,' Shirley declared. The thought of keeping vigil hadn't occurred to her until this moment, but there was no way she was going to bed and leaving her mother alone. 'I'll fetch a couple of blankets down and keep the fire going.'

So, for the rest of the night, mother and daughter sat huddled in blankets in front of the fire, waiting for news. And just the other side of the wall, Lil, too, sat in her chair by the fire through the interminable night, longing to be with her friend and yet too afraid to do anything about it.

*

As the pale light of Christmas Eve morning crept across the cold North Sea, two fishing boats edged slowly into the Grimsby dock, one towing the other and coming in on the tide.

From the shadows, Ursula watched as the men, cold and hungry, walked down the gangway. The skipper of the first trawler stayed on his bridge, but Ursula was sure it was Archie. She left her place where she had been standing for most of the night and, moving stiffly, went to meet the fishermen as they came ashore. As she moved closer she could see that it was Archie's ship, *The Havelock*.

'What happened? Why are you so late back?'

Most of the men glanced at her and walked on, not slowing in their haste to reach warmth and a good, hot meal, to say nothing of letting their anxious families know that they were safe. Only one, a young boy of sixteen or so, stopped to speak to her.

'Our ship's engine failed,' he jerked his thumb towards the vessel that had been towed home, 'and Mr Kelsey was fishing nearby. He came to our rescue. But for him,' he grinned, 'we might have been spending Christmas at sea.'

'Is everyone all right?'

The boy nodded. 'Aye, every one of us – thanks to Mr Kelsey.' The boy turned away and hurried after his shipmates.

'Happy Christmas,' Ursula called after him and the boy turned round briefly to shout, 'It will be now, miss.'

No one else seemed to be leaving the two trawlers and Ursula could see that Archie was still busy aboard his ship, so she turned and left the dockside to go home, but first she must go and see Shirley and her mother.

*

The knock at the front door startled both Shirley and Edie. They had been dozing in their chairs and now both woke with a start at the sound. For a moment they stared at each other, horror-stricken. No one ever came to the front door unless it was as the bearer of bad news. Except Ursula. Ursula always came to the front door. Oh please, let it be Ursula knocking, Edie found herself praying as she struggled to her feet. But she found that her legs wouldn't work and it was left to Shirley to open the door. Edie held her breath, listening intently for the sound of a man's voice – a man who would have come to tell them – but a grinning Shirley was leading a smiling Ursula into the room.

'He's all right, Mam, he's safe.'

Edie's wide eyes went to Ursula's face and the girl nodded. 'It's true, Mrs Kelsey. I have seen him myself.'

'Sit down here, Ursula, and tell us.'

She sat down in the chair where Shirley had spent the night and held out her hands to the fire. 'I stayed all night and about an hour or so ago, I saw two ships coming in. One – your husband's – was towing the other one. Mr Kelsey is still aboard his ship, but I spoke to a boy as he came ashore. It seems the other trawler's engine broke down and your husband towed them back home. That's why they were so late and one of the men told me that they couldn't send word because the ship-to-shore radio wasn't working properly.'

Edie collapsed against the back of her chair and closed her eyes. 'Oh thank God, thank God.'

When at last Archie arrived home it was to a rapturous welcome from his wife and daughter. Even Ursula stood behind them smiling widely. Edie shed a few tears against his shoulder.

'Now, now, love, what's all this?' he said, patting her shoulder, a little embarrassed by her display of emotion in front of a comparative stranger. It wasn't something Edie did very often.

'We parted on a quarrel. I'd never have forgiven myself if – if—'

'Everything's all right, love,' he said softly in his deep voice. 'And I've got a whole week off, right over Christmas and New Year. My ship's going in for repair. I'm sorry you were so worried because I couldn't send word.' He gave a wry laugh. 'So much for modern technology – never works when you really need it.'

Edie drew back and wiped her tears. 'Never mind, it's all right now, but just for a while there I thought you weren't going to come home either. Still, we can have a nice Christmas now – well, as good as we can make it without half the family – but Ursula's going to join us, aren't you, love?'

Archie tried to smile and nod his approval. He was grateful to the girl who'd brought the good news to his wife and daughter. And yet, somehow there was something about her that still didn't sit easily with the intuitive fisherman.

Christmas was a quiet affair in the two neighbouring houses, where once, laughter, love and friendship had flowed between them in abundance.

Edie, taking a few moments alone in her bedroom whilst Shirley, Jessie and Ursula did the washing-up and Archie and Harry snored in the front room before a roaring fire, shed a few tears for her missing family.

Laurence, whom she mourned with an aching sadness; Frank, who'd written only spasmodically throughout the whole time he'd been away, was now being kept away by his unfaithful wife; and Reggie, well, he was just an ungrateful little beggar. He could have come home, but he'd chosen strangers over his own flesh and blood. And as for Beth, well, Edie really daren't think about her. But in the New Year, she promised herself, she would make some enquiries. She would start by writing to Alan Forster; she had his address in London. Yes, she comforted herself, that would be a good start. Things couldn't be allowed to drift on any longer. They'd left it long enough – too long – as it was, hoping each day that they would hear something and not daring to find out what might be the dreadful truth.

If it hadn't been for Tommy running freely between the two houses this Christmas, Edie didn't know what she'd have done. But she had to put on a brave front and try to make the two days a happy time for those who were with her. And Ursula, too, for the poor girl couldn't be with her family. Never let it be said, Edie thought, that the Kelseys didn't make a lonely young woman welcome at Christmas.

And Lil? Edie shied away from thinking about her, unable to admit even to herself that she missed her friend sorely.

'But now,' she said aloud to the empty bedroom, 'you'd better get yourself downstairs and play charades with Shirley, Jessie and Ursula.'

Forty-Nine

They hadn't seen Ursula since Boxing Day, but on the morning of New Year's Eve, she arrived early in the morning at Edie's front door, looking flustered and wide-eyed. 'May I come in, Mrs Kelsey? I – there's a man following me.'

Edie poked her head out and scanned the street. 'Is there? I don't see anyone, but come in anyway.' As she led the way into the living room, she asked, 'Do you know him?'

Ursula shook her head as she removed her coat and hung it on the pegs behind the door. 'No. I've never seen him before.'

'Mm.' Edie eyed her speculatively. 'You ought to be more careful about the company you keep. Archie's seen you around the docks. It's not a good place for a young lass to hang about on her own.'

'I'm only trying to find stories – articles – for the paper.' She glanced round the room. 'Where are Mr Kelsey and Shirley?'

'Shirley's gone into town. She wanted a few bits and pieces before she goes back and Archie's just nipped down to see Harry.'

'I – I thought he might have gone back to sea.'

Edie shook her head. 'He's not going back until after New Year and Shirley's to go back the day after tomorrow.'

425

'Ah, yes, I remember now,' the girl murmured, still seeming distracted.

'And then I'll be on my lonesome again. Still, we had a nice time at Christmas, didn't we? Even if it was a lot quieter than it used to be. What we would have done without young Tommy to brighten things up, I don't know. And you, of course, love,' she added hastily, anxious not to let the girl think she hadn't been welcome.

Ursula smiled weakly. 'You've been very kind to me. All of you.'

'Sit down and I'll make us a cuppa.' Edie was glad to have someone with whom to share of cup of tea and a natter. If only Lil . . . But she closed her mind to thoughts of the countless cups of tea she'd shared with her friend over the years. That was all in the past, she told herself, but her heart ached with loss.

They chatted for a while, but Ursula seemed on edge; she was not as comfortable as she had been at Christmas. Then she had laughed and joked over the dinner table and played board games with Shirley and Tommy in the afternoon and even joined in the inevitable game of charades. But now her thoughts seemed elsewhere and when the back door rattled, Edie noticed that she drew in a breath and held it until Archie appeared from the scullery.

He nodded to her and sat down at the table, as Edie rose to make a fresh pot of tea. 'And I'd better get the dinner started,' she murmured, trying to give their visitor the hint that she should leave. But Ursula remained seated, looking down at her cup and twisting it round and round on its saucer.

'There are three policemen at the top of the street,' Archie said, deliberately making his tone casual, but his keen gaze was on Ursula. 'Just outside the house where you live.'

Ursula's head snapped up, she gasped and her eyes widened in terror. 'Oh please, don't tell them where I am.'

Edie, halfway to the scullery, carrying the teapot, turned and gaped at her. 'Why?'

When Ursula didn't answer, Archie said slowly, 'I think our young friend here has reason to believe that the police might be looking for her. Am I right, Ursula?' he asked softly, 'or is that not your real name?'

She stared at him for a long moment before she dropped her head. Her shoulders slumped and she said flatly, 'It's – it's Helga.'

'That's a German name, isn't it?' Edie gasped, coming back to the table and sitting down again, the fresh pot of tea forgotten.

Ursula – for that was the name they knew her by – nodded.

'And are you, as I suspect, a German spy?' Archie said.

'An agent – just like you've been sending over to France for years.'

'But why here? Why Grimsby?' Edie asked, but it was Archie who answered her.

'The shipping, love. Movements of the minesweepers, for one thing. And I'm sure there've been other bits of useful information she's been able to pick up.'

'So that's why you've been hanging round the docks,' Edie began and then frowned. 'But you can't still be spying; the war's over.'

'I was trying to get home.'

'She's been asking various skippers to take her across to one of the German ports. Bremerhaven was the favourite, I think, wasn't it, Ursula?'

'And no one would,' Edie murmured without Archie having to tell her.

'No. Word got round and someone went to the police.'

'Was it you?' Ursula asked.

Archie shook his head, 'No, it wasn't, though I can't say I'm sorry that someone did. I did have my suspicions about you, I must admit. So, what are you going to do, because I have to tell you now, we're not going to hide you. You can leave by the back door, that's as much as I'll agree to, but if the police come here, I shall tell them—'

As if on cue, someone battered at the front door. Ursula gave a little squeak of alarm and turned white. 'They will hang me,' she whispered.

Archie did not move to answer the door. Then, suddenly, he stood up and grabbed her coat from the peg and pushed it towards her. 'Go on, out the back way and run. For God's sake, run, girl.'

She hesitated for only a moment and then was out of the door and running down the yard and out of the back gate. Both Edie and Archie stood staring out of the window overlooking the yard.

'Archie Kelsey,' Edie said at last, as an even louder knocking sounded on the front door, 'you've just aided and abetted a criminal.'

'I know,' he admitted solemnly.

'You've shocked me. You're the most law-abiding citizen I know. And what are you going to tell them? You're going to have to answer the door else they'll batter it down.'

'I will. Just – give it another minute or so, eh?'

Now Edie turned to him. 'But she was a *spy*, Archie. She could have told the enemy all sorts of things. Mebbe it was her what told them where to drop their bombs. Have you thought of that?'

There was another banging on the door and Archie turned slowly to Edie. 'Just go along with whatever I say, all right, love?'

Edie hesitated for a moment. She had such a strong sense of right and wrong that all this went against her nature, against her instincts. But she didn't want to see a young girl hanged whatever she'd done. The war was over and surely it was time to forgive . . . The thought came unbidden and a little voice reminded her *What about you doing a bit of forgiving, then, Edie Kelsey?* Her wandering thoughts were brought back to the present by Archie whispering urgently, 'Edie, I can't give the girl away – I'm not going to lie but let's just act stupid as if we know nothing about her. Let's just give her time to get away.'

'But she's a criminal, Archie,' Edie hissed. 'We ought to hand her in.'

Archie stared at his wife and then touched her hand gently. 'And is that what you'd've wanted the French to do with our Beth?'

'Beth? What d'you mean, Archie? What are you talking about?'

Archie sighed. The knocking had stopped for the moment. Maybe they had a few more minutes before someone came back to try again.

'I think Beth may have gone over to France as a British agent. You know how well she spoke French. She was just the sort of person they'd have been looking for.'

Edie sat down suddenly as if the strength had drained out of her legs, but still she was staring open-mouthed at him. 'Beth – our Beth – an agent?'

'Of course, I don't *know* that's what she's been doing, but don't you think it strange that she's never been home over the last four years? And only a measly post-card now and again. Don't you remember how her first letters were full of everything she was doing – at least what she could tell us? The people she'd met, the friends she'd made. And then it all went very quiet. Her letters were stilted, not a bit like our Beth, and then the post-cards started arriving with a strange regularity. Now, we both know that Beth's letters were spasmodic, to say the least.'

'I – did notice, yes,' Edie admitted, 'but I just thought she was like the rest. Caught up with – with other folk. Like Frank, who doesn't want to come home – and I can't blame him for that, but Reggie . . .' She shook her head sadly. 'He didn't even want to visit his mam and dad at Christmas.'

Archie squeezed Edie's hand, knowing how much she'd missed the family this week. Christmas had height-ened the fact that there were faces missing around the table.

'So, you see, love, I couldn't turn the lass in – what-ever she's done, just in case . . .' He said no more, letting the words hang between them. But Edie knew what he meant. Just in case, somewhere in France, Beth had been in exactly the same position.

'But what are we going to do? We'll get done for helping her, won't we?'

'Oh, I'm not going to lie to them. I won't go as far as that. I'll answer their questions truthfully. I'm just not going to tell them that we knew what she was, because until five minutes or so ago, we didn't. Not really. So, here's what we'll do, when they come back – and they will – we'll say she was here but that when

430

she heard there were police in the street, she ran out of the back door. All right?'

Edie nodded, biting her lip. She wasn't very good at lying. She was sure the policeman would see it in her face.

The anticipated knock, not so loud as before, came about twenty minutes later, as if they'd reached the end of the street and turned back to try again at the houses where no one had answered the first time.

'Evening, Archie,' a deep friendly voice said when he opened the front door. 'Could I come in for a minute?'

'Hello, Bill. Of course – come in. The wife'll make you a cuppa, if you've time.'

'Oh aye, I've time now. We've apprehended the person we were looking for.'

Archie's heart sank. 'And who was that?' he managed to ask cheerfully. Walking in front of the officer he managed to pull a face at Edie to warn her that Ursula had been caught.

'A young woman,' Sergeant Bill Fenton began as he sat down and laid his helmet carefully on the table. 'We've been interested in her for some time. She lodged at the top of this street and we're just asking everyone if they know owt about her.'

'What's her name?'

'Helga Wolff, but we understand she was living here under the name of Ursula.'

'Good Lord!' Archie exclaimed and Edie, despite the seriousness of the situation found herself having difficulty in stifling hysterical laughter. She'd never known Archie had such acting skills. 'She's a friend of our daughter's. She spent Christmas with us. What's she been up to?'

The policeman sighed. 'We have no proof – yet. But we believe she may have been working as a spy.'

'A spy?' Now Edie was able to give vent to her laughter. 'In Grimsby? Never!'

But the policeman's face was solemn. 'Grimsby's just the sort of place, Mrs Kelsey; the movements of shipping and suchlike would be useful to the enemy and we're not a million miles from Hull, are we? And Hull's been a prime target for their bombers.'

'We've had our share.' Edie was indignant.

'Exactly,' the sergeant said solemnly. 'So, tell me what you know about her. You say she's been friendly with your girl. Shirley, isn't it? How did they get to know each other?'

Archie glanced at Edie. 'I don't rightly know, Bill. I'm away such a lot. When I came back after a trip, she'd been here to tea and it' – he shrugged – 'sort of led on from there.'

This was the truth so Edie felt able to take up the story. 'I think Shirley just happened to get to know her because she lived in our street. She asked if she could bring her home to tea. We felt sorry for her because she couldn't be with her family, especially at Christmas and that.'

'Did she tell you where she was from?'

Now Edie was on safe ground. 'Switzerland,' she said promptly. 'From Zurich and that explained her funny accent because she told us that they speak German there.'

Bill Fenton nodded. 'I believe that is correct, but as yet we have been unable to verify her story.' He smiled grimly. 'We're fully aware of the sort of cover stories agents use.' He shrugged. 'Our own Special Operations Executive was very creative in the tales they dreamed up.'

Archie and Edie dared not look at each other. Beth,

they were both thinking. Is that what our Beth's been doing?

'Do you know if she had a job?' Bill asked.

'She told us she was writing articles for the *Telegraph*.' Edie glanced at Archie. 'We know she used to hang around the docks. I warned her about it' – Edie waved her hand vaguely – 'you know what folks might have thought about her, but never this. It never entered my head.' Of the two of them, Edie at least could speak the truth here. She'd never thought to question what the girl had told them. She was too trusting by half, she told herself angrily. To think she'd let Shirley go about with someone who was a spy. For the first time, Edie was thankful that Shirley had gone away from home and at least put some distance between herself and Ursula.

'Ah yes, the newspaper. It was the editor who first alerted us,' the sergeant said. 'Someone asked him why he was employing a girl with a foreign-sounding accent, which, as it turns out, he wasn't. He'd never heard of anyone called Ursula and he'd certainly never employed her – not even as a freelance. So – he got in touch with us.'

There was a slight pause whilst Bill wrote some notes in his book.

Archie cleared his throat. 'What will – um – happen to her?'

'They won't execute her, will they?' Edie couldn't stop the question.

'I shouldn't think so for a moment,' the sergeant answered. 'We've still got agents over there who haven't come home yet. Maybe some sort of exchange will be arranged. I really don't know. But first, we want to find out – if we can – just what sort of information she gave away to the enemy, though I suppose,' he sighed again, 'it's all a bit futile now. Anyway, we would like to speak to your daughter – just a formality, like. Ask her to come to the station in town, will you?'

'I wouldn't like to think they'd hurt her,' Edie murmured. 'I know she might have worked for our enemy and maybe she'll have to face some sort of imprisonment, but – but' – her head dropped – 'it was war. She was only serving her own country, wasn't she? Like – like . . .' Now her voice faded and she turned away lest the two men should see the tears in her eyes. Oh Beth, Beth, is this what you've been doing? And have you been caught like Ursula? Are you languishing in some filthy jail somewhere or – or has a worse fate befallen you?

Fifty

When Shirley breezed in from her shopping expedition, gleeful at the range of goods that could now once more be found in the shops, though there were some things that were still in short supply, Edie said, 'Sit down, love, I've got a bit of news and I don't think you're going to like it.'

As she recounted all that had happened that morning, Shirley's mouth fell open. 'Oh Mam,' she said at last. 'I've been such a fool, so gullible. I never thought—'

'Neither did I, love, so don't blame yourself.'

'Oh heck, d'you think I'll be in trouble for consorting with – with a spy? I mean, we're always being told to watch out what we say and to whom we say it. We're not even supposed to tell our families much. Oh Mam . . .' Tears filled Shirley's eyes. 'I could be in real trouble.'

'If you're asked, love, just tell the truth.' Edie leaned closer and lowered her voice, almost as if she feared someone might be listening. 'You didn't tell Ursula – I still can't get used to calling her by her real name – anything about what went on in the ATS, did you?'

Shirley shook her head firmly. 'No, I do know that. Ever since we did the training, I've watched what I've said to anyone, never mind her.'

Edie laughed, trying to lighten the moment. 'Well, then, you've nowt to worry about.'

'But – but I might have told her things about here – about Grimsby – when I first met her. After all, I thought she was a journalist.'

'I don't reckon you knew owt top secret, now did you? The only ship you knew anything about was your dad's and he was only a fisherman. His trawler wasn't even a minesweeper, now was it?'

'I suppose not – but it's a bit scary to think I was going around with – with a *spy*.'

'The police do want to see you.' Shirley's eyes widened fearfully as Edie went on, 'They asked us to get you to go to the police station.'

'Will you come with me, Mam?'

'It'd be best if your dad went with you. He'll advise you what to say.' Edie laughed wryly. 'I never knew your dad was so good at – well, not lying exactly, but bending the truth a little.'

Shirley smiled tremulously. 'I'm glad he did. I still can't help liking Ursula. She was a good friend to me, when I didn't have anyone else after Beth and Irene had gone away.'

Archie and Shirley went to the station later that afternoon. 'Better get it over with, love,' Archie said to the anxious girl, 'and then we can all settle down and enjoy New Year's Eve and next year things will be a whole lot better.'

Shirley grimaced. 'Mam doesn't think so, if none of us come to live back at home. She's going to be awfully lonely, Dad. I know that, but I do love the life in the ATS. They're already saying it might be disbanded but that if it is, there might be some other sort of military service women can join. That's why I'm so worried I'm going to get a black mark against my name for this.'

'Here we are, love, we'll soon know now, and don't

forget your mam and me will stand by you whatever happens. We know none of this was your fault. In fact, we're as much involved, if it comes to that. We welcomed her into our home.'

'But you had your doubts, didn't you, Dad?'

'Yes, I did,' Archie admitted. 'But I didn't do anything about them – and that's nearly as bad, if not worse. Come on, lass, we'll face this together.'

Strangely, Shirley felt comforted; she had never felt closer to her father than in this moment of crisis.

'I need a drink,' Shirley said with heartfelt relief as they stepped out of the police station.

'Let's get home, then,' Archie began, but Shirley shook her head.

'No, Dad, I mean a real drink – in a pub.'

'Eh?' For a moment, Archie looked startled and then he grinned. 'My little girl all grown up. Well, well. Come on, then, we'll go to our local. It's nearly opening time. Harry might be there and we've something to celebrate.'

Shirley had told the police all she knew about Ursula, which, when it came down to it, wasn't very much, but Sergeant Fenton could see that she was being truthful.

'You might be called upon to give evidence if it comes to a trial, but I can assure you that you're not in trouble, Shirley. Far from it, because you've come forward of your own free will. You go home and enjoy your New Year with the family.'

'Except that there won't be many of the "family" home, will there, Dad?' she said as they walked towards the pub.

'No, love, but I expect Harry will first foot for us,

just like he always has. They'll be round for a drink just after midnight. In fact, there he is, look, making for the same place as us. We'll ask him.'

They sat at a table in the corner, their drinks in front of them, as they filled Harry in on the excitement that had happened earlier in the day.

'Poor lass,' was Harry's only comment, 'she was only trying to do her duty by her country, same, perhaps, as—' He stopped and glanced at Archie and when the other man gave a slight shake of his head as if to say 'not in front of Shirley', Harry said no more.

'I can't tell you how relieved I am.' Still wrapped up in her own worries, Shirley hadn't noticed the look that had passed between the two men. 'I really love the service life and I don't want to get chucked out just because I was friendly with her. Though I was a bit naïve, I have to admit.'

'You weren't to know,' Harry reassured her. 'We were all taken in. Even us old 'uns.'

'Well, I know now and I'll certainly—' Suddenly, Shirley stopped speaking. She was staring at the door, her eyes wide and her mouth dropping open. 'Well, well, well, just look who the wind's blown in.'

'Who?' Archie glanced up towards the door. For a moment, he, too, stared and then he was on his feet and shouting across the room. 'Frank! Frank, lad – over here.'

Frank, dressed in his army uniform, removed his cap and threaded his way amongst the tables, his progress hampered by greetings from all those who knew him. At last he reached their table and was hugged by Shirley and shaken hands with by his father and uncle.

'What'll it be, Frank? This one's on me,' Harry said, slapping him on the back. 'By, it's good to have you home.'

'It's not for long. I don't get demobbed for a few months yet. But I asked for leave. I needed to come home.'

There was silence; none of them knew quite what to say and Frank's expression gave nothing away as to how he was feeling about his wife as he sipped his beer and closed his eyes for a moment with obvious satisfaction. 'By, I've waited a long time for that, I don't mind telling you.'

'Are you back in this country now?' Shirley asked. 'You won't be going abroad again, will you?'

Frank turned to her and seemed to realize for the first time that his little sister was in uniform. 'Hey, you joined the ATS, Shirl. Good for you. What about Beth? Did she join up? Is she home yet?'

So many questions and yet they were all shying away from the one topic that was uppermost in all of their minds; Irene and her baby. Even Shirley, for once, held her outspoken tongue in check.

Archie sighed as he said heavily. 'Beth went off to London, we thought to work for that feller whose kiddies she looked after. Alan Forster. But he was something in the war office and I – I have my suspicions she might have ended up working for them too.'

Frank stared at his father and then at Shirley as she added, 'We haven't heard from her at all for ages and before that, it was only a measly postcard about once a month.'

Frank frowned. 'That's not like Beth. She was always writing home when she was in France. Long newsy letters about all she was doing, about the children and – oh, everything. Postcards, you say? Was that really all she sent?'

Shirley nodded and added quietly, 'I don't think the

last ones were from her. You know how she always used to sign off with "Stay safe"? Well, that wasn't on any of the last few cards.'

'Ah.' Frank was thoughtful, gazing down at his beer and twisting the glass round in his hand.

They were silent for several minutes as if not one of them wanted to be the first to voice their fears. At last, Archie said, 'I just wonder if she was involved in some sort of secret work in France. You know, because she could speak the language so well.' He glanced at Shirley as he added, 'We've just had a bit of that sort of thing here, haven't we, love? You tell Frank all about it.' So, haltingly at first and then with increasing confidence, Shirley told him about Ursula.

'It's possible, I suppose,' Frank said slowly. He looked straight into his father's eyes as he said softly, 'And you haven't heard from her recently, not even since the war ended?'

Unable to speak now for the lump in his throat, Archie just shook his head.

'Look,' Harry said, getting up. 'It's time I was going. And your Aunty Jessie will be so pleased to hear you're home safe and sound, Frank.' He put his hand briefly on the young man's shoulder. 'Night, all.'

'Shirley, love, would you go home ahead of us and tell your mam?' Archie said, 'She'll be thrilled, but it'll be a bit of a shock all the same.'

'Oh – yes, right you are, Dad.' Where once she might have argued, Shirley now understood what Archie meant. Edie needed to be prepared to greet Frank and perhaps, too, Archie wanted a quiet word with his son before going home. 'I'll tell her to get the kettle on, shall I?'

'And tell her I'm famished, an' all,' Frank said, grinning up at his sister. 'That'll keep her busy.'

As she passed by his chair, Shirley paused and looked down at him. 'Frank, I'm sorry if I did the wrong thing writing to you like that, but . . .'

Frank looked up and smiled at her. 'I'm glad you did, Shirl. It helped me get things right in my head before I came home. I know now what I'm going to do, so thanks.'

'Really?'

'Really.'

It was the second huge wave of relief that Shirley had felt that day.

Left together in the pub, Archie leaned forward and said, 'I know it's nowt to do with me, lad, but if you want to talk things over, I'm here.'

'Nowt to talk about, Dad. I've made me mind up and no one's going to persuade me different, so let's have another one and then we'll get going.'

They talked some more over their drinks and then Frank made a move to go. As he stood up, he glanced down at his father. 'Dad, just between ourselves, I've been no angel while I've been away. It's hard when you're separated for years on end like me and Irene have been.'

Understanding, Archie nodded and added, 'You go, lad. If you don't mind, I'll sit here for a bit. It's been a busy old day and I'd just like to be left alone with my thoughts.'

'I'll see you later, then.'

Archie sat for another hour and then, reluctantly, he left the pub and walked up the street towards his home, quite expecting to walk into a full-blown row between Edie and Frank. But he opened the back door to the sound of laughter and, walking into the living room, it was to see Frank sitting at the table attacking a huge plate of bacon, eggs, fried bread and sausage.

'Where on earth . . . ?' he began, but then he looked up to see a grinning Reggie standing behind Frank's chair.

'Joe Schofield brought him. He's staying a couple of nights with us.' Edie was somewhere between laughing and crying with happiness. To have her two boys home unexpectedly was almost too much to bear at once, even if the reason for Frank's return was not a happy one. 'And he'll fetch him again on Wednesday morning.'

'Ah, I see now where all the food's come from. That was very kind of them.'

Shirley came in from the scullery carrying a sponge cake filled with cream. 'And just look at this, Dad. Mrs Schofield sent this too. Would you like some bacon and egg? There's plenty.'

Archie pulled out a chair across the table from where Frank was devouring his meal. 'I wouldn't say no, lass. Thanks.'

Shirley disappeared back into the scullery and they soon heard the spitting of bacon frying. The smell drifting into the room made Archie's mouth water. When Shirley set it in front of him, Archie said, 'By, this is a meal fit for a king.'

'I've done you some fried bread too. I know how you like it.'

The two women helped themselves to a piece of cake. 'What about you, Reggie love?' Edie said. 'You've brought all this and yet you're the one not eating.'

'I'm fine, Mam, ta. I had a big dinner before we set off.'

Frank sat back and gave a sigh of satisfaction. 'I don't reckon I've tasted food as good as that for five years or more.'

Edie watched him, willing him to talk about the one

subject that was on everyone's mind, but Frank seemed content to drink his tea and talk about the rest of the family. Anything, it seemed, other than about his wife.

'I can't believe how you've grown, young Reg. Are you staying in the country, then?'

Reggie beamed and his eyes lit up. 'Mr and Mrs Schofield want me to stay and work on the farm. And it's what I want to do.' He glanced at Archie as he added, 'Sorry, Dad, but I really don't want to go to sea.'

'I'm glad, Son. It's been a good life for me, but it's not for everyone.'

'What about you, Frank? What are you going to do when you come home?'

It seemed as if everyone in the room was holding their breath, but Frank only smiled and said, 'I expect it'll be the sea for me. It's all I know.'

Edie could contain herself no longer. 'What are you going to do about' – she gestured with her head towards the wall between the houses – '*her*?'

Frank frowned, but before he could answer, Archie said firmly, 'Now, now, Edie, leave it, love. It's for Frank and Irene to talk things through. It's nowt to do with us.'

'It's everything to do with us, Archie. She's no better than a—'

Edie wasn't allowed to finish her sentence as Frank put up his hand to silence them all. Then quietly he said, 'I've already made up my mind what's going to happen and it will all be sorted out in the morning. It's too late tonight. The children will be in bed. It'll wait another few hours. In the meantime, can you put me up for tonight, Mam? If not I can—'

'Of course I can. I wouldn't hear of you going

anywhere else. The beds are all made up in the attic bedroom.'

Shirley chuckled as she put in, 'Just as they have been ever since you both left.'

They all stared at Edie, who wriggled her shoulders in embarrassment and said, 'Well, I never knew when any of you might come home unexpected-like, did I? I've kept them well aired.'

Archie got up and went to kiss his wife on her cheek. 'And now you've got three of 'em home, all at once.'

'Yes, yes, I have,' Edie said happily, trying hard to keep her mind off what would happen the next day.

Frank had still given them no clue as to what he intended to do.

Fifty-One

Lil rushed into the house and slammed the back door behind her, leaning against it. She was trembling, her heart hammering nineteen to the dozen, as the saying went. She put her hand to her chest. The shock of seeing him was so unexpected. And now she must tell Irene.

When she'd calmed herself a little, though her hands still shook, she opened the door into the living room and sat down opposite Irene, who was giving the baby her last night-time feed beside the fire. Tommy was already in bed. Irene glanced up and saw the anxiety in her mother's eyes.

'What is it, Mam? Has that old biddy next door been having a go at you again?'

Lil shook her head. At last she burst out, 'He's home, Irene. I've just seen him going in by their back door.'

The colour drained from Irene's face as she whispered. 'Frank?'

Lil nodded.

'Then – then he'll be coming here.' There was a slight pause before she added, almost pathetically, 'Won't he?'

'I – I expect so. But probably not tonight. He – he's a thoughtful lad. He'd not want to upset Tommy this late.'

Lil and her daughter stared at each other, both knowing that neither of them would sleep this night.

*

His decision made – and he intended to stick to it whatever anyone said – Frank slept soundly, but in the next room, Edie lay awake, staring into the darkness and listening to the baby crying through the wall. What was Frank going to do? Surely, surely he wouldn't think of taking her back, would he? No, no, she wouldn't let him. He'd listen to his mam. She still knew what was best for him – for all her family. And yet, Edie was forced to admit that one by one they seemed to be slipping away from her, making their own decisions and living their own lives.

But Frank was different; he would take notice of her. Shirley had always been a bit of a madam and as for Reggie, well, she blamed the Schofields. He'd gone to them at an impressionable age and impress him they certainly had!

Edie slept restlessly and woke with a headache. Frank was late up and both Shirley and Reggie had gone out by the time he appeared downstairs, needing a shave at the sink in the scullery.

'Breakfast?' Edie asked sharply, her nerves on edge. She could see trouble coming today. There'd be tears from Irene and that would likely set Tommy off and she wasn't even sure that Archie agreed with her. He'd been round to Lil's a lot recently – ostensibly to see Tommy or to take him out – but he'd seemed to stay sometimes far longer than was strictly necessary to collect the boy or see him home again. Archie was sitting in his chair reading the morning paper when Frank, clean-shaven and dressed in his uniform trousers and shirt, sat down at the table.

'So,' Edie said bluntly, as she pushed a cup of tea towards him. 'What are you going to do?'

'Talk to Irene,' Frank said, 'and then we'll see.'

'I think I'll have a walk up to the pub,' Archie said, heaving himself out of his chair. Coward, Edie thought to herself, wanting to snap at him, but she remained silent. Archie hated family rows and there was every possibility that there was going to be some sort of ruckus today. He reached for his muffler and cap and left by the back door.

Frank finished eating, stood up and went out into the backyard. Edie held her breath as she heard the wooden door between the two houses open and close again. Then there was silence as she waited – and waited. After what seemed an age to her, though in reality it was only a few minutes, Frank came back.

'Well?'

'Irene's coming round here in a minute, Mam.'

Edie stared at her son and pursed her lips. 'I don't want that little trollop in my house, I—'

'Mam.' There was a warning note in Frank's tone. 'Me and Irene have got some serious talking to do.'

'You are going to divorce her, aren't you?'

Frank shook his head.

Edie sank down into a chair and rested her arms on the table. 'Aw, Son, you're never thinking of taking her back. Not after—'

Frank held up his hand, palm outwards, to halt whatever his mother had been about to say. 'That's for me and Irene to sort out, Mam, there's a love.'

Edie opened her mouth, but whatever she might have been going to say – and Frank was sure he knew just what it was – was halted by a tentative knock at the back door. That alone spoke volumes. Ever since she could walk, Irene had come into Aunty Edie's house, often without even knocking, but now . . .

Frank wagged a cautionary finger at his mother and

moved to open the door, flinging it wide in a clear gesture of welcome.

'Hello, duck, come on in.'

Edie stared open-mouthed, but she said not a word as Frank reached out to take the little girl from Irene's arms.

'I'm sorry, Frank,' Irene said hesitantly, 'I would have left her with Mam, but she was crying – and then Tommy wanted to come too.'

'Of course he did. Come on in – all of you.'

He carried Marie towards the hearth and sat down in his father's chair with the baby on his knee. He stroked her blond curls and smiled down at her. Solemnly, she gazed up at him. Tommy sidled to stand beside his father's chair and leaned against his shoulder. He had no early memories of the man, but he'd taken to him instantly; Frank was the only one who'd shown Tommy's sister any kindness. Except his Granny Lil, of course, but she didn't count. You expected grannies to love you. Mam had told him that this man was his dad. It was all a bit confusing. He'd thought Ken – the man in the blue uniform they'd known at the farm – was his father but his mam had warned him that he must never mention the handsome airman's name again.

'You're a pretty little thing, aren't you?' Frank was saying softly to the little girl, who was gazing up at him with wide blue eyes, but it was Tommy who smiled and said innocently, 'She's my sister.'

Without looking up, Frank said gently, 'I know, lad, I know.' Then he looked up to see Irene still hovering uncertainly in the doorway. 'Come on in, Irene. Mam won't bite.'

Edie gave what sounded suspiciously like a snort, but she said nothing as her daughter-in-law moved hesitantly further into the room. Edie knew Frank wanted to talk to his wife on his own, but stubbornly, she refused to move. This was still her house, her home and—

'D'you mind, Mam?'

Edie opened her mouth to say, yes, she minded. She minded very much but something stopped her. Maybe it was the look on Frank's face, maybe it was the sight of him dandling the baby girl on his knee – the way he was smiling at her, his arm protectively round her and Tommy standing close to him. As Irene sat down on the edge of the chair opposite him, they looked like a family – a complete family. Edie felt something swelling in her chest. It was a feeling she didn't understand. Was it fear of what she now knew, without a shadow of a doubt, Frank was going to do? Or was it – strangely – an overflowing of pride in this man who was her son; a real man in every sense of the word who was prepared to forgive his wife in a way that she, Edie, had not been able to do?

Archie had said as much only last night as they were getting into bed. 'Our Frank'll know his own mind. He'll do the right thing and we'll abide by it, Edie,' he'd said. 'You hear me?'

She hadn't been prepared to listen to her husband then, but seeing them together now, she knew she had to do what Archie had said.

If Frank could forgive, then so must she. Slowly, she rose to her feet on legs that were a little unsteady. 'I'll – um – leave you to it then,' she murmured, but Frank and Irene didn't seem to hear her or even notice her slip out of the back door and make her way to her neighbour's back door. It had been a long time – far too long – since she'd spoken to Lil and she regretted all the harsh words.

She took a deep breath and opened the back door.

'You there, Lil? Get the kettle on, duck, I've summat to tell you.'

Archie had escaped to the pub; he hadn't long to wait until lunchtime opening. He'd known what was going to happen that morning and he'd wanted to be out of the way. Late last night Frank had confided his intentions in his father and had been given his blessing. Archie was happy about the outcome. They'd lost too much already in this war to bear grudges and carry bitterness for years to come. He mourned the loss of his eldest son and would do so until his dying day. And there wasn't a day went by without him thinking about Beth. And he was sure it was the same for Edie though they didn't speak about her much now. As for Reggie, he was well settled in the countryside. It was a good life and Archie was content to let him stay there, though he wasn't so sure that Edie was happy about it. So, all in all, Archie was ready to move on, to embrace whatever the future held for them all and if that included welcoming a baby, who wasn't of his blood, into the family, then so be it.

And yet, for all his decisions, he was still unsettled. As if there was still something else that was going to happen. He couldn't relax in his usual seat in the pub, he wasn't even enjoying his favourite beer. He was restless and he didn't know why. Archie sighed. Time to go home. He reckoned he'd given them enough time now. He stepped outside and nodded to one or two of his acquaintances before turning towards home.

It was when he turned the corner that he caught his breath. He stopped and stared the length of the street at the figures of two young people – a man and a woman – walking slowly towards him. The man was dark haired and wearing, of all things, a beret. The type, Archie knew, that Frenchmen wore. In one hand he carried a suitcase, but his other arm was protectively around the young woman, almost as if he was helping her to walk. And indeed, she did appear to be limping a little.

And there was something familiar about her, something . . . Archie's heart began to thump and he put out a shaking hand to the nearest wall to steady himself.

Could it be? No, it wasn't possible, was it?

He pushed himself away from the wall and began to walk towards them on legs that were trembling. Still, he wasn't sure. But then, as they drew nearer, the young woman looked up. Her hair was short, incredibly short, for she'd always been so proud of her long, curly brown hair. And she was thinner – much thinner – and she was definitely limping. And then, as she noticed him, she pulled away from the man's arm and began to hurry towards Archie. And now he knew for certain.

'Beth,' he whispered, the tears in his eyes almost blinding the sight of her. He brushed them aside impatiently. 'Oh my Beth!' He stretched his arms out towards her. 'You've come home.'

Jenny's War
Margaret Dickinson

Love, hope and courage in a time of war . . .

Is it possible for a ten-year-old girl to fall in love? Jenny Mercer thinks so. Evacuated to Lincolnshire from the East End of London at the outbreak of war, she is frightened of the wide open spaces and the huge skies. But the kindly Thornton family soon makes her feel welcome. And no one more so than Georgie, the handsome RAF fighter pilot who is caught up in the battle for Britain's survival. When Georgie is posted missing, presumed dead, Jenny is devastated.

More heartbreak is to come when Jenny's mother Dot decides that she wants her daughter home and Jenny is forced to come back to live in the city which is now under almost daily attack from enemy bombers. Dot's 'fancy man', Arthur Osborne, treats Jenny kindly. But is Arthur only interested in the girl because she can be useful to him? No one will suspect a ten-year-old girl of being involved with the Black Market . . .

When the law comes a little too close for Arthur's comfort, the family flees the city and head towards the hills and dales of Derbyshire. There, Jenny is caught up in a life of deception. All she really wants is to go back to Lincolnshire. For Jenny has never given up hope that one day, Georgie will come back . . .

ISBN 978-0-330-54430-6

The Clippie Girls
Margaret Dickinson

Sisters in love. A family at war. A city in peril.

Rose and Myrtle Sylvester look up to their older sister, Peggy. She is the sensible, reliable one in the household of women headed by their grandmother, Grace Booth, and their mother, Mary Sylvester. When war is declared in 1939 they must face the hardships together and huge changes in their lives are inevitable. For Rose, there is the chance to fulfil her dream of becoming a clippie on Sheffield's trams like Peggy. But for Myrtle, the studious, clever one in the family, war may shatter her ambitions.

When the tram on which Peggy is a conductress is caught in a bomb blast, she bravely helps to rescue her passengers. One of them is a young soldier, Terry Price, and he and Peggy begin courting. They meet every time he can get leave, but eventually Terry is posted abroad and she hears nothing from him. Worse still, Peggy must break the devastating news to her family that she is pregnant.

The shock waves that ripple through the family will affect each and every one of them and life will never be the same again.

ISBN 978-0-330-54431-3

Fairfield Hall
Margaret Dickinson

A matter of honour. A sense of duty. A time for courage.

Ruthlessly ambitious Ambrose Constantine is determined that his daughter, Annabel, shall marry into the nobility. A self-made trawler owner and fish merchant, he has only his wealth to buy his way into Society.

When Annabel's secret meetings with a young man employed at her father's offices stop suddenly, she finds that Gilbert has mysteriously disappeared. Heartbroken, she finds solace with her grandparents on their Lincolnshire farm, but her father will not allow her to bury herself in the countryside and enlists the help of a business connection to launch his daughter into Society.

During the London Season, Annabel is courted by James Lyndon, the Earl of Fairfield, whose country estate is only a few miles from her grandfather's farm. Believing herself truly loved at last, Annabel accepts his offer of marriage. It is only when she arrives at Fairfield Hall that she realizes the true reason behind James's proposal and the part her scheming father has played.

Through the years that follow, Annabel will know both heartache and joy, but the birth of her son should secure the future of the Fairfield Estate. Yet there are others who lay claim to the inheritance in a feud that will not be resolved until the trenches of a bitter world war.

ISBN 978-1-4472-3724-2

FOR MORE ON

MARGARET DICKINSON

sign up to receive our

SAGA NEWSLETTER

Packed with **features, competitions, authors'
and readers' letters** and **news of exclusive events**,
it's a must-read for every Margaret Dickinson fan!

Simply fill in your details below and tick to confirm that you would
like to receive saga-related news and promotions and return to us at
Pan Macmillan, Saga Newsletter, 20 New Wharf Road, London, N1 9RR

NAME

ADDRESS

POSTCODE

EMAIL

[ ] *I would like to receive saga-related news and promotions (please tick)*

You can unsubscribe at any time in writing or through our website where you can also see
our privacy policy which explains how we will store and use your data.

At Bello, we believe in the timeless power of books, and our extensive list of classic fiction has something for everyone. Whether you want to indulge in a heart-warming tale of life in the Hebrides from Lillian Beckwith's *The Hills is Lonely*, read a classic Yorkshire saga from award-winning author Brenda Jagger, or escape to the scandalous world of Renaissance Italy in Sarah Bower's *The Sins of the House of Borgia*, we've got the book for you.

BELL◉

panmacmillan.com/bello

@bellobooks   bellobooks